"I am not of a mind to kiss you now, so you should not anticipate that I will," Lily said.

"But I can anticipate that you mean to do it eventually, is that right?"

"Yes."

"Then I will require your assistance negotiating the route back to the inn, for I am weak-kneed."

"Fool."

"Quite possibly."

He was so cheerful about this assessment of his character that Lily reversed her own decision. She found a foothold for her heels between the stones and stood, then before he backed away, she steadied herself by placing her hands on his shoulders. She pressed her mouth to his and found at once that this was most sincerely more to her liking.

"You do not mind that I am kissing you?"

"No. I am perhaps too tolerant in this regard, but I do not think I will alter my views just yet."

This time when Lily kissed him it had all the sweetness of her smile. She worked her mouth over his, paying particular attention to his lower lip.

"You will think I am splitting hairs," she whispered against his lips. She flicked her tongue and it caught the upper curve of his mouth. "But I find I want the taste of you again . . ."

Books by Jo Goodman

The Captain's Lady
Crystal Passion
Seaswept Abandon
Velvet Night
Violet Fire
Scarlet Lies
Tempting Torment
Midnight Princess
Passion's Sweet Revenge
Sweet Fire
Wild Sweet Ecstasy
Rogue's Mistress
Forever in My Heart
Always in My Dreams
Only in My Arms
My Steadfast Heart
My Reckless Heart
With All My Heart
More Than You Know
More Than You Wished
Let Me Be the One
Everything I Ever Wanted
All I Ever Needed
Beyond a Wicked Kiss
A Season to Be Sinful

Published by Zebra Books

A Season to be Sinful

JO GOODMAN

ZEBRA BOOKS
KENSINGTON PUBLISHING CORP.
www.kensingtonbooks.com

ZEBRA BOOKS are published by

Kensington Publishing Corp.
850 Third Avenue
New York, NY 10022

All Kensington titles, imprints, and distributed lines are available at special quantity discounts for bulk purchases for sales promotion, premiums, fund-raising, educational, or institutional use.

Special book excerpts or customized printings can also be created to fit specific needs. For details, write or phone the office of the Kensington Special Sales Manager: Attn. Special Sales Department. Kensington Publishing Corp., 850 Third Avenue, New York, NY 10022. Phone: 1-800-221-2647.

Zebra and the Z logo Reg. U.S. Pat. & TM Off.

ISBN 0-8217-7775-0

First Printing: August 2005
10 9 8 7 6 5 4 3 2 1

Printed in the United States of America

For Aunt Ev and Uncle Bill
Love, Snowball

Prologue

L'Abbaye de Sacré Coeur, Avril 1810

"What about that one?"

The question startled Sister Mary Joseph, though she doubted her companion was aware of it. There had never been any pretense on his part to give her his full attention. He suffered the tour of the ruins, the walk through the scrupulously tended garden, his introduction in each of the classrooms, and finally the journey along the stone corridors to the old chapel, the stones themselves worn to a faintly concave smoothness by the silent, shuffling passage of penitents like her for more than two centuries.

Now Sister Mary Joseph's pale green eyes shifted first to the man at her side, then to the object of his interest.

Lilith Sterling knelt at the rear of the chapel, her head bowed, the slim, fragile stem of her neck revealed by the thick plait of hair that had fallen forward over her left shoulder. Her head was covered by a fine white shawl that muted the dark copper color of her hair but did nothing to conceal it.

Sister Mary Joseph gave the young girl full marks for not looking up. At some other time, Lilith's pious posture would have brought a skeptical, though tender, smile to her lips. That was not the way of it now.

Softly, indicating they should have a care not to disturb Lilith's prayers, Sister Mary Joseph said, "No, she is just a child."

The Right Honorable Lord Woodridge arched one brow but did not turn away from his regard of the girl. "I have children," he said. "My daughter is eleven, my son, three. I think I know the difference. She will suit admirably."

"I am sorry, my lord, but she is already promised."

"Promised?" He frowned. "I would know the name of the man. Is he French?"

"No, my lord."

"English, then. That is good. I do so dislike negotiating with the frogs at every turn. It is invariably unpleasant." He ignored the slight stiffening that the sister could not conceal. He considered apologizing and immediately dismissed it as unnecessary. Mary Joseph was, after all, as English as he, which is why the Reverend Mother had chosen her to accompany him. Impatiently, he inquired again. "His name?"

"She is promised to Our Lord, Jesus Christ." Sister Mary Joseph took considerable delight in offering this answer, though she was careful not to give herself away. She would confess the lie later and pray that she would be forgiven.

Wycliff Standish, Baron Woodridge, said nothing for a long moment as his attention returned to the girl. Each line of her face was finely drawn; there was a purity in her profile that he found much to his liking. Except for the faint movement of her lips as she prayed, she was as still as stone. The serenity that surrounded her was almost tangible.

It was difficult to suppress the shiver of pleasure he experienced at the thought of having it within his reach. Mayhap it could be touched. *She* could be touched, of that he was certain. She was young, yes, but not too young. Possessing her would bring him a measure of peace, at least for a time. And when she had served her purpose, been used, destroyed, and finally discarded, he would know his greatest satisfaction.

"Ridiculous." His lips moved around the word much as hers did, giving virtually no sound to the pronouncement. That he offered it with a certain finality, as though it put a period to his prayers, was not lost on him. He had, after all, his own god to appease. "She is wasted on the church."

Sister Mary Joseph hardly knew how to reply to that. She underscored her lie by telling it a second time. "Still, my lord, she is promised."

Woodridge's thin upper lip curled. "A bride of Christ? No, it is unthinkable." Tapping the tip his crystal-knobbed walking stick sharply against the stone floor, he was not surprised when the girl flinched. Appearances aside, she was not in a trance at all, certainly not lost in applying herself to her penance. "*Venez ici, mademoiselle.*"

Lilith froze.

"We should not disturb her," Mary Joseph said quietly. It was the most she thought she dared say. Lord Woodridge was more than a visitor to the abbey. He was a guest, invited by the abbess at the most particular suggestion of the bishop.

Woodridge ignored her. He was not accustomed to repeating himself, but he did so now, making allowances for the fact that he was not master here. "*Ici. Tout de suite.*"

Lilith came to her feet slowly, awkwardly, bracing her hand on the back of the pew in front of her so that she might have more support. She never straightened entirely; the pronounced curve of her spine would not permit it.

Sister Mary Joseph pressed the back of one hand to her lips to suppress the small gasp that hovered there. When Lilith limped heavily toward them, Mary Joseph realized her hand was insufficient to cover the bubble of nervous laughter that was lodged at the back of her throat. She coughed several times instead and drew out her handkerchief from beneath the sleeve of her habit.

Woodridge was caught. His distaste for the creature in

front of him was palpable. In other circumstances he would have concealed his disgust. Had he been observed by anyone save the sister and the cripple, he would have schooled his features and made some pretense of sympathy. He might have even deigned to touch the girl, though he would have carefully calculated the benefits of doing so against the possibility that he would be sick.

Lilith approached. The drag of her right foot on the stones echoed eerily in the chapel. She stopped more than a yard in front of his lordship, halted by what she spied in his ice blue eyes. Here was aversion in its purest form. She had given him disgust of herself, not for who she was, but for what she appeared to be.

Her curtsy was as awkwardly accomplished as her rising had been. The slight grimace about her mouth was not feigned. It was painful to be in his presence. "*Monsieur.*"

"Does she speak English?" he asked the sister.

"Very little."

He would have overlooked this deficit of education if she were not deformed. Indeed, he knew he would have found a certain enjoyment expanding her vocabulary. Those words shared between lovers, in particular, would have given him pleasure. To hear them whispered haltingly in his ear as he buried himself inside her . . . he reined in those thoughts before he was ill. Already he could taste bile at the back of his throat.

"What is wrong with her?" he demanded, though to his own eyes the answer was obvious. She was spoiled in the most fundamental way. If she was as pure as her profile had suggested, it was because she had no choice to be else. All that would be left to him was to defile her spirit, her soul, and it was not enough. It was his desire to begin with the butterfly, not the moth, and certainly not with this misshapen chrysalis. "Was she so deformed at birth?"

"No, my lord." That, at least, was true.

"An accident, then."

Sister Mary Joseph watched the baron closely. He seemed

to be satisfied with his assumption and did not ask for the particulars. She tried not to consider the nature of his thoughts. That he was repulsed by what Lilith had become was clear to her and must be so to Lilith herself. His lordship's reaction bore out all that Mary Joseph had supposed to be true about him in the first few minutes of their introduction. Upon taking his hand, she had felt a chill slip from his fingers into hers, then burrow under her skin until it raised the fine hairs on her arms and at the back of her neck. Time spent in his company had not altered that impression.

It would be difficult to ask for God's forgiveness when she had no remorse for lying.

"Tell her to leave us," Woodridge said suddenly. "She is an abomination."

"Reverend Mother has often said the same." Mary Joseph offered this observation quietly. Here again was the truth, something the Reverend Mother and the baron could agree upon were such a thing needed, although they had decidedly different perspectives on why the uncomplimentary description was also an accurate one. Turning to Lilith, Sister said, "*Allez! Vite!*"

Lilith hurried from the chapel as instructed but not before she risked a glance at the baron. He was no longer looking at her, but through her, his lips pursed in a rictus of a smile. Stepping to one side, he gave her a wide berth as she passed. She thought she felt him shudder but allowed that it could have been her imagination. She did not, however, imagine her own response.

For a moment, she'd not been able to breathe.

Woodridge waited for the uneven footfalls to recede before he spoke. This was not done because of any regard for the departing girl's sensibilities—he was quite certain she had none—but because he needed a moment to recover his own fine ones.

"That was extraordinarily unpleasant," he said without inflection.

"I am sorry you found it so." Sister Mary Joseph's eyes

were downcast. She had replaced her handkerchief inside her sleeve, and now she lightly fingered the beads of her rosary.

"Are there no other girls? I was led to believe I would find a suitable governess for my daughter here."

Would that were all he wanted, Sister thought. "You have seen all of them and dismissed each in turn." She did not add thank God, but it was that sentiment that was in her heart. In truth, he had expressed no interest in any of the girls until his cold study had fallen upon Lilith. There were girls here who would have been flattered by the Englishman's attention, taken with his fine patrician looks and distant regard. They would be frightened also, but excited as well, and as one emotion provoked the other, they would be made vulnerable.

Sister Mary Joseph understood that it had always been thus, but her knowledge of scripture and profound faith provided only one aspect of her understanding. She knew these things in a deeply personal way, and this she kept carefully guarded from everyone save her Lord.

"You will want to speak to the bishop again," she said.

"You can be certain that I will."

She nodded faintly, wishing it were otherwise. It was likely he had already made a substantial donation to the bishop, though perhaps not the church, in anticipation of finding *la jeune fille* who would fulfill his requirements. Sister Mary Joseph took a step toward the candlelit corridor and was brought up short by Woodridge's next words.

"I wish to see the Reverend Mother before I leave."

Hoping that he would not sense her distress, Sister Mary Joseph turned to face the baron. "Of course," she said, bending her head slightly as she acquiesced. "This way." The weight that had so recently been removed from her shoulders returned, redoubled this time so that her small frame could not support it. Long before they reached the Reverend Mother's study, it had settled quite heavily around Mary Joseph's heart.

* * *

The Reverend Mother's study was as severely appointed as the woman herself. Strong, angular lines defined her features, and the same was true of the room where she spent most of her time. Books neatly lined three shelves on either side of the stone hearth, the volumes arranged by the height and thickness of the burnished leather spines rather than by subject. Still, the Reverend Mother could find any book she wanted in a matter of moments, and no one wondered, even upon brief acquaintance, if she had read them all.

She looked up, quelling her displeasure at the interruption, and carefully placed a red ribbon between the pages of her missal to mark her place. The door began to open in spite of the fact that she had given no indication that she welcomed the intruder. That breach alone told her who would cross the threshold.

"*Ah! Bonsoir, monsieur.*" From behind the ornate and imposing mahogany desk, the abbess stood. She accepted his lordship's greeting, noting again that while he spoke with perfect grammatical correctness, his cadence was labored and there was effort applied here. She had little doubt that it was not to his liking to continue in French, but she would not speak English to put him at ease. There must be some small penance on his part for the rather bold manner in which he had shown himself into her private sanctuary.

The Reverend Mother's eyes slid briefly to Sister Mary Joseph, who remained hovering on the threshold. "*Pourquoi est-ce que tu ne partes pas?*"

"She doesn't leave," the baron explained in his stilted French, "because I do not wish it."

"Ah." The Reverend Mother shrugged, then motioned Mary Joseph to enter and close the door behind her. "She is to be a witness to our discourse, then."

"*Exactement.*"

"Please, won't you sit?"

"*Non.* I will be brief."

He was rude, but then she had expected nothing else. If his manner was offensive, his money was not. That was the bishop's reasoning and, finally, her own. She inclined her head, inviting him to speak.

"I was led to believe I would find a suitable governess here. Bishop Corbeil was fully aware of my requirements and assured me there was just such a young woman at the abbey. I do not think I am mistaken that he had someone in mind when he spoke to me."

Reverend Mother chose her words carefully. "He recommended no particular young woman to me, rather he shared the essential qualities you were seeking."

"Then he told you I must have someone of more than moderate intelligence? My daughter is intelligent herself, you understand."

"*Oui.*"

"And that the young lady should have experience instructing your younger students?"

The Reverend Mother inclined her head again, assuring him this had been related to her.

"He told you also that she must possess a modicum of grace and comport herself with dignity befitting a companion to my daughter?"

"Just so."

"You understand that I am seeking someone who will have more than a little influence with Mina?"

"That was made clear to me."

"Then you can appreciate that I desire a young woman of a certain moral character, preferably one that places her above reproach not only in my regard, but in the regard of society, and most especially of the *ton.*"

The Reverend Mother did not permit herself the luxury to bristle at this statement, but said calmly, "You may be certain that all of our young women, whether or not they will choose to serve God as a member of our order, are possessed of unimpeachable moral character."

Woodridge did not trouble himself to hide the fact that he

remained unconvinced as to the truth of this, but he did not press it further. Perhaps the Reverend Mother did not know, or care to know, that one of her young novices was *enceinte*. Granted, the pregnancy was in its earliest months, but the misshapen belly was there if one had but the eyes to see it. He had those eyes. He said nothing of this, however. It would be revealed soon enough to everyone that the girl was a whore and provide a delicious comeuppance to the supercilious mien of the abbess.

"For obvious reasons, I insisted that *la jeune fille* must enjoy good health. Corbeil promised me this would present no obstacle."

"*C'est vrai*. Fresh air. Daily walks. Hard work and prayer. None of us are prone to illness."

"If it is all as you say, then where is my daughter's governess? Are my standards so exacting?"

The Reverend Mother's dark eyes slid to Sister Mary Joseph, the merest question in the tilt of the glance. "No, they are not," she said slowly. "Your tour was thorough?"

The sister pressed her lips together and nodded.

Returning her inquiry back to the baron, the abbess said, "Then I can only suppose that there is some particular you require that is yet unknown to us, perhaps even to yourself. Given what you have said, we have many suitable candidates for the position of governess."

"Really? Like the redheaded cripple? Pure at first blush but clearly touched by the devil's hand." He paused, drawing on his recollection of something Sister Mary Joseph had said to him. "You cannot deny it, for I understand it is also your opinion that she is an abomination."

This time the Reverend Mother could not mask her surprise. Her nostrils flared with her sharp intake of air, and her regard for Mary Joseph was stern. Still, it was with a mixture of tenderness and resignation that she asked, "What has Lilith done now?"

*   *   *

Lilith stared at the traveling and identification papers that Sister Mary Joseph thrust into her hands. It was after midnight, and a stub of a candle was all that illuminated Lilith's cell. She had made room for Mary Joseph by sitting cross-legged at the head of her cot. Her thin cotton shift was pulled taut across her knees, and it served to catch the papers when they fell through her nerveless fingers.

"*Je ne comprends pas*," she said, pushing the papers off her lap and onto the cot. Her spine was no longer the curved deformity she had shown to the baron, but ramrod straight.

"Quietly," Mary Joseph whispered. "And in English, please. We do not want to be overheard, but if we are, it would be better if we were not well understood."

Lilith nodded. Everyone spoke some measure of English, but even Reverend Mother did not have the facility with the language that she and Mary Joseph enjoyed. They could speak rapidly and employ phrasing and cant that was often incomprehensible to those for whom *l'anglais* was a second language.

"But why am I being sent away?" Lilith asked with all the plaintiveness of a child questioning the fairness of her punishment. "I do not want to go. This is my home."

Mary Joseph shook her head, her eyes sad but resolute. "No, it is not your home. You have always chafed at the restrictions of the abbey, and you would not want to live out your life here. Some of us have spirits that are set free in the service of our Lord. The abbey does not confine us as much as it defines our work."

"But I want to serve our Savior." Unfortunately, even to Lilith's ears this statement was marked by a certain defensive desperation that undermined its truthfulness. "You are my family," she said, taking a different tack. "You. Sister Carmel. Sister Angeline. And Sister Mary Claire. Sister Agnes."

Mary Joseph held up one finger before Lilith named everyone who lived at the abbey as well as those who served it, from the groundskeepers to the groomsmen. "Shh. I know what we mean to you because I know what you mean to us."

In spite of the raised finger, Lilith was compelled to name one more. "Even the Reverend Mother," she added quickly.

This last elicited a gentle smile from Mary Joseph. "Of course, the Reverend Mother. She loves you, dearest. We all do." She gathered the papers, squared them off so they fit neatly inside a slim leather packet, then placed the packet on Lilith's lap. "There is not much time, and there are many details to attend. I must have your full attention and your promise to commit what I am telling you to memory."

Lilith was not yet prepared to listen. "I do not want to go with him. He frightens me. I saw how you looked at him. It was the same."

Mary Joseph did not deny Lilith's observation, only her assumption. "I am not here to arrange your departure with the baron. Is that what you have thought all this time? No, don't answer. I can see that it is. When he returns in the morning, it is my hope that you will be gone. That is important, for I am unsure that once you are in his company you will be able to get away. We are fortunate, indeed, that Reverend Mother insisted that you remain here this evening to make your farewells. More fortunate still that his lordship acquiesced."

This confused Lilith. She could not be certain what Sister Mary Joseph was telling her. Was she suggesting that the Reverend Mother had given her tacit approval to some alternate plan, or that they were about to take advantage of her kindness? The farewells, for all that they had been appreciated, had also been difficult. Lilith knew that with the exception of a few of the sillier girls, no one was truly happy for her.

The sisters said the right things, of course—that this was a great opportunity, that she would have her eyes opened to the world, that she was blessed to be offered a position that would no doubt prove her mettle. They pointed out that the time she spent in Paris with the baron and his children would provide a lifetime of memories. They were much less effusive about the certainty that she would eventually go to London to live. The one moment of respite came when Sister Angeline announced that it was her fervent wish that the baron's daughter would bless Lilith with the same challenges and rewards that Lilith had bestowed upon all of them.

Lilith had laughed then, knowing it was true that she had been up to every sort of mischief. Now, however, the memory of Sister Angeline's words were bittersweet, and she bent her head to shield tears from Mary Joseph. One dripped onto her unsteady hands but neither of them acknowledged it. "What would you have me do?" she asked with a calm that surprised her. "If I am not to be here when the baron returns, where will I be?"

"On your way to Le Havre, I hope."

"Le Havre?" It was so far. Impossible.

"Then across the channel and eventually to London."

"London?" In her terror she was becoming as silly as Justine Derain, the one they all called *l'écho*. Perhaps it was only that Justine was afraid, too, Lilith thought, and she kept her head down, this time with a sense of shame. "But I know no one there, and the baron—"

"The baron will remain in Paris for months yet, mayhap see out the year there. Do you understand his purpose in France?"

Lilith shook her head.

"He is trying to effect a peace here. *Détente.* The emperor merely suffers the Englishman and the others like him, of course. They amuse him, I think, and there are always advantages to keeping one's enemies at hand."

Glancing up, Lilith asked very softly, "Is that what we are, Sister? The emperor's enemies?"

"*Non. Jamais.* Do not think it."

"*Mais, je suis l'anglaise. Vous aussi.*"

"English, remember? Yes, we are English, but we are also French. Chameleons, both of us, and survivors as well. It is not politics that interest me, or governments. They are institutions of man, not God."

The church, Lilith thought, might be sanctioned by God, but it was most assuredly an institution of man. She sighed suddenly, knowing that her ability to entertain that thought was further proof that she could not live the abbey life. Survivors, Sister Mary Joseph had named them both. For the nun it meant embracing the protection of the abbey walls, but Lilith understood finally that for herself, it meant escaping them.

"What would you have me do, Sister?" she asked at length.

Mary Joseph nodded faintly as she leaned forward and grasped Lilith's hands in hers. "I have a brother, dearest Lily," she said. "You must go to him."

One

His nibs was a watchful one. She'd give him that. Most of the young bucks strolling through Covent Garden after the theatre discharged its patrons gave their full attention to the muslin set and never took notice of the footpads brushing their elbows. Some nights it was so easy to lift the contents of a gentleman's pocket that there was no sport in it.

She had never cared for the sport of it overmuch. *Snick. Snack.* A flick of the wrist and two swipes of a finely honed blade were usually all that was required. The threads, even the finest silk ones, could be sliced as easily as butter. Sometimes the money purse jangled, especially if it was nicely weighted, but by then it was already too late. Fleet of foot and as unpredictable in their movements as quicksilver, the thieves were already plunging through the crowd, hiding behind skirts as well as under them.

The gentleman—and she could tell by his negligent confidence that he was at the very least a gentleman—inclined his head toward the woman on his arm as she spoke. The nature of the comment was not clear to her, as the gentleman's features merely remained politely fixed. The woman evidently thought her observation was worthy of some sort of response because she raised her brows expectantly. His nibs remained unmoved. This seemed to cause his companion some distress as the curve of her dark red mouth faltered, then fell. Lest he miss the point, the woman underscored it by pursing her lips, not with disapproval, but petulance.

It was not a look that sat well on the woman's narrow features, she thought as she advanced on them, but that expression had arrested the gentleman's attention and neither he nor his lightskirt made any attempt to evade her approach.

She saw the buzz-gloaks coming at him from three directions, moving purposely through the crowd but without hurry or menace, cautious in the way they were proceeding to deliver the rum-hustle. Indeed, if she had not been looking for them, they might have easily escaped notice. It was all part and parcel of their plan, a plan they had executed successfully more times than she cared to contemplate. One would rub elbows with their quarry, one would beg his pardon, and one would step smartly on his ladybird's ruffled skirt. They would move on quickly, but not at a run. They were boman prigs and knew their craft too well to draw more attention to themselves than was strictly necessary. If their victim realized his purse had been lifted and gave chase, *then* they would run. It would require more luck than determination to catch them, for they had a lightness of foot that equaled the lightness of their fingers and putting hands on them was like trying to snatch quicksilver.

Her attention was all for them, gauging the moment they would strike, her deliberation matching their own. It surprised her, then, that she should notice anything at all outside the trap that was about to be sprung. Perhaps it was because she knew the players so well that one more or less in the drama gave her pause. It was as if Iago had made his entrance with Queen Titania's fairie court; one knew immediately that Othello's villain had no place in *A Midsummer Night's Dream*.

She did not mistake the man's nature by naming him a

villain. Although he was a brutish sort, with broad, uneven features and a heavy gait, he was in every way the equal of the dangerously sly and manipulative character that Shakespeare had perfectly penned.

These thoughts flitted through her mind so quickly that she barely grasped their import; acting on them was impulsive, accomplished more by instinct than plan. She had arrived in this place with only one purpose: to stop the three young ruffians from picking the gentleman's pockets. Once she saw the glint of the attacker's blade, she was helpless to respond in any way save to stop him from slitting the gentleman's throat.

Launching herself forward at a run, her lithe body defied gravity as it took flight. For a few moments she was actually suspended above the crushed gravel path, then momentum brought her crashing into the gentleman, bearing him hard to the ground.

Lady Georgia Pendelton, Countess of Rivendale, pressed her hands to her heart in what an idle observer might have determined was a dramatic, perhaps overwrought, gesture. Those fortunate people who numbered themselves among the lady's dearest friends knew the sincerity of such gestures and would always recognize them as a sign that her sympathies were deeply engaged.

"Never say you were hurt, Sherry. I do not think I can bear it if you say you were injured." Her pale gray eyes narrowed as she made a complete survey of her godson. He had suffered a measure of this scrutiny when he crossed the threshold into her sitting room, but then she had not known he had had an adventure. Now she must assure herself that he was none the worse for it, dear boy.

That dear boy, Alexander Henry Grantham, Viscount Sheridan, was in his twenty-eighth year, and he was as kindly cooperative of his godmother's second study of his person as he had been her first.

This inspection was nothing new. He had been all of five the first time he was aware of it. On that occasion Lady Rivendale had swept into the nursery, his own mother a few steps in her wake, and made an extraordinary fuss over him. There had been comments about the unfortunate darkening of his hair, from toffee brown to bittersweet chocolate. And was there nothing anyone could do about the cowlick that surely pointed due north like a compass needle? His eyes, she also noted as she raised his chin, had lost every hint that they might be green or hazel and now were as deeply brown as his hair. Why was he so pale? she wondered, and because she was Lady Rivendale, his mother's great friend from childhood and his own dear godmother, she felt free to wonder this aloud.

There was also a critique of the shape of his nose, which was pronounced as substantial as an eagle's beak by his godmother and aquiline by his mother. "Just like his father's," Lady Sheridan had said. "Yes," his godmother had replied, "but one hopes that can be changed."

She said nothing about his mouth, which he remembered thinking was a kindness, for surely his lower lip had been quivering by then. Still, he stood there and accepted it, watching her gravely from eyes that she had already pronounced too large for his thin face.

She liked the way he stood, though, and complimented him on his soldier's bearing. "Come, give us a hug," she said, and enveloped him in her arms. For a long time afterward Sherry had thought the "us" he was hugging were the soft twin pillows of her breasts.

"You must call me Aunt Georgia," she told him. Of course he did. How could he refuse a woman with such important breasts?

She would disappear for months, sometimes years, then announce herself without advance notice or invitation. She was always welcome. Presents arrived at odd times, never for the usual celebratory reasons like birthdays or Christmas, but simply because she thought of him. Later, when his younger sister reached the great age of six and exchanged the nursery for the schoolroom, Lady Rivendale proclaimed this also made her of interest and showered her with attentions that had been formerly reserved for him.

He did not mind overmuch. His godmother was in every way generous with her affections. The more she gave of herself, the more she seemed to have to give. For proof of this, he had only to think of the visit she made to Eton in the month following the death of his parents.

A great-uncle on his mother's side was now guardian to him and his sister, but the charge lay heavily on his shoulders, more burden than privilege, and he gratefully surrendered all duties to Lady Rivendale when she applied for them. At the funeral service he had been overheard to say, "Deuced irresponsible of Sheridan and my niece to die with their children yet to be raised. What am I to do with the two brats? Oh, it is a simple enough thing with the lad. He is at Eton at least, and his future is set. But the girl? I can get nothing from her save tears."

When Lady Rivendale arrived at Eton, she had his sister in tow. It was one of the few times she did not inspect his person before enveloping him in her plump arms and plumper breasts; it was also the first time he was called Sherry.

Viscount Sheridan. His father's title, now his, but somehow uniquely his. No one had ever call his father Sherry, not even the dauntless Lady Rivendale.

On the occasion of that visit she had announced they would be family now, and she said it with such practicality that Sherry and his sister never questioned the good sense of it.

It was not a matter of becoming a family; they just were.

"I am all of a piece," he said, returning to the present before she placed the back of her hand on his forehead. "The ill effects were confined to my frock coat, which split at the shoulder seam, and the backside of my trousers, which was pitted with gravel. Kearns says the frock coat will be repaired to its former fit; the trousers have already been surrendered to the ragpicker."

"I am certain your valet has your wardrobe well in hand—
he has never failed to turn you out impressively—but what
of your backside?"

Sherry blinked. He should not have been surprised by the
remark, for Lady Rivendale always spoke her mind. Most
often it was a refreshing discourse. He found, however, when
the subject was his backside the notion of such plain speaking was rather alarming.

"You are really quite charmingly priggish," she said, dropping both hands from her heart to lay them lightly on his
forearm. "I have always thought so. No, you must not take
offense, for none was meant."

"Saying that it is charming does not mitigate the prig-
gishness."

Lady Rivendale smiled deeply. She loved his wry tone.
Sherry might be a tad high in the instep, but at least he had
the good sense to know it. "I will not be persuaded to allow
my question to go unanswered."

Sherry regarded her gravely. "When I said I was all of a
piece, dear heart, all the pieces included my backside."

Clapping her hands together smartly as she laughed, her
ladyship sat back comfortably on the settee. "Splendid. That
is perfectly splendid. Now, what of your companion? I suppose she emerged unscathed."

Had his sister made the remark he would have reproved
her, but this was his godmother and he found himself chuckling instead. "You will be disappointed to learn it was just
so."

She did not deny it. "Bother. I would not wish her any
grievous injury, of course."

"Of course."

"But the thought of Miss Dumont tumbling head over
bucket, especially if it were done with little grace, well, it is
a delicious image."

Sheridan's manner of collecting himself until he could
make a considered reply was to lift a single dark eyebrow in
a pronounced arch. In that fashion he could communicate re-

proach, caution, or even carefully measured astonishment. If the dark glance that accompanied it was equally persuasive, the recipient of this look simply ceased to speak. There were times, though, when Sherry's deeply brown eyes were only amused, and the effect of the raised brow was to lend his expression a touch of the ironic.

"I did not realize you were acquainted with Miss Dumont," he said mildly.

"Acquainted? With your mistress? Hardly, Sherry, and you well know it." To give her hands something to occupy them, Lady Rivendale picked up her teacup and sipped. "But aware? Yes, indeed, how could I not be? She has been your consort these last three months. I believe I learned you intended to set her up in that house in Jericho Mews before she knew the same."

"You have never said anything."

"It is not at all flattering that you can scarcely credit it. I have always maintained that you should have some secrets from me."

"Or at least the illusion that I have them," Sherry said dryly.

Lady Rivendale had the grace to blush. Suffused with pink color, her remarkably smooth countenance hinted at the complete beauty she had been in her youth. In her fifty-second year, she was still a handsome woman by any of society's standards, though proportionately rounder. The visible markers of her advanced age were the graying threads of hair at her temples and the faint but permanent creases at the corner of her eyes. Because she had earned the latter by laughing at the vagaries of life, and the former by surviving them, she accepted both without regrets or any thought of concealment. A military man did not conceal his ribbons, and it was no different for her. Life was a campaign.

"You are put out with me, Sheridan," she said. "Do not deny it; I can see that you are. Although I abhor defending myself, I cannot abide that you might think I spy on you. What particulars reach my ears concerning you are never

sought by me." Over the rim of the delicate bone china
teacup, Lady Rivendale saw her godson's brow rise a fraction higher. "Almost never," she amended. "Certainly that is
true in the case of Miss Dumont. I might have happily lived
the rest of my life without knowing you had an arrangement
with this woman, but no less a personage than Lady Calumet
repeated the *on dit* within my hearing. Deliberately done,
make no mistake, but entirely for my benefit. She knows I
dote on you."

"Then perhaps I should extend my thanks. Will a note be
enough, or should I call on her?"

Her ladyship went on as if Sherry had not interrupted. He
meant not a word of what he said, and they both shared that
understanding. "I doubt that Miss Dumont is even French,
so if she has tales of escaping the Terror or of connections to
the Bourbons to retain your sympathies and lighten your
pockets, it is all lies and nonsense. Miss Duplicitous is what
the baggage should call herself."

Sherry was glad he was holding his tumbler of whisky
and not drinking from it. By only the narrowest bit of luck
did he manage to swallow his laughter rather than choke on
it. "Pray, do not mince words. If you have an opinion, I should
like to hear it."

Unlike her beloved godson, Georgia Pendleton had never
held back laughter in her life, and she was not inclined to
begin now. It was no polite, trilling titter that escaped her.
When she laughed it was an abandonment of genteel sensibilities in favor of a full-throated, husky shout of her delight.
Her shoulders and bosom were engaged in the activity, heav-
ing once, then merely shuddering until the first wave of amusement passed. There was little delicacy in the movements,
though in the end, when she dashed away the tears that had
collected at the corner of her eyes, it was accomplished with
a certain *gravitas*.

"You are an evil boy," she said without rancor. "I am certain I knew it from the first. Look, you have made me spill

my tea." Since every drop had been neatly caught by the saucer, her accusation did not have the weight of a rebuke.

At once solicitous, though with an exaggerated formality that made his gesture a parody of concern, Sheridan leaned forward and took the cup and saucer from her hand. He tipped the saucer so the droplets of tea slid onto the serving tray, replaced it under the cup, then added a generous pour of whisky from his own tumbler to her tea.

"For your nerves," he said. "Drink deeply."

Lady Rivendale was immediately alert. "What is it? Never say you mean to marry the girl."

"No," he said firmly. "I confess, the idea has never occurred to me. It is not a done thing."

This time when her ladyship's plump bosom heaved, it was with relief. She could point out to him that it was indeed a done thing, though perhaps not very well done. As annoying as Sherry's perfect sense of propriety could be on occasion, there were times, such as now, that it was a most comforting aspect of his character. He actually looked a bit affronted that she had even briefly entertained the notion.

"I am heartily glad to hear it," she said. She raised her cup and took a deep swallow. The whisky blended nicely with the tea's piquant flavor and admirably warmed her. She regarded him expectantly. "Well?"

"Last evening's incident at the garden was not without bloodshed."

The whisky kept Lady Rivendale's complexion in the pink. He was right to suspect she would need it. "But not yours," she said, eyes narrowing again.

"No. Not mine." Before she could interrupt, he hastened to add, "And I did not do murder, though *that* thought did occur to me. It was the fellow who bowled me over who was stabbed."

"Hoist with his own petard, I'd say. He meant to rob you."

Sherry nodded thoughtfully. "It appears that way."

"You are entertaining some doubts?"

"No, not really. It all happened very fast. Most of the crowd scattered. Perfectly understandable. You can imagine there was a great deal of screaming."

"A fair amount of it from Miss Dumont's substantial lungs."

He confirmed his godmother's observation with a faint grimace. The memory of Francine's shrill vocalizations following the attack still echoed in his ears unpleasantly. "It was generally agreed by those witnesses who were in the least reliable that the fellow tripped in his approach and was caught by his own blade."

"A grievous wound?" she asked. "Or will he hang for surviving it?"

"I'm afraid I can answer neither of your questions. While I was being attended to, and Miss Dumont was being quieted, he was carried off."

"Carried off? Whatever do you mean?"

"Just that. Taken away."

"By the parish watchmen?"

"No, not the Charlies. By his accomplices, I should think. Except to remove his person from mine, no one evinced concern for him. That he was wounded was apparent. There was the knife hilt under his ribs and blood seeping on the stones. Hoist with his own petard, as you said. Onlookers moved in closer, and when the area was cleared again, he was gone."

"Then mayhap he was not hurt at all."

"I cannot conceive of a reason for such an elaborate ruse, but it doesn't matter. His wound was real enough. The blood on my waistcoat and shirt was quite real."

"You did not mention blood before."

"We were speaking of my injuries then," he said with perfect calm. "And I will remind you that there were none. In any event, the waistcoat and shirt went the way of my trousers. Kearns insisted."

"As well he should have." She gave him a considering look. "I did wonder why you so easily accepted a whisky this morning. It is not generally your way to drink this early."

Sherry had only accepted the tumbler because he knew

most of it would be used to lace his godmother's tea, but if she thought he required Dutch courage or the hair of the dog to set last night's adventure before her and behind him, he would not correct the assumption.

"It was good of you to come and tell me the whole of it, Sherry," she said. "I shudder to think how the story will be perverted by the time I hear it again from Lady Calumet."

"Yes, there is that."

"Hmmm." Georgia's gaze became a little unfocused as she regarded a point in the distance beyond her godson's shoulder and set herself to the task of perverting the facts to fit her own sense of how the tale should be told. "I shall have to put it about that you gamely acquitted yourself. One does not like to think that you simply *lay* there under that unfortunate person. Do you ever carry a blade, Sherry?"

"I do not."

She sighed, expecting just that answer. "No matter. It is perhaps better that you had no weapon. Placing yourself between the cutpurse and your lady friend is romantic nonsense, of course, but just the sort of thing a doting mama with a daughter on the marriage mart will want to hear. Are you certain you were with Miss Dumont, dear? Mighten it have been Miss Harriet Franklin who accompanied you? I think you will agree she is likely to inspire more gallantry than Miss Dumont."

"What she inspires is indigestion."

Lady Rivendale frowned. "Truly? That is too bad. I admit to having some hopes in that direction."

Sherry merely shook his head and set himself comfortably back in the wing chair, though if she had offered him another pour of whisky he would have seized it with the alacrity of a man going under for the third time.

Mrs. Nicholas Caldwell, née Cybelline Louisa Grantham, brushed past the butler in the foyer of her brother's town-house and summarily announced herself in Sheridan's library. He was caught between pleasure and dismay in the same manner he was caught between standing and sitting behind his polished cherry wood desk.

Cybelline did not expect ceremony from her brother, though she knew he was hard pressed not to offer it. "Oh, do sit, Sherry, if that is what you intended. I am quite content to come to you." She briskly unwrapped the paisley shawl from around her shoulders and unfastened the ribbons of her straw bonnet, then tossed bonnet and shawl in the direction of the damask chaise, all the while advancing on the desk as if she were a regimental standard bearer. She stopped only when she was inches from the chair into which he had slowly lowered himself. "Perhaps you'd better stand," she said. "I will have to see for myself that you are unhurt."

"Would you be offended," he asked mildly, "if I snapped to attention?"

"Beast."

Sherry pushed back his chair and stood, allowing himself once again to be the object of a loved one's careful scrutiny. Cybelline's study was only different from his godmother's in that her eyes were a steelier shade of gray. "You are looking well, Cyb," he said. "You are glowing, you know."

"Glowering."

"That also, but I choose to comment on what is lovely about you."

The glower went completely out of her. She rested her hand lightly on the gentle swell of her belly. She was only three months into her pregnancy and would have welcomed more proof of it. "How is it that you know precisely the right thing to say?"

"The same instinct that sends a fox running to his earth: self-preservation."

She tapped him lightly on his arm with her fist. "You really *are* a beast, Sherry." Assured now that he was in every way unharmed, Cybelline backed away and bade him sit once more. She chose the damask-covered chair for a resting place, fitting a small pillow in the curve of her back and placing her feet on an upholstered stool. When she looked up she saw his expression had arrested on her. She laughed. "Yes, Sherry, I *am* going to have a child. Truly. Did you have doubts?"

He blinked. Raising one hand to his dark hair, he plowed through it with an apologetic, if somewhat perplexed, manner. "No doubts," he assured her. "But I think it is only now penetrating the gray matter."

She nodded wisely. She knew the look and the feeling. It was akin to her own experience but even more closely mirrored her husband's. "It was the same for Nicholas. He accepted the news easily enough, but I know the exact moment he actually *understood* it. Astonishing, really, when you think about it, since it is the natural course of things. You do realize you'll be an uncle?"

"I knew that at the outset, but you will understand that until a moment ago it was an abstract concept." He regarded his sister's lovely, familiar features. They were set more softly now than they had been when she entered the room. Then they could only have been described as militant. At this moment a slight smile lifted the corners of her mouth, and the color in her cheeks was as pink as a perfect English rose. Curling tendrils of hair the color of honey framed her serene countenance like a golden nimbus. She did indeed glow.

"Uncle Sherry," he mused aloud. "It suits me, I think."

Cybelline let her hand flutter over her belly again. "Certainly it does. You will be a wonderful uncle." The timbre of her voice dropped slightly as it took on a husky, hopeful quality. "Marriage . . . babies . . . your turn as uncle might yet inspire you."

He grunted softly. "You have surely been talking to Aunt Georgia."

"She is entirely sensible on the subject, though that is not why I came here today."

Sheridan was certain that was so, but wondered now if he should be glad of it. Sighing, he forged ahead. There was no point in avoiding the subject any longer. "What have you heard, and more significantly, from whom did you hear it?"

"I should have liked to have heard it from you," she said reprovingly. "Since you failed to deliver the details yourself, I had the tale from Miss Arbuthnot and Mrs. Dorsey."

"Then it was your ladies' literary circle that was titillated by the story. I suppose I may take some solace in that. If my poor adventure is going to be embellished, the best minds should have a crack at it. Come now, out with it."

"The particulars are these," she said, raising one slim hand to tick them off on her fingers. "You were set upon by footpads in Covent Garden." Tick. "You dispatched one by planting him a solid facer that broke his nose and the other by using his own knife to gut him." Tick. Tick. "Miss Dumont made a cake of herself screaming like a banshee while you were attacked." Tick. "And when it was over you gave the Charlies enough coin to see that your erstwhile victims were properly cared for." Tick.

Sherry regarded his sister's open hand for a long moment before he spoke. "My. The wags have had a good run with it. Aunt Georgia weaves a story with considerably more warp than weft. I suspect by the time I arrive at the club this evening, modesty will prevent me from admitting that I dealt soundly with a half dozen of London's worst sort."

"None of it's true?" Cybelline asked.

"You are crestfallen," he said, observing the way her mouth pulled at the corners. "And I am sorry for that. You must feel free to make more of the tale if the fancy strikes you."

"I am *not* disappointed," she said stoutly, "and I will have nothing to do with perpetuating the lie. What is the truth?"

He told her. When he finished he could see clearly that she could no longer deny her regret. "It is singularly unheroic, is it not?"

"You were simply knocked down?" she asked.

"Flattened."

"You did not try to move Miss Dumont out of the way?"

"She stepped aside easily enough. The fact that she was screaming like a banshee did not dispose me to save her."

"Then that part is true."

He tapped one of his ears lightly with the flat of his hand. "Sadly, yes."

"You did not gut your assailant?"

"I do not clean my own fish."

"I wondered about that."

He watched her carefully. "Should you have liked it better if the tale were true?"

"No!" The response was forceful and surrendered a shade too quickly. "No," she said more convincingly a moment later. "You had no opportunity to defend yourself."

"Perhaps I would not have."

"I don't believe that."

He shrugged. "When the choice is put to you that it must be your money or your life, there is only one sensible answer. I do not like it that the question was not even posed. It seemed rather ill mannered that he would simply run at me."

"Ill mannered?" Cybelline said weakly. "That is your characterization of the footpad's methods? You *do* admire good form."

"I do not deny it. Why should I? Every profession must have standards, else how to judge one's success?"

"Why, Sherry, you are disappointed that he was not better at it!"

While it was clear his sister was astounded by this notion, Sherry did not understand the why of it. "Certainly. How else was I to properly acquit myself? I might have wrestled him on the path and taken the upper hand. Not dignified, mayhap, but preferable to lying under his dead weight with my lungs absent of breath. We might have grappled for the knife if it hadn't been buried to the hilt in his side. He was so inept that he tripped while advancing and plunged the thing in himself."

Cybelline frowned. "You're certain you had nothing to do with that? It seems deuced odd that he would have been able to manage the thing." Standing, she crossed the short distance to his desk and picked up the silver letter opener that was lying squarely at the center. She held it by the embossed hilt as if to make a stab at him, then puzzled over how she would do herself in with the same blade. She reversed the opener in her hand so that she gripped it by its sharper end and tried again.

"Bloody hell," he said.

She looked up, startled, and realized he had been watching her closely. "Why, Sherry, you never swear."

He did not apologize for it. "Do give it over before you do real damage to yourself and my niece or nephew."

Glancing down, she saw she still held the pointed tip of the opener mere inches from her right side. "This is what you were doing before I came in here," she said. Certain that she was in the right of it, she did not wait for his confirmation. "You were wondering yourself how it was accomplished."

Sherry held out his hand and waited until she slapped the letter opener smartly in his palm. To quell further temptation, he opened a drawer under the desktop and slipped it inside.

"It is merely a curiosity," he said by way of explanation. He waved her back to the chair before he returned to his seat. "As I mentioned, it all happened with surprising speed. It is difficult to order the particulars in one's mind."

Cybelline did not think Sherry had ever experienced this difficulty before. He was maddeningly analytical. Aunt Georgia despaired that it was a flaw of character, though she cheerfully exploited it when Sherry's assistance was required to solve some nettling problem. Eyes narrowing, she asked, "You were not foxed, were you?"

"No." That she would ask, surprised him. "You know I do not drink to—"

"Excess," she said. "Yes, I do know. Clouds the mind; dulls the faculties. Bad form and so on."

It pricked him a little to have his views on the subject repeated to him in such a dismissive fashion, but other than a fractional lift of one of his eyebrows, he made no response. In any event, Cybelline was honing the point of her discourse and would not be easily stopped.

"I was wondering about the influence of Miss Dumont. She is a person known to invite—"

"Excess?" Sherry inquired mildly.

"Excitement." She cleared her throat and plunged on. "I realize you think it improper for me to raise the subject of your mistress, but I—"

"Improper *and* distasteful."

"Very well," she said, accepting the quiet reproach as due. "Improper and distasteful. Still, it does not mitigate the necessity of plain speaking. I love you to distraction, Sherry, and I would have you do so much better for yourself than Miss Dumont. By reputation she embraces all the things you despise. She has no heart, Sherry. Opportunity, not principle, guides her."

"At the risk of encouraging you to continue swimming in these dangerous waters, Cyb, permit me to say that I have no interest in Miss Dumont's heart, and I would not be flattered if she were to attach herself to mine. You are wrong, though, that she lacks principle, and correct that she sets her course as opportunity presents itself. They are not mutually exclusive."

"I cannot like her influence," Cybelline said tartly.

There was a moment's pause, then Sherry gave a shout of laughter. "I confess I have been slow off the mark, but I see your argument has nothing at all to do with Miss Dumont's influence. My ignominious brush with footpads is only an excuse for you to once again enumerate the reasons Miss Anne Meadows must be of interest to me."

Cybelline's blush made denial a hopeless defense. "You have admitted yourself that she is passingly lovely."

"I believe I said she is lovely in passing."

"You paid her the great compliment of not being without intelligence."

"As are even God's lowliest creatures."

"When you partnered her at Almack's you stated quite convincingly that she was accomplished."

"At counting the steps," he said. "Not in their execution."

Cybelline tried to pin Sherry back with a flinty, accusing glance, but it was useless. His smile melted her resolve to press on. "I shall be wary of all compliments from you from this point forward."

"Why? I say precisely what I mean."

"But not all you mean. I am understanding therein lies an important distinction."

One corner of his mouth lifted as he regarded her with approval. "You are also not without intelligence."

She laughed and reached for her bonnet. "I will take my leave before you toss more insults in my direction."

Sherry stood. "It was good of you to come. I would have called on you later today, you can depend upon it."

"I know," she said softly, knotting the ribbons to one side of her chin. "But the *on dit* was as frightening as it was delicious, and I could not wait to have the whole of it from you." She hesitated. "You will be careful, won't you, Sherry? I do not think I could bear it if you came to harm."

He rounded the desk and went to stand before her. He took her hands in his and gave them a small shake. "Look at me, Cybelline." When she did, he set about easing her fears. "Miss Dumont is in no way at fault for what happened last night. The theatre was my idea as was the walk afterward. I was bracing myself for the inevitable bad end to the evening, for I was determined to break things off with her. Now, are you quite satisfied? I have told you more about my private affairs than I intended, and I am telling you not because you asked but because I abhor the notion that either you or Aunt Georgia will congratulate yourself for influencing exactly this end."

Sherry did not miss his sister's small start, though she was making an admirable attempt to school it. "There," he said, amused and accusing at once. "I can see that you will take credit notwithstanding my efforts to the contrary. I advise caution, however, because I have not made the break yet and might be moved by purely spiteful motives to reconsider."

"You would not," she said certainly. "You have not a spiteful inclination in your head."

"Perhaps," he said, "but you would do well not to plant the seed there."

Standing on tiptoe, Cybelline raised her head and kissed his cheek. It was easy for her to forget what a tall, impressive figure he cut. Reaching for him reminded her. He gently steadied her until she was grounded again.

"Will you come to dinner this evening, Sherry?" she asked.

He picked up her shawl and fixed it about her shoulders. "I am playing cards at the club, then I have a business matter to which I must attend."

She realized he was speaking of Miss Dumont. Strange, she thought, that one's arrangement with a mistress was naught but a business matter. Was it always thus? she wondered. Or always thus for Sherry?

Sherry did not like the speculative look that came into his sister's eye. He gently took her elbow and steered her toward the door. When she was moving briskly on her own, he let her go.

Cybelline did not pause until she was standing on the threshold. She did not turn completely but rather glanced over her shoulder at him. "Do you know, Sherry, that I will think Miss Dumont the veriest fool for giving you up."

Francine Dumont was no one's fool. Sherry had considered this carefully when choosing the piece of jewelry that would serve to end their association in an amicable fashion. He counted himself as fortunate that he had not been robbed last night. The hapless footpad might have made off with the velvet-lined box he had carried with him to the theatre and the emerald earbobs that were the box's valuable contents. The loss would hardly have been worth his life, though he was not certain that Francine would not have thought so.

He lay in bed, sated, if not precisely satisfied, and stared at the ceiling. At the bedside, the candle flame flickered, creating the play of light and shadow across the plasterwork that claimed his attention.

"You are zinking about last night, perhaps?" Francine Dumont propped herself on one elbow and regarded Sherry's profile. "What is it, Sheridan? You have deep thoughts, *non*?"

"No."

"Zen not so decent thoughts, eh?" she teased, her accented English thickening. "*D'accord*. I have a fondness for your not-so-decent thoughts. You will like mine." She placed two fingers on his bare chest and began to walk them slowly toward his groin. She frowned when he caught her wrist just as it slipped beneath the sheet. "*Qu'est-ce que c'est?* Are you not well?"

Sherry released her wrist. "This is the last time I will visit here."

"*Est-ce que c'est vrai?* Zis is true?"

"Yes."

She sat up. Her breasts lifted invitingly as she tossed her hair over her shoulder. She noted with some satisfaction that his eyes followed the movement, and she stretched deliberately, arching her back to entice him with her rosy, beaded nipples.

"I never said you were not without your charms," he told her.

The absence of inflection in his voice warned her she was defeated before she could fire the first salvo. To salvage a measure of pride, she said, "I can make you want me."

"Never doubt it." His cock was stirring now. Leaving her was not about what she could give him but about what she could not. He did not try to explain this to her; she would not understand. Indeed, his arrangement with her came about in no small part because she *could* not understand. She was not

complicated that way, and he did not desire a complicated
life. A straightforward agreement was what he required and
precisely what he received. To that end, it was very good.
Very, very good.

Sherry watched her flatten the generous line of her mouth.
"*Tu es agitée*," he said softly. "*Je comprends, et je regrette*."

"*Merci*."

Chuckling deeply at the back of his throat, Sherry pushed
himself upright. "You will be wise to spend some of your
earnings on French lessons. I said that you are annoyed and
that I understood and that I'm sorry. It was not precisely a
compliment."

"Then you shouldn't make it sound like one," she snapped.

Sherry smiled now. Her lamentably accented English was
noticeable for its absence. "The trickery was always beneath
you, Fanny."

"Oh, do not call me that. I detest that name."

"It is a perfectly fine name. Is it really yours?"

She reached for the silken robe that lay at the foot of the
bed and slipped it on. "Yes," she said, biting off the single
syllable as she knotted her belt. "Not Francine or Francesca
or even Francis. Fanny."

"And your last name? Is it Dumont?" He actually blinked
at the glare she served up. "Oh no," he said, thinking it
through. "Never say . . . *du mont* . . . mountain . . ." He was
tempted to raise a hand to ward her off. He could not acquit
her of wanting to scratch out his eyes. "Hill," he said. "You
were born *Fanny Hill*."

Sherry did have to move quickly then, for she threw a pillow at him and was scrambling for her brush on the bedside
table. He ducked when it came flying at his head. "Have off!
A truce." This would cost him dearly, he suspected, but it
was worth every farthing he'd pay out. He regarded her almost as warily as she regarded him. "Finished?"

Fanny relaxed her grip on the mirror she held. It was a favorite of hers, and she would not have liked to see it broken.
That, more than Sheridan's call for a truce, decided her. "I

am not *that* Fanny Hill," she said smartly. "She was . . . she was . . . *common*."

"Of course, you are not." He did not point out that John Cleland wrote *Memoires of a Woman of Pleasure* more than fifty years earlier. He wondered if she had read the book or if someone had told her about the erotic adventures of its heroine, Fanny Hill. He decided it was the latter, else she would not have characterized the fictional Miss Hill as common. It had always seemed to him that Fanny Hill was unburdened by regrets and liberated by pleasure, which made her a decidedly uncommon woman in any time. "I understand that you would not approve of comparisons," he said, "but she is not a woman without her virtues."

Fanny's suspicious glance did not waver, but she did finally set the mirror down. "You will not tell anyone?"

"A gentleman doesn't."

Inexplicably, Fanny thought she would cry. She hardened herself against that urge and moved off her side of the great bed. "I will want the house for at least another month, perhaps two."

Sherry found his drawers and put them on. He was of the unwavering opinion that negotiations were better conducted with one's trousers on. "I am willing to give you three, but I am unconvinced you will need so much time to find another protector."

"Oh," she said, interested in spite of herself. "You have heard something?"

"Something," he repeated. "You are acquainted with Makepeace?"

"Sir Charles Makepeace?"

"The very one."

"He is looking for an arrangement?"

"I cannot say if that is so, but surely how it turns out has something to do with you. I know that he is at loose ends."

She considered this. "A man never does well in that state."

"My thoughts exactly. We are at our most vulnerable."

"Not you, Sheridan. You are ruthless in your own fashion.

I do not believe you have ever been at a loose end. You would cut it off rather than have it exposed."

She was closer to the mark than he had thought possible. Before she made the logical leap and realized that was precisely what he was doing now, he pointed to his frock coat. "I brought you a gift." He saw her eyes brighten and knew there were no more thoughts of loose ends. Avarice was perhaps her most honest emotion, and he did not fault her for it. He watched her search the coat and laugh delightedly when she found the box.

"Oh, Sherry," she said on a breath of sound, awed by the emeralds. "What beautiful jewels!"

He crossed the room to stand beside her. "*Regardes-moi, mon petite*." He touched the tip of her chin and tilted her enchantingly greedy face toward him. "Francine Dumont would say it just so: *Quels jolis bijoux!*"

It required only three days for Sherry to set his other affairs to right. None of them involved a woman, so choosing presents as carefully as he would choose his words did not delay his departure for the country. He canceled all his engagements for the next month, sending his regrets unaccompanied by any explanation. He knew the wags would have it that he was leaving because he had killed that cutpurse. There was never any chance of turning that story, and Sherry did not even try. He returned to the site of the failed robbery for clues about the thief, but no one he suspected of having information would speak to him long.

The gangs from the meanest streets of Holborn, the ones that roamed Covent and Vauxhall, and the pupils from the schools for thievery that were instituted in St. Giles-in-the-Fields and St. Martin's, were a closed bunch. Talking to them was a challenge, for when they did not wish to be understood, they spoke in a cant that was impenetrable to his ear. It was English, to be sure, but the phrasing and meter was more foreign to him than French was to Fanny Hill.

Inquiries about the thief, even the most inoffensive ones about his health, were met as often by blank stares as they were by suspicious ones. There was no one he could give money to for the man's care. There were plenty who would have taken it; indeed, he had to check his pockets constantly to be certain he still had it, but he had no faith that his sovereigns would ever be used to improve the man's care if he lived or provide a Christian burial if he didn't.

In the end there was nothing for it but to cut the loose end. Miss Hill was correct in her judgment that he had no use for them. It was just as she had said: he was ruthless in his own fashion.

It mattered not a whit to Sherry that the *ton* assumed he was running from something. The truth was that he was running to it, and he had made the decision a full month before the evening at Covent Garden. Arriving at the decision had actually led to that night at the opera, not the reverse.

London never held the appeal for him that it did for so many others in his set. He liked the card play well enough, the camaraderie of the clubs, the politics in or out of Parliament, the women in or out of bed, the occasional ball, and less occasionally a turn on the floor, but the carousel-like quality of it all bored him near to madness. He kept the house because it belonged in the family, and he could not ignore all the responsibilities of his position in town, but it was only at Granville that he could renew his spirit.

He needed to breathe unfetid air, paint as the mood seized him, ride hell-bent-for-leather across green fields, bury his hands deep in the fecund soil of the farm, and renew acquaintances at his leisure, not on demand.

Sherry stood with his back to the library entrance, making a last inspection of the shelves to see if he had missed a volume or two that he would enjoy taking with him. The carriage had been drawn up to the front of the house, and Kearns would arrive soon to inform him that all had been made ready.

The commotion in the hallway did not make him turn toward it. The brief attention he gave it was to suppose his housekeeper would see to it. Mrs. Ponsonby knew her duties and knew what he liked. There had never been anything she couldn't manage.

The shout, when it came, gave him some concern, but he let it pass. He did not recognize the voice. It had a youthful timbre and all the outrage that only youth can fully express. It actually made him smile. A lad from the kitchen, no doubt, unhappy with some duty he was expected to perform and too foolish to realize Mrs. Ponsonby would never let him out of the kitchen again.

There was another shout, more of a cry this time. A different voice, though. And then another cry, yes, definitely a cry this time. Mrs. Ponsonby, he decided. A yelp, a squeal, caterwauling, cursing, and still more shouts, some of it sounding as if spoken in a foreign tongue.

Unable to imagine the thing that Mrs. Ponsonby could not manage, Sherry turned and walked slowly to the open door. His presence and a single raised eyebrow had the desired effect: immediate quiet. The problem was that it did not last nearly long enough. In the space of a single heartbeat, three of the scruffiest street urchins he had ever beheld pushed past Mrs. Ponsonby and charged at him. He neatly stepped aside so when they skidded to a halt they were trapped in the library.

"I'll send for the authorities," Mrs. Ponsonby said.

"A few moments," Sherry told her. "I'll tell you when." He was already backing into the library when Mrs. Ponsonby's lower jaw sagged. He firmly shut the door on her gaping countenance and turned toward his uninvited guests. As he suspected, they all began speaking at once, and he didn't understand a word of it.

Two

Sherry learned quickly that a raised brow was ineffective with these young squatters. They'd already seen the limits of its use in the hallway and were apparently willing to take their chances that the other eyebrow was similarly without consequence.

"Bloody hell," he said under his breath. His language did not give them pause. If they heard him at all, which was doubtful given the volume of their own declaratives, it was a certainty they had heard far worse.

They were a motley trio. Poverty clung to them so aggressively they were barely distinguishable as three separate souls. Each of them was painfully thin. Sherry suspected that under the uniformly dirty rags they were wearing, they were all sharp angles, with knees and elbows shaped like the hard, knobby head of a walking stick.

He could not make a proper guess as to their ages, only that little in the way of months or years separated them. One of them always had his mouth opened, and Sherry had not yet glimpsed a full complement of teeth. Except for his own experience as a child, he knew nothing about them. When did they lose their teeth? he wondered. Were these young ruffians missing theirs as the natural course of maturing or was poor diet the culprit? Given their tendency to caterwaul at length, it occurred to him that a less patient man might have simply knocked them out.

At his back, Sherry turned the key in the door and locked it. He pocketed the key but doubted it was safe there. Any one of them looked capable of getting it out again, probably without his noticing. It was a lowering thought that he could be so easy a mark. He pushed away from the door and crossed the room to his desk. He would not have counted himself as surprised had they followed, but when he turned they were still planted in the center of the room regarding him cautiously. For the moment at least, they fell quiet.

Sherry showed them the quill he had selected from the pen stand. For most of its length, the striations on the feather were brown and black. Only the tip was white. He ran his index finger along it, bending it slightly to demonstrate its resiliency. He also showed them by pressing the nib against the tip of the same finger that it was not overly sharp.

Taking advantage of their silence, he said, "When the feather is in my possession, I may speak. When the feather is in your possession, you may speak. I am not using the words *you* and *your* in the collective sense, but in the singular; therefore, having the feather in your possession is not an invitation for three or even two of you to speak at once."

To a person they simply stared at him. Sherry sighed, then said, "It would appear we are divided by a common language." He approached the trio and extended his hand with the feather in it. "Which one of you will be first?"

He watched the boys exchange glances, nudge one another with those sharp elbows, then apparently arrive at a decision as the middle urchin stepped forward. That this was accomplished without a word passing between them impressed Sherry. "What a fine example you fellows could set in the Parliament." He dangled the feather in front of the boy. "I will have your name, young sir."

"Pinch," he said, lifting the quill smoothly from Sherry's grasp.

"Apropos," Sherry murmured.

"You don't 'ave the feather, guvnor."

"What?"

Pinch swiveled his head in the direction of each of his companions and rolled his eyes. "'E made the rules and 'as no respect for them. That's a swell for ye."

Sherry could not recall receiving a more righteous setdown, or perhaps one that was so well deserved. In observance of his own rules, he made to take the feather back. Pinch quickly put the feather out of reach behind him, and Sherry realized it must have exchanged hands in a nonce because the child on Pinch's left spoke up.

"Dash, 'ere."

There was another smooth exchange, and the boy on the right announced himself. "I'm Midge."

The feather was returned to Pinch. He revealed it to Sherry, twirling it in his fingertips, but made no move to offer it. "We know who yer lordship is," he said with a touch of defiance. "We come for the coin ye offered t'other day. If ye meant it sincere, then ye won't 'ave a second thought about givin' i'tover."

Givin' i'tover. Sherry winced as he translated. *Giving it over.* He held his hand out for the feather.

Pinch hesitated, but only briefly. He was not entirely proof against Sherry's implacable stare. "'Ere. But if ye keep it overlong, the bargain's struck down."

"We did not strike a bargain," Sherry said once he was in possession of the feather. "I suggested a means of conducting our business in a civil manner, Master Pinch, and you accepted. Matters of trade, diplomacy, and even parley between scurvy-riddled pirates require attention to certain niceties of deportment. I am the Viscount Sheridan, and you will address me as befits my title. As to this notion that I should give you funds, you will have to offer more in the way of explanation, otherwise Mrs. Ponsonby will be instructed to send for the watchmen, and I will give testimony against you at the assizes myself."

Holding out his hand again, Sherry offered the feather for the plucking. It was a long moment before it was taken. He was not sure if he had shaken their confidence or befuddled their young minds.

"Beggin' yer lordship's pardon," Pinch said, striking a note of credible deference. "We meant no disrespect." He shifted uncomfortably under Sheridan's sardonic gaze. "That is, we meant no *sincere* disrespect. There ain't much in the way of time left. Wouldn't 'ave come if it 'ad been else, but Dash 'ere followed you 'ome t'other day as we knew it might come to this. So here we are, come for the coin you promised so we can get a surgeon. Nothin' will be right again, I can tell ye, if we don't."

Midge took the feather. "Nothin', yer lordship."

Dash reached around Pinch and lifted it from his friend's fingers. "Nothin's been as it was since yer lordship plugged 'er with yer shiv."

Sherry frowned as the feather was held out to him. For a moment he simply looked at it dumbly and knew his own senses to be well and truly befuddled. These young ruffians had a way of dishing out twice what was served to them once. He took the feather. "'Er?" he asked, his voice not much above a whisper. "You are speaking of a female?"

There was some eye rolling before Pinch reached for the feather.

Sherry held it out of the way. "I think we can dispense with this," he said, tossing it aside. "It has served its purpose." He put the question to them again when they fell quiet. "Female?"

Pinch snorted. "Blimey! She's a girl, right enough, if that's what yer lordship means. Thought ye'd know that when ye put the knife to her."

"How would I know?"

Dash frowned. "Bubbies." In the event his host did not know the word, Dash cupped his dirty hands over his chest and pushed upward. "Bubbies."

Sherry actually felt himself pale. "A *young* girl?" he asked.

It was Midge who answered. He lifted his hands to his thin chest in the same manner his friend had, but he made bigger cups of his palms.

"A woman, then," Sherry said. It made him feel not a whit better. "My assailant was a woman?"

"Miss Rose," Pinch told him. "'Ere now, do ye need to sit? Midge, get 'is lordship a chair. Push it right up under 'im."

Midge started forward, but Sherry waved him back. He was all too aware that they were watching him closely, prepared to show no mercy for weakness.

For his part he was finally able to make some distinctions between the boys. Pinch's face was the narrowest, his features tight to the bone, the dark eyes keen with distrust. He might have taken the moniker Pinch because of his profession, but it was equally suited to his look.

Master Dash, in contrast, was not simply pale but fair skinned. There was evidence of a towhead beneath his battered cap and a substantial amount of grime. The boy evinced a natural restlessness, shifting his weight from one foot to the other, curling and uncurling his fingers. The temptations of the library, with its bone china vases and jade figurines, the crystal decanters on the sideboard, and the wealth inherent in the leather-bound books, were positively fraying the child's nerves.

Then there was Midge, the one Sherry took to be the youngest, if not in years, then in necessary experience. He was smaller of stature and held himself with less confidence. His eyes were a shade wider than the others, deeply blue, and more curious than cautious. He was easily the most vulnerable and accessible of the trio.

It was to Midge that Sherry looked. "Miss Rose?" he asked. "She is your sister perhaps?"

"Teacher."

Sherry did not miss the elbow jab that Midge was served for his answer. "You are all apprentices of Miss Rose, then," he said. "She runs a school for thievery?" There was no answer forthcoming; indeed, he had not expected one. They had already risked a great deal to come to their teacher's aid. They were not likely to put the whole of it at his feet. "Very well. Let us decide what is to be done."

"Yer coin," Pinch said, lifting his narrow chin sharply. "Then we'll fetch a surgeon for 'er."

"Make 'er right agin," Dash said. "Like she was afore ye stuck 'er."

Sherry was compelled to defend himself before Midge echoed Dash. "Contrary to what you think you know, I know I did not *stick 'er*. Your Miss Rose stuck herself. With her own blade, I might add, because I do not carry one." He was uncertain if this impressed his guests or made him seem foolish. No matter, it was the truth.

"Miss Rose don't carry one either," said Pinch. His chin was still up, challenging Sheridan.

"She did that night," Sherry said. "Because I did not."

Pinch did not back down from his assertion, and the other two squared their shoulders in support of it. "So you say."

Sherry was unused to having his word disputed; to have a child gainsay him was the end of enough. He was prepared to call for Mrs. Ponsonby—certain she was standing at the ready on the other side of the door—when the shutter dropped from Pinch's dark eyes and revealed nothing save his fear. The sharp breath Sherry had drawn to summon his house-keeper lodged in his throat. He released it slowly, long after Pinch had drawn the shutters up again, but he knew he had not imagined it.

There had been a moment when he had felt that fear as his own.

Sherry returned to his desk, hitched one hip on the edge, and crossed his arms in front of his chest. "We will have off with the accusations," he said firmly. "I will not give you coin for a surgeon but will summon my own physician in lieu of that." He absorbed their blank stares. "In lieu of . . . instead of." Comprehension brightened their eyes. "You will have to take us to Miss Rose. There is no getting around that.

I cannot send Harris off alone even if he would agree, which he will not."

"Then ye've kilt her," Pinch said. "We can't take ye."

"Do you think I mean to have her arrested?" They looked at one another uncertainly, then back at him and shrugged. "I don't," he said. "Neither do I intend to expose her school. The watchmen know where you live and have never been moved to run you out."

"Sure, and donchaknow, we give 'em a share of our pickins from time to time."

Of course, Sherry thought. The Charlies were paid little enough; the bribes they received were probably pathetically small. "Well? What is it to be?"

Pinch's glance was suspicious. "'Ere now, why do ye care?"

Sherry inclined his head slightly in a nod of approval. "You are the first person to put that question to me, Master Pinch, and the answer will surprise you: I do not care."

"Oooh," Pinch said, raising his hands in mock astonishment. "There's a surprise, right enough. A toff who don't care about us who's less fortunate than 'imself."

Sherry waited for Pinch's cynical amusement to quiet, then said, "I am no social reformer. I do not care about your school, or your teacher, or how many pockets you pick, but I cannot shed myself of the peculiar notion that I am in some way responsible for the injury that was done, and that, young master, is what offends me and what honor demands I correct."

"Responsible?" Pinch asked. "O'course yer responsible. Ye plunged yer shiv in her."

Sherry said nothing. His refusal to mount another defense left them wondering and uncertain. They were unused to extending trust outside of their small group; perhaps it was a rare thing extended inside it as well.

"No tricks?" Pinch's eyes narrowed to slits. "You won't 'urt 'er?"

"You will accept my word?"

Pinch glanced at his companions. They nodded slowly.

When he looked back at Sheridan he said gruffly, "Aye. We'll accept it."

Sherry stood and offered his hand. "A gentleman's agreement, then." There was some hesitancy, then they came forward one at a time and surrendered their grimy fingers to the grip of his long, elegant ones. When this solemn business was concluded, Sherry resisted the urge to reach for his handkerchief or check his timepiece to see if it was still attached to the fob. The trust they tendered was not necessarily reciprocal, but he had no wish to underscore that point. He unlocked the door, pocketing the key again.

"Mrs. Ponsonby," he said, his voice raised just enough to be heard into the hall.

The housekeeper appeared in the doorway immediately. Also in the frame behind her were his valet, the cook, and his driver. "Yes, m'lord? Shall I fetch a watchman now?"

"No. The physician, please. Be most particular to inform Harris that he should come immediately and will be well compensated for the trouble I am going to put him to."

Her eyes widened a fraction, but to her credit Mrs. Ponsonby kept her jaw firmly set. "Here, m'lord?"

"Here." He pointed to the space directly in front of him. "Also, a hack. I assume my trunks are already on the carriage."

"Yes, my lord." It was the driver, Mr. Pipkin, who answered. "But I can—"

"It will not be necessary to unload it. A hack will do. Of necessity my departure will be delayed. A few hours, I should think. No longer." Sherry's eyes swiveled to the cook as he addressed her. "Some repast for my guests, Renwick."

"You want me to feed them in my kitchen?" She was patently horrified by the idea and took no pains to hide it.

"No," Sherry said patiently. "I want their food brought here."

"Begging your pardon, my lord, but they are . . . they are . . ."

"Crumb-catchers?"

Pinch took immediate and powerful exception to this. "Now, see 'ere. There's no cause for making light of us. Midge is an erriff, true enough, but then he's only ten, workin' 'is way to becoming a fair to middlin' bulker. Dash 'ere's a bung-diver—one of the very best—and me own rum daddles make me a regular boman prig. So on no account should yer lordship be callin' us crumb-catchers."

Mrs. Ponsonby stepped forward. "Should I be washing his mouth out with soap, then?"

"I have no idea," Sherry said truthfully. It was difficult to imagine that Pinch's mouth was dirtier than the rest of him. Out of the corner of his eye he saw that all three boys were edging away at the idea of a good drubbing. "Let's let it go this time, Ponsonby, shall we?"

She nodded, though somewhat reluctantly, and began backing out of the room. The servants behind her scattered, each moving to their next task, all of them wondering what queer notion had seized their master.

"Why am I doing this, Lord Sheridan?" Harris asked, clutching his black leather bag in his lap. The three pick-pockets were riding on the roof of the hack, but the doctor was unconvinced they would not get it from him anyway. He leaned forward and tried to get a look at the roof from another angle. "You will have to explain it again."

Patiently, Sherry raised his beaver hat a fraction so that he might see Harris more clearly. The interior of the cab was dim. Outside, dusk was not yet upon them, but the narrow streets and oppressively close construction of the warehouses and tenements allowed little sunlight to reach them. "Because I am paying you an obscene amount of money for your ser-vices and your silence. Considerably more for the latter than the former."

"There is that." Although not placated, he was glad of the reminder. "You know I might not be able to do anything.

Judging by what you said about the location of the wound, it is likely infection has set in."

"Very likely. I'm certain her worsening condition is what brought the children to my doorstep."

"You will allow it's peculiar, my lord."

"I will allow that it's a great deal more than that."

"I shouldn't be at all surprised if they don't return to your home."

"I am hoping to be absent from it."

"You'll be missing the wash off your line and the pewter pots from your railings."

"I will be fortunate if that is all I'm missing," Sherry said with imperturbable calm.

Harris rubbed the rounded point of his chin with the back of his knuckles. His eyes darted left, then right. "They might accost us here," he said.

"Probably not while we're moving."

"You are armed, I hope."

"I am not a fool, Harris."

Which was not precisely an answer, the physician noted. He opened his mouth to say so, but Sherry cut the response by nudging his hat forward so that it shaded his eyes. At least, Harris thought, it was not that damnable eyebrow.

The establishment Pinch led them to was a more reputable place than Sherry had allowed himself to expect. The heavy wooden sign suspended on chains above the door identified the tavern as the Blue Ruination. The proprietor, Sherry decided, was possessed of a sense of humor, though such was not in evidence when Pinch led his parade inside. The great bull of a man wiping down the bar looked as if he meant to use Pinch to do the job on the next pass.

The child's *sang-froid* was quite remarkable, however. If he thought he was in danger, he didn't show it. Instead, he marched to the bar and climbed on a stool. As all seven of the tavern's patrons had fallen silent, he was forced to whisper.

Every crag in the owner's face deepened as he listened to Pinch's discourse, and Sherry was aware the man's eyes did not stray. Sherry realized he was being sized up as a threat, though what the proprietor thought he could do to challenge the peace and dignity of the Blue Ruination did not occur to him. At his side, Sherry felt the doctor take a step closer. The man's hands were shaking, a circumstance that did not inspire confidence.

Straightening as Pinch scrambled down from the stool, the proprietor wiped his hands on the towel and pitched it aside. "Pub's closed," he announced. "Out! The lot of ye! Go on. Don't like it? Take it up with the owner." He laughed heartily. "Oh, that would be me. Don't like it?" Still laughing he raised two meaty fists. "Take it up with these."

Harris was already in full retreat toward the street when the man bellowed, "Not you! Them!"

Seven tankards thumped to the tabletops. Benches scraped hard against the roughly hewn floor as five men and two women got to their feet. There were varying degrees of inebriation present, noticeable as soon as they started for the door. There was some bobbing and weaving, a few staggered footfalls, lurching, and help for a friend who could not manage his exit alone. The women took their leave more gracefully, adding a provocative sway to their hips as they brushed past Sherry.

"Shut the door, Midge, and bolt it."

Midge hurried off to do just that.

"Name's Rutland. Blue Rutland. Born that way. Blue, that is. Don't know why, just know it was so." He bobbed his head. As a sign of deference to quality it lacked genuine appreciation. "Pinch says you're a surgeon."

"Physician," Harris said weakly. He remained half a step behind Sherry.

"No sawbones, then. Well, we'll see what you know,

won't we." Rutland's discriminating glance went to Sherry. "You're Lord Sheridan?"

"I am."

"The one that gutted her."

Sherry didn't deny it. "Is she here? Show us to her. There is always time later to assign blame."

Blue Rutland considered this. It struck him as true. He nodded once. "This way," he said. "Have a care. The stairs are steep."

Sherry saw their host's shoulders filled the narrow stairwell. The steps made a tight curve as they climbed. Unused to the exertion, Harris's breath was labored. Sherry tried to ignore the puffing but knew that apoplexy was not outside the question.

Abovestairs, Pinch and Dash squeezed ahead of Rutland, then raced to the last door on the right and threw it open.

"Have a care," Rutland called after them. "It won't bother me to put you out, and she's in no condition to object."

Pinch caught the door before it banged against the far wall. He and Dash posted themselves with stiff, military bearing on either side of the threshold.

Sherry smelled the infection before he had fully entered the room. He heard Harris's steps falter and the man curse softly under his breath. To his credit, he did not hesitate. He brushed right past Sherry and went straight to the bed where his patient lay and the smell of putrefaction was the strongest.

Rutland hung back now. Sherry questioned the wisdom of approaching himself, then the matter was taken out of his hands because Harris asked for assistance.

"Remove these blankets," he ordered. "They're as dirty and infested as she is." He shot an angry, impatient glance at Rutland. "Was nothing at all done for her?"

The big man's broad face turned ruddy. "Got the knife out," he said. "Sewed the wound myself. Stitches are good, you can see that. I served on one of His Majesty's ships. I know a thing or two about stitchery."

Harris grunted as he lifted his patient's shirt. Blood stained the garment where it was rent. "This is the same thing she was wearing the night she was injured," he said.

"She wouldn't want me to ruin another."

The physician muttered something unintelligible under his breath. The stitches had been neat enough when applied, but they were stretched fair to bursting by the swollen discolored flesh. "My bag, Sheridan. I will require the scalpel." To Rutland, he said, "Whisky or something like it. Unopened if you have it. Nothing cut with water." When the barkeep hesitated, Harris snapped, "Now, man!"

Sherry almost felt sorry for Rutland. "What would you have me do?" He had already pitched the blankets in a corner.

"Take her wrists." He gave Sherry a short strap of leather. "If she tries to bite, put this bit in her mouth. Otherwise, keep her as still as you can. It will be a mercy if she doesn't wake." His tone made it clear he was not confident.

Sherry knelt at the side of the narrow bed near the head. The angle was awkward but he managed to secure her wrists. They were thin, fragile really. He was afraid that if she struggled he would snap them. The leather strap that he might require for a bit was tucked in his trousers where he could quickly reach it. He did not think he could be more prepared than that.

Shuffling at the door caught his attention, and he looked up. Pinch and Dash were no longer outside the room but in it. Midge was craning his neck between them. Their faces were grave, frightened. Sherry had not properly appreciated how important this young woman was to them until now. It had been on the tip of his tongue to tell them to leave. He did not. They had much more right to be here than he did.

He loosed a wrist long enough to remove his hat. When he bent his head again, a lock of dark hair tumbled forward over his brow. He let it lie there.

Even now she did not look like a female, but more like a child of indeterminate sex. He imagined in the last few days that she had lost at least a stone and nearly all of her strength. As slight of build as she was, it was hard to believe she had been able to knock him down. It was like a butterfly felling an oak.

Her hair was unnaturally dark, cropped short, and thickly matted to her head. Bootblacking, he suspected, though he wondered why she'd used it. Days ago, perhaps before she had taken to the streets, she'd covered her hair with the stuff. She'd been cautious enough to make swipes across her eyebrows, too, but close to her scalp where the sweat of her fever had diluted the black paste, and along the curve of her lashes, he glimpsed a hint of the penny copper color she had meant to conceal.

He watched her face as Harris worked. She didn't stir when the physician split the stitches with his scalpel. The odor from the pus was so intense that Sherry pressed his face into the sleeve of his coat until the urge to vomit passed. Her perfectly pared nose did not twitch.

Her skin was pale to the point of translucency and pulled taut over the high arch of her cheekbones. A faint blue web of veins was visible at her temples. Her mouth was full, a sweeping curve that lacked resiliency, animation, and virtually all color now. There was a deep hollow at the base of her throat caused in part by the prominent collarbones. Her breath came shallowly, and beneath his fingers he felt her rapid pulse. It thrummed against him with the lightness of a hummingbird's wing.

He could not guess at her age. She might have been as young as twelve or as old as five-and-twenty. The bubbies that Dash and Midge had outlined to indicate womanhood were bound tightly beneath a strip of linen wound several times around her. Her erstwhile caretakers had respect for her modesty, if not for her comfort.

No sound emerged from her parted lips as Harris cleaned the wound. Rutland arrived with a small, unopened cask of French brandy. No one raised any questions. Napoleon had escaped Elba earlier in the year—Wellington and Blücher were preparing to defend the Continent against the rise of a second empire—but Blue Rutland's smuggling was not the subject of recriminations.

Harris directed Rutland to unplug the cask. The physician plunged his hands into the golden liquid, rubbed them together, then poured a good handful into his patient's wound.

The keening cry arrested them all for a moment, but it did not come from the girl on the bed. Blue Rutland looked as if he might weep like a babe for the waste of his fine brandy.

"That's enough," Harris snapped. "Put it down." He went back to work, debriding the lacerated and devitalized tissue around the wound. His fingers were thick but deft, and he cut away her damaged flesh with ruthless efficiency. "It's deep," he told Sherry. "But not so deep as I feared from your description. She was struck at an angle, and the blade missed the vital organs."

"How do you know?"

"She's still alive," he said dryly. He dropped bits of putrid flesh into a basin. The first blood flowing from the wound was thick with the yellow-white fluids of the infection. Harris cut and pressed and cut and pressed until the only blood she gave up was bright red. "A cloth, Sheridan. A clean one. I've none left in my bag."

Sherry looked around. The room had little in the way of furnishings. There was no trunk or cupboard that might be a repository for linens. The sheet that had been removed as well as the one under her was stained. The blankets were filthy. "May I release her?"

The physician nodded. "It is unlikely she will wake now."

Sherry's fingers uncurled around her wrists. He stood and removed his frock coat, then his waistcoat. At his beckoning, young Midge came forward to hold them. Sherry unknotted the cravat that his valet had creased and arranged so carefully and added it to the pile in Midge's outstretched arms. He loosened the tails of his shirt, then pulled it over his head. Starting a tear with his teeth, he rent the linen until he had four neat strips.

Harris used the material as it was handed to him to staunch the flow of blood and finally bind the wound.

"You are not going to stitch it?" asked Sherry.

"Not now; not when the opportunity for infection is so great. This air is of the foulest sort, my lord. She will require poultices to keep it out of the wound, and they will have to be changed often. If she is to have improved odds for recovery, she cannot remain here."

Sherry did not hesitate, though it surprised him that he did not. "Then we will take her to my home."

Harris shook his head. "A charity bed in one of the surgeries will suit. The sisters at St. Luke's are admirably tolerant of all God's creatures."

"That arrangement will not suit me." For Sherry it was the end of the argument.

The physician realized it also. "Very well. Then we must apply ourselves to the problem of how to move her."

"Can she survive it now?"

Harris's regard of the room revealed his distaste. Littered as it was with the discarded blankets and revealing impoverishment in its singular lack of amenities, there was nothing to recommend it as a place of healing. Still, moving her too soon would no doubt kill her quicker.

Sherry had no difficulty reading his physician's thoughts. "Another day here, perhaps?" he asked.

"Yes." The response was reluctantly given. "If she survives the next twenty-four hours, I will judge she can be moved."

The matter of her care until then was Sherry's gravest concern. "You will take the hack and return to my home. Apply to my housekeeper for clean bedclothes, bandages, and whatever else you think is needed for your patient's comfort. Kearns will pack a valise for me. Direct the driver to unload the carriage as my departure to Granville will be delayed. I want brooms and scrubbing brushes. Lye would not come amiss. Combs also. As many as it will take to remove the nits from her hair." He looked significantly at the boys. "And theirs." To Rutland, he said, "There is someone nearby who will clean for hire?"

"Aye. The Widow Meeder could use the coin. Her daughter will help."

"Then I trust you will see to their employment." When Rutland did not move, Sherry added, "Now."

Blue Rutland picked up the valuable cask of brandy and secured it under his arm. "What about my customers? I can't keep them away all evening, not even for Miss Rose. More talk if I tried."

"I agree. Open your establishment. Do you let out the rooms up here?"

Rutland nodded. "There's some trade, if you take my meaning."

"I do." He calculated quickly what it would cost him to keep peace abovestairs. "I'll take all your rooms for the night. Seven pounds?"

"Nine."

Sherry did not haggle. "Seven," he said.

Rutland gauged his opponent's resolve. "Seven it is."

"Good." He raised one dark eyebrow. "Widow Meeder and her daughter?"

"Right away, m'lord." Turning sharply on his heel, he hurried out of the room. The bargain he struck with Lord Sheridan would net him a profit of five pounds on the rooms. Miss Rose, bless her, was still earning her keep.

"You paid him twice what he would have gotten for letting the rooms," Harris told Sherry.

Shrugging, Sherry said, "I shouldn't be surprised if it were three times that. Worth all of it, I think, for the peace it will afford. Which boy will you want to take back with you?"

"What?" Harris looked up from winding the bandage. "You're truly not going?"

"One of us should stay behind. I believe you would prefer to go."

For the sake of good form and honoring his profession, Harris considered mounting an argument. Then he remembered the rough trade that would be returning to their tankards, the smuggled brandy, and the three young pickpockets hovering nearby, and decided he possessed insufficient resolve to make a convincing protest. "I'd prefer we both go," he said at last, "but since you are determined to stay, I suppose the one called Pinch will do well enough as an escort."

"Master Pinch?" Sherry asked. The boy stepped front and center. "Did you hear?"

He nodded. His eyes darted to the bed where Harris was dressing the wound. A touch of color came into his cheeks, but the color was green.

Sherry waved him away from the bed. "You will see that Dr. Harris is not accosted. I am depending on you to secure another hack. I am in no expectation that our driver still remains on the street."

Dash went to the window, threw it open, and leaned so far out he was in danger of tumbling. "Right you are, guvnor," he said, craning his neck for a view of the front street. "I mean yer lordship. The bloke's gone. I suppose it weren't worth the extra shillin' ye give 'im to twiddle 'is thumbs waiting for us. There's people here'd just as soon slit 'is throat for it."

"Present company excluded, I'm sure," Harris muttered with heavy irony.

Sherry's slight smile was appreciative. "Come back in here, Master Dash, before you fall on your head and the doctor has two patients to attend."

It was hours after nightfall that the room, the patient, and all of her protectors were finally settled. After returning with Pinch and all the items on Sherry's list, Harris stayed long enough to examine his patient and enumerate the reasons Lord Sheridan should *not* spend the night. One of the things

Sherry had not requested was the services of his valet, but that stalwart had arrived with an underfootman, two valises, a trunk, and enough fresh bedding to open an inn.

As the entourage grew, so did the need for more clean rooms. The widow and her daughter earned three months' wages in the course of the evening, sweeping, scrubbing, and scraping the dirt from the floors, beating the bugs from the mattresses, and finally snapping clean white sheets over the beds.

Rutland did not warm to Sherry's permitting Pinch, Dash, and Midge to take one of the rooms, and Sherry did not favor the three urchins going to bed dirty, but by midnight there was little argument left in anyone.

Sherry's room adjoined Rose's. He'd had his bed moved to the wall that separated them. Now that he lay atop the unevenly filled mattress, he realized the noise rising from belowstairs would never permit him to hear her if she required help. It seemed rather far-fetched that she would. Harris had said it was unlikely that she would wake soon. Sherry suspected the physician meant to say that it was unlikely that she would wake ever, but at the last moment reconsidered this pronouncement.

What had he brought down upon his own head? he wondered. Although it was not his way to blame others, on this occasion he had not even the luxury of contemplating it.

It had begun simply enough with the desire to return to his country estate. A rather quaint longing, he thought. Would he be here this evening if he'd had desires of a different sort? What if it had been his inclination to spend more time in the gaming hells or if he had decided against ending his arrangement with Fanny? More to the point, what if he had chosen a different entertainment for their last evening together? An intimate dinner in her home to set the stage for the break. A private musical performance. Vauxhall Gardens instead of Covent.

What if he had . . . what if . . . what . . . if . . .

The cry made him bolt upright. He was unsteady at first and shook his head to clear it. Had he been sleeping? Dreaming? He had no memory of falling asleep but knew he must have. The tavern was markedly quieter now, the patrons having imbibed enough liquor to gradually pass from rowdy to stuporous. The crescent moon was no longer framed in his window, and there was a hint of starshine to replace it— more evidence that time had passed.

The cry, then. What was it?

Sherry cursed under his breath. In a single motion he pushed himself out of bed and grabbed the robe at its foot. He shrugged into it as he headed for the door. The windowless corridor was dark as pitch, but it was only a short distance to the next room, and he found his way with a minimum of groping along the wall.

He carefully let himself into her room. His crossing to the bed was not soundless. The floor creaked as his weight further depressed the sagging boards. Candlelight flickered when the wobbly bedside table shuddered.

Sherry lifted the candlestick and held it over her. She was quiet again; indeed, he was uncertain now that what he'd heard had come from this room. "Was it you?" he asked quietly. Her translucent skin seemed to reflect the flame's pale yellow glow rather than absorb it. He moved the candlelight over her face and down the length of her unnaturally still form.

She looked only marginally less feverish than she had earlier. Sherry thought any improvement was more illusion than real and credited the comb that was run through her matted hair and the change of her bed linens for bringing it about. Kearns had removed her stained shirt and soiled trousers, but it had been Sherry who cut away the strip of linen binding her breasts and who dressed her in his own nightshirt.

"What were you doing there that night?" he said. It was ridiculous, he supposed, to pose the question when there was no reason to expect she would answer him. "Did you mean to rob me?" He paused as though giving her time to consider her response. "Or kill me?"

The widow's daughter had found a chair in one of the other rooms and suggested they place it near Miss Rose's bed. It lightly scraped the floor as Sherry pulled it to him. He protected the candle flame as he sat. In profile she was as still as death.

"I'm done with that life, you know."

She didn't know, of course. He'd only recently decided. Saying it aloud to her, to someone who was insensible of him and of that profoundly secret life he'd led, was a test of his own resolve. That he felt not the slightest regret proved that he'd made the choice he could live with.

He wondered about the life she had been living. Teacher of young thieves. Participant in the abovestairs trade at the Blue Ruination. What cause had she to bind her breasts and dress herself in boy's clothes when she ventured into the street? And the blacking in her hair? What purpose had that served?

He had not known she was female when she lay full on top of him, but he had known she was French.

"Je n'avais pas un couteau. Quel dommage!"

The words, her last before she slipped into unconsciousness, revealed something more than her disguise had hidden. The accent was impeccable, the ironic intonation perfect. Why wouldn't she speak these words, he thought, the ones she believed might well be her last, in her native tongue?

"I didn't have a knife." Then even more softly, confirming her regret, *"What a pity."*

For days he had considered what she had been trying to tell him. As last words, their absurdity could not be questioned. As the truth, well, as often was the case it depended on one's perspective. The knife she said she did not have was buried deep in her side. Perhaps she was only communicating surprise and a sense of loss that it was no longer in her hand.

Sherry did not like that explanation. The ironic edge to her words still gave him pause. It was almost as if she were castigating herself for not having a weapon. That at least would fit what Pinch had said and his companions had supported: Miss Rose did not carry a blade.

It was this construction that troubled him. He knew he had not put the knife to her, and if she had not caused the injury herself, then . . .

The most logical conclusion was that there had been a third party involved. When Sherry considered the number of people rubbing elbows that night, the idea of identifying a single suspect was daunting. As little as a week earlier he would not have been caught so unaware or unprepared. He would have noticed individual faces in the crowd and not been fooled by his assailant's less than perfect disguise.

But by then he'd made his decision to leave London for Granville. That night he had been strolling in Covent Garden, it was as if he'd had one foot and almost all of his mind in the country. Now he was fair on his way to believing that his life had been turned by this moment's inattention.

What he did not know, *could* not know, was if he had truly been the target. Miss Rose was engaged in dangerous practices; she may well have been the mark. Another attack on one of them would certainly answer that niggling question, but waiting for it was not his way. Ignoring the possibility that the blade had been meant for him, however, was foolish in the extreme.

"You have the advantage, Miss Rose," he said quietly. "You know something I do not." One corner of his mouth lifted, the expression more considering than gently amused. "Your recovery would be of great service to me, although I cannot promise that it will not end at Tyburn for you." An eyebrow lifted as he regarded her pale, immobile features. "It is not so much the choices we must make but the choices we are given. Scylla. Charybdis." He turned his hand over, then over again, as though examining two sides of a coin. "They are not so very different, are they?"

She remained quiet. He could not hear her breathing, but the rise and fall of her chest assured him that she was. Her slender arms lay at her side outside of the blanket. His shirt was absurdly big for her. The sleeves were rolled three times and still the cuffs rested just above her wrists. The shirt's neck was open, slightly askew, and the sharp line of one collarbone was visible. Her skin was drawn so tightly over it, it looked painful.

He had revised his ideas about her age. Once her bindings had been removed, he knew she was much closer to twenty than she was to twelve. He and Kearns had made every effort to preserve her modesty, but he was keenly aware that Midge had been correct in his assessment of his teacher's physical attributes.

The boys seemed to have found nothing odd about her attire that night, yet they knew very well that she was a woman full grown. Did they understand the purpose of her disguise? Sherry realized he had never asked them. Recognition of this oversight changed the shape of his slight smile so that it became more derisive. How many more mistakes could he make before the full weight of them was brought to bear?

Sighing deeply enough to make the candlelight flicker, Sherry wondered about his next course of action. He would permit her to recuperate in his home, if she survived the journey there. To protect his reputation and that of his family, some measure of secrecy would be required, but he was practiced at secrets. He had already decided that moving her into his residence would best be accomplished at night and through the servants' entrance. His neighbors were unlikely to notice anything untoward, but their retainers were infinitely more alert to activity out of the ordinary. He would rely on his own staff to quell rumors. It was to their benefit to do so. There was no standing in being associated with an employer—even one with a title and fortune—who had gone queer in the head.

Sherry leaned toward the table and set the candlestick down. He started to rise, glimpsed a faint movement from his patient, and dropped back in the chair. At first he didn't know what it was he had seen. Her breathing seemed unchanged by any exertion or flutter of awareness. Then he caught the quarter turn of her wrist. Her fingers began to curl with aching slowness until her hand formed a loose fist. She did it several times over before he realized she was trying to tug at the blanket covering.

"Uncomfortable, are you?" he asked. "That is something I *can* fix." He lifted the woolen blanket carefully where it had bunched under her hip and retucked it under the mattress. "Better?"

The question was not meant to elicit a response, so Sherry was surprised when two of his fingers were caught by hers. She squeezed lightly at first, so lightly that he thought he imagined it; then he saw the change in the shape of her knuckles and knew it was true. His eyes went to hers and saw they were still closed, but when his gaze dropped to her mouth he witnessed the parting of her lips and the effort to form words.

"Qu'est que vous faites ici?"

He thought she might ask for something to moisten her dry lips. A sip of wine perhaps, or tea. What she wanted, though, was to know what he was doing here. She had definitely stolen a glance in his direction. His response was in French, although he didn't answer the question she put to him. "Do you remember me?"

"Oui, vous étiez au théâtre."

Her voice was whisper soft, and he had to lean closer to hear. "Yes," he said, in French again. "I do go to the theatre. Is that where you saw me?"

Her lashes lifted a fraction in response, as though it were too great an effort to nod. She touched the tip of her tongue to her lips. Instead of wetting them, it seemed to cling there. *"J'ai soif."*

"Of course you're thirsty. I have wine for you. The water is not fit to drink." He did not inform her the wine also had tincture of laudanum in it. The wine bottle was sitting on the windowsill. Sherry retrieved it and filled a third of a glass. Slipping an arm gingerly under her shoulders, he helped her rise just enough to tip the glass against her bottom lip. "Sip."

She pursed her lips, breathing in the wine more than drinking it. When she tried to reach for the glass to hold it herself, he would not let her. Instead, he made sure she was resting the weight of her shoulders fully against his forearm and kept the glass firmly in place.

"*Fermez vos yeux,*" he told her.

The corners of her mouth tilted upward even as she complied and closed her eyes. "*Quel jour sommes nous?*"

"*Mercredi,*" he said. Wednesday. Then he realized the lateness of the hour and corrected himself. "*Non, c'est t'aujourd'hui jeudi.*" He could not tell if she was in any way surprised by this intelligence; her pale and placid features gave nothing away. Five days had passed since the stabbing, but it was likely she was aware during some of that time.

"Thursday," she said on a thread of sound. "Thursday's child has far to go. It is as good a day to die as any, I suppose, and mayhap heaven is no greater a distance to journey than hell."

The movement of her shoulders was what he always thought of as the quintessential Gallic shrug. The words, nevertheless, were spoken in English, and the accent was the perfectly pitched inflection of the *ton*.

Three

Sherry sat, stunned. Her command of the King's English was flawless. The tone and cadence of her speech would have allowed her to converse among the guests at the Court of St. James without arousing suspicion. She spoke English as fluently as she did French, a talent mastered only by those young women with an exemplary education or a demanding tutor. At present, Miss Rose did not strike him as one who had had benefit of either.

After picking up the wine bottle, Sherry permitted himself a long pull. He watched her for several more minutes, the bottle neck dangling between two fingers, before he got to his feet. He went to the window, set the bottle down, and braced his arms against the frame while he stared out. It was a cool night. The light from small fires flickered along the street. People gathered in twos and threes to keep warm; some found respite in the protected doorways of taverns or under the canted bed of a produce wagon. He heard a bottle crash against the cobbles, then the sound of cursing followed by raucous laughter. There was a scuffle, muffled oaths, and then blessed silence. Sherry supposed the combatants had finally felled each other or made amends.

It was a hard life here, he reflected. Even the meanest

structure became someone's home, and usually it became home to more than a single someone. The *Gazette* reported of tenements that accommodated thirty people in their cellars. It was in his lifetime that there had been mass open graves within sight of where he stood. Rats had roamed the streets with impunity. The graves were finally covered; the rats were only marginally less bold.

Sherry leaned forward and pressed his forehead against the glass. He closed his eyes and allowed himself to consider the fate of the woman he knew only as Miss Rose. In spite of his intervention, it was a very real possibility that she would die tonight. He had known it, accepted it, at the moment he'd approached her foul-smelling quarters. Now he wondered if he was prepared to accept as fully the possibility that she might live.

He was brave enough to pose the question to himself but unwilling to hear his own answer. Pushing away from the window, he straightened and wearily rubbed the back of his neck.

He returned to the chair and sat. He would keep vigil here, he decided, and offer her what comfort he could. To that end, he took her hand in his.

He was of the firm opinion that no one should die alone.

Pinch opened the door just enough to slip inside the sickroom. Dash and Midge followed. They tiptoed to the bed, although their stealth was unnecessary. They were so slight of build that their weight did not cause the boards to creak.

Dash took his place on the floor near the head of the bed and leaned sideways so his cheek rested against the mattress. Pinch knelt beside the chair where Sherry slept. He edged his fingers close to the handclasp. Midge carefully crawled into the bed and lay down. He did not mind that she smelled like the advent of death.

* * *

When Sherry woke it was with the instant knowledge of changed circumstances, the least of which was the presence of the three dirty urchins in varying states of repose. What pulled his eye was the flush of color in his patient's cheeks and the uneven rise and fall of her chest. He eased his hand from around her fingers and touched her forehead.

The beginnings of a fever were upon her, but then so was the beginning of a new day.

She had survived the night.

Sherry stood and reached over her to lift Midge off the bed. He had to untangle the child's fingers from where they were wound in her hair. Turning, he made to set Midge in the chair and paused when he heard movement outside the door. A moment later, Kearns stepped into the room and was arrested by the sight of his employer holding a child in his arms while two others knelt sleeping at his feet.

Sherry sighed. "I cannot explain it myself."

"One frequently cannot, my lord," the valet said briskly. He advanced to assist Sheridan with Midge, steadying the chair while Sherry placed the boy on it.

Once Midge was set down, his pointed chin fell heavily and jabbed his chest. This seemed to be enough to trigger an abrupt snore but was insufficient to wake him.

"Little baggage," Kearns said.

One of Sherry's brows lifted at the tone of this observation. There was tolerance here—and if he was not mistaken—a hint of something that might be approaching tenderness. "You are demonstrating remarkable forbearance, Kearns."

The valet sighed. "I cannot explain it myself."

Chuckling wryly, Sherry stepped away from the bed and pointed to their patient. "I think she's coming into a fever. Will you send the footman for a basin of water and some clean cloths? Tell him to wake Mr. Rutland if he must."

Kearns nodded. "And you, m'lord? I have your clothes in the—"

Sherry dismissed this with a wave of his hand. "If a tub can be found, I think these three should be introduced to it.

The addition of soap and water and a scrub brush would not be amiss. Mrs. Ponsonby will bar the door and every window if we do not apply some spit and polish to them." Sherry gave his valet full marks for the attempt he made at schooling his features. "You have some thought on the matter, Kearns? I should like to hear it."

Uncomfortable, Kearns cleared his throat. "You mean to take them to your residence."

"Yes. I mean to take her," he said, gesturing to the bed. Then he indicated the three awkwardly positioned, exhausted boys. "Do you imagine these lads will stay away?"

Kearns looked from one child's bent head to the next. Although they were all sleeping, their posture and attitude was reminiscent of prayer. "I take your lordship's point."

Sherry nodded. "The tub, then."

"I shall see to it immediately."

Harris arrived before the noon hour. The first thing he noticed was what wasn't present. The nearly overwhelming odor of decay had disappeared, and it gave him hope.

"Well?" Sherry asked as the physician made his examination. "Is she improved by the fever or made worse by it?"

"A moment," said Harris. He tapped her chest and listened to her lungs and heart. He smelled her breath, nodded to himself, then laid two fingers along the pulse in her neck. "You have been keeping her warm?"

"Yes. She does not always appreciate the effort, but she has little strength to fight me."

Harris nodded. His eyes fell on the basin of water on the table and the cloths lying along its rim. "And her brow cool?"

"Yes," Sherry said with a touch of impatience. "What I want to know is if it has been efficacious."

Carefully peeling back the blankets and sheet, Harris took his first look at the wound through her nightshirt and bandage. He would not be pressed by Sherry's chafing. He answered cautiously, "It is a good sign the wound is not weeping overmuch. The shirt is largely unstained." He rolled the hem upward until the bandage was exposed. "Are you aware if she awakened at all?" he asked as he began to loosen the cloth wrap.

"Yes," he said. "She also briefly spoke."

"She was lucid?"

"Yes." Sherry did not offer to introduce their conversation, and Harris did not ask.

Harris stopped his examination to retrieve a tincture from his bag. He applied it to the ragged edges of the wound. "Hold her down," he instructed as his patient began to thrash.

Sherry knelt at the head of the bed as he had done the previous day and took her wrists. Although he had been gentle on that occasion, he saw now that he had also been firm enough to leave faint bruises. For entirely selfish reasons he hoped she would not fight him.

"Hold her," Harris repeated, looking pointedly at Sheridan's loosely engaged fingertips. He grunted, satisfied, when he saw the grip tighten. "You won't break her. Or if you do, it will be far and away less painful than this." He poured more of the tincture into the wound, causing his patient's slight frame to seize.

"Bloody hell, Harris," Sherry said under his breath. He felt every line of her body tense as though the physician had poured liquid fire into her blood. She arched, her back rising off the bed. Her knuckles whitened. In the last moment before her muscles exhausted themselves she ground out her pain between clenched teeth. Part whimper, part outrage, it was all wounded animal.

Sherry grimaced.

The doctor winced.

They both remained dedicated to their task.

"There," Harris said, satisfied with his work when a white froth bubbled from the wound.

"What *is* that?" Sherry asked as the physician stoppered the small vial.

Harris shrugged. "Something the chemist has encouraged

me to try. A compound that may have healing properties."
He wiped the froth away. "Never fear, I intend to use a poultice and bleed her. I do not abandon old treatments for untried ones, yet if one never tried anything new there would be no advancements."

Frowning, Sherry regarded the wound. "Can you say there will be no unfavorable consequences as a result of combining both treatments?"

"Nothing is certain."

Sherry considered this. "Then don't bleed her. Surely that was done to great effect by the nature of her injury. As to the matter of the poultice, I will leave that up to you."

"I am gratified to hear it," Harris said wryly.

"Do you think I overstep, Harris?"

"Not at all, my lord."

Sherry knew it was a lie. The physician had not established his successful and lucrative practice without learning how to placate his patients, most of whom were members of the *ton.* "I am paying you for the best application of your knowledge and judgment," Sherry told him. "Not for you to accede to mine. What is your opinion about bleeding her?"

"It is necessary for the removal of the impurities that remain in her blood; however, delaying the procedure until she is abed in your residence is the proper course of action here. In that environment there is less risk that infection of the blood will fix itself a second time."

"Very well." Sherry realized he was still holding her wrists. He let her go while Harris redressed the wound. "I have given some thought as to how we will get her out of here. Since we cannot negotiate her descent on those stairs with a litter, I suggest we make a sling and lower her out a window."

Harris's glance went from his patient to the window and then to Sheridan. "Her weight will not present much problem. You can rig such a thing securely?"

"I have spoken to Mr. Rutland about it. He assures me he learned more than stitchery in His Majesty's service. He

knows a thing or two about knots and rigging. He sent the
boys out to get the proper ropes."

"Steal them, you mean."

"Very likely."

Harris withheld comment and concentrated on the care of
his patient. Sherry fell silent, watching.

Unnoticed by either of them, the young woman's eyelashes fluttered once, twice, then quieted again. She offered
no opinion of the plan.

The boys returned late in the day with something more
than the ropes they were sent out to find. Their patient sur-
veillance of the harbor had been rewarded with an opportunity to board the *Gallant* unnoticed. From the fo'c'sle they
carried off ropes, a hammock, and one luckless sailor's extra
pair of wool socks. Without fanfare they laid their booty at
Sheridan's feet. He hardly knew whether to praise or punish
them, and since they seemed to expect neither, he simply
nodded and set about preparing the rigging.

They waited until night fell before they tested the contraption. It was decided that Midge and Dash together weighed
only a little more than their teacher. If the hammock held
them and could be lowered safely to the ground, then it was
agreed it would work for her. Sherry was struck by the fact
that neither of the boys showed fear as they situated themselves in the hammock. Their heads lay at opposite ends, and
they wriggled a bit when their arms and legs tangled, but
they were considerably less lively than a catch of fish when
Rutland and Sherry lifted the hammock to the window and
began lowering it by means of the stolen rope.

Pinch was waiting for them on the ground with Sheridan's
footman nearby. He had given the all clear signal to begin as
soon as the alley was deserted while the footman kept a watchful eye out for drunks, whores, and stragglers. When Midge
and Dash were safely on the ground, Pinch helped them out

and gave the contraption a hard tug, then they all watched while it was quickly hauled back inside.

"I'd like it better, Kearns," Sherry said to his valet, "if you helped Rutland lower her, and I stood below. I grow concerned that Dunnet will be heavy handed trying to carry her to the hack alone. She is likely to suffer less if we sling her between us to transport."

It occurred to Kearns that his lordship would be better satisfied if he could find a way to be on both ends at the same time. The valet had the good sense not to point this out. "As you wish," he said.

The boys and the footman returned then, were apprised of this change in the arrangement, and set off on the new assignment of procuring a hack and loading it with everything that had been carried in the previous day. Blue Rutland voiced some regrets when the beds were stripped of their linens and carted off, but Sherry did not choose to make a gift of them. The proprietor was being well compensated for his part in this night's work and double that to hold his tongue regarding it.

Sherry was not so foolish as to believe the money alone would ever buy Rutland's silence; he trusted it was the man's odd affection for Miss Rose that would encourage him to remain quiet.

The children had to be persuaded that their attendance upon the hack and its nervous driver was more important than standing under the hammock. The moderate level of cleanliness that had been achieved this morning under Kearns's watchful eye and Dunnet's fierce scrubbing was no longer in evidence, and they set their dirty faces stubbornly when Sherry pointed them toward the hack. When they slunk off grumbling to themselves, it was borne home again to Sheridan that they were proving infinitely more adept at taking things than taking orders.

Upon arrival at his residence, he would be fortunate indeed if his most trusted retainers did not mutiny.

When everything—and everyone—was judged to be in

readiness, the transport began. The boys directed the hack driver into the alley, and under cover of darkness Kearns and Rutland slowly lowered the hammock down the side of the building. They all considered the largest danger to the operation the patient herself. If she awoke in the middle of the transport it was easy to conceive of her crying out and calling attention to them or, even worse, doing herself more injury.

Their fears did not come to pass. She was in every way as cooperative as Midge and Dash had been during the testing of the system, though this was purely the result of her being insensible of it.

Sherry and Dunnet made short work of the knots securing the hammock. While the ropes were being hauled back into the upstairs room, they carried the sling to the hack. It was not so easy to get it inside without jostling their cargo, and they were aware of every utterance of pain, no matter how small its whisper.

The hack's bench was nowhere near long enough to allow her to fully recline. Sherry set himself in one corner and supported her as best he could. When Kearns joined him, he took the opposite bench while the footman climbed up beside the driver and gave the address.

Rutland ventured out long enough to wish them well. "Ye'll be sending her back to me now, once she's right and tight, I mean. She's got a way about her that the customers like. Fair popular, she is."

Sherry wondered if it was a question being put to him or a statement of the proprietor's expectation. His response was noncommittal. "Let us see how she fares," he said.

"The lads, too." Blue Rutland pointed to the roof where the children were riding with the luggage. "They've yet to prove their full worth, but there's promise there."

"The same has occurred to me," Sherry said. He thanked Rutland for his help and directed Kearns to pay the man what was due him; with that transaction completed, the door was closed and the driver took his cue to depart.

* * *

Their arrival in the mews behind Sheridan's Bentley Square address was accomplished in relative quiet. From time to time a stray cat found itself underfoot as the hack was unloaded, but that howling was nothing that excited interest from the adjoining houses.

Sherry's servants received his valet's announcement that there would be additions to the household with equanimity. It said something about the lateness of the hour that there was not even mild rumblings among them. None of them had been awake. To a person they had been roused from their beds to help with the unpacking and make the rooms ready.

Mrs. Ponsonby made her assessment of the patient and suggested quartering her in the same attic room shared by the cook's twin helpers. "They're decent enough girls," she told Lord Sheridan, "and they won't let her stray."

Sherry rubbed the back of his stiff neck and sought a measure of patience. "You will put her in my sister's former bedchamber," he said. "When her health is improved we will discuss moving her. As to the boys, what arrangements can be made for them?"

The housekeeper wanted to suggest that the tower had room enough, but she held her tongue. "There's sufficient space in the cupboard under the stairwell."

"Large enough for three?" He remembered hiding from his tutor in that cupboard. It was perfectly suited for the purpose to which he put it, but he did not think that it would accommodate three.

"They'll be fine," Ponsonby insisted.

Sherry agreed because he knew the boys would not remain there all night. "Very well. See to it." He turned and tiredly mounted the main stairs to his own room.

Kearns was waiting for him with fresh water for performing his nighttime ablutions and clean bedclothes. Sherry was grateful to be able to remove the assaultive odors that clung to his person, though he suspected the memory of them would linger in his nostrils for days. Holborn was not so easily shed as his clothes.

He desired nothing so much as to lift the covers that had been invitingly pulled back and crawl under them but permitted himself only a brief glance of longing. He asked for his robe instead and slipped into it when Kearns held it out. "Find your own bed," he told his valet. "I am for mine as soon as I see that our guest has been made comfortable."

"If your lordship doesn't mind, I'll tidy first."

Sherry offered a slight smile. "As you wish." He left the room and went down the hall and across it to the room his sister occupied before her marriage. He supposed Cybelline might have something to say about the use he was making of her old bedchamber, but she had a kind heart and would acknowledge that she really no longer had any say in the matter. Her concern, should she ever be in a position to raise it, would be that he was not fully in command of his faculties. She would look at the pathetic creature lying on the bed and demand that he account for his thinking on bringing the thing about. "A bit drafty in the upperworks, aren't you?" she'd say.

All things considered, he'd have to concur.

He waved the maid and Mrs. Ponsonby away from the bed while he leaned over it. She looked smaller and even more fragile against the expansive background of the crisp white sheet and lacy pillow shams.

"What is it?" he asked when the housekeeper cleared her throat behind him.

"I'd like to have one of the girls wash her hair on the morrow. The paste that's been mucked over it is staining the good linens."

"Dr. Harris will be here. You can put your question to him. I do not know what he will think about her having a wet head. He wants to bleed her."

Ponsonby wondered that the woman had any to give, but this observation was not spoken aloud. "Will there be anything else?"

"No. You can go."

The housekeeper hesitated, waiting for Sheridan to step away from the bed also. When he didn't, she realized it was not his intention to leave so quickly. She nudged the maid at her side and indicated they should leave. The maid would have liked to have caught her eye, but Ponsonby would not disrespect the viscount by entertaining speculation with an underling. She would have a word with Kearns later and see if the man would tell her what was toward.

When he was alone, Sherry drew the rocker abreast of the bed and sat. She appeared to be all of a piece to him but knew himself reluctant to leave her alone. He supposed he could have had the maid remain with her, but then the children would not have been able to take up their vigil. The maid was certain to disturb everyone's slumber if they tried.

For a time he was content to observe her sleep; then at last he rose from the chair and went to find the comfort of his own bed and dreamless repose.

Sherry resisted the idea of waking. He shook off the hand on his shoulder and turned over, burying his face in his pillow. There was more pounding, this time at the center of his back. He cursed his valet roundly and threatened to let him go without a character.

"God's truth," Sherry protested. "It is not yet daybreak."

"She must 'ave the doctor," he said. "She must 'ave the doctor. She must 'ave the—"

Sherry groaned loudly. The chanting was making his head pound. "Have off, Kearns. I can't—" He stopped, understanding at last the meaning of the words. He struggled to rise under the heavy weight on his back.

Midge pitched to the floor as Sheridan threw him off. He scrambled to his feet without any complaint for the bump to his head. "Come, guvnor." He grasped Sherry's hand and tugged. "This way. She must 'ave the doctor."

Sherry stood, shook off the dregs of sleep like a sheepdog

shakes off the wet, and allowed Midge to lead him from his bedchamber. Not surprisingly, Dash and Pinch were hovering beside her bed.

"It's the fever," Pinch said. He held up a candle so Sherry could see for himself that her condition had worsened. "She's shakin' wi' it, sir."

So were the bed curtains. Sherry cautioned Pinch to hold the candle steady and have a care not to drip wax on her. He pulled back the covers and laid his hand lightly over the bandaged wound. He could feel the heat of the fever through her nightshift. Calculating how long it would take to rouse Harris and bring him to the house, Sherry realized they had no time for indecision. His tone was brisk, decisive, and brooked no argument.

"Midge, do you know where the footmen sleep?"

"Aye, m'lord."

"Good. Wake Dunnet and say I have need of him. If he tries to clobber you, have at him the way you did me." He turned to Dash as Midge ran off. "Do you remember the location of the library?" Dash assured him that he did. "Bring a decanter of spirits here." To Pinch he said, "There should be a basin and pitcher of water in the dressing room." He did not have to say any more.

Sherry turned back to his patient. He raised her gown the least amount that was necessary to permit him to reveal the bandage. Slipping two fingers under the strip of cloth, he began to gingerly peel it back. Harris had applied a poultice to the wound during his afternoon visit. He informed Sherry that its purpose was to draw the poison and keep out the foul air. Sherry's observation was that its effect was exactly the opposite. He removed the poultice and smelled the malodorous vapors escaping.

Pinch wrinkled his nose as he presented the water-filled basin and cloths to Sheridan. He accepted the poultice in exchange and dropped it into the chamber pot in the dressing room. When he returned to the bedside, Sheridan was wiping seepage from the wound. "It's bad, isn't it? We should 'ave left 'er where she was. Leastways it was wot she was used to. That counts for something."

Sherry was not sure that Pinch wasn't right. To distract them both, he asked, "How long have you known her?"

Pinch shrugged. "Most o' me life it seems. 'Ard for me to remember a time when she wasn't at the Blue Ruin."

"I see."

"If ye'll pardon me for speaking plainly," Pinch said, then went on without any allowance from Sherry that he should do so, "it's been my experience that most people don't see at all when they say that."

"And you have a great deal of experience."

"More than yer lordship, I'd wager."

It would be an interesting wager, Sherry decided. "How did you become her pupil?"

"Oh, there's nuthin' 'ard to understand abou' it. She coaxes us in with sweet words and a proper warm meal, and then she gets us to do things for 'er. Can't refuse, really. She 'as a sweet voice, though don't expect ye know that about 'er, and she just gives ye the urge to want to please 'er. Even Blue'll do things for 'er, and most folks in Holborn think 'e's a proper villain. 'E give 'er a room of 'er own to use."

Sherry saw the blood around her wound was flowing clear again. He staunched it with a clean cloth. "Then she lives there."

"No. 'E give 'er a room to use, not to live in. Didn't ye 'ear me say 'e's a proper villain? Lets out 'is rooms, but 'e gives 'er one when there's one gone beggin'."

"I see," Sherry said quite deliberately.

Pinch frowned, uncertain how to take Sheridan's comment. He thought he saw one corner of his lordship's severe mouth lift ever so slightly, but he couldn't be sure. He was saved from making any reply with the arrival of Dash.

Sherry saw the decanter and realized Dash had managed to seize his only bottle of French brandy. Wouldn't Blue Rutland love to see him weep over it. "Bring it here, lad. You've good taste in drink."

"Smelled them all," Dash said proudly. "This is what Blue gave Dr. 'Arris."

Sherry almost groaned aloud. So it wasn't happenstance at all; the urchin had a nose for the bouquet. "Serves me right for having the stuff," Sherry said under his breath. He passed the basin to Pinch and took the decanter from Dash. He was tempted to take a swallow for himself but resisted. He soaked the last clean cloth he had with a generous pour of brandy and pressed it against the wound.

She bucked, almost dislodging him from the bed. Midge arrived in that moment, Dunnet on his heels. The footman saw the problem and went to stop her from thrashing his master.

Sherry waved him aside. "Don't worry about me. I want you to wake Dr. Harris and ask him for the vial of medicine he poured into her wound this afternoon. If he doesn't have any more, make him give you the name of the apothecary. Bring that vial here. Also, a tincture of laudanum would not be amiss."

Dunnet started to go, then paused. "You don't want me to bring the doctor himself?"

Sherry shrugged. "If he wants to come, I won't turn him out. Go on. Go. Pinch, come closer. Take her hand. Perhaps it will calm her." Pinch did as he was told while Sherry removed himself from the bed. He padded into the dressing room with the basin, emptied it, and poured fresh water from the pitcher. He searched the cupboard and found more cloths. When he returned to the bed, Pinch was no longer the only one at her side. Dash had her other hand in his, and Midge was sitting at her feet.

"Do you say prayers for your Miss Rose?" Sherry asked. "They could certainly do no harm." Their silence did not trouble him; their guilty exchange of glances did. "What is it?"

Midge bent his head and stared at his hands. "Lily," he said.

"Midge!" Pinch snapped at him.

"Midge!" Dash cried.

"Midge?" Sherry asked softly. "What is this about Lily?"

Pinch and Dash tried to talk over him, but Sherry wouldn't let them. Squeezing cool water from a wet cloth, he quelled them with a glance. "Say what you like, Midge."

The boy looked neither right nor left at his friends but directly at Sherry. "'Er name is Lily. It is 'er own name, 'er secret name. Not many know it, but God does, and we should use it proper when we talk to 'Im."

"Lily." Sheridan looked from Midge's earnest face to the young woman's deeply flushed one. Beads of perspiration were visible above her lip. The impossibly dark hair lay damp against her scalp and forehead. "Lily," he repeated, and permitted himself a small smile as he wiped her brow and an errant thought crossed his mind.

"'Ere now, wot's this?" Pinch demanded, his dark eyes narrowing on Sheridan's smile. "Wot's amusin' about 'er name?"

"Not a thing, Master Pinch. I was thinking that Shakespeare was in the right of it when he penned, 'What's in a name? That which we call a rose by any other name would smell as sweet.' "

Pinch frowned deeply as he considered the import of what Sheridan was saying.

Sherry was careful not to allow his smile to deepen. "It means that whether Rose or Lily, she is still the same person."

"Oh, I understood that well enough. It was wot you said about 'er smellin' sweet that didn't set right wi' me."

Sherry's sudden bark of laughter caused all three boys to rear back in surprise. In turn, their wide-eyed, open-mouthed expressions made it difficult for him to rein in his amusement. For Sherry, there was no clearer indication of how tired he was than to have to work at tempering his laughter. It required looking down at Lily to sober him. There was nothing about her condition that invited amusement, and her gravely still features and the protective hovering of the boys was a forceful reminder.

He bent his head to feel her breath on his cheek. At this angle he could once again make out the shallow rise and fall of her chest.

"Is she all right?" Dash asked. "I mean, she's not—"

"She's sleeping," Sherry told him. He had no better description for her condition. "If you boys want to remain here, then bring the bedding Ponsonby gave you. You can make pallets on the floor. There is nothing more to be done until Dunnet returns with the medicine." Sherry hoped they would be sleeping soundly by then and would not have to witness her agony of feeling as he applied it. "Go on. I'm not going to leave her."

As proof of that, Sherry moved the basin and decanter from the bed to the nearby table, tucked the covers about her, then eased himself into the rocker at her side.

The boys ran off to gather their bedding, and Sherry prepared himself to begin another death watch.

She was floating in a sea of cream and white silk. Her body was weightless. She drifted without direction. Her hair fanned out around her like the radiant red rays of dawn. It rippled and dipped on the undulating tide of the milky sea.

She let herself be carried away by the slow-moving current. Turning. Bobbling. There was nothing to stop her. Nothing that could stop her. She was insubstantial, a spirit now free of her corporeal self.

It was curious to her that she could sense this so clearly, still more curious that she could observe it at the same time. It was as if she had two perspectives at once: one from within and one from above.

Thinking about it disturbed the flow, and for few moments she bumped along unevenly. It ended only when she set her mind at peace again and allowed herself to be carried away. Her brief exposure to the turbulence had placed the fullness of understanding in her mind. There was a direction she was taking. Her journey had a purpose.

All that was required of her to be on her way was that she not resist.

Bloody hell.

Lily sucked in great draughts of air as she tried to catch her breath. She coughed, choked, and thought she would finally retch in an effort to clear her lungs for the air she needed. Her body ached. There was no part of her that did not feel battered or bruised, but it was under her ribs that she felt as if she'd been skewered with the heated end of a poker.

She drew her knees up and bowed her head. She would happily become a hedgehog and reveal only her prickles, never the soft underside of her belly. Had she ever promised herself that before? She thought she might have. She thought she might have broken her promise.

She was weak willed, she realized, without the resolve that marked a person of good character. Already she was thinking about the currents of heavy cream and how she would let them carry her away if she could find them again. She would drift toward the light if she could catch that tide a second time.

The tide she caught was one of pain. There was nothing for it but that she ride it out. Her dry lips parted on the sound of her gasp. She thought there might be tears, but none came. That made her feel better, stronger somehow. She could manage as long as she did not give in to tears. There was some part of her that recognized it as a sea she could drown in.

Lily's eyelashes fluttered, then lifted. A sliver of sunlight was revealed by a narrow part in the curtains. Her eyes followed the beam of light to the floor where it brightened a patch of burnished gold fringe on the area rug. She contemplated the light and the fringe and the rug for a long moment before allowing her vision to broaden and absorb far more of her surroundings.

Below the bank of windows a niche was carved out for an upholstered bench. Its blue-gray damask covering matched the curtains there and the ones drawn back at the head of her bed. The fabric was embossed with a swirling pattern of willow leaves that the light breeze from an open window seemed to set in motion.

The room's wainscoting was a darker shade of walnut than its appointments. The top of the vanity was neatly arranged with several small crystal perfume bottles, an intricately tiled wooden box, and a vase filled with a spray of freshly cut lilacs. An oil painting of a grand country estate in summer, vibrant with its verdant hillside and halcyon sky, had been placed above the mantelpiece, a position of some honor in the room.

There was an escritoire situated against the wall near the windows. Books and figurines were kept in the glass case above the desk. From the middle shelf, a porcelain doll peered out, her head cocked at an angle so that her painted expression made her seem at once wise and amused.

Lily returned the doll's stare and foolishly wondered if she had a name. Perhaps she had once, but she probably had not been called by it for a very long time. The thought made her unaccountably sad, and she recognized the ache at the back of her eyes for what it was. She blinked, pressing tears back, and settled her gaze on the scattering of paper and quills on the desktop. A few crumpled sheets of vellum lay on the floor, the evidence of a writer's frustrated attempts at expression.

The pair of wing chairs in front of the fireplace had been pushed together so they faced each other and their cushions formed a small bed. Midge was sleeping deeply there in spite of the awkwardness of his repose. One leg dangled over the arm of the chair. An elbow jutted in the air. His neck was bent at an angle not so different from the doll's.

Pinch and Dash shared a pallet on the floor beside him. They were sprawled across the covers, not under them—one on his back, the other facedown—and the tangle of limbs and blankets made it almost impossible to put parts to the right boy.

"They shined up nicely, don't you think?"

Lily nodded slowly. Since waking she had avoided looking too closely beside her. She was aware of the rocking
chair, the moment it ceased to move, the moment its occu-
pant left it behind to sit on the edge of the bed. She ignored
his weight reshaping the mattress and the way he turned to
balance himself, angling his knee and hip closer, but she
found it impossible to disregard his presence when he spoke
to her. She remembered that voice, the quiet cadence of it,
the husky undertone that tripped lightly down her spine like
a delicious shiver.

She remembered, too, when it had been fierce, not angry,
but insistent. The cursing had been his, not hers, but somehow he had given sound to what she had been thinking.

Bloody hell.

Lily turned her head and stared at him, as wary as she
was curious. He did not so much return her regard as present
himself for her inspection. She took full advantage, letting
her gaze wander over his thick, dark head of hair, a disheveled
thatch now from repeatedly plowing his fingers through it.
His eyes were the color of bittersweet chocolate, a near match
for his hair. Above them rested nicely spaced eyebrows, one
lifted a fraction higher than the other to affect . . . what? she
wondered. What was it she observed there? Amusement?
Satisfaction? Interest? Contemplation?

Her eyes dropped to his nose. He turned slightly, purposely,
she thought, so she could see its curve in profile. He held the
pose just so, as though his likeness had been struck on a coin.
He seemed to be well aware the aquiline appendage had that
sort of stature. The light self-mockery in the gesture made
her think well of him, though it simply hurt too much to smile.

He had no such difficulty, she noticed. It was no broad
smile, but his mouth was lifted sufficiently at the corners to
draw attention to it. She studied the placement of his lips,
equidistant of his nose and chin, generous enough in their
line to be called sensual.

It was a handsome face that he revealed unselfconsciously
to her, the features bold but not aggressive. His shoulders

were broad rather than heavy, and he sat with a certain casualness of posture that she decided he did not indulge in often. It was not that it was out of character, she thought, but that it was an aspect of his character not often expressed.

A flight of fancy on her part, Lily knew, to draw such a conclusion on so little evidence. Here, then, was an aspect of her own self revealed, the slightly whimsical, romantic side that was not out of character but nevertheless was ruthlessly suppressed. Lest he see it for himself, she turned her head away and let her cheek rest once again on the pillow.

She regarded the children again. None of them had been disturbed by her movement or his. Their faces were scrubbed free of dirt; their hair shone. They wore clean white nightshirts that swallowed them in a cloud of soft cotton. Their features were untroubled, even serene. It was an expression she'd hoped to see on their faces and had despaired that it could ever be so.

"I did not know they could sleep so soundly," she said. Getting the words out was harder than she expected. Her throat felt as if it were filled with gravel.

Sherry reached for the tumbler of water on the bedside table. "Drink this." He slipped one hand under her hair and gently helped her raise her head. He pressed the glass against her bottom lip and tipped it so she could sip. "They've finally exhausted themselves."

The same could be said of him, she realized, though he had not yet surrendered to it. There were faint shadows under his nearly black eyes and darker ones along his jaw because he had neglected to shave.

Sherry set the glass down and eased her back onto the pillow. "I was not certain you would come around again."

"Again?"

"We spoke before. Do you remember?"

She closed her eyes briefly, urging the memory to come forward.

"No matter," Sherry said. "It will come in time. In any event, more than a sennight has passed since then."

"A sennight. Can it have been so long?"

He cocked an eyebrow. "I assure you, I have no reason to lie." He picked up a damp cloth from the table and used it to erase perspiration from her face. The unnatural flush of fever was gone from her features, and the translucency had returned to her complexion. Her eyes, though, were sharp and intelligent, evincing strength where she'd had none before. "May I examine your injury?"

Lily's hand strayed under the covers to the site of her sharpest pain. She laid her palm over the bandage protectively.

"I have seen it before," he said. "Nevertheless, if you like, the examination can wait until the arrival of the physician. He usually attends you late in the morning."

"Then you are not a physician."

Amused, he shook his head. "Lord, no. I haven't the constitution for it nor any appreciation of the quackery. Dr. Harris has seen to your care. I have merely seen that his care didn't kill you."

"Oh." She bit her lower lip.

"A little while ago I thought you would leave us," Sherry said. He would not press to examine her, though if her reluctance was rooted in modesty, he did not understand it. "It seemed the fever would carry you away." He raised his hands, palms out. "Then it broke. Snapped like a dry stick."

"You cursed," she said, recalling the voice that had spoken for her. "You said, 'bloody hell.' "

"I probably did, though I have no recollection of it. I imagine I said a lot of things in the frustration of the moment. You have not been an easy patient, you know. After so long, it seemed rather ungrateful that you would give up." He indicated the sleeping children. "I should not have liked to face them."

"Then you should not have given them hope."

Sherry blinked. Her response was not what he had supposed it would be. She was clearly leveling an accusation at him. "You are of a practical nature, then."

She shrugged, then winced as the movement caused her to recall all the ways her body ached. "Some things in life are better met if one knows no better."

"Ahh," he said thoughtfully. "You make the case for lowering expectations."

"Surely it is a reasonable safeguard against disappointment."

"Perhaps," Sherry said, rising to his feet. He dropped the damp cloth back into the basin, then loosely tied the belt of his robe. "The last time you woke we spoke of a knife you said you didn't have. Now we touch on matters of philosophy. You have curious conversational gambits." He watched her eyes widen and waited to see if she would say anything. When she didn't, he went on, "You are tired. More than that, you are weak. For all that you have done nothing but lie abed since you were injured, I think it will still require rest for you to regain your strength. I will return later to see how you fare, but for now, I am for my own bed." Under his breath, he added, "Finally."

Lily had only a vague memory of the physician's visit, but she supposed he had truly been to see her since it was dusk now and she had been told he attended her in the morning. She did not think he spoke to her but made a brisk examination, which included some prodding and a bit of pain, then addressed his questions and comments to others present in the room. She was not certain who joined him, except that none of them was Pinch, Dash, or Midge.

She eased herself into a sitting position, rested for a time against the headboard, then slipped her legs over the side of the bed. Her feet dangled a good three inches above the floor. There was a stool nearby but not close enough for her to reach. She supposed that if she planted her feet and her legs would not support her, the worst that would happen was that she would fall back on the bed. She did not anticipate listing to starboard so quickly and with so much force. She managed to wrap her arms around one of the bedposts and hang on until the world righted again and the wave of nausea passed.

It was her experience that channel crossings were not so difficult as negotiating her way to the chamber pot.

When she was finished making water, Lily rested on the stool beside the commode. The dressing room also held a large armoire and a hip bath, both of which she regarded with a sudden surge of yearning that was as powerful as hunger. With difficulty and no little resentment, she squashed it. It was as she had told her host: some things were better met if one didn't know better.

Using the commode to brace herself, Lily rose to her feet once more. She caught her reflection in the mirror before she turned away. Someone had washed the blacking from her hair, and now dark copper curls framed her face. The smudges she had made across her eyebrows had also vanished. She had always hated the paste in her hair, but now that it was gone she felt uncomfortably exposed. How long had others been looking at her as she was now? It seemed wrong—a violation of her person—that she'd had no choice in how they saw her.

Lily wondered what else they had seen. She drew up the hem of her nightgown with her fingertips until it was bunched just below her breasts. Glancing in the mirror, she realized that she was not tall enough to view her injury. The stool she'd been sitting on was too high, but the one by the bed was exactly right. She tottered back to the bed, retrieved the stool, then returned to the dressing room. After setting it firmly on the floor in front of the commode, Lily stepped on it and judged herself to be at the right height. She raised her nightgown again and regarded herself in the mirror.

Her first thought was that it was surprisingly small for the pain it had caused. It could not be more than two inches in length. The stitches were neat, exact. She remembered Blue had closed it up once, giving her a good cuff on the chin when she had called him all manner of foul names. Well, good for

Blue, she thought, but these weren't his stitches. She'd been sewn up again, though she had not the memory of it. Perhaps she'd been walloped hard before she got around to calling this tailor names.

She ran a finger along its length. The skin was puckered around the threads, reddened a bit, but she could see for herself that the flesh was knitting. That was good, then. She'd be able to leave soon enough, with her legs firmly under her, instead of her arse.

"You understand I am in want of a good explanation."

Lily jerked in surprise. Instinct had her turning toward the doorway, all sense that she was standing on the narrow pad of a stool forgotten. Her nerveless fingers dropped the hem of her gown, and the legs that she'd hope would hold her soon were not up to the task now. She offered a rueful, apologetic smile when they folded as easily as paper and squeezed her eyes closed as the floor rose up to meet her.

Four

Lily's graceless fall to the floor did not occur in the manner she anticipated. She was saved from the impact with that hard surface when Sheridan rushed to her aid. The point of impact, though, was him, and for Lily it was not all that different than meeting up with the floor. He was a man of many hard surfaces, and she seemed to be pressed flush to all of them.

For Sherry's part, he had not expected she would be quite the handful she was or that the stool she'd been standing on would overturn and trip him up. The unfortunate result of this was that his rescue was as graceless as her fall.

"In my defense," he said wryly, "it must be pointed out that I did manage to take the brunt of it."

Lily raised her head a fraction so that she might stare down at him. "As well you should have. You caused it, you know."

"I see you mean to give me no quarter, though I can't say I blame you. Are you quite all right? The stitches?"

Carefully inserting a hand between their bodies, Lily pressed her fingertips against her injury and explored the line of stitches. "I seem to be all of a piece," she told him.

His regard was suspicious. "Can you move?"

Wriggling fingers and toes, she nodded.

"Can you move off of me?"

Lily flushed deeply and tried to scramble off.

"Easy," Sherry said, catching her elbows and securing her again. "You forget how little strength you have. Let us try again, shall we?" He eased his hands to her shoulders and held her while he rolled them both until they were lying side by side. "Steady?" When she nodded again, he released her and sat up. He did not miss the tightness around her mouth as he pulled her into a sitting position beside him. He also noticed she did not complain.

Sherry rose to his haunches, then to his feet, and contemplated the best way to put Lily on hers. She took the matter out of his hands by tucking her knees under her and hauling herself up, using the corner of the commode stand for support.

"You are rather more self-sufficient than is strictly proper for a damsel in distress."

"I beg your forgiveness, then," Lily said. Her hand rested over the placement of the stitches.

"It was merely an observation," Sherry said, watching her closely. The slight curve of her mouth was more wince than smile. He pointed to the site of her injury. "I think I shall have to have a look at that."

She shook her head. "It is nothing. Merely a stitch in my side."

"Self-sufficient *and* a wit."

Lily chuckled at his arid tone and immediately was sorry for it. She pressed her palm tighter still to her side and sucked in a short breath. Before she could mount a scold, she was plucked off her feet and cradled in Sheridan's arms. "You are determined that I should require your assistance," she said. "It is really very curious."

"I know. You cannot imagine my surprise."

She bit her lip to keep her amusement in check. "Then you are not by nature chivalrous."

Sheridan carried her toward the bed. "Most certainly not.

You will not like to hear it, but there is no precedent for my behavior."

"It must be disconcerting for you then."

"Astonishingly so." He set her on the bed and helped her slip a pillow comfortably under her head. "You will allow me to examine the stitches."

Lily studied his face, taking his measure. Absent from his features was any hint of amusement. The dark eyes were implacable, the mouth stubbornly set. She was quite certain she was seeing something that *was* part of his nature: getting precisely what he wanted.

Sheridan placed his hand on her side just below the injury. He felt her skin retract as she sucked in a breath. For a brief moment the dark centers of her green eyes widened so that her study of him became unfocused. He almost drew back. His hesitation lasted just long enough that she calculated his resolve to be unyielding and finally gave her permission.

"This will take but a moment," he told her.

Lily closed her eyes. Her brow knit as she felt him rise from the bed. The movement was unexpected, and she was curious enough to risk a peek in his direction. From behind carefully shaded eyes, she watched him cross the room to the vanity and open the small wooden box resting there. She could not see what he removed, but she saw him pause to examine it. He seemed satisfied with the object, for he palmed it and closed the lid.

Lily's fists curled lightly at her sides when he sat down again. She expected to feel his knuckles brush the length of her leg as he raised the nightgown or feel his fingertips on her skin at her neckline as he lowered it. In some ways it was worse that neither of these things happened. Anticipation made her light-headed; her breathing quickened. She wondered if she would scream and if he would cuff her as roundly as Blue.

She raised her lashes only that fraction necessary to see what she was about. What she glimpsed made her go entirely still. In his right hand he held a shiv and was directing it toward her injury. There could be no mistaking that he meant to plunge it in her side.

Lily threw herself sideways and rolled toward the far edge of the mattress. She felt him reach out for her, but she eluded his hands—and the shiv—by dropping over the side of the bed in a crouch. She stayed low and heard him curse softly and only once, then wondered why he did not fill the air with more expressions of his frustration.

She listened for some sign that he meant to give chase. When there was no movement, she slowly raised herself so that she could see over the bed's horizon. He was sitting almost exactly as she had left him, turned slightly sideways with his knee drawn up for balance. He still held the shiv, but he was contemplating it now, turning it over in his hand as he did so.

She supposed that he caught her movement out of the corner of his eye, for his head swiveled in her direction. She did not make herself a better target by rising higher but remained in the half-crouched position in spite of the pressure it placed on the stitches.

"Do you think I mean to gut you?"

That he would put the question to her so baldly made her begin to doubt that she'd drawn the proper conclusion from his actions. She regarded him and the shiv warily. "Don't you?"

"If that is what you believe, I cannot comprehend what I can say to persuade you that is not my intent."

He made an excellent point. The thing of it was, she realized, she *was* disposed to being persuaded. "I suppose you are of the opinion that I am behaving foolishly."

Sheridan shrugged. "I do not judge you harshly. I can only imagine what you have been made to suffer at the hands of men. You know the truth. It seems you have reasons for expecting the worst even when you have been shown only kindness."

Lily rose a bit higher. She found his argument disarming.

It was true that she had not taken what she knew of his character into account. She had not considered the question of *why* he would want to do her such grievous harm. She had only reacted.

"You said you were going to examine my injury," she said.

"That was my design."

"Why do you need a shiv to do it?"

Sheridan glanced down at the thing in his hand, considered it again, and nodded thoughtfully. "You thought this was a shiv?"

"It *is* a shiv."

"It is also a tool to tear threads and fabric. I took it from my sister's sewing box."

Eyes narrowing, Lily examined the weapon he dangled from his fingertips more closely. For the first time she saw it possessed an oddly shaped end, more like a claw than a single point. "A seam ripper?"

"I have heard it called so," he said mildly, drawing it back. He set it down on the bedside table.

Lily gripped the edge of the mattress and pushed herself to stand. The question of what he had intended to do with it remained uppermost in her mind. She hazarded a guess as to his purpose. "You were going to remove my stitches, perhaps?"

Sheridan sighed. "It is a temptation to name you the most foolish female of my acquaintance, but it has been my misfortune to know a number who surpass you in this regard."

"That must indeed be a trial to you."

"I have always thought so." He smiled a little unevenly in her direction. "At least you had the good sense to move out of the way when you believed you were threatened."

"These women you would name as more foolish? They would have fainted?"

"I'm afraid so."

"That does seem to show a considerable want of good sense."

"My thought also." He pointed to the seam ripper. "I was going to use it to make a small tear in your nightgown so that I could see the condition of the stitches. I thought you would find it preferable to raising or lowering the shift. You affected such modesty that it seemed only proper that I make an attempt to preserve it."

Lily's brows rose a fraction. "It is not an affectation," she said. "I am modest."

"Yes, well, I admit to some curiosity on that count. Mayhap you will later explain it to me."

She blinked at him widely. "Explain modesty? Have you none yourself?"

He waved her questions aside. "I will call upon Mrs. Ponsonby to make the examination. I should have done so at the first. It is only that I have become accustomed to caring for you myself. I do not say that to defend my actions, merely to explain them. Of course I will no longer do so."

"Take care of me?" she asked with a touch of derision. "Or explain yourself?" She smiled a little when she saw his mouth tighten with annoyance.

"Do I amuse you?" he asked.

Lily's wistful smile vanished immediately. How easily she had forgotten herself. She could hardly tell him that his high instep could benefit from a good trouncing now and again. "No," she said quietly, lowering her eyes. "I am sorry if I gave offense."

Sherry studied her bent head, the contrite posture. "You are ill suited to that penitent pose, so have off."

Lily's head snapped up, her lips parting.

He almost laughed aloud at her perfectly expressed astonishment. Instead, he said, "It is your hair, I suppose. A most unfortunate color."

Her eyes narrowed. "It used to be black."

"You are accusing me of something, I collect."

"I—I . . . no."

Sherry did not think that words often failed her, and he counted it as a small victory of sorts to have brought the thing about. He made her the subject of his most withering regard. "You are a singular creature, are you not?"

Lily made no response, but neither did she look away.

"Better," he said, one corner of his mouth lifting. "I will ring for Mrs. Ponsonby."

She expected that he would summon her from the bed-chamber, so she was at once relieved and puzzled when he quit the room. She pushed herself back onto the high bed but didn't lie down. That he should have named her a singular creature was rather like the hedgehog finding fault with the thorn bush for being prickly. Did he know that? she wondered. Or was he supremely unaware of all the reasons she could say the same of him?

He seemed to be blithely—perhaps arrogantly—un-concerned that she did not even know his name. She did not know where she was, except that it was most likely his resi-dence. That particular circumstance was more than passing strange. Even on such short acquaintance, she compre-hended that he set his clock by the conventions of society. He'd admitted as much to her, and yet he had taken her in, made provisions for her care, and now seemed bent on . . .

What? she wondered. To what purpose had so much been done for her? She had not asked for it and certainly did not deserve it. The only explanation left was also the most obvi-ous one: he wanted something in return. This was not a revelation but more of a disappointment. No matter how often she was reminded that kindness in the larger world was made in trade, not given freely, she continued to hold out hope that it would be different.

"Foolish," she said under her breath. Still, although she had learned that she could not reveal this optimistic sense of self to others, she also could not imagine embracing an al-ternative view of life.

The question of what he would demand in return was left unanswered for the moment. Lily's attention was diverted as the door opened and a woman of middle years and unsmiling disposition entered the room.

"He said you might not be abed," Mrs. Ponsonby announced without preamble. "At least I can report you were not on your feet. Lie down, girl. Or is it that you mean to injure yourself again?"

Lily blinked.

"And I have no use for owlish, wounded looks. His lordship may have taken you in like a queer notion, but those of us who serve him still have our good sense. You would be mistaken to think you can overstay your welcome by feigning injury or bringing it about in fact."

Quite unbidden, tears welled in Lily's eyes.

"Oh no." The housekeeper held up one hand. "Those will not work, and I haven't the patience for them. Lie down. Let's be done with this."

Lily sniffed inelegantly and knuckled away the tears. How to explain them? she wondered. It was unlikely that Mrs. Ponsonby would want to hear that she put Lily in mind of Sister Agnes or that the scold was reminiscent of so many she had received at the abbey. It was not what the housekeeper said that provoked Lily's tears but the manner in which she said it. Like Sister Agnes, Mrs. Ponsonby employed a termagant's temperament to good effect. As a child, Lily had felt both distress and defiance. Now she felt only an unexpected sense of longing and deep, abiding loneliness.

The unwelcome tears welled again.

Lily quickly averted her glance and lay back as the housekeeper directed. To avoid another accusation that she was trying to elicit sympathy, Lily closed her eyes and placed her forearm across them. She ignored the housekeeper's skeptical grunt and remained quiet during the examination.

"You have indeed split two stitches," Mrs. Ponsonby said as she drew the nightgown down. "His lordship will want to send for the doctor."

Lily tilted her forearm so she could see the housekeeper. The eyes that regarded her remained disapproving. "Oh, surely not."

"I think I know his mind on this better than you."

"I didn't mean—"

"No, of course you didn't."

"We do not have to tell him."

Mrs. Ponsonby's eyebrows rose halfway to her graying hairline. "You'd like that, wouldn't you? Keeping something from him, I mean. That's not how I've ever managed his lordship's household, and I'm certainly not going to begin now. I don't suppose a baggage like you thinks much of us that deal honestly with others, but there you have it. It's clear you'll need close watching." She turned away from the bed and started to go, shaking her head as she spoke to herself. "A young woman no better than she ought to be living under his roof . . . turning the house on its head for her . . . it's the devil getting his due, and that's a fact . . . it's not—"

The door opened and closed, ending the housekeeper's harangue. Lily simply sighed. It was difficult to find fault with Mrs. Ponsonby's suspicions. She was right to entertain them, and the firmness with which she expressed them reflected well on her loyalty to her employer. Lily decided his lordship might benefit from adopting his housekeeper's way of thinking.

Oddly enough, his nibs was too trusting.

Lily carefully pushed herself upright, resting once again against the headboard. She could not quite tamp her smile.

His nibs. So he was a gentleman and something else besides. She was not surprised. He was toplofty enough to be a prince, though of a certainty he was not. Mrs. Ponsonby had not referred to him as his grace, so he was not a duke. A marquess? Earl? Viscount? Was his nibs a baron? A baronet?

It did not bode well for her that he was a titled gentleman. She had reason to know that there were few strangers among the noble inner circle of the *ton*. They were not merely connected by bloodlines; they were often bound by them. Observing the strictures of that small society had become an end unto itself, and the severest consequences were meted out to those whose behavior brought embarrassment upon them all. They could close ranks quickly in order to put a period to a scandal that might threaten their sense of the social order and their position as arbiters of what was right and proper.

It once again begged the question of what his lordship wanted from her. He had risked something of his reputation by not only bringing her to his residence but allowing her to stay as long as he had. He had not given her a room in the garret or one belowstairs. The bedchamber she occupied had belonged to a person of some importance. Clearly he must know she was not such a person. Just as Mrs. Ponsonby had said, she was no better than she ought to be. If she were, his nibs would not merely be risking a nine days wonder, but a scandal of some middling proportions.

He might not become a pariah in his own society, but neither would he be warmly welcomed. He would find his life could be made most uncomfortable. Lily did not think he would like that in the least.

Woodridge had not.

"You are wool-gathering."

Lily's head came up sharply. His nibs was standing in the doorway, watching her. He looked as if he might have done so for some time. "It is not well done by you to enjoy a laugh at my expense." She rubbed the back of her head where she'd thumped the headboard hard enough to make it shudder.

"I am remarkably tightfisted," he said easily, entering the room. "Better a laugh at your expense than my own. Have you raised a goose egg?"

"No." Lily lowered her hand. "It is nothing."

Sherry stood at the foot of the bed. "Ponsonby reports you have torn two stitches."

"That is the same she said to me. I do not want you to send for the physician. There really is no need."

"She told me you would say that."

"Your housekeeper is very thorough."

"I believe she is, yes." He regarded her a moment longer. "Are you certain there is no urgency? Has the tear caused you no distress?"

"There is discomfort. Pain, if I am careless, but you know I am no hothouse flower, my lord, and I would prefer that you did not treat me as such."

There was a pause as he considered the request. "As you wish." He clasped his hands at his back, rocking forward just once on the balls of his feet before he was still. "It occurs to me that there have been no introductions," he said. "I am Sheridan."

"M'lord," she said, inclining her head respectfully.

"You will not give me your name?"

"You must know it. The children will have told you."

He shrugged. "I should like to hear it from you."

Sensing there was a trap here, Lily still did not know how to avoid it. "Rose," she said carefully. "I am called Miss Rose."

"I did not inquire as to how you are called," he said mildly. "I asked for your name."

Color flushed her cheeks. "You think I am lying."

"Not at all. I am quite certain you have told me the truth, but it also circles a truth you do not wish to reveal."

Lily said nothing. She did not want to look at him but knew she did not dare look away.

"Do you deny it?"

Instead of answering, Lily's small chin came up. She challenged him. "Does it matter what I say? I think it is your intention to discredit me, else why would you ask a question to which you seem to believe you know the answer?"

Sherry smiled faintly. "Parry and thrust. Conversing with you has rather a lot in common with a fencing match."

"You wound me, my lord."

His dark eyes saluted her. "Touché, Lily."

For a moment she simply could not breathe, then she drew her knees back, closer to her chest, and tucked the tented coverlet under her. The effect, she supposed, was like a fox seeking the safety of its earth. It chipped at her pride to know Sheridan would also see it in that light, yet she doubted she could have done it differently.

"The children told you," she said without inflection.

"Yes. But only because they thought you were dying." When he saw her faint, mocking smile, he added, "They believed God should hear prayers said to your true name."

The smile vanished. "Mayhap you wish they had been less earnest."

A small crease appeared between Sherry's brows as he considered the sudden flattening of her mouth at this mention of prayers. "It did not occur to me. May I have leave to call you Lily?"

She shrugged.

Sherry waited. "Shall I call you Miss Rose, then?"

"I suppose you may call me whatever you wish."

"You have still another name, Miss—?"

"Rose," she said, responding to his questioning inflection without hesitation. "No other names. I am Lily Rose."

He was tempted to salute her for the alacrity of her response. There was a certain sly lilt in her voice that fairly challenged him to take exception. That alone decided him not to press. "Very well," he said. "Miss Rose."

Lily thought she should not be so pleased to have diverted him, or at least that she should not show it. It was no easy thing to temper her smile.

"Gloating is unattractive," he said.

"Of course," she said, composing herself. "You are right."

"Thank you."

Lily's eyes narrowed slightly. She thought she detected a hint that he was amused by her. He was much better than she in schooling his features, and he had perfected a shuttered glance that gave little away and a maddeningly neutral tone of expression, but she could not acquit him of enjoying himself once again at her expense. She might have accused him of such if her stomach had not rumbled uncomfortably. Knowing that it was a perfectly natural response to hunger did not lessen her embarrassment.

She drew her knees closer to her chest. "Pardon me. I do not—"

Sherry waved aside her apology. "It is the exact purpose of my return," he said. "To discover if you are prepared to eat something. Ponsonby says she did not inquire."

The anticipation of food caused Lily's stomach to rumble again. "I should like something, yes." She realized she did not even know when she had last eaten.

"Of course. Cook will prepare something for you. You've had little more than broth spooned into you for far too many days." He inclined his head and prepared to make his exit.

He was half the distance to the door when Lily's softly spoken thank you reached his ears. She knew because it caused him an infinitesimal pause in his step. She thought he might turn—hoped that he would—but he didn't, and then he was gone.

Staring at the closed door, Lily was uncomfortably aware that she suddenly felt more lonely than alone. Because nothing good could come of dwelling on it, she ruthlessly pushed the sense of it aside and opened her mind to the important matters that must occupy her.

Chief among them was her own survival.

There was no question but that she would have to leave. Less clear was whether the children should accompany her. It was not unreasonable to suppose that Sheridan would instruct his housekeeper to find some position for them. They might shovel coal and fill his fireplaces. Midge could blacken his lordship's boots. Dash could run errands. And though he might chafe at being forced to wear the livery, Pinch would make an excellent tiger.

It would be a good life for them, better than she dared hope and beyond their expectations. By every sensible measure, they should leap at the opportunity for such good fortune. Lily was less certain they would do so.

Bringing the thing about would take considerable cleverness on her part. They were children, so they could behave foolishly, but they were not fools. She would be lucky if she could manage to stay even a half step in front of them.

Then there was the complication of Sheridan. His lordship would not be easily gulled if it came to that. Everything must needs be his own idea, or at least he should believe it was.

Closing her eyes, Lily sighed. It was all very tiring. She simply hadn't the strength of body or will to stand long against an opponent like Sheridan. They had fenced, sure enough, but Lily knew better than to believe he had not also been considerate of her and that he was simply assessing her skills. If he had judged her to be a stronger opponent, he might very well have run her through.

The thought of being stuck again did not in any way please her. She placed one hand over her injury, reminding herself that he'd played some role in her acquiring it. She should have already told him how it had all come about. That was no secret she meant to keep, but whether or not he believed her was entirely his choice.

The arrival of her repast ended Lily's musings. It was brought to her by a young woman possessing both brisk efficiency and a suspicious temperament. Lily immediately felt the housekeeper's influence.

She unfolded her knees so the maid could place the legged tray over her lap. When the cover was lifted, Lily breathed deeply of the aroma of warm milk and porridge. What she lifted first to her lips, though, was the cup of tea.

"Thank you," she said. "You are very kind to bring it to me." Lily saw her thanks did nothing to allay the maid's distrust. If anything, the girl was given to deeper suspicions.

"I'm doing what I was told," she said. "There's no cause for you to be thanking me."

"I would have gladly taken my meal in the servant's hall."

"What makes you think you'd be welcome there, a baggage like you?"

Lily's fingertips tightened on her cup, but she did not respond to the provocation. "Are the children about?" she asked instead.

"Underfoot, you mean."

Lily did not contradict her. "May I see them?"

The maid was at the foot of the bed now, smoothing the blankets and remaking a rumpled corner with a neat tuck. She paused. "That's not for me to say, is it? They come and go as they please, so it's up to them, I suspect."

That surprised Lily and concerned her as well. "His lordship does not allow them free rein of his home, I hope."

"Do you take him for a fool, then?"

"No, I—"

"Because he's not."

Lily thought the maid's stout assertion was in aid of convincing herself. "I only meant the boys are likely to get up to some mischief if not taken in hand."

"Mischief? Now, if that ain't calling a downpour a bit of drizzle, then I've never stood in the weather."

Alarmed, Lily set down her cup. "What have they done?"

"What haven't they done is more the thing. Into the larder, they were, and the meat safe, and Mrs. Renwick's tarts and custards. They put sugar in the saltcellars and salt in Mrs. Ponsonby's tea. They rearrange the linens, smudge the silverware after it's been polished, and drop coals like bread crumbs when they're carrying the scuttle to the hearth."

Lily was very careful not to smile. "So it is the servants' hall where they've been allowed free rein." She watched the maid stiffen indignantly, but there was not much she could say when it was patently the truth. Lily suspected Sheridan's staff was in no small way responsible for provoking the boys.

"They are the very devil's seed," the maid said.

Ducking her head quickly so she would not catch the girl's eye, Lily applied herself to her meal. She felt the maid's hesitation, as if she wanted to say more, but then she seemed to think better of it and backed out of the room. Her hasty retreat made Lily smile. "If they are the devil's seed," she said, a chuckle softly edging her voice, "then surely I must be his handmaiden."

Sherry had forbidden the boys to go to Lily's room the night before. This was not done as punishment for any particular offense—indeed, he was blithely unaware of their offenses against his staff—but because he had determined his own brief encounters with Lily had exhausted her. He had no doubt she would disagree with his estimation, which further supported his decision not to include her in making it.

The boys knew, though, that she had been awake long enough to get herself out of bed and into trouble and that she had been served her first meal. Such particulars as they had about her condition were courtesy of one of the maids, and they were fairly dancing with excitement to see Lily when they applied to Sherry for permission to do so.

Sheridan was not optimistic that they would obey him, so he was pleasantly surprised when he found them huddled outside the door to her room the following morning. He was certain one of them had had an ear pressed to the door a moment before he'd stepped into the hallway. They came to attention rather too quickly to have been applying themselves to some good purpose.

Sherry subjected them each to a careful examination. They were clean, if not polished. Tucked in, if not neatly pressed. They had parted their hair crookedly, but that was less important than the fact that they had combed it. It was a good effort by three children who had not seen the sense of it before.

"Impressive," Sherry said. He could see the compliment pleased them, but they were far too anxious to offer more than an uneasy smile.

"Do ye think she'll know us?" Midge asked. "Dash 'ere thinks we look like toffs an' she won't see us for 'oo we are."

Sherry gave them all a second critical glance. "I do not like to disagree with Master Dash, but I believe you have not yet achieved membership in the Brummel set."

They regarded him blankly.

"It means she will recognize you."

"Oh, then yer lordship should 'ave said that."

"I thought I did," Sherry said, but his comment was meant more for himself than for them. "Is Dr. Harris with her?"

Pinch nodded. "'E's been in there ever so long. Wot do ye make of it?"

"I expect it's because he is thorough."

"We should go in," Dash said. "'E might need us to fetch something." To support this point, he added, "You did."

"I am certain Harris has all his medicines and tools in his bag."

Dash looked as if he might object, but laughter from inside the room arrested his attention. "Oh, she will pop 'er stitches for sure. On no account should 'e make 'er laugh like that."

Sherry was inclined to agree, though he also had the unexpected and unwelcome thought that if there was going to be laughter, then it should be he, not the physician, who aroused it. Unwilling to make that notion the subject of contemplation, Sherry placed his hand on the doorknob. It turned under his palm without effort from him.

Harris opened the door wide. "So it is just as we thought," he said. "Four of them come to beg an audience."

Four? It was not what Lily thought. She had anticipated only three. When the physician stepped to one side, she saw Sheridan was with the boys. Lest the children doubt that she was happy to see them, she thrust aside her regret that they were not alone and opened her arms wide.

"She will be overrun," Sherry said to the doctor as the boys bounded for the bed.

Harris turned to observe the reunion. All three boys clambered onto the bed, and all of them stopped short of throwing themselves into that welcoming embrace. "It appears your worries are without foundation. The lads show remarkably good sense."

Sherry had to admit that they did. Instead of dropping like felled trees, they wound themselves around her as gently as ivy. Pinch got the half circle of her right arm, Dash and Midge the left. It was impossible to know who was truly clinging to whom, and Sherry concluded that in the end it was of no consequence. One was vine. The other lattice. He supposed it was the need of one for the other that was important.

"Makes me quite envy them," Harris said, glancing sideways from the affecting scene on the bed to Sheridan. "I didn't think that was possible."

It made Sherry feel like an intruder as well. He tilted his head toward the hall and indicated they should both step outside. When the doctor followed, he closed the door.

"I have missed you terribly," Lily said.

"We wasn't the ones gone away," Pinch reminded her. "Ye left us."

"I suppose I did."

"'Ow'd ye let 'im stick ye," Midge asked. "Ye always was as light on yer feet as I am wi' my fingers." He held five digits up for her inspection and wiggled them. "So 'ow'd it 'appen?"

"He didn't stick me."

"No," Dash said. "Pull the other one, it's got bells on."

Lily lowered Midge's hand and held up her own. "I swear it's true. Do you think I'd allow a macaroni like him to plunge his shiv in me?"

Dash giggled. "'E is a toff, right enough, but not a bad sort. Still, I didn't believe 'e was innocent, even when it looked like 'e was 'elpin' ye, I was wonderin' if 'e still meant to finish wot 'e started at the Garden."

"That's why we stayed wi' ye," Pinch said. "In case 'e decided to try an' make a proper job of it. Slept right 'ere in this room every night but last."

"Why not last night?"

"'E forbid it."

Lily's head lifted along with the eyebrows. "You thought he might still mean to kill me, but you stayed away because he *forbid* it?"

"Well, 'e 'as a way about 'im that ye don't want to cross," Pinch admitted sheepishly. "And we was comin' to trust 'im a little."

Lily knew precisely what Pinch meant. "It's all right." She gave his narrow shoulders a light squeeze. "I don't think he's a bad sort either. He seems to have treated you well."

"Except for the proper drubbin'," Midge said. "There was no cause for 'im to 'ave us scrubbed until we was as white as the Dover Cliffs."

"You've never been to Dover, Midge."

"No, but I 'eard ye tell about it. The cliffs are fair to gleamin' in the sun, you said, and so were we. Everyone stared."

She laughed. "What torture has been inflicted on you poor boys. You have my deepest sympathies, but you will find them insufficient to release you from telling me what you were doing in Covent Garden that night."

"Wot night?" Dash asked.

Lily caught him by the chin and made him look at her. It was enough.

"Oh, *that* night."

"Hmmm. Why were you there? I thought I had your promise." She glanced at each of the others. "And yours. And yours, too."

"Ye did," Dash said. "But we give our word to Ned Craven as well. 'E 'ad need of us that night. Said we should find a mark wi' a quid that wouldn't be missed."

"Ned? Then why was he . . ." She stopped herself from

asking the impulsive question and chose another tack. "Did Craven say why he needed a quid?"

Dash shrugged. "Why does 'e ever? Drink or gamin'."

"'Ores," Midge said. "Sometimes it's 'ores."

"Thank you, Midge," Lily said wryly. "I will speak to Craven about releasing you from your word. You can depend upon it." Even if the boys were able to secure employment with Sheridan, there were hundreds more like them in Holborn for Craven to exploit. She could manage perhaps another three or four under her protection. "So Lord Sheridan was the mark you chose."

It was Pinch who nodded. "I fancied 'im to be good for the quid. We all did. Couldn't expect wot come of it, though. That was a bit of an eyepopper, seein' you fall on 'im that way."

"For me also," Lily said.

"So 'ow'd ye get stuck?" Pinch asked.

"Inattention, Pinch."

"But 'ow?"

"And 'oo?" asked Midge. "If it wasn't 'imself wot did it, then 'oo?"

So they hadn't seen everything; she had wondered. Then she wondered if they would tell her. Mayhap silence was best for all of them. "I have nothing else to say on the matter until I've spoken to his lordship." She ruffled Dash's flaxen hair with her fingertips. "Tell me about him. What title does he possess?"

"'E's a viscount."

"How do you know?"

"'E told us the day we come 'ere. I think we must 'ave tweaked 'im proper because 'e puffed 'imself up a bit and told us 'e was the Viscount Sheridan. Midge was impressed, but I knew it wasn't the same as if 'e was a duke."

Lily could only imagine Sheridan's chagrin if he heard the boys talking now. "Well, it is still an important title. Have you learned his name?"

Pinch looked puzzled. "Lord Sheridan. That's wot they all call 'im."

"That is like you calling me Miss Rose when my name is Lily." She saw their eyes dart away and their heads bow. "Yes, I know about that. Never mind, it is done with. You will continue to call me Miss Rose, and we will not speak of the other again. I only mention it because it is a respectful address in the same manner Lord Sheridan is a respectful address. He has another name. Norbert Pennywright perhaps. Or Neville George Whittington."

"William Toplofty," Pinch said.

"Simon James Toggery," Dash said.

Not to be outdone, Midge offered, "Arthur Macaroni."

They rolled away from Lily, holding their sides as they laughed at their own delicious wickedness.

"Actually," came the smooth voice from the doorway, "it is Alexander Henry Grantham."

There was immediate silence. Unlike the boys, Lily did not blush. She regarded Sheridan with perfect frankness and was emboldened by the presence of the children to take him to task. "Do you find knocking a terrible inconvenience?"

He raised a single brow at the chilly tone she adopted. "In my own home, yes."

"Eavesdroppers hear no good of themselves."

"I was not eavesdropping. None of you noticed me standing here."

"You might have announced yourself."

"I thought that is what I just did. Alexander Henry Grantham, Viscount Sheridan. I shall keep that appellation, I think, though I admit to some fondness for Arthur Macaroni."

Midge burrowed his flaming face in a pillow.

"We didn't mean yer lordship offense by it," Pinch said. "It was all in the way of fun."

"Do you think I'm offended?" Sherry asked.

Dash felt like burying his head with Midge, but he risked a glance in Sheridan's direction. "'Ow would we know? Ye always look like ye do now."

The irony of Dash's observation was that it had a powerful effect on Sheridan's countenance. He blinked widely, boggle eyed. Even the line of his taut jaw became a fraction slack. His nostrils flared and his lips parted. From somewhere under his intricately tied neckcloth a wave of red color washed over him and settled most distinctly in the tips of his ears.

Now it was Lily who clutched her side as the laughter she could not hope to restrain truly threatened to burst her stitches.

Watching her, the niggling thought returned to Sherry that it was no hardship to play the fool. Her laughter did not disturb him in the least this time. As was often the case, he reflected, one's disposition could be favorably bent by which side of the door one was on. He liked being on this side.

Sherry walked to the foot of the bed just as Midge was crawling out from under the covers and Lily was knuckling tears from her eyes. Midge handed her a corner of the sheet he had tucked in his hand.

"Don't you have a handkerchief, Master Midge?" Sherry asked.

"Yes, m'lord, but it's mine." He glanced apologetically at Lily. "We're not allowed to use our sleeves 'ere. Dunnet cuffs us if we do."

Lily glanced sharply at Sheridan and he raised his hands, palms out. "This is the first I've heard of blows being struck."

The boys laughed in unison, but it was Dash who explained the reason for it. "'E don't swipe at us 'ard. Miss Rose 'ugs us 'arder than Dunnet pops us."

Now it was Sherry who gave Lily the significant glance. "Please give Miss Rose your handkerchief, Master Midge. It is always the politic thing to do to offer a lady one's handkerchief."

"'E means it's good form," Pinch said. "Go on."

Midge retrieved his handkerchief and looked at it rather longingly before holding out it to Lily. "Thank you," she said gravely. "It is enormously kind of you." Unfolding it, she couldn't help notice its crisp and pristine condition. "And so clean."

Midge's shrug had overtones of guilt. "I mostly use my sleeve. Ain't comfortable blowin' my nose in something wot's so pretty."

Lily was able to use the handkerchief to shield her smile as she dabbed at her eyes, but Sherry had to be more circumspect. He studied the carving on the walnut headboard beyond Lily's right shoulder and worked very hard at not catching her eye.

When Lily was finished, she folded the handkerchief carefully and began to return it to Midge. Before he took it, the boy looked to Sheridan for direction.

"You may tell her to keep it, or take it back for yourself. If it makes a difference, I will see to it that you get another."

"Oh, that's all right, m'lord. I know 'ow to get more. Fogle-'unting is wot us errifs learn first."

Lily was fortunate to still have the handkerchief. She crushed it in her fist and pressed it against her mouth. Even so, she looked as though she might choke trying to contain her amusement.

For his part, Sherry had to make do with a good effort at looking appalled. "Fogle-hunting. Is that cant for drawing out a handkerchief?"

Midge nodded.

"I see. I believe you are a thorough scoundrel, Master Midge."

"Yes, m'lord. I am that."

It was no good. Sherry surrendered to the shout of laughter that was pressing at the back of his throat. "Go on," he said when he was able to catch his breath. He jerked his head toward the door and watched them scramble off the bed. In their haste to leave, they jostled him as they swept past. It was like being in the center of a whirling dervish. "There must be something for you to do in Renwick's kitchen," he called after them. "Pots to scour. Vegetables to scrub. Tarts to steal."

That stopped all three of them in their tracks. "'Oo do you think told 'im about the tarts?" Dash whispered to Pinch.

Sherry rolled his eyes at Lily but addressed the boys who were now behind him. "No one told me. It was a carefully reasoned guess."

"I told ye 'e was a clever one," Pinch said, nudging Dash. "Can't be too careful 'ere."

Midge was impressed. "Do ye think 'e knows about the custard?"

"I do now," Sherry said dryly.

Pinch, Dash, and Midge fairly tripped over each other to get out the door.

"Are they gone?" Sherry asked Lily.

She leaned slightly to one side to see around him. They waved to her from the hallway, then disappeared. "Yes."

"They didn't shut the door, did they?"

She shook her head.

He sighed. "I suppose it would have been too much to expect." Turning on his heel, he crossed the room to close it. When he returned to Lily's bedside, she was regarding him with an expression that was at once contemplative and amused. "What is it?"

"You like them," she said.

"Are you accusing me?"

"I think I might be."

"Then *mea culpa*."

Lily smiled. "They are perfect scoundrels. You were right about that."

Sherry leaned his shoulder against one of the posts at the end of the bed. "What about you, Miss Rose?"

There was a small catch in her voice. "Me?"

"Yes," he said. "Are you a scoundrel?"

"No. I don't think so."

"A thief?"

"Pinching purses. Shiving the froe."

"Shiving the froe?"

"Cutting a woman's pockets off with a razor."

Sherry wondered at her calm admissions. "You teach the boys what you know?"

"Yes."

That was when he pinned Lily back with a dark, implacable glance and asked with remarkable indifference, "Are you a whore, Miss Rose?"

Five

Lily remained singularly self-possessed as she considered his question. "A whore? There are some that would say so."

"What is your opinion?"

"I do not consider myself such." A strand of dark coppery hair had fallen across her cheek. She tugged on it idly, straightening the curl before tucking it neatly behind her ear. "You will allow this is a curious interview."

He gave no indication that he was willing to admit as much.

"Then it is your practice to put these questions to all your guests. In that case, I should wonder that you have any."

Sherry went on as if there had been no interruption. "Are you French?"

Lily frowned. "Why would you think so?"

"It seems to me that is the question you should have posed when I asked if you were a whore. It is more than a little peculiar that you would practice prevarication when the subject is your origins and speak quite frankly when you are asked about your morals."

"I am responsible for my morals," she said. "I cannot help the other."

"Then you *are* French."

"I did not say so." Lily drew her knees up and laid her forearms across the top. "I cannot imagine of what import it is. It was not to my particular liking that you put questions to me about thieving and whoring, but I could understand their relevance. Certainly the circumstances of our meeting would permit you to make some assumptions about my character, but I cannot fathom what has suggested to you that I might not be one of His Majesty's subjects."

Sherry could not help himself. Incredulity caused him to grin quite openly at her. "Why, you are offended," he said, shaking his head. "Do you think you will stand accused of being some sort of spy?" He watched her cheeks pinken and her eyes dart away. "Bloody hell. You do. What sort of maggot have you got in your head that would make you think that?"

The deep rose color in Lily's cheeks continued to blossom. She shrugged.

"I doubt that Boney sends his female spies to Holborn. To the Court at St. James, mayhap, but not Holborn or even Covent Garden. It would be ill-advised of them, and they are damnably more clever than that. Do you think they give so much as a fig that Blue Rutland is in receipt of smuggled brandy? That is the sort of intelligence our own excise men would like to know, while the French are happy for his industry as it supports their efforts to overrun the whole of the Continent."

Sherry finished his discourse abruptly when he saw she was regarding him worriedly. He held up his hands, palms out, and adopted what he hoped was a more reasoned tone and tack. "If I promise that I acquit you of being a spy, will you admit that you are French?"

"No."

He sighed. Perhaps appealing to her reason was not the better course. He tried approaching the thing directly. "Then how is it that you are fluent in the language?"

Lily's lashes flickered. "Does someone say that I am?"

"I do."

"I don't suppose there is a maggot in *your* head?"

"No. No maggot." He watched her chin come up and cautioned her. "Think carefully before you answer, Miss Rose, especially if you mean to tell me you don't speak the language." When her eyes darted away, he knew he had been right to suppose she meant to lie. The long silence that followed made him wonder if she would speak to him at all.

"*Je suis anglaise,*" she said finally. "*Le même que vous. Je parle français parce que j'étais ene élève à l'Abbaye de Sacré Coeur. J'y suis arrivée avant de la mort de mes parents, mais j'y restais pendant dix année. L'abbaye est dans la compagne en dehors de Paris. Es-ce que vous la connaissez?*"

"*Non.*" He had never heard of the abbey where she said she'd spent ten years after the death of her parents. He imagined there must be many like it in and around Paris.

"*C'est une école sans importance avec seulement vingt-cinq étudiantes et quatre enseignante avec la Mère Révérends.*"

He wondered why she'd left and put the question to her. "*Pourquoi est-ce que tu as partir?*"

"*Vous parlez bien le français, mais vous parlez mieux l'anglais.*" Lily switched effortlessly to English after this critical assessment of his French. "I was sent away," she said. "I could not live out my life there, not without taking my vows and joining the order. It was only because the abbey had been my home longer than it had not that I contemplated remaining. I believe the Reverend Mother was horrified that I might not be dissuaded." The shadow of a wistful smile momentarily changed the shape of her mouth. "You can appreciate, I think, that she was of the opinion that I was ill-suited to that life."

Still leaning against the bedpost, Sherry folded his arms in front of him and studied her. It was true that on their short acquaintance he had glimpsed a hint of mischief in her eyes. There was also that impish, slightly reckless smile of hers that would give a more prudent man pause. Her hair, with its extraordinary deep copper coloring, would not be tamed by the close cropping she'd given it or straightened by her frequent tugging on the curling tendrils. He tried to imagine it tucked under the severity of a wimple instead of as a halo about her heart-shaped face and found his imagination failed him.

Perhaps it had been the same for the Reverend Mother, though if that were true, the judgment struck him as having no real substance. Shouldn't it have mattered more what was in Lily's heart? "I think I understand her counsel," Sherry said at last, "but was she right to advise you to leave?"

"Never say you doubt it? I am far and away more astonished by what I have become than she would be."

"But if you had not left . . ." He let his voice trail off, prompting her with his silence.

Lily shrugged. "I think I would have been content."

Sherry considered this, wondering as much about what she'd told him as what she'd left unsaid. "It does not seem that—" He stopped because she was shaking her head slowly and had lifted a cautionary finger. "You are tired," he said. "I have taxed your strength."

"You have taxed my wits," she said. Her faintly amused smile faded, and now she regarded him with solemn purpose. "You have been most gracious to me, my lord, but not even for you will I reveal more. If you cannot accept this, I truly understand. Naturally you have the right to know the character of those you invite into your home. I think you have already made a great allowance on my behalf because you brought me here in spite of all you suspected about mine. I honestly cannot say that if our positions were reversed that I would have done the same."

"You are firm on this?"

"Yes." She was certain he didn't like it, and she did not expect him to. Her only regret that she must be adamant was because of the children. She knew he liked them well enough, but she was less confident that he would take them in if she was not cooperative. "There is one thing I would tell you, though."

Sherry cocked an eyebrow at her. "Oh?"

"It has very little to do with me and everything to do with you."

"How so?"

Lily pushed her back more firmly against the headboard, bracing her spine and shoulders, screwing her courage to the sticking place. "I find it odd that you have asked me nothing about Covent Garden. I recognize you from that night, you know."

"I know. You told me as much when we were yet at the Blue Ruination." Her look remained blank. "You don't remember, do you? I had begun to think that must be the case, else you would not have hesitated to answer my questions regarding your fluent French."

Lily understood at last what she must have done. "*J'ai parlé française à vous.*"

"You did indeed speak to me in that language. You asked, '*Que faites-vous ici?*' "

Feeling weak of a sudden, Lily translated quietly, "What are you doing here?"

Sherry nodded. "I could have concluded from that that you recognized me, but you will understand that I wanted to be certain. I asked the question plainly, and you confirmed it. You pointed out that I go to the theatre. Do not strain your gray matter trying to recall our conversation. It was cogent but disappointingly brief."

"I did not say anything untoward, did I?"

"You were discreet. It seems you are of a mind to reveal very little in any language."

Lily discharged a breath she hadn't realized she was holding. "That is something at least."

"Relieved?"

"Yes."

The bed shuddered as Sherry pushed away from the bedpost. He regarded his choice of chairs and selected the Queen Anne at the escritoire. He carried it back, placed it at Lily's bedside, then set himself comfortably upon it, folding his arms again and stretching his long legs before him. In every way he gave the impression of a man prepared to hear a story. Whether or not he would believe it was less clearly defined. The tilt of his head and the thrust of his chin spoke to some measure of skepticism, while his dark eyes were more warmly inviting.

"We have established that you recognize me from Covent Garden," he said as if there had been no interruption. "Perhaps you should proceed with how you came to be there. You were not at the theatre yourself, I collect." He was immediately sorry for provoking her with this last observation because the splendidly curved line of her mouth flattened. "Very well. You must tell the tale in your own way."

"I have been to the Royal Opera House," she said with quiet dignity. "Perhaps you think it is the sole province of the *ton* or that it would be better if that were so."

"I beg your pardon," he said. "I meant no slight."

Lily cast him a sideways glance to gauge his sincerity but had to accept his words for what they were. Sheridan did not seem to know how to affect an expression of contriteness. She supposed it was because, like so many others of his class, he seldom believed there was a need for it.

"However," Lily said, neither accepting or dismissing his apology, "I was not there that evening. I followed the boys to Covent Garden because I do not trust them. They are as likely to end up on a transport ship to Van Diemen's Land as any I've known, perhaps more so because Midge is eager to prove his worth to the other two."

"Pinch and Dash?" Sherry asked. "How skilled are they?"

"Expert enough to take your handkerchief without you knowing."

"I doubt that."

Lily simply raised one eyebrow and leveled him with a significant look.

"Surely not," he said, unfolding his arms to check for his handkerchief. It was gone. "The devil they did. When did they—"

"They gave you the rum-hustle on their way out the door. Pinch was the bulker, and Dash did a bit of fogle-hunting. He gave your handkerchief to Midge, though, which I thought was generous. Midge waved it at me from the hallway."

Sherry remembered his back had been to the door and that he'd asked Lily to tell him if the boys had gone. "You didn't say a thing."

She raised her hands helplessly and shrugged.

Sherry plowed his fingers through his hair, supporting his head in his palm for a moment as he considered his response. "It is difficult to be annoyed when one is also damnably impressed."

"Yes," she said. "One frequently feels that way about them."

"Nothing is safe here, is it?"

Lily did not lie to him. "I suppose that depends on whether Ned Craven finds out that they're here. Left to their own devices, they'll be satisfied with tarts and custards."

"And handkerchiefs," he said wryly.

"Just to keep their hand in."

"I forget you are a wit." He folded his arms again. "Who is this Ned Craven?"

Lily had wondered if Ned might be known to Sheridan. Discovering he was not made her tread carefully. "I suppose it is best understood if you know that he enjoys some influence in Holborn. He trades in favors, large and small, and he expects a fair tribute for what he does—or what he doesn't do. The boys steal for him when he asks."

"They wouldn't refuse him?"

She shook her head. "That is never wise." She gave him time to think over her full meaning, then she went on. "Pinch told me this morning that Ned was in want of some funds that night, and that's why they went to the Garden. Since it was a quid Ned was demanding, there was probably a gaming debt he wanted to settle."

"So the boys are there because of Craven, and you are there because of the boys."

"That's right."

"And I am their mark."

"Yes. I saw Dash first from one direction, then Pinch from another. They are so small and slippery that it was not easy to follow their movements. It was when I spied Midge that I was finally able to make you as their target."

"I am curious about that," he said. "Why did they choose me?"

Lily suspected Ned had been more particular about the mark than the boys had led her to believe, but she did not explain this. Keeping it from him, however, did not give her any measure of peace. "You will have to ask them. I would not have."

"Why not?"

"Because you were watchful. I do not think the boys notice such things yet, but I saw how your eyes moved over the crowd. It was not merely in support of casual interest, and neither were you trying to catch anyone's eye. I do not believe you offered a polite greeting to a single person in all the time I observed you."

"Truly?" Sherry asked, fascinated. "You noticed all this?"

"Of course. One must."

"So it would seem. Pray, continue."

"The woman at your side," Lily said, "she is your . . . ?"

"Miss Dumont," he said.

Lily was not surprised that he did not reveal his relationship to the woman, but she was disappointed. "Yes, well, Miss Dumont said something that took your attention. It is possible the boys observed this earlier and chose you because they knew you could be easily diverted. They also know that when it comes to making the rum-hustle a gentleman will have more care for his lady than himself."

"It would seem that gallantry makes one vulnerable."

"Indeed."

Sherry set his heels on the bed frame and tipped his chair back, balancing it at a dangerous angle. "Go on."

Lily felt a twinge in her side as she drew in a breath. Not wanting to distract Sheridan from the story, she said nothing and let her hand idly drift downward to where she could place pressure on the injury. "You were distracted, the boys were moving closer, and I only wanted to stop them. I started to duck and weave in the crowd, hoping to reach you before they did. I would have let you go unmolested; they only had to see me there to do the same."

"But you didn't. You attacked me."

Lily nodded. "I did, but not to hurt you. There was someone else. Someone with a blade. I confess, I remember very little about it, and almost nothing about him, but I swear to you I didn't have a knife." She shrugged, hoping the truth would shield the lies. "More's the pity."

Sherry set his chair down on all four legs. "That is what you said when you fell on top of me with the blade buried in your side."

"I did?"

"Mmm. Except you said it in French."

Lily's green eyes widened a fraction. She could think of nothing to say.

"It was surprising," he said lightly. "Especially when your speech was without accent."

"It must have raised a great many questions in your mind."

"A great many. Most of which you have since announced you will not answer."

She did not apologize for it. He would have known it was insincere.

Sherry applied himself to all the particulars she had set

before him and wondered which ones he could trust as facts. It was perhaps too convenient that she did not remember the last moments of the attack very well. "If you saw the man's weapon, how is it that you got caught by it? Was there nowhere for you to move?"

"It was moving that caused him to stick me," she said. "Do you not understand, my lord? The knife was meant to split your ribs, not mine."

When Lily had considered how she might tell him the whole of it, she had entertained some notions regarding his response. It had occurred to her that he was likely to be appalled, perhaps incredulous. When she painted the same picture with less bold strokes, she thought he might be dismayed, mayhap wary. What she had not been able to anticipate was his unemotional and unequivocal acceptance.

"You knew," she said. It was an accusation.

Sherry corrected her. "I suspected."

"Why did you permit me to prattle on?"

"I needed to learn what you knew," he said. "And in the event you could tell me nothing substantive, there is still the fact that you are vastly entertaining."

Lily made to speak, then decided she didn't know what she might properly say. Had she been insulted? Or was there a compliment paid? In truth, she did not know if she was annoyed or flattered.

"You wish to say something?"

She shook her head.

"Than perhaps you will permit me to explain." He tipped the chair back on its hind legs again. "You denied having a knife. You spoke a foreign tongue. Plainly, a knife was in your side and plain to me at least was the truth that I didn't put it there. Your body was spirited away before the crowd was cleared, and yet there were no witnesses. I think you will agree, it is a peculiar set of circumstances. I made a good effort to ignore the whole of it. A day passed before I ventured back to Covent Garden and into Holborn. I was looking for you, certainly, but for answers also. I did not know if you still survived, and I particularly did not know that you were female. There were not many people who were willing to speak to me."

"Did you offer coin?"

"For your care if you were alive. For your burial if you were not. I demanded proof of either."

"Then you never spoke to an informer. Any one of them would have told you where I was for very little of the ready."

"Perhaps none knew."

"There is always one who knows, and it takes only one. It can't be helped." But Lily knew why no one had come forward—and it wasn't because of her. She felt a small stab of conscience, then another in her side as she shifted her position to put more weight on one hip. It was sharp enough to make her breath hitch.

Sheridan's dark glance was shrewdly assessing. "You have been sitting there too long." He dropped his feet to the floor and stood. "Harris says you're healing well enough on the outside but that it will take considerably more time to heal what none of us can see." He held up the covers so she could stretch out more comfortably under them. "Not on your side," he said. "Your back."

"I will get a crick in my neck trying to look at you if I lie on my back."

"I am not staying. You are going to rest, perhaps even sleep."

"I am bored with resting and tired from so much sleep. I cannot stay bed-bound. Nothing good can come of it."

"That is my opinion also, but walking about is something to begin this afternoon." She looked as if she meant to continue arguing, and Sherry held up a hand to stop her. "I mean to have my way on this."

Lily could not think of any situation thus far in which he had not had his way. She would have dearly liked to point this out, but he was already quitting the room and her wide yawn precluded speech of any kind. She would not be at all surprised if she was asleep before he reached the stairs.

Sherry was in want of a diversion. It occurred to him that he might have been too hasty putting a period to his liaison with Francine. He had not accounted for the possibility that his journey to Granville would be delayed. Now he was at sixes and sevens, reluctant to venture out to the clubs and risk another flurry of invitations that would require answering but equally dissatisfied with the prospect of remaining indoors.

The solution that he arrived upon was to do something out of the ordinary. He would go out but not to any of the haunts he typically frequented. There was a certain freedom in that, being unburdened by the expectations of others. It was what he'd hoped to accomplish by going to Granville. It was no small revelation to find the same could be accomplished in Holborn.

Sherry counted five patrons in the Blue Ruination. Rutland was setting drinks on a table between two of his customers when Sherry walked in. The tavern received little in the way of sunlight through the glass at its front, and the gloom shielded Sherry from immediate recognition.

He chose a table as far from the other patrons as was possible and sat on the bench that would put his back to them. Blue was not long in coming over.

Sherry glanced up when Rutland demanded his order.

"Demmed if it ain't you." Blue wiped his hands on his apron and struck a small bow before he joined Sherry at the table. "What are you doing here?" He looked about. "Miss Rose? You ain't here to tell me you killed her, are you?"

"No. I'm here for a pint of ale."

"Pull the other one."

"It's true. Join me."

Although suspicious, Blue got up and poured Sheridan a

pint and one for himself. When he returned to the table he pocketed the coin that was put out for him and sat down. "You'll tell me how she fares?"

"Well enough."

"You ain't chased the lads out yet, leastways they haven't come round here."

"Would they?" asked Sherry. "Come here, I mean."

"They might," Blue said cautiously. "I have work for them now an' again."

"Fogle-hunting?"

"Not bloody likely. I don't deal in stolen goods, but if I had a mind to do it, I'd make a proper job of it. Fogle-hunting's sport for children. I'd set up the drag sneaks and snoozers, that's who get the goods."

"Drag sneaks?"

"With all your fine talk of fogle-hunting," Blue said, "I thought you knew the cant."

Sherry ignored Rutland's mockery. "I'm learning. Tell me about the drag sneaks."

"They take luggage from coaches and carts. Snoozers are about the same, but they sleep close to the hostelries along the road and steal the luggage straightaway from the rooms."

Sherry thought of the rooms Blue had abovestairs. He did not suppose those who took one for the night ever had much in the way of trunks and bags. "What do the boys do for you?"

"Wash the cups. Sweep. They take a meal and bit of grog for that. I give them coin for catchin' rats."

Although he tried, Sherry could not imagine Blue Rutland offering any employment because of a generous nature. It seemed more likely that Lily's fine hand was at work here. "Do the boys work for anyone else?"

"Couldn't say. I ain't their wet nurse."

"What about Ned Craven?"

Blue choked on a mouthful of ale. His eyes watered, and his complexion grew as ruddy as an old salt's as he coughed hard over his drink. More than a minute passed before he recovered. Making a frank assessment of Sheridan, he slowly wiped his mouth with his sleeve. "You'd do well to be cautious there," he said. "He's not a bloke you want to cross."

Sherry shrugged. "How would I find him?"

"You wouldn't. He'd find you."

"Does he come here?"

Blue looked around, gauging the notice his other customers were taking of his conversation. "You a thief-taker?"

"A thief-taker? What manner of sneaksman is that?"

Rutland's lip curled; his expression hovered on contemptuous. "Here's a piece of advice for you, m'lord: go on back to your fine house and your fine life and be happy with the education you got. You don't know enough about what happens here to keep your wits about you. Some would say it's easier to bash a man's brains in, then pinch his purse, than it is to pinch his purse."

Sherry didn't blink. As warnings went, it was a good one. "What is a thief-taker?"

Rutland chuckled, albeit without any genuine humor. "My conscience's clear. I give you my best advice." He took a long swallow of ale. "A thief-taker's a hunter. He's after the criminal, you see, and when he finds one with a proper reward on his head, he takes him off to court. There's a good livin' to be made from it. A fellow can prosper if he don't get himself killed." His eyes narrowed as he put forth his question baldly. "So what I'm askin' you is this: are you one of them? Perhaps they go by a different name where you come from."

Not a different name, Sherry had good reason to know. There simply was no name. It did not follow that the profession did not exist. It would have been a grave error to make that assumption. Rather, the absence of a name for it was quite deliberate, for there was inherent power—and mystery—about something of which no one could properly speak. Silence was all but assured.

In Sherry's society the thieves taken in were no drag sneaks and snoozers. Governments did not concern themselves overmuch with fogle-hunters and pickpockets. To the extent that the apprehension of these petty criminals provided great spectacle as they were marched aboard the transport ships and fostered the quality's belief that their leaders were responsive to this threat from the lower orders, the Parliament passed laws and assigned judges to mete out punishment.

It was Sherry's observation that governments were not interested in merely protecting the citizenry from threat but in removing those souls who through persuasion or force threatened the government's very existence.

Dissidents. Assassins. Traitors.

And in time of war, foreigners.

To combat the danger and eliminate each threat in turn, a confederacy was created and made almost invisible to those outside it by its lack of a name. In secret, its members acted on orders from the king and prime minister when they were working in concert and on orders only from the king when they were not.

These confederates were the thief-takers, hunting their quarry in places not frequented by drag sneaks and snoozers but by gentlemen of quality and sometimes of rank. Once captured, the traitor rarely was asked to account for his actions in a public trial. Instead, justice was routinely served by offering him a ball and pistol and an honorable end by his own hand.

Sherry regarded his pint of ale a long moment before he met Blue's gaze directly. "A thief-taker? Me? You cannot imagine what amusement that would be to the people who know me well. No, Mr. Rutland, it's a life of regularity and routine that I enjoy. What you're describing is certain to be fraught with risk and offers little reward."

He held up a hand as Blue made to object to this last. "I heard you say a man can prosper in the profession, and I say this next not as a boast, but as a point of fact: I am already a prosperous man."

Blue grunted once. "Aye. I meant no offense putting the question to you."

"None taken." Sherry set his forearms on the rough table and leaned forward. "Now what of Ned Craven?"

"He's all risk, m'lord. You won't learn about him from me, so I don't mind asking what your interest is."

Sherry made a careless shrug. "I understand the boys work for him from time to time. It has occurred to me that he might press them into service while they are yet under my roof."

Blue offered no comment. He stared at Sheridan over the rim of his tankard.

"I wondered if he might be someone who can be reasoned with." Sherry waited until Blue's hoarse and hearty laughter died before he spoke again. "I believe I take your meaning."

Grinning, Blue answered, "Aye. You take it right enough. An' bribery won't work. Not that Ned wouldn't be happy to take your silver, but once he has a taste for it, he'll empty your pockets." His grin faded and his broad features turned grave. "There's only one way of ending an arrangement with him, m'lord. Seein' how you say that you like things all regular and routine, it don't occur to me that you'd be the one ending it."

"You're saying he'd bleed me."

"In every way a man can be bled." Blue lifted his chin and gestured toward the door. "Better if you take your leave now and don't come here again. Bad for business if word gets around that I been talkin' to a toff."

Sherry nodded. He finished his ale. "About Craven—"

"I won't be tellin' anyone you was inquirin' after him, same as I ain't told a soul where Miss Rose or the lads have gone."

"I will depend upon it." Sherry started to rise, then paused quite deliberately. "Oh, and I should like to take delivery of some of your fine French brandy."

Sheridan handed over his hat and gloves to his butler, then waved the man off when he would have spoken. "It's all right, Lane. I saw her carriage outside. I'm not certain that a plague of locusts could have turned her away." He gave Mr. Lane a sidelong glance. "Though you'll try that the next time, won't you?"

The butler nodded, the grim features of his narrow face brightening by the merest fraction. "I shall indeed, my lord. Just the thing, a plague."

"Good man. Where is she?"

"I suggested the drawing room."

"Then she is . . . ?"

"In your library, m'lord."

"Of course. I am certain you did your best." Sherry did not like his sanctuary being breached but lay none of the blame at his butler's feet. The man's formidable presence had never had the least impact on his godmother. Sherry was not at all certain she ever noticed he *had* a butler. "Some refreshment, Lane. Tea for Lady Rivendale, I think."

"And you, m'lord?"

"Hemlock." Striding away, Sherry did not glance back to see if Lane's composure was broken by this last, although he was sorely tempted. The man's gravity unsettled him on occasion, so how his godmother remained perfectly oblivious to him was a puzzler.

"Aunt Georgia," Sherry said pleasantly as he entered the library. "How good it is to see you."

"You are a dear boy to say so when we both know it is a lie," she said. "I forgive you, however." She proffered her rosy cheek as he approached the chaise longue. When Sherry bent and kissed her, she took his hand so that he could not easily move away. "Permit me to look at you," she told him as he straightened.

"Pray, could I stop you?"

"Don't be impudent." She made a thorough study of him, pronounced him in good health, and only then released his hand. "What is toward, Sherry? I had it directly from you that you were going to Granville. I don't think you can properly appreciate my surprise when I learned that your physician has been visiting daily for more than a sennight. Yet here you are, gone from home when I arrive and in the very pink of it upon your return. What does Harris say about your condition?"

"That I am recovered, of course." Sherry pushed aside a ledger on his desk and hitched his hip on the edge. "In the very pink, as you pointed out."

"But what *was* it? Something serious, I'll wager, since it delayed your departure for the country."

Sherry realized he should have been prepared to dissemble about his condition. He quickly turned over the possibilities in his mind, looking for one that would satisfy but not alarm. "Pleurisy." As soon as he saw Lady Rivendale fashion her eyebrows in a dramatic arch, he knew he had overshot the mark. "A mild case only," he said, soothing her. "I assure you, I am well."

"Cough."

"I beg your pardon."

"Cough. I want to hear you cough. How can I know that your lungs are perfectly clear if I don't hear you cough?"

"Because Harris is satisfied that they are?"

"Hah! As if I would depend upon a physician's word on such a matter. Now, cough."

Sherry raised his hand to cover his mouth and coughed.

"You sound sickly," Lady Rivendale said. "I don't like it, Sherry."

"That was the polite version."

"Then, by all means, let us have some gusto."

"Gusto. Yes, of course." It occurred to Sherry that it was prudent of him not to have told her he had the pox. This examination was nothing to what she would have wanted to do in that event. This time when his hand came up, it was to cover his smile. He coughed hard into it, then looked to her for a verdict.

"I detect some fluid," she said firmly. "You should be abed."

"I cannot help feeling very well loved by your fussing,

Aunt Georgia, but I will put you out of my house if you try to order me to bed."

She blinked. "You would do it, too, you beast." Lines of concern about her eyes and mouth softened as she affected contriteness. "I am very sorry, Sherry, but in my defense I have had only a short time to accustom myself to the fact that you were ill. Why did you not send word? Does Cybelline know?"

"I would not have had you troubled," he said. There was an excuse with no legs, he knew. His godmother was not likely to accept something so lame. He went on quickly. "Nor Cybelline either. She would also have wanted to be here, and need I remind you that she is *enceinte*. Her husband is a most amiable fellow, but he would not have thanked me for exposing his wife and child to illness."

"That was sound of you," her ladyship said, at least partly placated. "But you will call upon me next time so I might send my own physician."

"Very well."

"Your word, Sherry. I see you only mean to pacify me now and will do as you please should these circumstances arise again. I would have your word."

"You have my word," he said dutifully.

"Good. Now permit me to tell you who arrived in town this morning." She regarded him a shade guiltily. "If it will not overtire you, that is."

Sherry thought of Lily abovestairs. He was neatly caught in the web of his own lie. If he admitted that such a discourse as his godmother suggested would tax him, she was certain to fret unnecessarily over his health; if he allowed her to relate the latest *on dit*, she would be calmed and he would be delayed in visiting Lily. Neither choice improved his mood, though he hid it well enough.

"By all means," he said as Lane entered to serve refreshment. With impeccable timing, Sherry thought, the hemlock had arrived. "You must tell me who has come to town."

* * *

It was after he had dined with Lady Rivendale that Sherry was finally able to bid her farewell. Unwilling to leave anything more to chance, he made certain her carriage was underway before he climbed the stairs to Lily's bedchamber.

He did, on this occasion, announce himself with an abrupt knock, though he entered before permission was granted. He stopped just on the other side of the threshold when he saw the bed was empty.

"Miss Rose?"

"Do not make yourself easy here," Lily called from the dressing room. "I am indisposed."

Sheridan was uncertain what this meant until he heard the telltale splash of water. "You are bathing? Is that advisable?"

"If I want to be clean it is."

"What about your stitches? Did Harris say—" He stopped. Even with the door to the adjoining dressing room opened only a crack, Sherry heard her sigh. "I will cool my heels in the hall."

"Please," she said. "Do that."

He made to step out when a sound that was most definitely not splashing caught his attention. It was laughter and it was cut off abruptly, but Sherry was certain he recognized the source of it. The overtones of youth and mischief were unmistakable. Although Pinch and Dash were good candidates, the most likely one to become discomposed was Midge. Pinch and Dash, he imagined, each had a hand clamped over their friend's mouth.

Sherry opened the door, then closed it firmly, but remained inside the room. The quiet continued for a few moments longer, and he could imagine they were listening with complete concentration, their heads cocked and their breath held in wary anticipation that they had been caught out. When only silence met them, they finally surrendered to the exhilaration of having made such a narrow escape of it.

There was another round of splashing, more giggling, and someone most assuredly was pressed under the water.

Lily scolded, but it was clear she had no real heart for it. A great deal of sputtering followed, then a thud. A bar of soap came skittering through the narrow opening in the doorway.

"Now see wot ye've done, Dash," Pinch said. "Ye'll 'ave to get it. Miss Rose can't be on 'er 'ands and knees goin' after it."

"Midge knocked it out," Dash said. "My aim was true."

"Didn't," Midge said.

"Get it," Pinch said.

Sherry let the door swing open just as Lily was settling the disagreement by upending a pitcher of cool water over the tub. The three young men inside it could not avoid the cascade. They ducked and squirmed and flailed their arms, but it was a squeeze equal to Almack's at the beginning of the Season, and they could not eject themselves.

"Perhaps a bit of soap?" Sherry stepped into the dressing room and held up the bar for their inspection. "Shall we see what happens when you're as slippery as eels?"

"Oooh," squealed Midge. "Now ye've done it, Dash. We're certain to get a proper scrubbin'."

Lily no longer held the pitcher above the boys. As soon as Sheridan entered the room she had withdrawn it and now cradled it protectively in front of her. Her expression reflected a perfect mix of amusement and consternation as he made his predatory advance on the tub.

The boys watched him warily, silent now, and continued to squirm ever so slightly in the hope that one or all of them might be wrenched free. For all their fixed fascination on the object in his hand, he might have been brandishing a pistol instead of a lump of soap.

When Sheridan began to drop to his knees beside the tub, they reacted instinctively, closing their eyes tightly, gulping air, then thrusting their faces in the water.

Lily stepped closer to Sheridan, thrusting one hand out to prevent his descent to the floor. "You musn't," she said. "You will ruin your trousers. It is naught but wet everywhere."

"So it is," Sherry said as though noticing this condition

for the first time. He glanced at Lily. "Then it is a very good thing I don't mind." He knelt in a puddle directly beside the tub. "I suppose they'll have to come up for air directly." His tone was entirely conversational. "Shall we wager who will be first?"

Clutching the pitcher more tightly, Lily simply stared at him. Everything about her revealed that she was regarding a man who was in all ways outside her experience.

Sherry's smile was perfectly genial, set on his face of a purpose to further confound her. In truth, he was infinitely unsettled by his own behavior. There was no way to explain what he was doing now. He had never entertained the notion of giving anyone a bath, and that he should have set himself on this course solely for their entertainment was vastly out of character. No one had ever made a misstep by depending upon him to show good sense and a respect for convention. Handsome enough to be a rogue, it was not a reputation that had ever been attached to him. Mothers with eligible daughters regularly brought them to his notice by arranging a first waltz with him or managing the seating at a dinner party. His conduct practically defined the acceptable standard. He was polite to a fault and took pains not to draw untoward attention, even when he wished himself anywhere but where he was.

It was more than passing strange that he wished to be nowhere but where he was just now, defying the expectations of even himself.

The high drama of some rather loud gasping distracted him from Lily and his own musings. Midge came up for air, and Sherry was on him like a mongoose on a cobra. He caught the young scoundrel by the scruff of the neck and lathered his hair, face, and shoulders with the soap. Midge gargled water and words, making his protests wholly unintelligible. Lily was easier to understand, though her concern was not for Midge but for Sherry's frock coat, which was already wet to the elbows. Water also darkened the front of his waistcoat and shirt and ran in fine rivulets down his face.

Sherry had to forego Midge's proper drubbing when Pinch surfaced. He had his hands full by the time Dash lifted his head for air.

Still hugging the pitcher, Lily eased herself onto the chair behind her. She watched the antics in and around the tub, fascinated and bemused. She could quite honestly say that she had never seen the like before: a man full grown at play with children. She was witness to a pitched battle of wills that had nothing to do with practices of cleanliness. The object of this exercise seemed to be about who could use a lump of soap to inflict the most distress.

Sherry lost control of the soap when he applied too much pressure around it. Its trajectory was high and narrow, and Pinch was the one to pluck it out of the air on its descent. He cupped it between his palms, aimed, and squeezed. It shot out of his hands like a cannonball and hit Sherry squarely in the chest. There was an audible grunt and some high-pitched laughter, and the game was on again. The soap changed hands so often it was sometimes difficult to know who had it. At one point, Sherry actually plunged his arms elbow deep into the water to join the frantic search for it.

Pinch's dark hair gleamed with droplets of water and suds. Dash's usually pale face was flushed with high color. Even Midge, who did not always demonstrate the confidence of his compatriots, sported a smile so broad it very nearly did not fit between his cheeks.

But it was to Sheridan's face that Lily's pensive gaze kept returning.

His deeply brown eyes were not merely brightened by laughter, they were warmed by it. His smile was easy, open, and laughter rolled effortlessly from him. It was not so much that he was transformed by the spirited play but rather that he was revealed by it. The nature of this man was something more than he lay open to the casual inspection of others, mayhap even to himself.

There was nothing toplofty about him now, no hint that he could be high in the instep or vaguely disapproving of nonconformity. His wet hair was plastered darkly to his head, defining the shape of his skull. Water dripping from his drenched frock coat and neckcloth beat a hard tattoo on the floor. His lopsided grin was entirely too devilish to be polite and too indulgent to be disagreeable.

In short, he had the look of an inordinately happy man.

Lily felt as if her heart were being squeezed. The ache was dull, yet insistent, and it pulsed slowly to other parts of her body. It became a lump in her throat and a pressure behind her eyes. Her limbs felt weighted, then numb, and at the periphery of her thoughts it was as if a dense fog were encroaching.

"Lily?"

She was aware of a stillness beyond her own, of a voice that was both gentle and stubborn repeating her name. There was little impact at first. The threads of her consciousness required steady tugging.

"Lily."

She opened her eyes, blinking widely, and knew a disorientation so complete that she thought she might be sick. When she turned her head to the side her view of the room was once again familiar.

"I say," Pinch said, morbidly fascinated, "you don't think she's going to turn up 'er toes?"

Sherry's darkening sideways glance silenced the boy. "She's simply fainted. Women are wont to do that when they observe men at rough play. They are of a delicate constitution, you know, and cannot abide bloodsport." He looked down at Lily and saw a measure of color had returned to her face, all of it indignant. That was good, then. "Can you sit?" he asked.

"With my delicate constitution? I am not certain."

Better. "Very well. Permit me." Before she could protest, Sherry slipped one hand under her back and lifted her into a sitting position. He was gratified to see that not only did the blood not rush out of her cheeks, there seemed to be a bit more bloom there. Cocking his head in Dash's direction, he asked the boy to turn down Lily's bed. "Trousers first, Master Dash." He looked significantly at the other two who were shaking water from their hair and naked limbs as they rose from the tub behind Dash. "Preserve the lady's modesty," he told them, "if not your own."

"Oh, Miss Rose 'ad an eyeful when we stripped to get into the tub," Midge said. "Didn't you, Miss Rose?"

"No, Midge, I didn't. As befits my delicate constitution, I closed my eyes."

As that was not the way of it now, Pinch, Dash, and Midge immediately clapped their hands over their private parts.

Lily averted her head and pressed one hand to her temple, a gesture that assured her fragile smile would not be seen and relieved the pounding in her head. She did not oppose Sherry when he helped her to her feet, then lifted her.

Dash narrowly beat them to the bed and turned down the covers. Midge plumped a pillow and pushed it under her head just as Sherry laid her down. It was Pinch who neatly tucked the blankets around her after Sheridan raised them.

"Go on," Sherry told the boys. "She's fine. I promise you that she is." He was not at all certain they would have obeyed him if Lily had not echoed his words, but once she did, they trotted off. Sitting sideways on the edge of the bed, he turned enough to watch them go, his amiable smile fixed.

It was only when they were out of hearing that Sherry's affability vanished. Regarding Lily again, he pinned her back with a narrow, studied gaze, and asked, "Is there to be a child?"

Six

Seemingly of its own accord, Lily's right hand smoothed the coverlet across her torso and stopped when it lay protectively over her abdomen. Bemused, she asked, "Why ever do you think there is to be a child?"

"You fainted," Sherry said. His regard of her did not soften. "And you said yourself that there are some who would name you a whore."

"I had hoped," she said with quiet dignity, "that they were not in this room."

Sherry was not entirely proof against this pointed verbal dart. For all that it was said in a voice barely above a whisper, he was certain she had meant to draw blood. He studied her less intently than before and permitted his gaze to wander from her stricken face to the slim hand that rested above her belly. "You have not really answered my question," he said, raising his eyes to her again. "You are rather skilled at circumnavigating the most direct inquiries. Are you carrying a child, Miss Rose?"

"No." She offered up her own candid gaze. "Do you want to know if I have ever done so?"

That she would put the question to him so baldly was unexpected, but then Sherry supposed it was no more than he deserved. It caused him more in the way of discomfort to admit that he did want to know and that not one of his reasons included simple curiosity. The silence following her question lay between them for a long moment as Sherry considered his response.

"Only if you want to tell me," he said at last. "Do you?"

"No."

"Very well." He owned to a measure of disappointment but no surprise. "Then we will not speak of it again." He noticed that she was not immediately relieved by his words but rather more skeptical of them. "I am not used to being disbelieved."

"And I have little experience believing."

Sherry was quite certain she had not meant to be affecting. It was perhaps that she offered these words in so matter-of-fact a manner that he found them as poignant an expression of one's aloneness as he had ever heard.

"It seems to me that it can begin now," he said a shade huskily. "Trusting and being trusted."

Lily searched his face. "Why?"

"Why should you trust me?"

"Why should I want to?"

"Ahh," he said. "Well, there you have me."

"My question does not offend you? I find that curious."

"So do I, but there it is. I cannot say whether your life will be in any way improved by trusting me, only that I will give you no cause to regret it."

"That is an expansive promise and perhaps more than you can properly deliver. You will be relieved to know that I will not hold you to it."

"So you are already choosing to mistrust me."

Lily's lips curved upward in response to his faintly provoking grin. "I suppose I am."

Shrugging amiably as if this were of no import, Sherry asked, "Why do you think you fainted?"

"I fear I exerted myself overmuch." It was not the truth as she understood it, but it was the only answer that would serve. She did not want to tell him that it had been emotion of a certain kind that had overwhelmed her, not exhaustion. "As I recall, you warned me against it." It was Lily's experience that appealing to a man's sense that he had been right was never wrong.

"So I did. I don't imagine you will be any more likely to take my good advice in the future."

"I don't suppose so, no."

"You are of a bloody independent mind, Miss Rose."

"Yes," she said. "Sometimes to my detriment." She gave him an arch look. "Is it so different for you, my lord?"

Honesty compelled him to admit that it wasn't. "But I believe it is a trait of character more suited to men than women."

"And I believe an orangutan will attack the town. That does not make it so."

Sherry grinned appreciatively. "One hopes not," he said, "but I take your meaning." His eyes wandered to her extraordinarily colored hair. The copper accents were turned a deep shade of red and orange by the candlelight. He noticed that short tendrils of hair at her nape and temple were darker at their tip, spiked rather than curling. Damp instead of dry. To be certain of what he was seeing, he lifted his hand and touched one such strand clinging to her cheek.

Lily flinched. "What are you doing?"

Sherry withdrew his hand, though not with alacrity. "Your hair is wet."

She used her fingers like a rake through her thick, unevenly cropped hair and found it was so. "Yes, it is."

"What possessed you to have a bath drawn for the boys here? Arrangements could have been made for them to—" He stopped. There was no change in Lily's features that pointed out the error in his thinking, yet he knew suddenly that he was in the wrong of it. "You did not order the bath drawn for them, did you?"

She shook her head. The small movement made her aware again of the ache at the back of her skull, and she slipped one hand under her nape to massage the area lightly. "I cannot imagine who among your servants would be moved to obey any order that I would give them," she said a shade wearily.

Sherry rose from the bed and used the bell pull to ring for a maid. Offering no explanation for his actions, he returned to Lily's side but this time chose the chair where he'd sat that morning. "So it was the boys who drew the bath for you?"

"Yes. Pray, do not punish them for it. They did not conceive the idea on their own."

"You asked them to do it?" Her slight hesitation led him to the truth. "I think I comprehend what happened," he said. "You mentioned that you would enjoy a bath, and that was sufficient to stir them to action."

Lily's faint smile confirmed that he had nearly divined how the thing had come about. "I am not certain I told them I would enjoy it, only that I envied them for having had one. They were complaining, you see, that someone named Dunnet was going to give them another proper scrubbing."

Sherry chuckled. "Is there anything so onerous to a boy than soap and water?"

"Even when the boy was you, my lord?"

Her patent skepticism made his grin deepen. "Never doubt it. In support of your surprise, I will tell you that I do not believe I was ever as dirty behind the ears as the lads are. Nanny Dory would have said they could feed an Irishman for a month with the potatoes they could grow. Her estimation of my own crop was that it would only serve that Irishman a week."

Lily did not try to modulate her laughter, though she knew it would set her head throbbing again. Still smiling through her pain, she removed her hand from under her neck and placed it across her eyes, then rubbed her temples with the thumb and middle finger. She heard the door to the bedchamber open and Sherry acknowledge someone's entry. Lily lifted her hand only that fraction necessary to see who it was.

"A packet of headache powders," Sherry told the maid.

"If Ponsonby has none, then see that some are purchased from the chemist straightaway."

"Yes, m'lord." She bobbed a curtsey and was gone.

Lily recognized the maid as the same one who had been moved to call her a baggage only that morning. She was not in expectation of receiving the headache remedy anytime soon. Lily let her hand fall away from her eyes once the maid was gone. She turned her head slightly to better see Lord Sheridan. "It was kind of you to ask for the powders, m'lord, but your servants can only resent such attention paid to me."

"What a ridiculous notion."

She shrugged.

"Why do you suggest it?" he asked.

Lily regretted that she had placed the idea in his mind. Clearly it would not have occurred to him. "Forgive me," she said. "I should not have done so."

Sherry was having none of it. "If there is something you are in want of saying, then say it."

"I should not be here, my lord, that is all I meant."

"Indeed, you should not," he said flatly. "You should be dead."

"I did not mean—"

His hand sliced the air, cutting her off. "There is but one reason that I have set you up here and that is for my comfort and convenience. A box bed in the servants hall might have been all that was required for your care, but it would have been deuced disagreeable for me to go there. If there is, as you say, resentment, then it is because I have not acknowledged to anyone that you saved my life, not because you are not deserving of attention."

Lily blinked. Her lips parted around a soft expulsion of air. "Oh."

He cocked one eyebrow. "Precisely." He stood then, responding to the scratching at the door, and crossed the room. After accepting delivery of the powders, he carried the packet to the dressing room and mixed the powder with water from the pitcher. Lily was sitting up in bed when he returned to her side. He held out the glass to her. "Drink it quickly before it settles. Every drop."

Lily did as she was directed. The bitter taste made her want to gag. She gasped a little, pulling a face as she swallowed the last mouthful.

Sherry took the glass from her, rinsed it out, and brought another with nothing but water in it. "This will help remove the taste."

She accepted it gratefully and drank. He was right; it did help. "Thank you."

He nodded and waited for her to drink her fill before he took the glass and set it on the bedside table. "You will rest now?"

Lily liked that for once he framed his order as a question. She glanced at the clock on the mantel. It was not so very late. If she were serving drinks at the Blue Ruination, the brawling would not yet have begun. "I think I will, yes." At least for a little while, she thought, until the worst of her headache passed.

"Good. I will express my wishes that you are not to be disturbed, especially by the young ruffians. I'm of a mind to make them say their prayers this evening. A cleansing on the inside will do them no more harm than one on the—"

"No!"

Sherry's astonishment was not feigned. Lily had thrown off her bedcovers and risen up on her knees. She was all fury and scorn, and it looked to him as if she meant to launch herself in his direction. He raised a hand to stay that precipitous action.

"You will not!" she said tightly. "I will stick you myself if you approach them about saying their prayers. I swear it." She edged closer when he did not back away. "Say you believe me. Say you know I will do it."

A shutter closed over Sherry's dark eyes, and a vertical crease appeared between his brows. He stood his ground with his hands open at his side, palms out, careful not to betray himself with any movement that could be perceived as a threat. The violent mood that was upon her was unknown to him outside of an asylum, yet there was a clear intelligence working here that he'd found lacking in the poor creatures at Bedlam. In contrast to those lunatics, Lily seemed to know what she was about. This was the bared-teeth ferocity of a mother protecting her young, of that he was no longer in doubt. What was less clear to him was how he had become a danger to her and, in turn, what danger she might be to him.

"I believe you," he said calmly. He watched Lily's fever-ishly bright eyes make a narrow study of him. He could not be sure she had even understood his response. She was judging him by the weight of his words, the gravity of his tone, and the manner in which he stood before her, open and clearly without intent to harm. "I know you will do it."

She said nothing for a moment but did not relax her posture. "If you would have someone say their prayers, then you will come to me."

Sherry judged it the wiser course to agree, but he had no clear understanding of her meaning. Careful not to reveal his confusion, Sherry maintained his neutral expression and nodded.

"I have already been taught how to pray," Lily said. "You will not teach the boys."

It was odd, Sherry thought, that she no longer spoke of the children *saying* their prayers but of *teaching* them to do so. He tried to make sense of the workings of her mind, of why prayer would raise such a fierce and incensed response. He wondered about those ten years she had spent in the care of nuns at the abbey school. *L'Abbaye de Sacré Coeur.* Had she thrown off all her religious instruction since leaving? He had no understanding of how she had come to London from Paris, and not just any part of London, he reminded himself, but the mean and squalid streets of Holborn. Living there would sorely test the faith of a devout man. Lily must have wondered if she have been abandoned by her Lord.

"I will leave their instruction to you," he said, still cautious of his tone.

Lily sneered. "As if I would instruct them in such. They are better served by pinching pockets than the other."

"Very well. It shall be as you wish."

It required a second thorough assessment before Lily nodded. She sat back a fraction. "We understand each other, then."

"We do," Sherry lied.

"Good."

Sherry had no familiarity with being dismissed in his own home—even Lady Rivendale and Cybelline were not so bold—but that was his distinct impression of what Lily had just done. Loath to make a retreat with his tail between his legs, Sherry nevertheless understood the wisdom of not provoking her further with his presence. He inclined his head, careful not to mock her with a smile, and bid her good evening.

It was only when he was safely on the other side of the door that he permitted himself the welcome relief of a steadying breath. Out of the corner of his eye he saw his valet step into the hallway from the servants' stairs.

"Is everything all right, my lord?" Kearns inquired as he approached. "If you will permit me to say so, you look as if you're sickening for something."

"Pleurisy."

"I beg your pardon?"

"I hope it isn't pleurisy," Sherry said, collecting himself. "I believe I will have a drink in the library, Kearns."

"Very good, sir. I understand the hemlock is of a particularly fine vintage."

Sherry did not fox himself on drink, though he had rather more than was his custom. The whisky fogged his mind more than cleared it. Occasionally he would arrive at some idea he considered particularly brilliant, only to discover that he could not hold it long enough to make it the subject of study. Worse, he sometimes realized there were but three ideas and he was simply returning to them.

He slept for a while in the large wing chair in front of the fireplace. When he stirred it was to find that someone—Lane most likely—had seen to it that a small fire was laid and a rug was placed across his lap. He was not comforted by this coddling of the servants—quite the opposite, in fact. That he was looked after in this way made him feel decades older than his twenty-eight years, well into decrepitude. He should be afforded the same opportunity to suffer the consequences of other young men who drank deep in their cups. There was a certain dignity, he was coming to understand, to being able to make a perfect cake of oneself. He had never done so, but he was fashioning the opinion that it might have something to recommend it.

When he woke again, he had a most painful crick in his neck. All thoughts of suffering the consequence of drink vanished, and he wondered why no one had thought to put a pillow between his head and the wing of the chair. Rubbing the back of his neck with his palm, his eyes fell on the small fringed pillow on the floor beside him. He smiled ruefully. It seemed someone had thought further to his comfort, and he had been too churlish to accept it.

"Ahh, you are awake."

Sherry blinked as Lily stepped out of the shadowed recess beside the fireplace. He did not have immediate recognition of her voice, but his eyes knew her. The embers backlit her hair and made it glow in a dark copper penumbra about her head. Her features remained largely invisible to him so it was his keen memory of them that drew in the outline of her lush mouth and the exotic tilt of her green eyes. He knew the shape of her cheekbones and the exact distance from the nose to her mouth and from her mouth to her chin. It was a face of perfect proportion and startling symmetry.

The lingering effects of drink allowed him to acknowledge what he had resisted before: she was easily one of the loveliest women he had ever seen, and he was drawn to her in a way that was outside his experience.

"I woke and could not find sleep again," she said quietly.

"I see it was not the same for you. You stirred once before. I thought you would rouse yourself then, but you went straightaway to sleep."

"The drink helped, I'm sure."

She nodded. "Are you still foxed?"

"I never was. I do not seem to have an intemperate nature."

Lily thought he sounded a shade disappointed. "Unlike me." For want of something to do in the aftermath of this confession, she tightened the sateen sash of the robe she was wearing. She'd found it in the armoire in her room and availed herself of its modest protection when she ventured downstairs. The sleeves were too long and the quilted cuffs lay against the back of her fingers. To keep from tripping on the hem, she had tugged the length of the robe upward and secured the extra fabric above the belt. "I hope you will not mind," she said, "but Midge told me earlier where I would find the library."

"You have been here long?" She'd said she had seen him stir before. How many minutes had passed since then? Judging by the stiffness in his neck, he had slept for more than a few.

"Not so long," she said vaguely. "I have been reviewing your collection."

"A better pastime than watching me sleep."

"More edifying, at least."

"I should hope so," he said slowly, uncertain what she'd meant by this last remark. Had she been watching him or not? "Have you made your selection?"

"I think I would like *Delphine*."

"Madame de Staël?"

"Yes. That is the one."

"Very well. Take it." He uncurled his legs from their awkward position under the chair and stretched. "It is in the original French, though I suppose that presents no problem for you."

"No," she said softly. "It doesn't."

"Who are you, Lily Rose?"

"It seems to me you know."

"Lily Rose is merely a name, perhaps not even yours. It is not you." He studied her a moment longer. "I want to know you."

"No, you don't."

"Contrary creature. Did I not just say so?" He did not think he mistook her smile for anything but rueful as she turned away. "You must have been a sore trial to the sisters of Sacred Heart."

Lily ran her index finger along the shelf where she remembered seeing the novel she wanted. "I possessed that happy talent," she said idly. "Here it is. *Delphine*." She carefully removed the book and cradled it in one arm as she lifted the cover and studied the title page. She glanced over at Sheridan. "Thank you, my lord. It is a great gift to be allowed to read again."

Sherry nodded, faintly discomfited by her gratitude. "I hope you will have joy of it."

"I will." Lily stepped forward, once again into the dim glow from the fireplace. "Have you need of anything before I go?" she asked. "Another rug? Perhaps I should add more coals if you are not going directly to your own bed. I used precious few the first time."

So it was not Lane who had directed that someone see to his comfort. Sherry required a few moments to accustom himself to that. Everything he'd thought when he'd believed his retainers had cared for him was challenged by the realization that it had been Lily. Where he'd found no comfort in their fussing, he discovered that he quite liked the idea that she'd thought to lay a fire for him and place a rug over his legs. Far from feeling as if he were in his dotage, he was warmed by the notion that she had wanted to make him easy. He wished now that she had been more insistent that he keep the pillow under his head.

To prove that he was appreciative of such efforts as she'd shown him, Sherry reached over the arm of the chair and scooped up the pillow. He slipped it behind his neck. "I believe all is well enough for me."

Worrying her lower lip, Lily nodded.

"What is it?" he asked. It was plain that she was teetering on the edge of something of consequence. "Is it that you want another book? Pray, do not make me suppose what it is. I am not foxed, but I am dull witted."

Lily's bare feet were rooted to the rug, but the rest of her slender frame inclined forward in a posture of earnestness. "I deeply regret my ill-advised temper," she said quickly. "It was unconscionable of me to speak to you so vilely. I don't think I knew all that I said until I was done saying it. I have had more than sufficient time to reflect on my words, and I cannot find them anything save appalling. I do not understand why you didn't cuff me. It would have been a mercy—for both of us."

"Hit you, you mean?"

She nodded and touched her index finger to one side of her chin. "Just here. It's a proper good clip, but it doesn't knock my teeth about." When he was silent for so long, Lily clamped her teeth together and drew back her lips in a semblance of a smile. "See?" she asked, speaking from behind the double row of pearlies.

Sherry knew himself to have an almost indecent desire to kiss her and something more besides. He was glad for the rug covering his lap, or she would have known it, too. What sport she might have made of that, he didn't want to think about. "Go to bed, Miss Rose," he told her with a credible show of weariness. "You have made a good apology, and I am accepting it. We shall endeavor to go forward."

Lily still hesitated, then gauging that he was impatient with her, she added quickly, "Then my immoderate behavior will not reflect poorly on the boys." There was the faintest inflection at the end that made it more question than statement.

Sherry was tempted to reach for the finger of whiskey left

in the tumbler on the side table. "I am not certain it even reflects poorly on you, so I am not inclined to say how it might affect my opinion of the lads." He could see that she was very clearly stunned by this intelligence. He sighed, not because he was in the least tired or out of sorts with her but because he wanted her to believe that he was. Every moment that she stayed, he felt a measure of his considerable control eroding.

Sherry did not permit his eyes to drop to her bare feet. Her toes, all ten of them, were as provocative peeping out from under the hem of her robe as her teeth had been when she flashed that absurdly artless smile. He could make a feast of those toes, he thought, sucking on one until all of them curled.

He reined himself in before he came out of the chair or his skin, the order of which no longer mattered. "When you said those things to me, Lily, I had the impression you felt threatened in some way. Was that true?"

Lily's breath hitched, but she stayed her ground and answered quietly, "Not for me, but for them."

"Yes," he said. "That was it. And everything you said and did was in aid of protecting them, isn't that also true?"

She nodded.

Sherry shrugged. "Then why should I reproach you for it? I admit to a lack of comprehension regarding the particular threat, but I acknowledge you perceived one. That being the case, you reacted with some courage." He smiled mildly, the warmth of it not quite reaching his eyes. "That confounds you, does it? Well, good. It seems a fair turn. What say you, Miss Rose; it occurs to me the time is finally upon us for you to say your prayers."

Sherry had meant the suggestion to put a period to their discussion and send her to her room. He was unprepared for her to drop his first edition, leather-bound copy of *Delphine* to the floor and approach him. Even more singular was the moment she parted his crossed ankles by nudging them with her toes and came to stand between his splayed legs. He was forced to widen his stance each time she stepped nearer.

Lifting his eyes, Sherry schooled his features so no thought or emotion was revealed. For once, Lily was his equal. Her face was pale, the eyes unblinking. There was little in the way of expression behind them. They darkened ever wider at the center until the deep green iris all but disappeared, and Lily with it. These black wells of the soul were empty.

Sherry reached for her but only grazed her upper arms as she dropped to her knees in front of him. His hands were still clutching air when she was already flinging aside the rug. He made to catch it, but it was a poor use of his resources. By the time he attended to her again, she was yanking the tail of his shirt out of his trousers.

"Lily!" Sherry grabbed her wrists, stilling them, and discovered quickly this grip did nothing to prevent her fingers from deftly unbuttoning his flies. He said her name again, as urgently as before, though with considerably more huskiness, and began to peel back her hands. For the first time he saw something in her face that he understood most likely mirrored his own: confusion.

"What are you doing?" They spoke the same words almost in unison, though Lily's voice was a softer echo of his.

Sherry still held Lily's wrists, but her fingertips grazed his heavy erection where it pressed against his drawers. If he relaxed his grip even a fraction he knew she would release him into her hands. He wondered if any man had had his resolve so sorely tried, then wondered immediately if it were not every man who met Lily.

This last thought was what made one corner of his mouth lift contemptuously. "This is what you do?"

Lily flinched, but then her chin came up. "You wanted this. How dare you scorn me for obedience. Or is it that you mean to test me again?" She stretched her fingers as far as she was able and scored the underside of his cock with the nail of her middle finger. The soft hitch of his breath was unmistakable. "You did ask me to say my prayers, didn't you? I'm not wrong about that. But perhaps it is only that you mean to test yourself. Can a pederast surrender his perversions to a woman's mouth? That is it, isn't it, my lord? You are a pederast who wishes above everything that you were not. Shall we see if mayhap the screw can be turned?"

Sherry had never struck a woman. Grunting softly with the effort not to do so now, he released Lily's wrists. In the moment before he took her by the shoulders and flung her away from him, he saw how she prepared herself to pray at the feet of men. In attitude she held herself as a model of piety, while the reality was that she mocked it. Bowing her head, she also lowered her eyes, and the faintly derisive curve of her lips faded until it was as serene as it was profane. Her hands came together, the fingers steepled around his cock as she made to take it from his drawers. Her mouth parted and . . .

Lily fell sideways to the floor. Sprawling at Sheridan's feet was not as humiliating as the surprise of it was. She drew her knees up and lowered her head toward them, curling instinctively in the manner of a wounded animal.

When he was free of her, Sherry catapulted out of the chair. He did not glance once in Lily's direction, concentrating instead on quieting his rough breathing and righting himself and his clothes. He went to the side table and lifted the tumbler with its single finger of whiskey to his lips. He did not drink but held it there a long time. Violent emotion ran the same course through his body as his blood. His fingertips pressed whitely on the glass, and his hand shook. Sherry thought he might crush it in his palm and realized the pain would not be unwelcome.

Lily hunched her shoulders and squeezed her eyes closed when glass shattered somewhere beyond her head. She heard the pop and sizzle of embers, the hiss of liquid on the flames, and understood that Sheridan had consigned his drink to the fireplace.

"Get up," he said without any inflection save weariness. "I am not going to beat you." He recalled her pointing out the sweet spot on her chin and hoped she would not do so again. He had no wish to further test his tolerance. "I have delayed my departure for the country long enough. I will be gone from here tomorrow. You may stay until Harris says you are sufficiently recovered, then you will do me the great favor of leaving. If there should be occasion again for you to save my life, I want you to resist it."

Save for her shuddering sobs, Lily did not move.

Sherry hardened his heart enough to finally look in her direction. She was the most pitiable of creatures, curled as tightly as a child in want of a blanket or a breast. "Get up," he repeated. "You cannot stay here for the servants to find."

Lily's effort to stop crying only created great, wet sucking noises and spasms of her head and shoulders.

"You cannot possibly carry on," he said. "You'll make yourself ill." There was no sign from her that she'd even heard him. That was when it was borne home that she *would* carry on regardless of whether she became ill or not, that she was helpless to do anything else. He had never heard the sound of a heart breaking, was not at all certain that her crying was the source of that vibration in him, but he understood her aloneness and that he could not abandon her to it.

Sherry crossed to her quickly enough, but it took longer to resolve what he must do then. Slowly, with considerable reluctance, he finally dropped to his knees beside her. Laying his palm lightly on her shoulder, he inched forward. Even through the fabric of her shift and robe, he could feel the heat of her skin and the taut bunching of her upper arm. The moment she was aware of his presence, of his touch, she tried to escape it.

He didn't believe that it was a thing done of conscious will. Lily was intuitively a survivor and most often acted in ways that supported the preservation of her own life. Perhaps the one time she had acted in opposition to her finely honed instincts was when she had leaped at him in Covent Garden.

A single moment's contrariness had set everything that followed in motion, and now she was lying on his floor, wracked by sobs and more surely troubled than he could properly understand, and certain to be sick on his new Aubusson rug.

There was nothing for it but that he take her in hand, which of necessity meant that he must take her in his arms.

She resisted at first, clenching so tightly that he thought she might snap her own bones. Sherry shifted his weight off his knees and leaned back against the chaise longue. He drew Lily up by the shoulders in much the same manner as he had flung her away earlier. Her strength was all turned inward, and she had little in the way of fight that she could use against him. She had no defense because he did not mean to hurt her. She had not learned how to fully arm herself against kindness.

"Poor Lily," he said softly, rubbing his chin against her hair. "You are hardly more than a child yourself."

"One-and-twenty."

"Hmm?" To Sherry's ears it sounded only as if she had hiccuped.

"I am one-and-twenty."

"Ahh, a great age, then." He wondered if it had passed her notice that he was cradling her like a child. When he felt her try to speak again, he simply bent his head and whispered against her ear, "Shh." She buried her face in the curve of his neck, and her tears dampened his shirt and cravat. "I cannot offer you a handkerchief," he said. "As Midge is still in possession of mine, you may use my sleeve." He thought she might have tried to laugh, but the sound was all watery snorting, none of it pleasantly musical to the ear.

She cried harder then, though Sherry wasn't certain how that was possible. He absorbed her shudders. His embrace was firm but not confining. Sometimes he placed one hand between her shoulder blades and passed it up and down along the length of her spine. He said her name softly and spoke of nonsensical things. His left thigh grew uncomfortably numb under her, but he was loath to move and upset the delicate balance he had struck with her. What he had to do was wait her out, and eventually he was rewarded for doing so. The shuddering diminished. There were longer intervals of quiet between the sobs, and her breathing steadied. By slow degrees he felt her relax in his arms.

For a time he thought she had fallen asleep, though he did not attempt to dislodge her from his lap. He found he still had the wherewithal to smile when he felt her fingers unfolding his damp neckcloth and drawing one loose end toward her eyes.

"If you mean to use it to blow your nose," he said in wry accents, "I beg that you remove it first."

Lily lifted her head and looked up at him. "You have a most curious sense of humor."

"Humor? I assure you, I am perfectly serious."

"I know. That is what makes it curious. There are your words, then there is your tone. One is frequently at odds with the other."

"I'm sure I don't know what you mean."

But there it was again, she thought, and he knew it too, whether or not he could be made to admit it. Lily let her hands drop from his shoulders and started to move away.

"What are you doing?" Sherry's arms did not release her.

"I am crushing you."

"Hardly. Crushing is what you did before I became numb. There is no reason you should move now."

"Do not be too kind to me," Lily said quietly. "I don't think I can bear it."

He nodded, understanding. "Then sit here. Beside me."

"On the floor?"

"That's where I am." This time when she began to slide away, he let her. The distance that she put between them was not so great that he could not have her back again if it was his desire and her need that he do so. "What will you do?" he asked.

Lily shrugged, not mistaking his question for real interest. "I suppose I shall return to Holborn. I have a room there if the landlady has not already given it to someone else. My rent was paid only for the week." Her mouth twisted in a rueful smile. "I think I have answered my own question about the room. A full sennight's passed since I gave her any coin."

"She will not make allowances? It cannot have escaped her notice that you have been absent."

"Nothing escapes Mrs. Cuthbert's notice. If she can be persuaded to return the room to me, then she will charge me for all the time I was gone from it even though you can be certain someone else had the use of it."

"What about your belongings?"

"Yes, well, that is the bigger blow, though I do not count myself as having many possessions. One doesn't, you know, not in Holborn. What can be stolen from someone else can be stolen from you."

"Honor among thieves?"

"A myth as there ever was."

"I see." Sherry rubbed the underside of his chin with his knuckles. "Then it will be starting over for you."

"Not precisely. I think Blue will have me back."

Sherry remembered that Rutland had said something in that regard when Lily was taken away. "I'm sure he will. He's not a rough sort, then?"

"Blue? No. He does not suffer fools, so there is no advantage to be gained by crossing him, but he has a reasoned sense of ruthlessness. I do not fear him, if that's what you were asking."

"I was." Sherry raised one knee and laid his forearm across it. His inflection was casual; his interest was not. "What about Ned Craven?"

Lily could not suppress a shiver. "I should not have told you his name. It is better left unspoken."

"There is too much power for him in saying nothing," Sherry said, "so we will speak of it."

She glanced sideways at him, intrigued that he would understand. "How can you possibly know that?"

"I know," Sherry said softly. "I just know. Ned is not so reasoned as Mr. Rutland, I collect."

"That's right."

"He is a threat to you?"

Lily hesitated. "No."

Sherry wasn't certain that he believed her, but this truce was too delicate to call her to task for dissembling. "What about the scoundrels? Is he a threat to them?"

She nodded.

Sherry slowly expelled a breath, then plunged ahead. "He is a pederast?"

Flushing deeply, Lily dropped her head. Her voice was but a thread of sound. "I should not have accused you of such."

He ignored that. "You are not answering my question. Is Craven a pederast?"

"No." She did not look at him, though she lifted her face again. "At least I've never heard of such. But he'll pimp the boys to men who are. They're of an age that is useful to him." Lily impatiently dashed away tears welling in her eyes. "It's happened to other boys. If they take to the life he fashions for them, they don't live long. If they refuse Ned, their lives are forfeit anyway, though perhaps it is a mercy."

Sherry wondered if that was what she thought about her own life, if it would have been a mercy to have been able to refuse what had been done to her and accept sure death as the consequence. "It is easier to understand why Rutland held his tongue about Ned Craven."

"You spoke to Blue?" Lily's head snapped around. "When?"

"This afternoon." He glanced over his shoulder at the clock that stood in the corner. It was long gone midnight. "Yesterday afternoon now . . . after I left you and before Lady Rivendale's visit."

"My God," she said softly, more to herself than Sherry. "You'd never heard his name until I told you the boys stole for him." At her sides, her fists clenched and unclenched. "Did you speak to anyone save Blue?"

"No."

"Did you never once think that your life might be forfeit? You are ill suited for making inquiries in Holborn."

"Ill suited?"

"Please, do not say I have offended you with that characterization. You must know that your presence in a place like the Blue Ruin cannot pass unnoticed. You might have been attacked again."

"I must point out that attempts on my life can be made anywhere. I am not in hiding. Further, I have only your word for what happened at Covent Garden. It may be that you were the intended victim. Have you considered that?"

"It is a ridiculous notion. I am no one."

Sherry considered that, the shadow of something like a smile passing across his dark eyes. Quietly, he said, "So am I."

It was as peculiar a thing as he had ever said to her, and Lily had no response at the ready. She drew her knees up and applied herself to smoothing her shift across them. "I hope you do not mean to go there again. I should not like to think that anything you've learned from me will turn you in that direction."

"My direction is set," he said. "Remember? I am leaving for the country."

Lily nodded. "Yes, of course. That is good, then."

"I am taking the lads." He placed his intention before her baldly and watched her out of the corner of his eye for reaction. He did not think she would accuse him of pederasty again, but some fresh charge was not out of the question. What he saw transform her troubled features was a fine mixture of resignation and acceptance, all of it bittersweet. He removed his neckcloth and handed it to her.

Lily offered an apologetic, watery smile and pressed the fine linen to her eyes. She held it there for several long moments, collecting herself. When she thought she could speak, she lowered it and idly began making new folds in the cloth. "It is what I hoped for," she said finally. She stole a glance at him. "Not when I thought you might be a—" She shook her head, unwilling to speak of it yet again.

"A pederast," Sherry said.

She nodded.

"It shows some great sense on your part." He watched her fingers made a second fold in the neckcloth and carefully crease it. She was no longer looking at him, but he had no doubt that she was hanging on his every word. "You will understand that I wish you had not accused me of such, although I do not acquit myself of helping to bring the thing about. It may be that I should have insisted you explain your earlier behavior, the exact nature of the threat you perceived, and in what manner I had provoked you. Still, your practice of saying whatever comes into your head is every bit as discomfiting as your practice of acting on it."

"Discomfiting?" she asked. "That surely understates it."

"And you make my point for me. Yes, it understates it. You would perhaps use words like *repulsive* or *revolting*. *Vile* and *loathsome* also come to mind. Indeed, I find your behavior all of that. Am I improved in any way by telling you so? I think not. And neither are you. Indeed, I have armed you with four more words with which you might bludgeon yourself." He took her chin in the cup of his hand and turned her face toward him. "You are none of those things. None. I am speaking of what you do, not what you are."

"They cannot be so very different."

Sherry released her chin. "You will consider, Miss Rose, my foot and my boot." He tapped his left foot on the floor to draw her attention to it. "The former is part and parcel of me, but I can change the latter anytime I choose to do so."

Lily considered the polished toe of his black leather boot. "I have but one pair, my lord. Change is not so simple a thing."

Sherry nudged her foot with his own. Her bare toes peeped out from beneath her gown, and he trod upon them very lightly. "Do not force me to belabor the metaphor. At this hour I have not the capacity for it."

Lily did something then that she had not believed she had the capacity for: she laughed. It lacked much in the way of robustness, but even soft and tremulous, it could not be mistaken for anything else. "Very well. I take your point, and it is most excellently made." She started to ease her foot out from under his, but he pressed a bit harder and kept her there, not hurting, but not releasing her either. Turning to face Sheridan, her own features still imprinted with a trace of her smile, Lily saw that his regard of her was intent once again. "You are staring."

"Yes."

"What is it?" He didn't answer immediately but continued to study her at his leisure and made no allowance for her own discomfort. She prompted him again. "My lord?"

"I'm not certain," he said at last. "In truth, I do not think I've seen the like before." He offered no elaboration but removed his foot from Lily's and rose in a single fluid movement. While she was still blinking up at him in some surprise, he quit the room.

Activity in the townhouse was orchestrated chaos, or at least it seemed so to Lily, whose vantage point was behind her bedchamber door. She heard the orders, the grumbling, the heavy footfalls and the light ones. A trunk thudded to the floor. Someone cursed. Valises thumped against the wall as servants made an awkward transport of them. There was only the occasional lull, and it was followed with a fresh surge of stirring by people filled with purpose.

With so much noise and no direction from anyone to curtail it, Lily surmised that Lord Sheridan was already gone from home. These final preparations for his journey to the country would have been accomplished a great deal more quietly if he had been in residence. Even shutting himself in his library would have provided little in the way of sanctuary this morning.

It had provided him little enough last night.

Lily's eyes dropped to the breakfast tray on her lap. She had known when the maid set it before her that she would not be able to eat, but she had not felt up to listening to the haughty complaining if she'd refused the repast. The fare was cold now. The egg yellows were congealed so thickly that poking them with a fork would not cause them to run. The thin slices of tomato were lying in their own red, watery juices, and the bangers were glued to the plate by their hard-cned drippings. The pyramid of burnt toast crumbs was larger than the two triangles of bread from which they were scraped.

Lily moved the tray off her lap and slipped out of bed. She padded to the window, knelt on the bench, and pressed her forehead to the glass. Disappointed that she could not see the street, she remained there nevertheless.

She imagined the carriage and four that were standing at the ready by the front entrance. The boys would be dancing with excitement, most likely getting underfoot as they assisted with the packing. To her knowledge they had never been gone from London. Except for their forays into Covent Garden, they rarely ventured out of Holborn. Their entire world was a tiny parcel of land bounded by wretched tenements and slop-strewn alleys. That they should have this opportunity to leave fairly took her breath away.

She could not cry, of course, when they came to make their farewell. She would make a convincing lie of it and tell them she would be joining them when she was well enough. Sheridan had not asked it of her—indeed, she had not spoken to him since his abrupt and confounding departure from the library—but Lily was of the opinion that she owed him a dignified exit with the boys and that any sort of high drama would have revealed a remarkable want of pride.

She had little enough of it left after debasing herself at his feet last night. Wishing the boys off with Godspeed was but one way that she could hold on to that small remaining measure.

Lost in this reverie and finally deaf to the noises beyond her room, Lily did not turn away from the window until the door to her bedchamber was flung open. The boys were almost upon her by the time she was sitting properly on the bench. She welcomed them, smiling gamely just in the manner she'd promised herself she would, then redoubled her efforts when she saw the scoundrels had not arrived alone.

Lord Sheridan stood on the threshold, filling most of the doorway that framed him. His dark eyes were perfectly unfathomable.

"How can it be, Miss Rose, that all of us are properly turned out for traveling and you are still in your bedclothes? You will find the journey considerably more comfortable if you are dressed for it."

Seven

The coach and four that Lily imagined would carry the boys and Lord Sheridan to Granville was in reality two coaches and a pair of beautifully matched cinnamon-colored horses for each. The equipage she was expected to ride in was as fine a carriage as she had ever seen in the theatre district or the park, with the exception of the prince's own.

She still had no proper understanding of how she had come to be aboard it.

The mechanics of the thing were comprehensible, of course. She'd been given the rum-hustle, or at least a version of it, for at the end of some gentle prodding, a bit of misdirection, and a great deal of artful evasion, she'd found herself being helped into the carriage by the footman Dunnet.

The scoundrels and Sheridan had left her long enough for two maids to attend her and turn her out. Then the prodding had been something less than gentle, and Lily had felt more in the way of being turned inside out. The clothing they'd carried in was not made for her, but of a size with the robe she had worn the night before. The maids were nimble with a needle and thread and made short work of the alterations, though Lily thought they too often found her a convenient pincushion.

They gave her hair a hard brushing, pinched her cheeks, and fussed with the fit of her dress across the shoulders and back. They critically studied the embroidered front of the shell pink jaconet muslin to be certain the line of it fell just so and showed no compunction about reaching inside the gown's bodice to yank on the undergarments to perfect the fit.

She had only a glimpse of the bonnet before it was placed on her head, but it appeared to be of the latest stare with its chimney pot shape and a splendid plume sticking out of the top like a sweep's broom. They gave her no opportunity in front of the cheval glass to be critical of either herself or their work. Once they had fastened the gray cottage mantle over her shoulders and turned back the collar to reveal the pink silk lining, they escorted her to the door and stood aside.

Lily judged herself to have made a good presentation because the boys stopped dancing about, and for once there was naught but silence from their open mouths. Although she was too bemused to fully appreciate their reaction, she nevertheless counted it as a good thing that Lord Sheridan no longer accompanied them. He had more in the way of good manners than to subject her to the same much-struck expression as the children, but no matter what his regard, she would have been more unsettled by it than flattered.

"I say, Miss Rose, this is a good piece of luck." Dash's speech had a slightly nasal intonation as his nose was flattened against the carriage window. "Would you look at that? That bloke's starin' at us just like we was toffs."

"He's staring because you're staring," she told him. "Please come away from there and sit down."

Dash peeled himself off the glass and dropped to the bench beside Midge. He looked pointedly at Pinch who was similarly pressed to the other window but had not yet drawn attention to himself.

"Pinch," Lily said. She caught him by the back of his jacket and tugged lightly. Grinning, he settled himself at her side. "We want to give a good accounting of ourselves and not abuse his lordship's generosity. He will not like it if people stare at us."

"'Ow would 'e know?" Midge asked. "'E's ridin' by 'imself on that great black beast."

"Killies," Pinch said. "'Eard 'im call the beast Killies."

Lily smiled. "Might he have said Achilles?"

"Might 'ave."

"Achilles was a warrior," she explained. "He fought with Odysseus at Troy. Do you remember what I told you about that war?"

They did, but they had no objections to hearing it again, and in this way Lily diverted them for much of the journey through London proper. They were well into the countryside before the adventures of the King of Ithaca began to pall. When neither the sirens or the cyclops could hold their attention, Lily let them amuse themselves at the windows again.

More tired than she cared to admit, even to herself, Lily removed her bonnet and rested her head back against the leather squabs. The boys chattered, traded views, dirtied the glass with their handprints, and occasionally squabbled. Sometimes they sighted Sheridan far ahead of the carriages, taking a turn in the road or going over a rise, and they would marvel at his mastery of the great warrior beast.

Lily listened to them with half an ear, not unhappy that they were more than a little in awe of Sheridan. She could own that it was not so different for her, though perhaps it was more unwise.

As Dash had said, it was a good piece of luck. All of it. She was not anxious to have another blade poked under her ribs, but it was difficult not to think of it now as providential. Lily had no clear sense of what Sheridan meant to do with them once they arrived at his country home, but for Pinch, Dash, and Midge it had to be better than anything they could expect in Holborn.

For herself, the future was not so easily divined. She hadn't the least idea what might be expected of her now. She was certain that he had meant to leave her behind, yet sometime over the course of what was left of the night, he had changed his mind. From Lily's perspective, there was no comprehending it. More to the point, she was not certain she wanted to. Distance between them was not only prudent, it was necessary. She had no wish to bridge it with the sort of understanding that would forever put him in her mind, or her in his.

Lily fingered the brim of her bonnet, turning it idly in her lap as she made an accounting of her prospects. Each time the carriage rocked, the bonnet's heavy plume fluttered so that the tip of it tickled her under the chin and distracted her from her musings. Perhaps if she'd had more prospects, or a more ambitious muse, the effect of the swaying plume would not have been hypnotic, but such was not the case, and it was not long before Lily surrendered herself to a very deep sleep.

Granville lay well north and west of London, a three days' journey on horseback if the horse was prime and the rider tireless. By carriage, the trip required a full sennight and that was dependent upon fair skies and the ease with which failures of either of the carriages might be remedied.

Sherry's desire to arrive at Granville was such that he contemplated riding far ahead of the carriages and coming to the residence a full four days before them. Because of the entourage he had acquired, he restrained himself, though his mood was in no way improved by it. Instead, he allowed himself no longer a leash than the distance to each night's lodging. He would arrive at the hostelry hours before the carriages, make arrangements with the innkeeper for lodgings, then find diversion in the nearest village. This often involved games of chance, card play, sharing a pint with the locals, and—on the evening of the fourth day—sharing several satisfying hours in the bed of a comely widow whose acquaintance he'd made on previous journeys.

"She is liberal with her scent, my lord," Lily said when

Sheridan called upon her room before retiring. "One can scarce smell the drink on you for the perfume."

Sherry decided the surest means of niggling her was offering no reply at all. He looked past her shoulder as she opened her door wider and saw the three scoundrels were already abed and sleeping soundly. "That bed does not look as if it will accommodate you and the boys. Shall I inquire about another room?"

Lily shook her head. "It is sufficient, even comfortable."

"The first may be true, but to say it is comfortable strains belief."

She shrugged.

Sheridan lifted his chin to indicate the sleeping children. "Midget seems to lay claim to more than his fair share."

Lily did not glance back. A small crease appeared between her brows. "What did you call him?"

"Hmm? Oh. Midget."

"I hope you will not call him such to his face. He is liable to forget himself and threaten to blacken your eye."

"He is not Midget, then?"

"No. Their names are all of a piece. Pinch. Dash." She paused deliberately, giving him another opportunity to work it out. "It is perhaps that you have never spent much time in any of your homes with your cooks. He is—"

"Smidgen." Sherry chuckled. "Of course."

"They were being chased for stealing spices from a baker's shop when I met them."

"You offered them sanctuary."

"After a fashion. They hid behind my skirts."

"All three?"

"Pinch and Dash. Smidgen was being carried off by the baker's wife." The memory raised a faint smile. "He wiggled out of his jacket and made his escape. It was quite something."

Sherry's gaze dropped momentarily to Lily's mouth. As quick as that, her smile disappeared, and Sherry was sorry for his lapse. It had occurred to him that she might have been persuaded to join him in the taproom for tea and conversation, but he knew now that the overture would be rebuffed. It was not that he smelled of another woman's scent that put him out of favor with her but that he smelled of drink. Lily was invariably wary when she thought he had compromised temperance, and Sherry acknowledged he was indeed too proud to explain that more was spilled on him than was drunk.

Knowing himself reluctant to take his leave, Sherry asked, "They have been with you ever since their narrow escape?"

"After a fashion. They have never lived with me."

"But they are under your protection."

"It is more accurate that I let it be known that I have an interest in the boys. I can provide precious little in the way of protection. If it were not for Blue, I would have already lost them."

"To Craven, you mean."

Lily nodded.

Sherry glanced at the boys again. Sometime during his brief conversation with Lily, they had managed to twist and turn and become a thorough tangle. "I think it is fortunate that they chose your skirts to hide behind."

"Actually," she said as pale pink color stained her complexion, "it was *under* them."

"Then I stand corrected, Miss Rose. The young scoundrels are damnably lucky fellows."

Granville Manor was the source of considerable speculation among the passengers of Sheridan's lead carriage. They could have gone to Sheridan, put their questions to him, and ended all their conjecture on the subject, but they were agreed it would also put a period to their fun.

Midge imagined a castle with turrets, a moat, crenelated battlements, and a dungeon. He was particularly anxious that Granville have a dungeon and hoped there would be at least one poor soul still in residence.

Pinch put forth the idea that it would be on a scale with the Royal Opera House. There would be so many rooms that they would not have to sleep in box beds. They would be able to hide from the housekeeper, butler, and cook without fear of ever being found, and in fact, they might be able to grow so old in hiding that no one would recognize them when they reappeared.

Dash envisioned dark halls and hidden passages. He would be very disappointed if there were no spirits in residence. He did not care if he had to sleep in a box bed, as long as it was in the same tower where he could expect to find the ghost.

Lily's expectations were not on so grand a scale, but the boys listened raptly as she spoke of polished granite walls that would reflect a pale pink hue at sunset and windows so tall she might stand tiptoed on the sill and not be able to reach the lintel. There would be a turret, just as Midge imagined, and the view from there would be the Granville estate for as far as the eye could see. And Pinch was correct that they might hide in the warren of rooms, but never so well that Sheridan could not find them. As for Dash's ghost, there was certain to be one, yet he had been an educated fellow and confined his incorporeal self to the library where he rearranged the books.

"The library?" Dash asked, suspicious. "Are you certain?"

"Quite."

"I don't think I like that."

And so it went, each of them elaborating a bit on the house at Granville, refining their vision aloud so that they all could share it, making small wagers when there were points of contention and allowing that it would be Lily who would settle disputes.

For the boys, their excitement was not so easily contained,

while Lily became more subdued with each milestone that was sighted and passed. She anticipated that when they reached the last inn on their journey, Sheridan would not hesitate to ride on to Granville. It seemed to her that he was wearing his skin less comfortably of late and that his desire to be at home was what made him restive. When he secured lodging for himself as well as everyone else, Lily wondered if he felt obliged to remain behind and what she might say that would ease his sense of responsibility.

To that end, she sought him out in the taproom once the boys were abed. The innkeeper had commented upon their arrival that there were few travelers availing themselves of his hospitality this evening, and Lily was gratified to see that even fewer were passing their time in his taproom. She recognized their driver, Mr. Pipkin, and the groom everyone called Tolley sitting at a table near the hearth. Mr. Kearns was noticeable for his absence, and Sheridan sat alone in the darkest corner of the room. He had a pint of ale in front of him, but for the time Lily stood watching him, he showed no interest in it.

"My lord?"

Sheridan turned slightly in his chair. "Miss Rose." He inclined his head politely but did not rise. "How may I be of service?"

"I wondered if I might speak with you."

"Here?" Without waiting for her response, he glanced around the room, assessed their situation as unlikely to command interest, and nodded. "Very well. Please, won't you sit?" He rose slightly and gestured to the chair at a right angle to his, holding it steady while she sat. "Shall I order you some refreshment?"

She regarded his ale with a rather wistful smile but answered in the negative. "Nothing, thank you."

Sherry indicated his tankard. "You drink ale?"

"Not so much as you have before you, but I admit to acquiring a fondness for it at Blue's."

"Not the French brandy? That is a pity."

"Neither my tastes nor my pockets supported the brandy."
Tilting her head to one side, she eyed him curiously. "You
are interested in Blue's brandy?"

"Indeed, though it is unwise." His mouth twisted wryly.
"Sometimes it is difficult not to be appreciative of the enterprise of the smugglers." He lifted his tankard, watched her
over the rim. "That surprises you, does it not?"

"A little."

"I am always admiring of enterprise, though I should not
admit it so easily when it flies in the face of society's expectations." He shrugged. "But I think we digress. There is something particular you require of me?"

When put before her so plainly, Lily found it difficult to
answer. She nodded, swallowing. "I would like to know your
plans for us. You have said nothing regarding your intentions.
It is not so much for myself that I ask, you understand, but
for—"

"The lads," Sherry said. "Yes, I certainly understand that.
Tell me, Miss Rose, have you considered even once what my
intentions toward you might be?"

"Yes. Many times."

"And?"

"I cannot divine them."

"Yet your primary concern is for the boys."

"Of course. They have seen a great deal and know very
little. To be so far from London, from the streets and life that
are familiar to them, well, they cannot fathom how different
it will be. I should like to prepare them. I thought that you
might speak to them, but tomorrow we will arrive at Granville
and you have said precious little to any of us."

Sherry set his tankard on the table and lightly rubbed
the underside of his chin with his knuckles. "I must allow
that I am curious. It seems to me that you have also seen a
great deal, and unlike the lads, you know a great deal
more. You are also far from London, yet you appear to
have some notion of what you can expect. I wonder how
that is."

"I lived outside Paris, remember. I have been to the country."

"You lived in a convent. *Out* of the country. It is not at all the same."

She merely returned his regard.

"You are determined to remain silent, I see. It intrigues."

"I do not mean to set forth a challenge, m'lord. I hope you will not take it as such." Beneath the table, Lily pleated a fold in the fabric of her gown. "Will you not say what it is that you expect of the boys?"

"I hope to find honest work for them," Sherry said.

"At Granville?"

"Yes, certainly. Did you truly think I would bring them so far only to send them away?"

"I didn't know. I wondered if there might not be a workhouse nearby."

He shook his head. "It never occurred to me that it would be a question in your mind. Have the lads wondered the same?"

"Not aloud, they haven't."

"Perhaps they trust me to deal fairly with them."

"More than I trust you to do the same." Lily's fingers stilled momentarily. "That is what you left unsaid."

"True. And you seemed to have arrived at my meaning anyway." Sherry's eyes darted past Lily's shoulder then returned to her. "Mr. Pipkin is preparing to take a pipe, and I have no liking for it. Are you well enough to walk with me, Miss Rose?"

Lily did not try to hide her surprise. "I'm well enough, but I don't have my coat."

"I shall lend you mine."

Her hand went to her head where she fingered the lace edge of her cap. "My bonnet is—"

"Wherever it is," Sherry said, interrupting, "it is better left there." He stood and touched the back of her chair. "Say yes, Miss Rose. Knowing how you chafed at being confined to your bed, you cannot have enjoyed passing this last week in the carriage, then your room." He paused. "If you are certain you can manage the thing."

Lily rose immediately. Her head came around at the sound of his low chuckle. "What is it?"

"Forgive me. It is only that I did not mean to set forth a challenge. I hope you have not taken it as such."

That he was looking at her with such perfect innocence did not change the fact that he had bedeviled her with her own words. "I suppose you are accustomed to people thinking you are vastly clever."

His chuckle deepened. "And I am certain you mean to come down firmly on the other side of that opinion." Sherry gave her a nudge at the small of her back. "Let us remove the debate to the out of doors."

Lily immediately stepped ahead of his touch, then forced herself to proceed without hurry to the door. Once they were beyond it, she put herself at better than an arm's length from him.

"Will you accept my frock coat?" he asked.

"No, it is not so chilly as I thought."

Sherry did not insist. He glanced around the inn's yard, looking for a suitable path they might follow. A large tabby cat approached him and wound herself in and out of his legs. Sherry hunkered down and idly scratched the tabby behind her ears. "There is a stone wall not so very distant," he told Lily. "The Romans laid the first of it. Perhaps we could set that as our direction."

Lily stood outside the light coming from the inn's windows, but it illuminated Sheridan's figure. She watched him absently stroke the cat as he continued to look around the yard awaiting her reply. He was in every way an enigma. "I should like to see this wall," she said, turning from him. It did not bear thinking why she suddenly felt like weeping. "Is it this way?"

Sherry set the cat from him and stood. "Yes. I would not

suggest it if there were no moonshine. I think if we walk along the road, the way will be clear enough. Do you require assistance?"

"No."

He fell into step beside her. "Then you are feeling more the thing. I wondered. You never complained at any point during the journey, but I was uncertain if that was merely a measure of your tolerance for pain or an indication of the absence of it."

"You might have been at Granville three—or even four—days past if not for insisting that Mr. Pipkin stop so often. I believe I am correct that it was done in aid of easing the journey for me. I cannot fathom why you would show me such consideration, except that it is in your nature to do so." Lily thought that in Sheridan's eyes she and the tabby were not so very different creatures. "You give it no more thought than drawing breath." She felt him falter beside her, but they were leaving the inn's torchlights behind them, and she couldn't be certain if he was simply less sure of his steps.

"Is that what you think?" he asked finally. "That I have a kind nature?"

"Yes."

"I am considerably less confident than you that that is the case. I think you would be better served not to trust it is my nature but that it is done of a purpose."

Now it was Lily who chuckled.

"What is it?"

"It is just that you are cautioning me not to depend upon your kindness. That is rather kind of you, don't you think?"

Sherry offered a reluctant smile. "Well, perhaps you have me there."

They passed from under the shadowed canopy of a large chestnut into moonshine. The road lay like a silver ribbon before them, and the bleached white stones of the ancient Roman wall were visible at the first turn.

"Is it too far?" Sherry asked.

"No. I wish I might have walked like this every day." Lily could not be entirely comfortable with the silence that settled briefly between them. The intimacy of it created a sense that they were of similar stations, perhaps of similar minds. She knew the falseness of both those things and spoke to cleanly cut the quiet and the mood. "I had not expected that you would take lodging with the rest of us tonight. Are you not anxious to arrive at Granville?"

"I am, but I am also desirous that everyone should make the journey safely."

"If you had only your trunks to consider, you would have gone ahead."

He shook his head. "You are in the wrong of it there. I place a higher value on retaining my possessions than is probably wise. Theft is not isolated to Holborn, you know. Highwaymen are common enough along this route. It is not only you and the lads whose safety concerns me, but there is Kearns and Pipkin and the grooms to consider."

Lily wondered if she could believe that, then decided she must. Hadn't she been the one refining upon his kindness just minutes ago? She sighed. "Very well. I only thought that . . . it seemed to me . . . I suppose I didn't . . ." She drew in a steadying breath, gathering her wits, and wished herself almost anywhere but where she was. The low rumble of Sheridan's laughter did not assist her effort to form a complete sentence out of the jumble of thoughts. "It is good to know that you have not been burdened overmuch by the addition of the boys and me."

"Just so. Is that why you followed me to the taproom? To tell me I was under no obligation to remain behind?"

"It sounds terribly presumptuous when I hear it aloud, but yes, that is what I meant to say."

"As long as you know it was presumptuous."

Lily gave him a sidelong glance. Moonlight lent his profile enough definition for her to make out the wry twist of his mouth. Caught by that aspect of his features, she did not realize how close he was until she felt his hand under her elbow when the road became uneven. This time she did not pull away.

"Why am I here?" she asked. "And, pray, do not mistake my meaning. I am not referring to this walk."

"Nor, apparently, to the larger question of your own existence." He gave her elbow a gentle squeeze before she could reproach him for his impoverished humor. "Very well. The answer to your question is surprisingly simple, though I doubt that it will satisfy. You are here because I desire it."

He was correct. As an explanation, it did not satisfy in the least. "But why?"

"Ahh, well that is more difficult. It cannot be because you are a restful person, or that you are tractable. I am uncertain that it has anything at all to do with your character, though perhaps it does, and what I wish for is something different than what I have known."

"*Ennui*? Is that what you are saying? You are bored? I am neither restful nor tractable, indeed, that is but the beginning of a long list of all the things I am not, and you are telling me you find that a welcome diversion?"

"Your inflection leads me to believe those are all questions. Are they rhetorical, I wonder, or must I answer?"

Lily was forced to press her hand to her side as laughter threatened. She was not surprised when he was immediately attentive to her health. "I am fine," she said. "Really. All of a piece, but it is very bad of you to make me laugh when it can still pain me to do so." She let her hand fall and looked up at him. "Though it would be far worse, I believe, if I could not laugh at all." Acutely aware of Sheridan's study of her, Lily's eyes darted away. She would have stepped back if not for the faint tightening of his hand at her elbow.

"I swear this was not my intent," he said.

It was only when he was kissing her that Lily realized that he hadn't been speaking of provoking her laughter.

His mouth was firm on hers and tasted warmly of ale. After the first moment, he did not press the advantage of surprise. He allowed her opportunity to become accustomed to his touch or draw back from it. Lily did neither. What she did was stand still for it, and when he finally raised his head after finding her wholly without response, she said, "Perhaps you will want to revise your opinion of my value as a diversion."

Sherry smiled, but there was no humor in it, only regret. "I most humbly beg your pardon."

Lily nodded. With a tilt of her head, she indicated the wall. "Shall we continue?"

"If you like."

When they had taken but a few steps, Lily asked, "Are you disappointed, my lord, that I was not more accommodating?"

Sherry didn't answer. He helped her over another rough patch in the road, then onto the grassy verge, and finally released her when they reached the wall. "It continues as far as the eye can see from here, past that rise and into the next shire. It was a fortification, though not as extensive or effective as Hadrian's in the north. Whole sections of it are gone now, carted away by crofters for building their homes. There are those of us who would like to see it preserved, but with no means and with no more compelling reason to do so than that it is part of our history, it will most likely disappear."

Lily ran her hand along the pitted surface of one of the stones. She was admiring of the moonlight that leeched color from each of them so that in the distance the wall was like a chalk line. "I think I should like to sit on it," she said, "but it feels curiously like a sacrilege."

Confounded, Sherry's brows rose in tandem. How was it possible that she sensed sacrilege here and barely a sennight earlier had knelt between his thighs without turning a hair? Because he doubted she would explain this bent of her mind to him even if she understood it, Sherry chose not to put the question to her. Instead, he placed his hands on either side of her waist and lifted her the few inches necessary to put her on top of the wall.

"You will be pleased to know," he said, "that you are sitting on stones stacked by the Roman invaders in the third century."

She once again regarded the length of it. "You will tell the boys about it tomorrow, won't you?"

"If you like."

"About the battles also. They are of an age when bloodshed intrigues."

"Then I shall give a good accounting of the gore."

She turned back to him and discovered his interest was not the wall, but her. "You do not mean to kiss me again, do you?"

"No, but then I did not mean to do so the last time. It just happened."

"I would not have reckoned you to be so impulsive a gentleman."

"I am having difficulty coming to terms with it as well."

Lily's eyes were made gray by the moonlight, and her complexion was without color. The effect lent her countenance preternatural gravity. "If you will allow that a kiss can be on my terms, then I think we might arrive at some satisfactory arrangement."

"Terms." He said it as though testing the word. "You have terms. Why does that not astonish?"

"Perhaps because you comprehend very well that I am not tractable."

"That must be it." He inclined his head. "Please, go on. I am frankly fascinated."

Lily's mouth flattened briefly, and her eyes reproached him. "I cannot know with certainty, but I think the kissing will be improved if I am permitted to begin it."

Sherry waited. When nothing more was forthcoming, he said, "You have but the one term? Then by all means, be—"

"I do not want your tongue in my mouth."

This last was said so rapidly that Sherry required a moment to interpret. "I was not aware that I—"

"You didn't," she said quickly. "It is just that you should

know at the outset that I don't want it there. And I won't put mine in yours either."

"Apparently I am not as fastidious as you, for I don't mind in the least." He held up one hand when she looked as if she meant to admonish him again. "Is there anything else? Perhaps you do not like it that I have been drinking spirits."

"No, that is of no consequence, though I shouldn't like it if you were foxed. I told you I acquired a taste for ale at Blue's." A half smile played about her lips. "I am not of a mind to kiss you now, so you should not anticipate that I will."

"But I can anticipate that you mean to do it eventually, is that right?"

"Yes."

"Then I will require your assistance negotiating the route back to the inn, for I am weak-kneed."

"Fool."

"Quite possibly."

He was so cheerful about this assessment of his character that Lily reversed her own decision. She found a foothold for her heels between the stones and stood, then before he backed away, she steadied herself by placing her hands on his shoulders. She pressed her mouth to his and found at once that this was most sincerely more to her liking.

Lily allowed her lips to soften and tilted her head a fraction. She touched the corner of his mouth so lightly that it was merely a promise that more was to come. She nudged his upper lip with hers. His mouth did not part but hers did. She nibbled at his lip with her own until she arrived at the other corner. Was he smiling? she wondered.

She drew back a fraction and regarded Sheridan. Turned away from the moonlight, his features were cast in shadow. His eyes were so dark as to be black, but nothing in his look suggested a predatory intent. There was curiosity there, and amusement. He was completely at his ease waiting her out.

She faltered a bit as she bent toward him. "Perhaps you will put your hands at my waist."

"Of course. There?"

Lily nodded. She felt the placement of every one of his fingers through her muslin gown. His hands were softer than hers and more elegantly tapered. She bit her nails, sometimes to the quick, while all of his were buffed and neatly trimmed. "You do not mind that I am kissing you?"

"No. I am perhaps too tolerant in this regard, but I do not think I will alter my views just yet."

This time when Lily kissed him it had all the sweetness of her smile. She worked her mouth over his, paying particular attention to his lower lip, worrying it gently between hers. The tip of her tongue ran along the line of it, but she did not thrust it in his mouth.

"You will think I am splitting hairs," she whispered against his lips. She flicked her tongue and it caught the upper curve of his mouth. "But I find I want the taste of you again."

Sherry felt a shudder begin at the base of his spine and slip all the way up to his shoulders. His voice was husky. "It seems I can adapt."

Lily wet her own mouth with the tip of her tongue then laid it gently over his. She felt his fingers tighten at her waist, not so firmly that there was discomfort, but enough to let her know he was not unaffected. Still, it was puzzling because he was not returning any measure of the kiss.

"You wish me to stop?" she asked.

"No. Does it seem that I do?"

"You're not kissing me back."

"I didn't know if it was permissible under the terms of the arrangement."

"Of course, once I begin the thing I am all for it."

"You might have been clearer on that count."

Lily did not explain that except for the scoundrels and her own father, she had never initiated any kiss. It did not seem likely that Sheridan would believe that confession, not after she had set herself on her knees before him.

"Lily?" Sherry lifted his head a fraction when he felt her entire frame stiffen. "What is it?"

She shook her head. "Nothing."

"Not nothing. I do not think you are ready for me to—"

Lily lifted her hands from his shoulders and plunged her fingers into his hair, cupping the back of his head to hold him steady. She slanted her mouth across his and felt his surprise, then his response.

His lips moved over hers, tugging at first, then sucking. She felt the dampness of his mouth, the rough edge of his tongue, but he never pressed more deeply than to trace the outline of her lips. A delicious frisson slipped under the surface of her skin, and moments later she was aware of a blossom of heat between her breasts.

This was better, Lily thought, infinitely better than anything in her experience. His teeth did not grind against hers, and he didn't mash her lips until they were bloodless. He did not bear down on her, did not force her mouth open. Whatever he did to her was what she had already done, so that his kiss was like an echo of her own. There was no coercion, no force, merely gentle persuasion.

Her fingers curled lightly in his hair. She brushed the tapering ends just above the collar of his frock coat and felt his breath hitch. It was as if he stole her breath as well, and Lily wondered how it was possible that she had not moved but had surely lost her balance.

It was Sherry who broke the kiss. He could no longer recall the terms of their arrangement, or if he'd ever agreed to them. He set Lily from him, drew a steadying breath, and said in mildly mocking accents, "Perhaps we need to clearly define the parameters of kissing. Duration. Frequency." He paused. "Intensity."

Lily nodded dumbly.

"But not at the moment," he said. "I am for returning to the inn and my bed." Sherry watched her pale eyes grow wider; fear made her blink. He realized that if he was not careful he would step into it again. "To the inn and my bed to sleep."

When this explanation did nothing to allay her suspicions, he added, "Alone. At least I will be alone. You will be with the lads."

"Oh." Lily wrapped her arms about her middle. "Then you will require nothing else from me?"

"No. And, Lily, I did not require that you kiss me. At any time."

She flushed a little. "I should also like to go back."

"Of course." He removed his frock coat and laid it across her shoulders. "Don't argue. It is plain to see that you are shivering."

She was, but it was not entirely from exposure to the chilled air. Lily thought he probably understood and was grateful when he made no mention of it. "Thank you."

"That was not so difficult, was it?" When she shook her head, several heavy curls slipped out from under her lace cap. Without thinking, Sherry reached out and removed the modest covering altogether. He pressed it into her hand when she held it out for it. "It is an affront to nature that you hide your hair. There is no one here to see and at the inn, no one who knows you."

Lily was so taken aback that she had to hurry to catch up with him. He shortened his stride once she was at his elbow. "What did you mean by that?"

"Merely that I would be in favor of a law that would make it a crime for you to cover that extraordinary hair."

"No, not that. The other thing you said."

"You can't have mistaken my meaning. Or did you think that it had escaped my notice that you're in hiding?"

"But—" She broke off when he paused in his step long enough to cock an eyebrow at her. Bowing her head, Lily studied the ground as she walked. "It is *not* what you think."

"You cannot know that."

"I am not a criminal."

"By your own admission you are a practiced thief, so it is disingenuous of you to proclaim your innocence. Nevertheless, that is not why you are hiding."

She decided it was better not to provoke him into putting the whole of it before her. If he did suspect the truth—and he could not possibly comprehend it in its entirety—her need for safety would still require that she lie, and she knew herself to be oddly reluctant to do that. She would also have to run. She could own that it held as little appeal as lying.

The best she could hope for was that he would lose interest in her—in every manner that such a thing was possible.

"What is it?" he asked, not breaking stride this time.

"Hmm?"

"You sighed. Rather heavily, I might add. Frustration or fatigue?"

It was disappointment, but the Grand Inquisitor himself could not have wrested that from her. "Fatigue," she said. There were lies, then there were lies worth telling.

And there were consequences for both, she realized, as Sheridan swung her easily into his arms. She sighed again.

"Frustration," he said.

Indeed it was.

Granville Hall was approached from the southeast by the route that skirted the lake. The boys had chosen to make this last leg of the journey perched atop the trunks and valises on the roof, and now they were exuberantly pointing out their discoveries.

"Look!" Midge cried. "There are fish in the lake! Did ye see that one jump, Pinch? I'll wager they are man-eating fish. Do ye think there will be a moat? Oh, I 'ope there is a moat."

"A tower!" Dash was up on his feet, straddling a bag and pointing to the distant house. The sun winked in one of the windows. "There! The ghost. I feel sure of it."

Pinch grabbed Dash by the back of his jacket and pulled him down. "Mr. Pipkin will 'ave yer guts for garters if ye don't sit."

Dash sat, but he was in no way subdued. "It's as grand as

the Opera House, Pinch, just as ye said. We're in for a bloody good time o' it, I tell ye. A bloody good time."

Below them in the carriage, Lily offered Sheridan an apologetic, if somewhat guilty, mien. "We have all been speculating about the house, you see. We made a game of it to pass the time."

Sherry glanced up at the roof. "They are sure to be disappointed. There is no moat."

"Midge is the only one set on a moat. The lake will do wonderfully well for him. I cannot say how he will take the news that there are no man-eating fish, but I believe that eventually he will find it a good thing."

"What about your own curiosity? I notice you have not looked out."

"You wouldn't mind? I confess, were you not here, I would have my face pressed to the window in the same fashion the boys did."

"By all means." He gestured toward the door. "You will have a good view of the hall when we make the next turn in the road."

Lily sat forward on the leather bench and braced herself with one hand on the curve of the seat and the other on the door handle. She was leaning toward the smudged glass just as the carriage began taking the slow, wide curve.

There was no rosy cast to the sky that could lend the pale ochre stones of Granville Hall more color, but it was of no consequence. The grandeur of the home was set first with its positioning on a verdant rise just beyond the lake. Like the facets of a yellow diamond, every window exposed to the southern view winked sunlight, and the three squared-off towers that were visible from this approach stood splendidly taller than the rest of the house, drawing the eye and supporting the setting.

"Are there ghosts?" Lily asked.

"I'm afraid not. Is it Midge who wants ghosts?"

"Dash. Besides the moat, Midge is set on a dungeon. Granville does not look as if it might have one."

"No," Sherry said. "No dungeon."

"Then you will have no hapless fellow manacled to a wall."

"Only if the housekeeper is having words again with the second butler."

Lily chuckled. Her gaze dropped away from the towers to the surrounding park. There were terraced gardens from the crushed-gravel drive all the way to the lake. Rows of neatly trimmed box hedges and topiary lined the walking paths. Openings in the rows were an invitation to step into one of the gardens where rosebuds, in their seemingly infinite variety of textures, fragrances, and shades, were beginning to bloom.

As the carriage made its slow arcing ascent to the house and passed the gardens, Lily pressed her palm to the glass. She stared out for a long moment, then closed her eyes and secured the memory. It would come to her again when she had need for it. Time would soften the colors but not change them. She would be able to feel the downy side of rose petals against her skin and know the individual scents or the redolence of the whole.

With these last memories captured in her mind's eye, Lily sat back. "Will you not also have a turn at the window, my lord?"

Sherry shook his head. He did not think he had ever seen his home more beautifully rendered than through Lily's eyes. Like her, he had also secured a memory, but his was of her hand splayed against the glass, the long, shapely fingers perfectly white at the tip with the pressure she applied. He would always know reverence by the fixed expression of Lily's profile, the parting of her mouth, the lift of her lashes and tilt of her eyes, the way her slim nose flared slightly when she drew in a hushed breath.

This is what he had imagined when he decided to leave London. This is what he had come home to.

"How is it you ever leave?" she asked.

"Duties."

"I suppose you have a great many."

"I have no idea. I have no sense how to measure them. They just are."

Lily considered this. She suspected he was not the sort of man to complain under the weight of duty. "They are not a burden to you then?"

"A burden? They are the responsibility of privilege. One does not accept one without the other."

"Truly?"

Sherry did not miss the cynical inflection. "I cannot speak for what others do, but it is my way."

She smiled a little. "Of course."

"Did I sound pompous just then?"

Lily worried her lower lip between her teeth. "A tad, yes, but I have always supposed it is one of the privileges of rank." When he offered no opinion save for a soft grunt, Lily bit her lip harder to moderate her humor. She thought it prudent to change the subject. "Who will be in residence?"

"No one save the servants."

"Well," she said, not troubling herself to conceal her surprise. "I suppose that means there will be no end of rooms for the boys to hide in. They will be glad to hear it. It is Pinch's fondest wish to avoid notice of the housekeeper, first butler, and the head cook until he is quite in his dotage."

Sherry laughed. "What about my notice?"

"Oh, you must not worry that any of us will ever be underfoot, my lord. Once we are assigned our duties, I suspect we will never cross paths. You have back stairs, do you not, for the servants to use?"

"Yes, but—"

"Then you will not be troubled by our presence."

"I see. It seems you have considered it all carefully."

"I have tried. I had hoped you would explain to me last night the manner in which we might serve at Granville, but I collect that you will leave that decision to your housekeeper or steward. They will know best how we should be employed, and I should not have pressed you in that regard."

Sherry tipped back the brim of his hat and regarded Lily with a hooded glance that was at once cool and considered. "So you do not think the boys will really shirk their duties."

"No, my lord. They will get up to tricks, I suspect, but they will work very hard for you. Please do not think they won't."

"And you, Miss Rose? If the scullery requires a maid for cleaning dishes and scrubbing pots, will my cook find you in a cupboard reading Madame de Staël's latest novel?"

"No. I mean to do whatever is required."

Sherry nodded slowly, in perfect tempo with the gradual halting of the carriage. "It is what I hoped for, then," he said. "The lads will be set up in the schoolroom, and you will see that no matter what tricks they get up to, no one is harmed."

"But—"

Sherry threw open the door of the carriage, pausing just once before he descended. He fixed Lily with his implacable glance. "Whatever is required, Miss Rose. You said it yourself. And what I require is a governess for the scoundrels."

Eight

Pinch's gaze wandered to the bank of windows in the schoolroom for a third time before Lily surrendered. She closed the book she was reading from with enough force to garner Pinch's guilty attention, then took the sting from her reproving glance by announcing they would continue their lessons out of doors.

"Science, I think," she told them. "There is a good breeze today. I believe we can do our wind and water experiments."

"Boat racing, you mean?" Midge asked, excitement bringing him out of his chair. "Oh, please say it is to be boat racing!"

Lily rose to her feet, her mouth set primly. "Water displacement and buoyancy. Wind direction and speed. Perhaps barometric pressure."

Midge actually went airborne. "That is boat racing!"

Laughing, Lily directed them to get their boats and promised she would inquire about a luncheon for them to take. She had to call after them as they went charging ahead to their own rooms. "Meet me at the tradesman's entrance and use the back stairs." She poked her head into the hallway in time to see Dash disappear into his bedchamber. "And whatever you do, do *not* go to the lake without me!"

Shaking her head, her smile happily indulgent, Lily returned to the classroom and straightened the table where they had been working. She stacked and squared off Pinch's papers, Midge's drawings, and Dash's primers, returned quills and ink pots to their stands, and pushed their chairs back into place. Before the last chair was righted, she heard the boys charging back into the hall, scrambling to see who would be the first to reach the stairs.

She followed at a much less hurried pace, stopping first in her bedchamber to retrieve her hat and shawl. With the boys gone, the entire east wing of the great house seemed inordinately still. Lily remembered assuring Sheridan that he would not be troubled by their presence, that neither she nor the boys would be underfoot. In the two months since their arrival at Granville Hall, she had never failed to be impressed by how easily that assurance was kept and how often the reverse of it was not.

In truth, Sheridan had never offered any promise of privacy. Naturally it was not something he needed to extend in his own home; he had a right to go anywhere. Lily realized early on that she'd made the faulty assumption that he would wish himself anywhere but where she and the scoundrels were. This did not turn out to be so. Although his lordship was not a regular visitor to the schoolroom, neither was he a stranger. From the outset he showed considerable interest in what the boys were learning, suggesting subjects and books, even casually testing them.

While the boys enjoyed his visits—even the testing—it was something of a reprieve for Lily that she had not seen Sheridan for more than a sennight. She did not inquire after him. She believed that such an inquiry demonstrated an unseemly interest that she was anxious to avoid, and moreover, it was always possible that he was actually in residence and merely tired of the schoolroom.

Pinch, though, showed no compunction about asking after the master of Granville Hall and had learned after the first day of missing him that Sheridan was gone from the estate. It seemed he was invited to a house party at the home of their neighbor Sir Arthur Meredith and had given no indication if he would be gone for a few days or a fortnight. Word had also reached Granville from London that Wellington and Blücher had defeated Boney at Waterloo, and Lily was aware that this news could also delay Sheridan's return as there would be extensive celebrating.

So it was with some confidence that there would be no interruptions that Lily had suggested the science lesson at the lake. The boys were waiting for her at their arranged place, and when she appeared with a large covered basket over one arm they whooped with excitement.

Dash offered to tote the basket, but Lily refused. Each boy was carrying a ship he'd built himself, and she had too much respect for the effort to risk damaging one of them. Even with three hungry lads anticipating a substantial luncheon, the basket was still the least valuable item being taken to the lake this afternoon.

Lily snapped open the blanket covering the basket and laid it out on the grass. The breeze was sufficiently strong for her to require help to keep it anchored. Midge set a plate at three of the corners, while Lily placed the basket on the fourth.

"Shall we eat?" she asked. "Or is it to be the races first?"

The response was unanimous and resounding. "Eat!"

Laughing, Lily knelt and began breaking up a crusty round of peasant bread still warm from the oven. She cut wedges of sharp cheddar, then sliced two pears in half so they all might have a taste of one. There was a large skin filled near to bursting with cool cider, and the boys dutifully held out their glasses while she poured.

They settled back and enjoyed their repast while the sun beat down on them and the wind lightly whipped their hair about. Occasionally a fish would jump in the lake, but this no longer elicited any untoward excitement as they had all learned none were man-eaters. A flock of geese roamed a nearby bank, poking at the grass and each other with their beaks. A few took to the air, circled overhead, then dove at the lake. They skimmed the reflective surface, splashing and stirring the water until they made a wake that resembled nothing so much as a trail of liquid diamonds.

Dash leaned back on his elbows and stretched his legs in front of him. Sunshine brightened his pale yellow hair and put pink in his cheeks. "I say, Miss Rose, it's a good life 'ere, ain't it? I guess we buggered ol' Ned Craven right enough, leavin' Lunnon the way we did."

Lily gave Dash a sidelong glance, but her reproach was less effective than the light cuffing he received from Midge and Pinch.

"Sorry," he said. "Wot's a proper word for bugger?" He received a second cuffing for that.

It was not surprising this form of discipline from his friends became a tussle. Lily let them go, watching them only to make certain the wrestling did not become a fight where blows were exchanged in earnest. The day was simply too splendid to take exception to their antics. They rolled in the grass, first away from the lake, then perilously close to it. Laughing and shouting, they had the tireless energy of puppies as they crawled over one another in an effort to scramble up the bank toward the designated safe spot of the blanket.

When they finally arrived, they were panting hard. They collapsed around Lily, covering the blanket with sprawling limbs. She merely smiled. It was indeed a good life here.

It was the light rumble of the ground under the blanket that caused them to finally stir. Pinch lifted his dark head first, looking immediately to the road for the source of the vibration. Dash popped up next, then Midge. They each cupped an ear for better reception of the familiar sound.

"Is it 'is lordship's carriage?" Midge asked.

"Don't know yet," Pinch said.

Dash rose to his knees. "I think it might be."

Lily pushed herself up to her elbows. She'd also felt the vibration caused by the approaching carriage, but unlike the boys, it was never a question in her mind that it was anyone other than Sheridan.

Dash jumped to his feet as the horses appeared rounding the curve at the far side of the lake. He was quickly joined by the others, and they remained standing, greeting the arrival with long, sweeping waves of their raised arms.

Pinch glanced over his shoulder at Lily. "Do you think he saw us?"

"If he's in the carriage, I'm certain that he did."

"You didn't wave." His tone was more curious than accusing. "Aren't you glad he's returned?"

"It's good that he's back safely, yes." It was not quite an answer to Pinch's question, but it was all that Lily was prepared to say on the subject. The boys fell on one another again just as if there had been no interruption. This time Lily stopped them, raising her voice just above their laughter. "Shall we begin the lesson?" she asked. "Gather your ships and let's go to the water."

That was where Sherry came upon them not long after. He stood higher on the bank and off to one side, loath to draw attention to himself while the boys and Lily were so engrossed in their activity.

They were all standing where the water could lap at their bare feet and ankles. Shoes and stockings had been flung in the grass just beyond the reach of the wavelets. Jackets lay scattered on the bank as well. The boys wore their shirts only loosely tucked, and there were large damp patches on each of them. The short pants were unbuttoned and rolled above their knees, and Midge looked as if he might have already taken a spill.

For practical reasons, Lily's attire was similarly disheveled. Her skirt and petticoat were hiked halfway up her slim calves and held in place by the shawl wrapped around her waist. She wore a broad straw hat and an apron to protect her calico dress, and she had her sleeves rolled back to her elbows.

It was Sherry's observation that not only did she look perfectly at her ease, but with no effort on her part she lent the notion of disarray a certain elegance.

He stood awhile longer, watching them huddle around the ships. Lily bent several times and fiddled with Dash's replica of the Egyptian single mast, adjusting the boom at its foot. Dash looked on worriedly, while Pinch and Midge impatiently shifted their weight from one foot to the other wanting the race to be underway. Their ships, a Roman merchantman with twin topsails and a long, shallow, square-rigged vessel like the Vikings might have used, were harbored safely between their legs.

"Is there a problem?" Sherry asked as he approached. The scoundrels greeted him with open smiles; Lily's was more reserved. It also seemed to him that she was no longer so completely at ease. It made him wonder if he had stayed away too long from Granville or not long enough. "May I see the ship? I should like to have a go at it."

Since Lily had the vessel in her hands, she began to move to the bank with it. The boys started to follow as well, talking over one another as they welcomed Sherry's return.

"Did ye see us waving?" Pinch asked. "We knew it was ye come back to Granville before we saw yer carriage proper."

"Like rumblin' thunder, it was," Midge told him.

Dash nodded. "But it was just under the blanket, rollin' through the ground. It's good o' yer lordship to come back for the races. 'Ow'd ye know they would be today?"

Pinch jabbed Dash with a sharp elbow. "'E ain't come back for the races. 'E come back because the bleedin' party's ended." He glanced guiltily at Sheridan. "Beggin' yer lordship's pardon."

Sherry schooled his smile and held up a hand. "You should be begging the lady's pardon, Master Pinch."

Pinch dutifully turned to Lily and made a most sincere apology. Not quite under his breath, he added, "I did 'ear 'im tell Mr. Kearns it would be a bloody dull affair, though."

Sherry cleared his throat and accepted Lily's gently arched eyebrow as the reproach that was due him. Pinch, he noted, escaped a reprimand for listening at doors *and* tattling. "Let's have a look at that boat, shall we?"

Lily started to approach, but Sherry stayed her when he began to unbutton his frock coat. "My lord?"

"Stay where you are, Miss Rose. I shall come to you." It was a bit of a struggle to remove the close-fitting frock coat, but he managed the thing just as Dash was about to step forward to tug on a sleeve. He handed it to the boy to place with the others, then dropped to the ground to remove his boots and stockings. Midge collected those items and tossed them up the bank away from the water.

"Yer stock, m'lord," Pinch said. "It'll fall as limp as a fop's wrist if you wade in with it."

"Pinch!" Lily said.

"Wot? It will." He waggled his wrist up and down to show the full effect of such limpness. "Just see if it don't."

"It's all right," Sherry told Lily quickly. To his way of thinking Pinch had shown remarkable restraint in not referencing any other part of a male's anatomy that had occasion to go limp. "I'm removing it now." He tugged on the neckcloth, loosed an intricate knot, then unwound it. Dash was at the ready to take it and pitch it up the bank.

Sherry stepped up to the water's edge, rolled his trousers halfway to his knees, then waded in. Silt squished between his toes. When the wind lifted, it pressed his shirt to his chest and rippled his dark hair. He grinned quite openly at Lily, holding out his hand for the ship. "You would do well to temper your astonishment, Miss Rose, lest a sand swallow mistake your mouth for a nesting place."

Lily's jaw snapped shut. She placed the ship in Sheridan's outstretched palms, almost daring him to repair the thing.

"It appears to be the boom," he said unnecessarily. He gave Lily full marks for not speaking from behind clenched teeth. "It was no easy task to secure the first time." He pulled it out and examined the end. "It requires a bit of trimming. Do any of you lads have a knife?"

It was Lily who produced one from inside her apron pocket. She accepted the ship back while he trimmed the boom.

"I think a notch is the answer here, Master Dash. It is too bad we did not arrive at that solution at the outset." From the corner of his eye he saw that Dash was fairly twitching in place, twisting one tail of his shirt in his hands and rocking on the balls of his feet. He was also studying the water, not regarding the improvement in the design of the ship. Sherry was late to the realization that Dash had not told Lily that there had been help with the project. From the manner in which Pinch and Midge had also fallen quiet, Sherry suspected they had kept the same secret.

"You will want to know, Miss Rose, that I pressed the lads to permit me to assist them with their ships. It is a particular fondness of mine, and they were good enough to indulge me."

"Truly."

Sherry decided the only way she could have served up more cynicism was if she had used a platter. "Certainly," he said. "When I was not much older than they are, I built an armada. Cybelline sunk the thing right over there." He pointed to a small outcropping of rocks where a pair of ducks were preening. "As I recall, it was revenge for some trick she thought I'd played her. I had not, of course, because one doesn't play tricks on women. Right, lads? One is fair minded and honest in their dealings with women."

There was a lot of nodding of heads and some cautious optimism that they would be out of Dutch and back in Lily's good graces. Lily, however, was made of sterner stuff.

"This principled conscience of yours," she said, "the one that compels you to deal fairly and honestly with women, would it make an exception, mayhap, when you wish to protect three young scoundrels who applied to you for help against the express wish of their governess?"

"Ye've done it now," Pinch said under his breath.

Midge nodded. "Riled 'er up good and proper."

Dash hung his head more pitifully than before. "Never knew anyone to 'ave the knack of it the way ye do."

Lily cocked an eyebrow at Sheridan. "It's no good, my lord. You cannot be both abashed *and* amused. One rather negates the other. You would do well to study these poor fellows and learn how it is done."

"You are a harsher critic than my own governess," he said. "She was taken in often enough."

"That is because she wasn't taught by the good sisters at Sacred Heart." Lily held out the model ship. "Can you repair it?"

Nodding, Sherry finished making the notch in the boom and reattached it. He tested it several times, saw it would hold, then raised his hands to indicate he was done.

Lily returned the vessel to Dash and accepted her knife back from Sheridan. "Thank you. It was good of you to lend assistance."

Sherry inclined his head. "Do we begin now?"

"You wish to stay?"

He did not mistake that she was not eager for him to do so. "Of course. It is to be a boat race, isn't it?"

"It's to be a science lesson disguised as boat race."

"Even better. Science is also a passion."

"Very well." Lily led the way to slightly deeper water and directed the boys to hold their boats for a moment. "Let us examine the hulls, shall we? Do you see why the Roman merchantman is called a round ship? Now look at the narrow lines of the Viking vessel. Can you tell me how they will perform differently in the water?"

Sherry stood slightly back from them, offering no comment but listening to everything. He observed that Lily did not condescend to her pupils. She challenged them. The questions she put to them had no simple answers but required that they consider ideas they had learned in the classroom and put them to use. If she addressed a notion they had not yet discussed, she required them to experiment and employ their own eyes to draw conclusions. They were allowed to ask questions freely; in fact, she encouraged them. When she didn't know an answer she applied herself to arriving at one by the same methods she asked them to use. If she was not satisfied with the breadth of her own knowledge, she was not so proud that she could not turn to him for help.

In precisely that fashion, Sherry found himself being included in the lesson, part teacher, part student, all admiration.

The boat races proved to be more exciting than any of them anticipated. The Viking longship, with its simple square-rigged sail and narrow hull, was the winner more often than not, though with no Lilliputian aboard to turn the deep oar, it frequently went off course. Since the Roman round ship and the Egyptian barge sailed off course as well, they had a good time of it predicting where they would run aground.

Midge fell into deep water first, though whether by design or accident was a question Lily raised when Sherry hauled him back safely. Pinch announced in dramatic tones that his ship was in danger of falling off the edge of the earth and promptly dove after it. Once again, Sherry was called up to make the rescue. When Dash slipped under, Sherry responded by bringing him up and promptly pushing him down again.

Lily waded away and sat down in the grass while the boys—and there were four of them now—splashed and leaped and dived and sputtered. They abandoned their ships first, then gleefully sank them. Hoisting each child in turn, Sheridan hurled them like cannonballs at the vessels.

"The captain goes down with the ship, lads. It's the law on the high seas."

"But we're pirates! We 'ave no 'onor!" Pinch's protest came to nothing as Sheridan tossed him anyway.

The splash was large enough to reach Lily on the bank. She didn't flinch from it. The spray of water stung far less than her tears.

* * *

It was little more than an hour after Sheridan took his dinner that he came upon Lily in the garden. Although he hadn't inquired, the boys told him where she was when he went to bid them good night. It was, of course, one of the reasons he sought them out.

She was sitting on a stone bench, looking out toward the lake. An unopened book lay in her lap, her place marked by the insertion of her index finger. Her posture was erect, even stiffly held, and he wondered if it had become so in anticipation of his approach. Surrounded on three sides as she was by the palest of pink roses and deep emerald leaves, the effect was rather like she was wearing them as a mantle.

"Miss Rose," he said quietly. "You are aptly named, I think, for your presence here compliments this garden. Will you permit me to join you?"

"Surely that is your choice." She did not turn to look at him. "I am not long for this place. It is growing too dark to read."

Sherry chose not to be put off by her lack of enthusiasm. "Then I will remain so that I can escort you back." He indicated the book in her lap. "Another novel?"

"No. *Chemical Philosophy*."

"Davy's work?"

She nodded. "There are many books like this in your library. You were sincere this afternoon when you said that science was a passion."

"I was, though you sound as if you cannot credit it. By my reckoning, you have been in residence at Granville every bit of two months. After so much time, how can you doubt that I am an enlightened, scientific farmer? I am certain I had less difficulty arriving at the conclusion that you were more in the way of a teacher than a governess." Sherry joined her on the bench, stretching his legs and bracing his arms slightly behind him. Infinitely more at his ease than Lily, he nevertheless looked out over the lake as she was doing. "I hope you will allow that I am more in the way of a farmer than a lord."

A smile flickered across her lips. "I will allow that it requires more study."

"That satisfies for the time being." He crossed his legs at the ankles. "Your lesson this afternoon was extraordinary. I have not been involved in the like since I was at Cambridge. Is that how you were taught at the abbey?"

"It was how Sister Mary Joseph taught." She regarded Sherry askance. "I imagine you would say she was an enlightened, scientific nun. She embraced faith and reason, though not without some argument from the Reverend Mother and Bishop Corbeil."

"She persevered."

"Always."

Sherry thought he caught a trace of wistful admiration in Lily's tone. "She is still there?"

"I don't know."

"You've never written her."

It was more statement than question, but Lily responded anyway. "Never." When Sherry said nothing, she found herself filling the silence. "I never judged it prudent to do so."

From Sherry's perspective it seemed a curious choice of words. "Did you run away from the abbey, Lily?" He was close enough to her to feel the slight tremor that slipped under her skin. Glancing down, he saw her slim fingers tighten around the book. "Are you still running from there?"

Lily stared across the terraced gardens. Dusk was leeching the color from the roses and creating gray-green shadows along the boxwoods. "Is it so important that you know?"

"Yes, I think it is."

"Why?"

Sherry regarded her profile. She was as still as the stone she sat on, perhaps just as cold. "Can you not imagine that I'd like to help you?"

"If it is because I took a shiv for you, it is not at all necessary. I did not mean to get stabbed, you know, only to deflect the villain's aim. If it will help you feel less beholden to me, then you should know that I am not at all certain I would do it again."

He merely lifted a brow.

His silence caused her to glance in his direction. "You don't believe me."

"I did not say so, did I?"

"You are maddening."

"Yes. And you are obstinate beyond reason." He paused a moment, then said quietly, "I find that I like you immensely, Lily. It also occurs to me that you will have more difficulty coming to terms with that than I did."

"Then you did not embrace the idea at the outset?"

"No. Heavens no."

She chuckled a little then. "Pray, do not spare my feelings."

The corners of Sherry's mouth lifted in a faint smile. "I embrace the idea now."

"You should not."

He shrugged.

"You will not change your mind?"

"About liking you? I think not. About wanting to help you? That answer is also no."

Lily stood so suddenly that she fairly vibrated. She turned on him. "I think you will," she said. Then she ended the discussion by abruptly walking away.

In some ways she was predictable, so Sherry did not evince any surprise when Lily let herself into his bedchamber several hours later. He was not yet abed but sitting in a wing chair near the window. A candelabra on the side table illuminated his still figure and the open book on his lap. He closed it slowly and set it aside.

"If you mean to stay," he said, "then shut the door."

Lily stood only a few steps beyond the threshold, more in

the room than not, but hesitant of a sudden. Her hand rested on the door handle; she twisted it absently.

"You must choose," he told her. "In or out."

She released the handle and gave the door a nudge with her fingertips to push it closed. "You have been expecting me."

Sherry almost smiled at her soft, accusatory tone. Instead, he made certain his expression remained as neutral and unrevealing as his voice. "It occurred that you might come, yes. Does that put you off your purpose?"

Lily shook her head.

"Very well. What is it that you require of me?"

"What do you mean?"

"Should I remain where I am so that you might say your prayers, or do you wish to have me on the bed?" He watched her eyes dart in that direction. "Kearns turned down the covers, but that is his nightly ritual and for my benefit. It was not done in anticipation that you would come here."

Lily caught her lower lip between her teeth. "Perhaps the bed."

"Of course." Sherry stood and moved toward it. "It will not have escaped your notice that I am not yet in my nightclothes. Will you undress me or should I manage the thing myself?"

Rooted to the floor, Lily took in a deep breath and let it shudder through her on release. "Why are you doing this?"

He cocked an eyebrow at her. "You will have to explain yourself."

"I thought you would . . ." She looked at her reflection in the dark mirror that the window had become. "I thought you would not want me. You did not before."

"Yet in spite of what you thought, here you are."

"Yes."

"Because you mean to seduce me."

She nodded.

"You mean to make me want you against my will."

Lily nodded again.

"And give me disgust of you. Perhaps you even hope I'll send you away."

Her eyes dropped to the floor. Her voice was but a thread of sound. "Yes."

"Then you have forgotten our kiss at the stone wall, Lily. I have not." Watching her, taking in the whole of the subdued manner in which she held herself, Sherry realized he had at last stumbled on the true purpose of her visit. Seducing him, giving him disgust of her, were but a means to an end. Now he needed to understand that end. "Why," he asked. "Why do you hope I will send you away?"

"Because I cannot go."

This admission was made so quietly it was more an exhalation of breath than speech. It was also reluctantly offered. Sheridan could only guess at the cost to her pride. "Look at me, Lily."

She lifted her head; her eyes were luminous.

"You must not depend on me to make you go," Sherry said. "You cannot seduce me, Lily. Nor give me disgust of you. You cannot make me want you against my will because I find that wanting you is in every way my will."

She blinked. Tears spilled over the rim of her lashes. "You do not mean that."

His gentle smile chided her. "I think I know my own mind." He held out his hand to her. "Will you not come here?" When she didn't move, not even to shake her head, Sherry's smile deepened. "Very well. It is better, perhaps, that I come to you." In only a few measured steps, he closed the distance between them and stood directly in front of her. He saw the effort she made to hold his gaze. Her hands twisted in the fabric of her robe, and her breathing came quick and shallow. "Take measure of my sincerity, Lily. I like you. I want to help you. I also want to lie with you. What we shall make of it, I don't know."

The honesty of this last statement simply stole her breath. The offer or a single promise about a future together would have been suspect. More than that, it would have been a lie.

Whatever they might make of one night together would not be a future, but another day. It might become a sennight, a fortnight, a month, then a season . . .

It was too much to contemplate, an impossible idea to hold before her. Feeling helpless in the face of it—and not liking any part of that feeling—Lily wished the ground would simply swallow her.

Her distress was so palpable that Sherry wondered that she remained standing. "I would like to hold you," he said. "May I?"

She pressed her lips together, then nodded once.

Sherry was skeptical; his eyebrows lifted a fraction. "It shouldn't be against your will."

Lily dashed away tears at the corners of her eyes. "It's not."

He still didn't move to take her in his arms, but watched her closely. It was not possible for him to know what held her back. He decided to risk a guess. "Are you afraid of me, Lily?"

"Of you, a little." She caught her lower lip between her teeth for a moment, then told him, "Of me? You cannot imagine."

Sherry laid his hands lightly on her upper arms. Although she didn't flinch, he could feel the tremor of her body under his palms. He let his hands fall down the length of her arms until he had her wrists. A tug was all it would have taken to pull her close, but he didn't do that. Instead, it was Sherry who took one more step forward, raising Lily's arms, and entered the circle of her embrace. When he released her wrists, her hands remained at his sides, and he slipped his own around her back.

Bending his head, he kissed the crown of her hair and breathed deeply of her fragrance. "You were sitting among the roses, yet your scent is lavender."

Lily turned her face and pressed her cheek against his shoulder. "Will you let me go?" she asked.

Surprised, he began to draw away. "Of course."

"No!" Lily tightened her embrace and did not release him. "No. Not now. I did not mean now." She waited until his hands returned to the small of her back. "If I must go, if I find that it can be no other way, am I free to leave at any time or will you . . ."

When she trailed off, clearly caught by some emotion Sherry could not name, he prompted her softly. "Will I . . . what? What do you need to know?"

"Will you hold me whether I wish it or not?"

Sherry realized then Lily was not speaking literally of this embrace but of something much larger. She was asking about her choices, her right to make them. She was asking about her very freedom. He could not help but wonder at the experience that pressed her to ask the question. "You may leave Granville at any time, Lily. I hope knowing that will prevent you from leaving in the dead of night without any word of your intent to do so. I would rather see you off safely than discover you've run away." He caught her under the chin with his index finger and tilted her head so that she might look at him. "Now, tell me that in this matter, at least, you will trust me."

With her chin poised on his finger as it was, it was not possible for Lily to merely nod. She must speak the words aloud—for him, certainly, but for herself, more importantly. He was something beyond clever; he was diabolical.

"I think you are used to getting whatever you want," she said, "but in spite of that, I trust you."

" 'I trust you' would have been sufficient," he said with a certain wryness. Still holding her chin at the desired angle, Sherry bent his head. When his mouth was but a hairsbreadth from her, he whispered, "I hope there are not a great many rules this time."

"No."

Her response presented him with her lovely open mouth just as he'd known it would. He kissed her lightly at first, then with mounting pressure, drawing her closer with a hand at her back while dropping the other from her chin. The taste of her was not precisely what he remembered, but something more besides. Not sweet, but sweeter. Not yielding, but giving.

She stood on tiptoe and leaned into him and was supported by his chest, sheltered by his shoulders. Her body bowed, pulled taut by her reach for him, then by her need. This experience of wanting was new to her. Did he know? She hoped he would know.

Her hands lifted to his head; her fingers threaded through his dark hair. She felt the tip of his tongue sweep across her upper lip. His teeth caught her lower one, and he bit down gently. Heat uncurled inside her so quickly, and with such force, that she gasped.

Sherry raised his head immediately. "Did I hurt you?"

"No." She pressed her fingers against his scalp with just enough force to bring him back to her. Her open-mouthed kiss rocked him back on his heels and lifted her off the floor. She engaged his tongue, teasing him at first, then with mounting urgency, and the fever pitch of wanting did not pass as she was maneuvered toward the bed. It was only when she felt the mattress at the back of her thighs that the enormity of what she would do with this man was borne home to her.

"Lily?" Sherry drew a ragged breath and forced a calm he did not feel. She was still holding him, still flush to his body, yet there was tension in her now that had not been there a moment ago. It was not the strain of wanting to be closer to him that he felt, but the resistance of someone who wanted to be away. He let his hands fall from her and took a step backward. This time she did not stop him. He did not miss that her own breathing was unsteady or that composure was hard won. "Do you mean to end it now?"

Her head snapped up. It had not occurred to her that he would think that. "Could I?"

"It will most likely kill me, but yes, you can end it and go now if you wish."

"I do not wish it."

His brow furrowed. "Then why are we not kissing?"

That was more difficult to explain. She had the sensation of the bed behind her again, of being forced down with him lying heavily on top of her. What she said was, "I should like it if you undressed now."

"Truly."

He offered this with such perfect blandness, his expression shuttered, that Lily could not tell if he was horrified or amused but thought it might be some part of each. "Yes," she said. "Truly."

"Will you assist?"

"If you like."

He did. "I think, Miss Rose, that you mean to seduce me after all."

Lily's eyes widened a fraction. "No, I just—"

"It's all right," he said. "I don't mind if you do. In fact, I believe when done by you, it has much to recommend it."

"It does?"

"Mmm." He tugged on his stock. "Will you help me with my neckcloth?"

Her hesitation was brief. "Very well." She stepped forward and brushed his hands aside. "Mr. Kearns ties a prodigiously intricate cravat."

"He would be pleased you think so. It is the Mathematical."

Lily's fingers deftly managed the knots and folds and at last removed the linen from around Sheridan's neck. "Perhaps you will be able to carry on."

"The coat is always deuced difficult to remove," he said. "My tailor likes a tight line across the shoulders. For the posture, he says. For the torture of the *ton*, I say."

"Deserved, no doubt." Lily unfastened the two brass buttons that closed his sage green frock coat and slipped her fingers under the fabric near the wide lapels. She lifted and nudged, moving it carefully over his broad shoulders. She could feel his eyes on her, could hear his indrawn breath. He helped her by shrugging, first one shoulder, then the other. Lily tugged on the sleeves at his wrists and finally removed it. When she would have taken it away to hang in the dressing room, he stopped her, plucked it out of her hands, and pitched it over his shoulder. It landed on the floor near the cold fireplace.

"Kearns will scold me," he said. "He will never know you are in any way to blame."

"I am *not* to blame."

He kissed her. Hard. Insistent. Pressing. It was meant to be brief, serving only as a reminder of all the reasons that she *was* to blame, but in spite of the intention, it lingered, softened, and became reason enough to continue in the same vein. Sweetly pliant and damp, her lips moved under his. She warmed to the kiss, returning it measure for measure, making it something that was not done to her but something that she was doing as well.

Her breasts swelled. The budding points of her nipples scraped against his waistcoat. The heat that she'd felt unfold before became a flush that rose from her breasts to her face. Her fingers tightened on his arms; she required his steadiness as she lost her way.

It was Sheridan who broke the kiss, his head rearing back as he caught his breath. If he thought she would not have bolted for the door, he would have carried her straightaway to his bed. "My waistcoat," he said as though it were a perfectly reasonable concern. "There is still my waistcoat."

Lily nodded. She laid her palms at the front of his chest, then slid them slowly down until she had the first button between her fingers. The tremor in her hands was invisible to the eye, but she could feel it under her skin. She slipped the first button through the opening, paused, then did the same to the second. In moments the waistcoat went the way of Sheridan's frock coat. She noticed he did not even glance back to see where it landed. Had there been a fire in the hearth, the garment would have been lost to him.

"Your lordship is careless with his clothing," she said.

"The shirt, Lily."

"Yes, of course. Will you raise your arms, or shall I rend it?"

"By God, you tempt me." He lifted his arms and bent slightly forward so that she might have her way with him.

Feigning more confidence than she felt, Lily caught Sheridan's muslin shirt at the waist, pulled the tails free of his trousers, and took it from him. She held it aloft, out of his reach, and made to throw it as he had done.

"Not my shirt," he said, making a grab for it. "It is from Thorndike's on Bond Street." When Lily hesitated, he stole it from her and tossed it over his shoulder himself. "You would never be able to face Kearns if you were careless with it."

"So you were saving me."

"Indeed."

It was that fractional lift to his eyebrow that made Lily's heartbeat trip over itself. She felt heat rising once again and knew her cheeks would be stained with color. He must wonder that she could be so easily unsettled. Flooded by a wave of panic, she blurted out, "I'm not a virgin."

"Neither am I."

She gave him full marks for not so much as blinking. Hers had been a breathless declaration, and he had handled it manfully, giving her the gallant reply. He might just as easily have reproached her for stating the obvious since he had once been moved to inquire if she was a whore. "That is good, then. There will be no surprises for either of us."

Sherry most sincerely doubted that. Though he hadn't moved, he was still reeling from her last ill-timed confession. He felt as though he should adopt the stance of a sailor at sea, legs parted, knees slightly bent, body turned from the wind, all of this in aid of keeping him upright in the face of Lily's unorthodox seduction.

"My boots," he said. "What is your pleasure?"

"What is yours?"

If she had not already dropped to her knees before him on another occasion, he might have found it erotic to have her there. He suspected now that nothing good could come of re-creating that scene. "I will remove them myself." He deliberately did not fall back into a chair but returned to the bed to sit. He raised his right leg, setting his ankle over the knee of the left, and took off the boot. His stocking followed, then he did the same with the other.

He patted the space beside him. "Perhaps you will join me here." Lily's gaze, he noticed, wandered everywhere but at him. When she was sitting at his side, he asked, "Is there anything at all you wish to tell me, Lily?"

She shook her head. "I should like to extinguish the candles, though."

"By all means." As soon as she rose again to do so, Sherry lay back on the bed and cradled his head in this clasped hands. He watched her snuff the candelabra on the side table, the candlestick on the writing desk, then draw the curtains before she arrived at the bedstand. When she extinguished this last flame the bedchamber was thrown into almost complete darkness. Only gradually as his eyes adjusted did Sherry see the slip of light coming through a part in the drapes and from under the door.

The light did not matter. He had already memorized the look of her. He had carried it with him when he left Granville for the house party at Sir Arthur's. Through better than a week of insipid conversation and predictable entertainments, made bearable only by the presence of Lady Rivendale and his host, Sherry had kept Lily's image in his mind. He did not question the unfairness of comparing her to every eligible female of his acquaintance during the rout, not when it was the company that he found lacking. Among his peers, she had none. Her conversation was more interesting, her mind more lively, and her hair in every way more extraordinary.

He was on the point of convincing himself he was misremembering the particulars of her, that perhaps her eyes were not so bright a green, nor her lips so lush in their line, when he arrived home and saw her by the lake. From the distance of the road he could make out neither eyes nor mouth, only the sweet curve of her figure in recline on the blanket, but he knew she was entertained by the antics of the scoundrels waving to him and rolling willy-nilly on the grass. No, he had not been mistaken about any part of her countenance.

He felt her come to stand beside the bed, and with some sixth sense, he found her hand. "Will you lie with me, Lily?" Sherry could not see her nod, but when she did not remove her hand from his, he knew what her answer was. He moved closer to the center of the bed and felt the depression at his side when she sat.

Lily bent her head and unerringly found his mouth. Her kiss was light, a mere promise of what he could expect. "You are a foolish man," she whispered against his lips, "to take me into your bed. And I am perhaps more foolish yet for allowing you to do it."

And lest there be even the smallest sting to her words, she removed it with a second kiss, this one in the shape of her smile.

Sherry's fingers undid the knotted sash at Lily's waist and pushed her robe over her shoulders. The slippery satin fell soundlessly to the floor, joining every other discarded garment. The light batiste of her shift was as insubstantial as a cloud. When she settled against him, he felt only the heat of her skin and nothing of the barrier that separated them.

Lily slipped her fingers through his hair. He had not had it trimmed since his arrival at Granville, and now it curled at his nape on the precipice of being unfashionably long. She let her short nails lightly scrape his skin and felt him shiver in reaction, then she lowered her mouth once again to his.

There would be no turning back from this.

She kissed the corner of his lips, his jaw. She nudged his cheek with hers, turning his head aside so that she might catch his earlobe between her teeth. Her tongue darted out, and she heard his low, throaty chuckle. She returned to his mouth, deepening the kiss until they were sharing a single breath between them, then she pulled back, slipped lower, and ducked her head against his throat and sipped his skin.

He arched under her, lifting her body but not overturning her. His hands caught her shoulders. He was careful to steady, not restrain. The way she moved over him was maddeningly thorough. No woman had ever been so openly curious about his body. There was no artifice here, no guile. She might know what would please, but she wanted to learn what pleased *him*. Until now, Sherry had not collected there was such a vast difference in the two.

It was the darkness, he suspected, that allowed her to touch him so freely. In his London library she had been bold, but she had also been angry and afraid. She was different now, driven by different emotions, and though he could not say with certainty what they were, he welcomed them over what had come before.

His skin retracted when her fingers slipped under his drawers. At her urging, he lifted and she drew them down. Her hand circled his erection. He groaned softly at the back of his throat as her fingers explored its length and girth. She cupped his balls, squeezed lightly, and swallowed the next sound he made by covering his mouth with hers. Her hand continued to move, stroking, massaging, wresting one guttural utterance from him after another and taking them all into herself. He was hard and heavy in her hand, hot with the surging and pulsing of blood. His upper lip beaded with perspiration. His hair clung damply to the back of his neck. The rhythm she found was his own, synchronous with his breathing, his heartbeat, the contraction of muscles. His hands fell away from her and clenched the sheets. His head tipped back, dislodging Lily's mouth but exposing his throat. She nestled her lips in the curve of his neck and sucked.

It was then he thought he would come out of his skin. Every muscle in his body tensed; his heels dug into the bed. She was leaving her brand on his throat, and her hand was still fisted around his cock, squeezing, sliding, milking him.

He reached for her, intent on finding her wrists and pulling her away. Or pulling her closer. He was not at all certain that he knew what he wanted better than she did. In the end it didn't matter because she eluded him, and he was left to clutch the sheets a second time, straining against pleasure on the verge of pain, almost shouting with frustration when she released him.

Every part of his body vibrated with tension she had created and now abandoned.

"Bloody hell," he whispered hoarsely. "Bloody, bloody—"

Smiling, Lily rose to her knees and straddled him. "Shall I take you inside, my lord?"

Nine

Lily lifted herself as though to move away. "My lord?"

Sherry realized the strangled sound he'd made was not answer enough for her. "If you do not, I am certain to die of wanting you to."

The rasp in his voice raised a shiver. She leaned over him, found his mouth, and made this kiss only about sustaining his anticipation a few moments longer. It was when she raised herself a second time that she took him in hand and slowly seated herself until he was deep inside her.

She remained still for a time, taking measured breaths, glad for the darkness that kept him from seeing her face. Accommodating the uncomfortable pressure of joining required that she bite her lower lip until she tasted blood. It seemed that her body remembered the act well enough but had forgotten the nuanced pain of it.

"Lily?" Sherry slipped his hands under her shift and found her thighs. He caressed her lightly from knee to hip, his thumbs running along the inner side until he brushed the soft curling hair of her *mons*. He meant to say something more, certainly he meant to hear her reply, but then she lifted herself, and his palms were under her bottom, helping her rise, and the pressure in his fingertips was communicating the cadence of the ride.

Closing her eyes, Lily moved slowly at first, guided as much by his breathing and the small sounds she wrested from him as she was by his hands on her hips and buttocks. While the sense of fullness never left her, she found she was able to tolerate it and that she could contract around him so that when his breath hitched and his fingers tightened, it was only pleasure that he felt.

She rose and fell and rose again, her rhythm quickening. He bucked, driving himself powerfully into her. She pressed her moan back by flattening her mouth and breathing through her nose and gauged his arousal by the movements he could not seem to help.

It was when his entire frame went taut under her that she drew him out again with an intimate contraction. His fingertips pressed whitely into her flesh and he arched, not to dislodge her but to take her as deeply as he could. She felt his shudder, the spasm of his body as he gave her his seed, then the quieting of his muscles as tension left them.

She made to rise a final time and found herself caught by his hands on her hips. He did not exert a great deal of force, indeed, she did not think he had the strength to do so, but it was enough to let her know he wanted her to remain exactly as she was. It occurred to her to remind him of his promise to let her go but did not say so aloud. She had not extracted that promise from him for a moment such as this, and using it now would be foolish when she was certain to have need of it later.

All that was required was that she wait him out. She was not unduly discomfited by remaining joined to him, and she liked the steady thrum of his heartbeat and the warmth of his body. Leaning forward a small fraction, she laid her palms lightly on his chest and ran them up to his shoulders then down to his waist. His skin was smooth, resilient. Her fingertips lingered over the contrasting textures of flesh over muscle and bone and the arrow of crisp hair that began below his navel and went to his groin.

"What is this?" she asked, tapping the star-shaped cicatrix just above his left hip. It had all the markings of a pistol ball wound. "Were you shot?"

"Yes." He removed her hand. In order to do so he had to release her hip. It was that moment's inattention that permitted her to lift herself away from him. "It is of no account."

Lily righted the hem of her nightshirt until it covered her knees, then she lay on her back beside him. No part of her touched him. "Was it a duel?"

"No." Sherry sat up, found the flint on the table, and struck it. He felt Lily stirring as soon as she realized his intent, but he was quicker bringing the candlelight to her than she was escaping it. He held the candledish aloft, out of her reach, and pinned her back with his hard, black glance. When she raised her hand, he suspected it was done more in the way of hiding her face than shielding her eyes.

Sherry was having none of it. He grasped her wrist and lowered her hand, easily overcoming what resistance she offered. She blinked up at him, and the wariness of her expression struck him as a blow.

"Was none of it for you, then?" he asked.

She frowned. "I don't know what you mean."

God help him, he thought, she didn't. Her face was pale, the flush of that first arousal had vanished under cover of darkness. Her bottom lip was swollen, though not with the bee-stung appearance of one who had been thoroughly kissed. Her own teeth marks were still imprinted in the line, and a droplet of blood welled up from a cut on the underside. Strands of hair clung damply to her forehead and at her nape. She did not seem to know that her eyes held proof of a wounded soul.

"You let me hurt you," he said. "No, don't deny it and lie to me as well as to yourself." He set the candle aside and threw his legs over the far side of the bed. "Do not move."

Naked, he padded to the dressing room and drew water for his own ablutions, then hers. He carried the basin back to the bed, wet the flannel and wrung it out, then gently pressed one corner of it to Lily's swollen mouth. He held it against the droplet of welling blood. "I wish you had stopped me, Lily. You could have, you know. At any time." She looked as if she might say something, but he halted her with a glance. "It was unfair of you to make me think it was what you wanted, too. That you took no pleasure in it is lowering enough. That it was painful for you shames me."

Sherry removed the cloth from her lip, dampened it again, then asked her to raise her shift. He watched her fingers curl in the batiste, but she didn't gather it up. "Did I rend you, Lily? I cannot see what damage has been done. No, do not clamp down on your lip again. We both will be better served by your answer than by more bloodshed."

"I do not think I am bleeding," she said, her voice not much above a whisper. "I told you I am not a virgin."

"That is of no account. You weren't prepared to take me; of course you can bleed." He took her wrist, pried open her hand, and placed the wet cloth in her palm. "I will give you some privacy." Sherry not only turned away, he left the bed and retrieved his robe from the armoire in the dressing room. When he returned, he did not glance at the bed but went straightaway to the window. After drawing back the curtains and securing them, he lifted the latch and pushed the window open. Moonlight glanced off the lake. A light breeze ruffled his hair. He breathed deeply of its freshness. Somehow it was the scent of lavender that was lifted to his nostrils.

"I am finished," she said. "There was only a little blood."

He nodded once but did not turn.

"I do not think there is any stain on the sheets."

Sherry swore softly. "God's truth, Lily, do you think I give a damn about the sheets?" He spun on his heel. She was sitting up now, her knees drawn to her chest and her shift pulled tightly across the tops. He recognized the hedgehog posture she used to protect herself. "Why did you not have the great good sense to stop? How long has it been since you had a lover?"

Lily's eyebrows lifted. "I have never had a lover. I have had men."

Sherry's gut twisted a little. Here was confirmation at last that there had been more than one. "Lovers. Men. What is the difference?"

She shrugged. "Perhaps it is only that I imagined there must be. You are the first man I ever had of my own choosing, so I thought you might also be my first lover. You are right that I allowed you to hurt me. That, too, was of my own choosing, and I do not regret it save for the fact that you do. It seems that in wanting to pleasure you, I have given you disgust of me after all."

Sherry pressed one hand to his temple and massaged lightly. He sighed. "You unman me, Lily, and you are right to do so. I have given no thought to any feelings save my own. I bear no disgust of you." Even watching her closely, he could see no indication that she believed him. "I want to be your lover. I want to know that when we make love that it is always of your own choosing and that you will never again exchange my pleasure for your pain. It can be no other way, else it is for all intents and purposes a rape."

She clasped her legs more tightly to her chest and nodded once.

"Is that all you have known?" he asked. "Has it been naught but rape, Lily?"

She was a long time answering. With great difficulty she admitted her deepest shame. "I did not always fight." Her eyes darted away from him, and she stared at the tops of her knees. "Toward the end, hardly at all. Perhaps not so often even in the beginning, though I'd like to think it was otherwise. It is not so easy to fight all the time, but you might not understand that. Men often don't, you know. Fighting is more in their nature, I suppose, than it is mine." She swallowed hard, dislodging the lump at the back of her throat to push the last words out. "There were too many times I just gave in."

Sherry went to the bed and sat down, swiveling sideways and drawing one knee up. "Sometimes surrender is the best fight you can make," he said quietly.

She glanced at him, uncertain.

"Could you have left if you'd never given in?"

A small vertical crease appeared between Lily's eyebrows, and she gave him her full attention.

"Where would you have found the strength to run?" he asked. "How would you have been able to plan to leave or take advantage of an opportunity to do so?" He laid his hand over hers. "You have nothing to be ashamed of, Lily. There is no reason for you to question your own courage when it is in every way the equal of men who stand on the front lines of the battlefield."

She looked from his face to the hand that covered hers. In light of what she'd told him, the fact that he was willing to touch her at all had the capacity to surprise. "You are good to say so, but—"

"I am not good, Lily. I am not even kind. I have committed acts that I once supposed would bankrupt my soul, and I did them for no other reason than I was asked. I had not even the courage of my own convictions, while you had no choice and never strayed once from your moral center. Do not suppose that you are the coward in this room or even the whore."

Lily cupped her hand around his and raised it to her lips. She kissed his knuckles, then turned his hand over and placed her mouth against the heart of his palm. "If you can think that I am no whore," she said, "then I can think you are a good and decent man."

Sherry stared at her, then nodded once. He used the hand she held to pull her away from the headboard and closer to him. "Will you let me love you, Lily?" He bent his head and whispered against her mouth, "Will you let me give you pleasure?"

She moaned softly. As a reply it was sufficiently eloquent. With only his mouth on hers he pressed her back to the sheets and stretched. She uncurled along the length of him, and her hands lifted to his shoulders. The silk dressing gown he wore was cool under her fingertips, but through it she could feel the heat of his skin.

"Tell me what you want," he said. He nudged her lips with his, wetting them with his tongue. "Do you like that?"

"Yes."

He did it again, flicking his tongue across her lips. "Will you like it inside your mouth?"

"I never have . . . save with you . . . ."

It was enough. He took advantage of the sweet opening she gave him and kissed her deeply. His tongue played over hers and drew out a response that he knew was genuine as her hips thrust forward and pressed against his groin. He slid one hand to her hip, stroking, but gentling also, and all the while he continued to kiss her.

He alternated the rhythm of the kiss, making it so languorous it was like a drug to the senses, then nibbling on her lips as though he meant only to tease a taste from her. "This?" he asked her, then his mouth found the delicate hollow just behind her ear.

"Mmm."

"And this?" The question vibrated against her skin as he went lower and sipped the skin in the curve of her neck.

"Mm-yes."

He dallied there for a while, using his teeth to worry her flesh then laving the spot with his tongue. Sherry felt her grow restless for something more, but he was content to remain where he was, making only short forays to her collarbone and the hollow at the base of her throat. When he finally pressed his mouth along the neckline of her shift her body fairly thrummed for him.

"Yes," she said without being asked.

He did not lift her shift or ask her to do so. His lips closed over her nipple through the batiste. He drew it into his mouth and sucked. Once dampened, the soft fabric became deliciously abrasive. He had only to drag it across her skin to make her feel as if his mouth was still there. It protected her when he rolled the bud between his teeth.

She made a sound that might have been a protest when he raised his head, but it died at the back of her throat as he bent again to give attention to her other breast. Her slender frame quivered. She did not know what to do with her hands.

"Hold on to me," he said. "I won't let you fall."

It seemed odd to her that it made sense. Her back was firmly against the mattress and she was in no danger of falling out of the bed, yet he had said the right words to her because he made her feel as if she were climbing. Pleasure rose like steps, and each time she placed one foot in front of the other she was also being lifted.

He had made her feel this heat in her belly before, and it had come to nothing. Now she felt it in her breasts, in her thighs, even in the tips of her fingers, and believed for the first time that there might be something more that would follow. The very air she breathed was warmer. The steady suck of his mouth was like a second pulse. Thin tongues of fire licked her skin, first over it, then under. Tiny darts of pleasure followed the same course as her blood, pooling between her thighs. The heaviness there was unfamiliar. So was the dampness.

She closed her eyes. Somehow he knew it was a mistake before she did.

"Look at me," Sherry said, his face hovering just above her. Her tension had been instantly communicated to him. "There is no one else here."

Lily pressed her lips together and nodded. "Your hand is—"

"Do you want me to remove it?" He began drawing it down her thigh toward her knee.

"No." It was no surprise to Lily that his hand was on her leg, only that it was on her *bare* leg. She could not remember him sliding it under her shift. "No," she repeated on a breathy sigh.

"And here?" he asked, slipping it over the curve of her thigh to her *mons*.

Her hips jerked, but it was not to get away from his touch. "That's right. Will you open for me, Lily?"

She had never been asked before. In that moment he gave her back some part of her self. Watching him, she slowly raised one knee. Her thighs parted, and his hand cupped her in a pocket of heat.

His kiss engaged all of her senses, and she rocked hard against his hand. She was glad she was holding on because she had not understood until she was falling just how high she had climbed.

This time pleasure was absolute in its release. No more tugging, no tiny darts. In free fall it spiraled out of control, and there was no part of her body left untouched by it. She inhaled sharply, then could not seem to release that breath. Caught by the need to move, she dug her heels into the mattress for purchase and finally cried out.

Sherry cradled her. Candlelight bathed Lily's face but did not account for the pink wash of color in her cheeks. She breathed softly and shallowly, and her mouth trembled as she sipped the air. This time when she closed her eyes, Sherry did not urge her to do otherwise. He held her in his arms long past the time she fell asleep.

When Lily woke she was in her own room with no memory of how she arrived there. Her recollection of detail until she fell asleep was remarkably clear, and she was grateful to have no time to dwell on it. She'd slept almost an hour longer than was her habit, and if she did not arrive in the schoolroom at the appointed time, the scoundrels would be upon her.

She washed, dressed, and decided to forego her morning

walk in favor of eating breakfast. The boys were helping themselves at the sideboard when she entered the dining room. Lord Sheridan, who normally took his morning meal in his room, was sitting at the head of the table sipping coffee and reading from a folded newspaper.

He lowered the paper just a fraction so that he might view her over the top. "Good morning," he said. His eyes fell back on the paper, and he resumed reading.

Lily wished him the same, though she did not think her voice was half so cool as his. She greeted the boys with more enthusiasm and helped herself at the sideboard when they moved on. Pinch was waiting for her at the table and held out a chair.

"Thank you," she said. "Master Midge, will you pass the jam?" She spread a dollop of it on a triangle of toast. "Have any of you given thought to where we might begin today? I am all for doing sums." She expected this would be met by some sort of protest, at the very least a groan from Dash who hadn't the same skill with numbers as the other two. Instead, they darted glances at one another, apparently looking for a spokesman. Lily watched this for a moment, then looked suspiciously toward the head of the table. Sherry remained behind his newspaper, but Lily was certain he was hiding now.

It was Midge, always the most vulnerable to a frontal assault, that Lily singled out. "What has his lordship promised you will do today?"

Midge's deep blue eyes could not hold Lily's direct gaze. Blinking rapidly, he began to sink in his chair.

"I say, Master Midge, buck up." This was from Sherry, and he had not come out from behind the paper. "She hasn't applied thumbscrews."

Midge gripped the sides of his chair. "Ye ain't lookin' at 'er," he grumbled softly. "She's got a way o' makin' a body go all melty."

"The brain, too," Pinch said helpfully.

Sherry's paper rattled a little as his shoulders shook, but he stayed where he was.

"Well, Midge?" asked Lily.

"We're to go to the village with Mr. Pipkin and Tolley and fetch supplies for Mrs. Bennet and Mr. Gant."

Bennet and Gant were the head cook and baker at Granville. Lily knew very well that there were helpers to manage precisely what Sherry was sending the boys to do. Had he not placed them in her charge in the schoolroom she would have been pleased to have them assigned such tasks.

"We have a list," Dash said. He lifted his right buttock and produced a paper from under it. He held it up for Lily to see and surrendered it when she put out her hand. "It is everything we require for Lady Rivendale's visit."

From behind the newspaper there was some throat clearing.

"Lady Rivendale?" asked Lily.

"'Is lordship's aunt," Midge said.

"Godmother," Pinch said. "She's 'is godmother."

"But he calls her Aunt Georgia."

Sherry lowered the newspaper long enough to say, "That does not give you leave to call her anything but Lady Rivendale."

Lily glanced down at her plate and realized she would never do breakfast justice. Her appetite had fled. It was with some difficulty that she was able to swallow the toast she'd already bit off. "There is to be a guest at Granville?"

Oblivious to her alarm, the boys nodded in unison. Dash spoke up. "She's a very grand lady—a countess, to be sure—and 'is lordship says we shall 'ave to be on our best behavior. And even if we are, she might pinch our cheeks anyway."

"Then it's good that you've come to have such plump ones."

Dash grinned in a particularly disarming manner, tempting Lily with those cheeks. It was Midge who caught one and gave it a twist. "Ow!" Dash elbowed Midge, knocking him sideways. Pinch swung his legs hard under the table, kicking them both. "Ow!" they cried together. "Wot was that for?"

Sherry set his paper down, and the boys came immediately to attention. With a bland smile at Lily, he raised his coffee cup to his lips.

Doing her best to ignore Sheridan, Lily encouraged the boys to finish eating. She returned Dash's list to him. Neither he nor the others seemed to be aware of how many sums they would be doing while completing the baker's order. It was further proof of his lordship's cleverness, though Lily thought she had had her fill of it this morning.

Once the boys were excused and their plates were cleared by the maid, Lily sat quietly in anticipation of Sherry making some explanation about his visitor. When he offered nothing save the paper for her perusal, she understood how little had been changed by the evening past. He was right not to engage her in conversation in front of the servants, not when the boys were absent and the topic would have veered sharply away from their lessons and progress, yet she could not deny that she felt his silence as a slight.

Sherry regarded Lily's full plate when he had finished his own. "You are not hungry, Miss Rose?"

"No, m'lord."

"Then you will not mind joining me in the library. Meredith made me a present of some primers for the boys when I remarked that I had them in residence. It has been many years since he taught, so the primers are old. Still, I believe they will be useful in the boys' lessons. Naturally, I should like your opinion."

For a moment Lily could not think who he meant, then she remembered it had been Sir Arthur Meredith's house party that Sheridan had attended. "Of course. You are always welcome to my opinion."

Sherry managed not to choke on his last mouthful of coffee, but it was a narrow thing. Butter wouldn't melt in her mouth was what he thought as he accompanied her to the library, and once they were behind the pocket doors, it was more of the same.

He sighed when she immediately put herself out of his reach. "If you mean to give me the sharp edge of your tongue, have done with it quickly. There is already precious little time for an explanation."

"Then you do mean to offer one."

"Certainly. Did you doubt it?" He held up one hand to forestall her reply and hitched his hip on the edge of his desk. "I see that you did. Will you not sit?"

Lily could not. Her agitation was so great that it was difficult not to pace. Sitting would have placed too much strain on her nerves. "Who is Lady Rivendale?"

"Very well, we go straightaway to the matter." He folded his arms casually in front of him. "She is as the lads reported: my godmother. She is no relation, but was the dearest friend of my mother, and Cybelline and I were always instructed to call her aunt. She is also good friend to Sir Arthur and perhaps something more, though that is my sister's speculation in her latest correspondence and none of my affair."

"Then she was present at the rout."

"Indeed, she was most likely the one who suggested the party to him. I have it on good authority—his—that he prefers a quieter existence in the country. My godmother, however, is a force of nature, and if Cybelline is correct and Sir Arthur regards her in a romantic light, then he is particularly vulnerable to lending his support to whatever notion takes her fancy. She had it in her mind to get away from London. Her cousin—he represents himself as a relation on her late husband's side—arrived in town shortly before we departed." He frowned slightly as he tried to recall the specifics of an earlier conversation. "Did I not mention she visited my home when we were yet in London? It was the same afternoon I went back to the Blue Ruination. She was waiting for me when I arrived home."

"You may have; I cannot remember. You will understand I was more concerned regarding your call upon Blue."

"That is only because you have not made Lady Rivendale's acquaintance," he said, more sincere than not. "The purpose of her visit on that occasion was twofold. First, she had learned that my physician was regularly attending me at the house and required the evidence of her own eyes that I was not dying, and second, she wanted to apprise me of her cousin's arrival in town. She has little regard for him, as his interest seems to be entirely about making a claim of inheritance. Since his connection to her is quite distant and was brought to her attention not above a year ago, she is out of patience with him and would put the whole of it on my plate."

Lily was now recalling more of her conversation with Sheridan that day. While she had been making him defend his trek into Holborn, he had also had these matters of family on his mind. He should have shown her the door. Even though she knew the risk to her own well-being, she felt her heart softening. "You could not tell her your plate was already quite full."

"No, that is not the sort of thing she would understand. She would encourage me to find a serving platter."

Lily smiled. "I see."

"You don't, but you will." Sherry riffled through some papers and cards on his desk until he found what he wanted. He waved the correspondence once before he set it back on the stack. "I received her letter this morning. Pray, keep in mind that I only left her yesterday, and she never once hinted at her intent to come here. She must have posted this before I was gone for it to arrive here in so timely a manner. She has left me with no opportunity to dissuade her from making the journey, which she knows I would have done if she'd told me."

"How would she know that?"

"Because I talked her out of accompanying me to Granville when she seized upon the idea in London."

"Oh."

"Precisely."

"She is cunning, then."

"Thoroughly."

"It is natural for her to be curious about the boys." Lily glimpsed something in Sheridan's expression that she could not quite divine. "She does know about the boys, doesn't she?"

"Not from me. Sir Arthur told her after I took him into my confidence."

"Ahh. Well, there you have it. You said yourself that he is vulnerable. I doubt it required any effort on her part to make him give you up. I'm afraid this is exactly what you made it: a fine mess." Her eyes fell on the short stack of books on a side table. "Are those the primers? May I take them with me?"

"You mean to go now?"

"Yes. I don't know what more you would have me say or do."

"Have you not considered that she is certain to be interested in you?"

"Me?" Lily had started to pick up the books; now she lowered them back to the table. "Why should I come to her attention? It is certainly remarkable for you to take three stray boys under your protection, but to hire someone to teach them is not in the least exceptional."

"She is certain to point out that a tutor would have been more the thing. Sir Arthur did."

Lily's mouth flattened momentarily. "Is there nothing you left unsaid to the man? Did *he* apply thumbscrews?"

"I thought I was speaking in confidence." He added a shade defensively, "And he *was* a teacher before distinguishing himself in matters of law, so his opinion was of merit."

Lily doubted that Sheridan said anything that was not of a purpose. She did not acquit him of contriving to bring about just this end. Poor Lady Rivendale was most likely the one being manipulated, which meant that she was being led about by the nose as well. "How long to do you expect her to visit?"

"She doesn't say. A sennight would not be unreasonable."

"I can arrange to be ill for that long," she said. "Something contagious, I think. Influenza?"

"It is not the season for it. And why should you go to any lengths at all to avoid her? I said she will express an interest in you, not want to live in your pockets. In any event, she is living in mine so you cannot have her."

Lily laughed outright. "Your lordship is a fraud. She is everything dear to you."

"I don't deny it. It doesn't mean, though, that she isn't also deuced inconvenient."

"And unlikely to change her ways." Lily picked up the primers and cradled them in the crook of her arm. "Perhaps leprosy will keep her from my door."

"Lily."

"Smallpox?"

He shook his head. "You will only make her more curious."

"A summer cold, then. A very bad one." She did not give him time to dismiss this idea as well. "When will she arrive?"

"Sir Arthur is one of my neighbors. His property abuts mine north of here. Aunt Georgia says she will leave on the morrow, but I think that means this morning. It is possible she will be here before the boys return with Pipkin from the village."

"But that is no time at all!"

"As you intend to merely affect an illness and absent yourself for a week, I cannot see any reason for you to make haste."

Lily's free hand went to her hair. "I must change this. I cannot hide it under a cap for a sennight. If she deigns to meet me, she will see through it straightaway."

Sheridan's brows lifted. "Dye it again, you mean?"

"I have no dye. I will have to use blacking, just as I did before."

"Like hell you will."

She blinked. "You cannot prevent me."

"I forbid it."

Lily stared at him, incredulous. "That is terribly high in the instep, even for you. You cannot mean it."

"I do."

She would have thrown a primer at him but had too much respect for the books to do so. "Has it not occurred to you that she might recognize me?"

"If that is even a remote possibility, then you lied to me. You are not *no one*. Aunt Georgia is not acquainted with *no ones*."

"I did not say we were acquainted, only that she might recognize me. I certainly do not know her, not by name. And I *am* no one. I have no title, no fortune. My parents are dead, and I have no brothers or sisters."

Sherry was not appeased. "That does not mean there is no family. Lady Rivendale does not know you from *L'Abbaye de Sacré Coeur*, I am certain of that."

Lily was certain of it, too. "I told you I left the abbey at sixteen."

"You ran away."

"Yes, but not because of anything that happened at the abbey, or rather not because of anyone there. I know you thought otherwise, and I allowed you to believe it because it is simpler that way."

"And safer?" he asked.

"Yes. For both of us."

"I do not require your protection, Lily."

"I have a scar beneath my ribs that speaks to the error in your thinking."

Sherry gave her a sour look. "That was an entirely different matter."

"Dead is dead."

"I should not have carried you back to your room this morning," he said, letting his eyes drop deliberately to her mouth. "You and I would still be abed, and I would be making love to you as I meant to last night. If I was considerably fortunate, Aunt Georgia would surprise us *flagrante delicto* and you—" He paused. "You know what that means, do you not? *Flagrante delicto?*"

"I could understand the gist of it, my lord, whether or not I knew Latin. As it happens, though, I know Latin."

"Yes," he said wryly. "You would. As I was saying, you and I would be forced to make some explanation that would satisfy, particularly if she did indeed recognize you, and the whole of it would be out."

"And then?"

He regarded her blankly.

"And then, what?" she persisted. "Once the whole of it is out, what is changed for the better? Do you think your aunt would condone an affair between us if she recognized me? I can tell you with complete confidence that the opposite would be true. She would drag me from the bed by my hair and send for a physician to examine you for the pox." Lily paused long enough to let that thought take hold and said, "I do not have the pox, by the way."

Sherry gave her no chance to escape. One moment he was leaning comfortably against his desk and in the next he was pressing Lily back against the pocket doors.

"My lord?" Her face was raised to his; her eyes regarded him warily.

"Sherry," he said.

"I beg your pardon?"

"Sherry. It is my name. I should like to hear you use it." Whether or not she would have said it then, he didn't know. He was not about to pass on an opportunity to kiss her parted lips. There was sauce enough that would come from them later.

He angled his mouth across hers and felt her immediate response. The books, the ones he was almost certain she'd considered throwing at him, thudded to the floor, and her arms lifted to his shoulders. He kissed her long and deeply, savoring the taste of her, remembering how she had lain so lightly in his arms. She did not feel insubstantial now. The languor that stole over her limbs made her require him for support, and he felt the comely shape of her pressed to him. Her simple muslin day dress was a suitably modest cover when viewed from any distance, but when she was flush to him, it was insufficient to keep him from knowing every long line and curve of her body. He felt the swell of her breasts above the neckline, the slope of her shoulder beneath the lace shawl. His knee insinuated itself between her legs, obliging her to stand on tiptoe. He welcomed the slim hands clinging to his neck and wished that she might always drink kisses from his mouth.

He lifted his head to inhale a shaky breath but did not draw back far. "Was this a mistake?" he asked. "Tell me this was not a mistake."

"Will you stop if it is?"

"No."

Her smile was a shade wistful. "Then it is of no consequence, is it?" This time she placed her mouth on his and kissed him with every bit of the yearning she'd felt since waking alone in her own bed. It was not sensible, or right, that she should like or even desire him, yet she could no longer pretend that it wasn't so, and there was no reason that he shouldn't know it. This risk was hers to take, and he couldn't forbid her feelings any more than he could forbid her to change the color of her hair.

She broke off suddenly. Still clinging to him, she said, "I must go."

He nudged her lips with his. "Of course."

In the space of a heartbeat she was made breathless again. She tore her mouth away from his a second time. "No, truly, I must go."

He nodded his agreement, but the movement of his head merely caused his lips to brush against hers. "Hm-hmm."

Lily simply held on. He raised his knee, lifting her, grasped her by the bottom and carried her to his desk. Resting her on the edge, he used one arm to sweep across the top of it, clearing it of papers and quills and sealing wax. He rucked up her gown and petticoat while she fumbled with the buttons on his trousers. He stepped closer, spreading her thighs to stand between them, then he pulled her tightly against him, grinding against her once but not entering. He looked down at her flushed face and saw the centers of her eyes were very wide. Moreover, he saw that even the irises had darkened from leaf green to emerald.

She stared up at him, waiting, then realized he was waiting for something from her. She let go of her bottom lip and nodded.

Sherry lifted her hips and thrust deeply and hard. She was ready for him this time, wet and warm, the musky scent of her sex inviting his entry. He withdrew slowly, watching her, then watching them. She made small contractions around him as he moved as though she meant to hold him to her.

Lily sought purchase for her fingertips on the edge of the desk, then found she could not hold on. She lay back, stretching, and felt him plunge into her again. Her head was thrown back, her neck arched. She felt his hand slide over the fabric of her gown from her breasts to her belly. She wished she were naked. She wished the suck of his mouth was on her breasts and that he would take a nipple between his teeth and bite very gently.

The vision in her mind's eye, as much as the rhythm he forced on her, made Lily's hips rise and fall. Her breath caught at the back of her throat. She pressed one knuckle against her lips and bit down to keep from crying out. Her heels banged the desk making it shudder under her.

Lily turned her head from side to side, not in negation of pleasure but in the acceptance of it. Every muscle in her body felt as if it were pulled taut. Last night Sherry had cradled her fall. This time he abandoned her to it. The strangled sound at the back of her throat was unrecognizable to her as her own voice. She gulped air, then held it as her body seized in the moment before her release. She arched, lifting herself up to him, wanting as much of him as she could take or he could give her. His thrusts quickened between her thighs, then he was in her one last time as powerfully as he was able. He gave a hoarse shout, then collapsed over her, taking his weight on his forearms.

Breathing hard, they stared at each other for a long moment, then began laughing.

"If I had known you would shout like that," she said when she could catch her breath, "I would not have bitten my own hand." She held it up for his inspection, showing him the knuckle she'd abused with her teeth. Lily was only slightly mollified when he kissed it. "Next time I will bite yours."

Sherry doubted he would mind, or even feel it. He said nothing to that effect, certain she would never allow him to have her on his desk again if she knew the extent of her power over him. He straightened, righted himself and his clothes, then helped her up. Since coming to Granville her hair had grown long enough to require a few combs to keep it neatly tucked. Two of the combs were loose, and one of them was lying on the floor. He bent and picked it up.

"I hope you will reconsider doing anything to change the color of your hair," he said.

She raised an eyebrow as she tucked the combs back into place. "So you are no longer forbidding it?"

"I lost my head for a moment."

Snorting delicately, Lily pushed her gown over her knees and stood. She shimmied once so that the hem fell neatly to the floor. "It would be better, perhaps, if you did not follow me immediately. I am certain to have a difficult time composing myself if I meet a servant in the hallway. It will be impossible if you are sniffing after my skirts."

"A coarse expression, but apt enough in this case. Very well. I'll let you go." Sherry straightened the shawl for her, fixing the tails so that they fell neatly between her breasts. "But you mustn't think things are settled between us, Lily. You always raise more questions than you answer. You have only whet my appetite."

She raised herself on tiptoe and brushed his mouth with hers. "And I was so certain I had satisfied it." Before he could respond, Lily ducked past him and hurried to the doors. On the point of leaving she paused only long enough to glance over her shoulder, cock an eyebrow at him, and make certain she had the last word. There was more than a trace of huskiness in her voice when she spoke it.

"Sherry," she said, then she was gone.

Lady Rivendale arrived late in the afternoon in a coach and four, followed by a second carriage with her servants and still more of her trunks. Sherry saw the coaches coming around the lake from his position in a field west of the house. He did not immediately ride out to meet his godmother; rather he finished his random inspection of the corn crop and judged the early plantings were ready for harvest. He communicated this to his land manager, discussed at some length the proper way to turn over the field, and bid good day to his tenant farmers. When he could find nothing else to detain him, he turned Achilles toward the hall and headed back.

By the time he appeared in the entrance hall, his godmother had already been shown to her rooms. The servants, hers *and* his, were still unloading the carriages and settling in with varying degrees of equanimity to this disruption in their own routines. He inquired of the butler as to the precise location of her rooms and was informed she was indeed pleased to have accommodations in his own wing of the house.

Upon hearing it, Sherry released a breath he hadn't known he was holding. He had had some concerns that she would choose to take up residence elsewhere, and it was his wish to keep her as far from the scoundrels and Lily as was possible when he was not present to observe and mediate. The size of the hall should have made that a simple matter, but Sherry knew from experience that Lady Rivendale, with the very best of intentions, could manage to insinuate herself and annoy like a strawberry seed in a wisdom tooth.

Lily was in the right of it when she'd said he loved his godmother dearly, but it was equally true that he could cheerfully throttle her when she got up to mischief.

Knowing he had tarried too long, Sherry took the stairs two at time on his way to greet her.

"There you are!" her ladyship cried, waving off her maid as Sherry poked his head in the open doorway. "Come in, you dear boy, and give me a proper kiss." She held out her arms in welcome and proffered her cheek.

Sherry took her hands, gave them a warm squeeze, and bussed her on both cheeks. "Can it be that you look lovelier than when I saw you last and that it was only yesterday morning that I took leave of you?"

"I detect flattery and censure there, Sherry. Flattery is all that is ever necessary. I do not accept criticism well, even from you. You must know I could not announce my intention to come here. You would fob me off again and feel very bad about it, I am certain."

"Then you practiced this subterfuge to spare my feelings."

"Yes." Lady Rivendale freed one of her hands from his so that she might pat his cheek. "How well you understand me." She looked past his shoulder to where her maid stood in the doorway of the dressing room. "Yes?"

"It's your ladyship's bath. It's been drawn."

"And still too hot by half. You can attend me in a moment, Digby." She waited until Digby disappeared again, then said to her godson, "I am favorably disposed to these rooms, Sherry. I don't recall that I've ever stayed in them before. I believe I've always had accommodations in the east wing."

"I'm glad you approve."

"You still have your rooms here, do you not?"

Sherry could feel that strawberry seed wedging itself between his teeth. "I do. I thought you should like to be close."

"You will not find that inconvenient?"

"In what way?" As a child he would have broken under her scrutiny, much in the way Midge had surrendered to Lily at breakfast, but he had had considerable practice in the intervening years shuttering his expression and was able to hold his own.

"Bah!" She freed her other hand and waved him off as cavalierly as she had her maid. "I see there will be nothing forthcoming from you. You always were a deep one, Sherry, but I used to be able to plumb those depths. I will tell you straightaway that I have every intention of meeting these lads you told Arthur about. I cannot imagine what you were thinking taking three creatures from the Holborn slums and putting them up in your home. They might come upon you in the middle of the night and slit your throat."

Sherry was very aware of the maid's presence in the adjoining room. "Please have a care, Aunt Georgia. Only the servants that came up from London with me know the precise origins of the boys, and they are under threat of being dismissed if it becomes fodder for all. If you have already made your distress known to Digby, then I would ask you to caution her as well."

"Why?" She lifted her chin a fraction, and her gray eyes flashed silver. "Why shouldn't people know what a good heart you have? In any event, there must be suspicion about them, or are their manners and speech so improved they can pass for children such as you and dear Cybelline were?"

Her point was well taken, though Sherry did not say so. "I will let you judge, Aunt. They will dine with us this evening."

"Oh, surely not."

"You would prefer to dine in your room?"

"I would prefer they dined in theirs. It is not the done thing, Sherry, for children to sit with the adults."

"It is done here at Granville. Not always, certainly, but on special occasions my own parents permitted Cybelline and me to join them. I seem to recall that you were present more than once."

"That was entirely different. We indulged you both, and you had the advantage of not being raised by wolves."

"Are you afraid they will snap and growl at you?"

"Do not be impertinent." She pursed her lips and leveled a reproving glance at him. "You might at least tell me their names, Sherry. Arthur said you were closed mouth there."

"Pinch, Dash, and Midge—the diminutive of Smidgen, not Midget."

"You cannot be serious."

He shrugged.

"Oh, Sherry, it is far worse than I imagined. In every way that can be conceived, this is a ramshackle affair." She breathed deeply through her nose, nostrils flaring slightly, and released the breath slowly. "What can you have been thinking?"

Since she had posed the same question before, Sherry believed this one was strictly rhetorical. In any event, he had no intention of answering. "Then you will not approve of this either, Aunt, but I am making arrangements to make them my wards."

Sherry had never considered his godmother faint of heart, but he was tempted to call Digby to fetch the smelling salts. He judged the moment as passing quickly and encouraged her to sit on the chaise longue to collect herself.

It was at the exact point of color returning to her face that the door to her room swung open hard and Pinch and Midge skidded breathlessly to a stop on the edge of the carpet.

"Beggin' yer pardon, but it's Miss Rose!" Midge cried. "She's taken a spill from the top o' the chestnut! Ye must come, m'lord! I fear she is broken!"

Lady Rivendale ignored the urchins dancing with anxiety on the perimeter of the room. She had eyes only for her godson's pale countenance, and upon seeing it, saw her greatest fears confirmed. Her dear boy wasn't thinking at all; he was besotted.

Ten

It required some effort of will for Sherry not to run. He had a view of the chestnut tree—all seventy-five feet of it—as he passed one of the arched windows on the main staircase landing. He could not see Lily because she was already surrounded by servants. Dash was visible, though, darting in and out of the servants' circle, anxiously looking toward the house.

Pinch and Midge slid past him on the banister and were out the door before the housekeeper finished scolding them. Sherry paused long enough to give her instructions, then he continued in the boys' wake.

When he was still better than twenty feet from Lily, he slowed the brisk pace he'd set and forced calm. It was not merely for himself that he did this, but for Lily. What reputation she had been able to establish with his retainers—and by all accounts it seemed to be a respected one—would be forever changed if it was suspected she was the recipient of some special feeling from him. Because his own reputation was sterling in regard to dalliances with those in his employ, and because he was the master of Granville Hall, Sherry knew he would be acquitted of wrongdoing, while seductress might be the kindest name she could expect.

When the circle of servants parted for Sherry, he saw that it was Mr. Penn, the groundskeeper, who was kneeling beside Lily. She was still sprawled awkwardly on the ground, her face devoid of color but not lacking for expression. What Sherry spied there was at least as much chagrin as pain. Mr. Penn released Lily's hand when Sherry hunkered down beside him. Sherry did not pick it up.

"Can you tell if anything is broken?" he asked, credibly composed now.

"My right ankle hurts abominably, but I think it is a sprain." When he glanced at her foot she rotated it slowly for him. "I do not believe I could do that if it were broken."

"No," he said. "I don't believe you could."

"No one has allowed me to move."

He nodded, understanding the servants' reserve. "That is because you have dislocated your left shoulder. That is, if it is not broken."

Lily twisted her head to look down at herself. She grimaced with the pain this small movement caused her. "I thought it was bruised. I'm afraid I somersaulted rather awkwardly when I landed. I think my shoulder took the brunt of the fall."

"That you rolled at all is most likely why you have a sprained ankle instead of a broken one. Let's have a look at the shoulder, shall we?" He explored the line of her collarbone and the ball and socket joint of her shoulder. "Kennerly." Sherry waved the head groom forward. The man had more experience than anyone with broken and shattered bones, albeit with four-legged creatures. "Tell me what you think."

The groom dropped to his knees and made his own assessment. His examination was less gentle than Sherry's and also more thorough, but his judgment was the same. "It's popped the socket," Kennerly said, sitting back. "No break, so that's a bit of luck."

"Then you won't have to put me down, Mr. Kennerly," Lily said. "I'd hoped you'd be more relieved."

Neither Sherry nor Kennerly responded to her wry humor. They merely exchanged dark glances, communicating what was to be done without a word passing between them.

Sherry slipped his hands under Lily's shoulders, raising her just enough for the groom to get the grip he needed. "I hope you will scream as loudly as you like."

Lily did not have time to ask him what he meant. Kennerly wrenched her shoulder and arm so hard that she nearly lost consciousness from the pain of it. She had no sense of herself screaming, but the vision of Dash and Midge clamping their hands over their ears was proof that she had.

"Sorry, Miss," Kennerly said. "It had to be done."

Her shoulder throbbed, but she was no longer being skewered by needles of pain. "I'm sure it did," she said, her voice still reed thin. "May I sit up now?"

"That'd be his lordship's decision."

"Are you able?" Sherry asked.

"I think it will make it easier to catch my breath."

Sherry gestured to everyone to step back. "Did you lose your breath in the fall?" he asked.

She nodded. "And again when Mr. Kennerly offered his cure." Out of the corner of her eye she saw two footmen approaching carrying a litter between them. "I won't need that. I am certain I will be able to walk."

"That is only because you haven't tried." Sherry instructed the footmen to place the litter on the grass beside Lily, then he and Kennerly gingerly lifted her just enough for the litter to be pushed under her. The onlookers dispersed to return to their duties, and Sherry and the boys accompanied Lily back to the house, taking up positions on both sides of the litter to make certain she didn't fall off.

"Who is going to tell me how this happened?" Sherry asked. "Midge?"

For once the youngest of the trio remained silent and stared at the ground.

"It's for me to tell," Dash said. He ran his fingers through his pale hair and glanced sideways at Sheridan. "We were in the tree, lookin' out for 'er ladyship. Like a regular crow's nest it is up there and wi' us bein' pirates and all, well—"

"You are *not* pirates," Sherry said in crushing accents.

"Right, but we were playin' at it, and my ship was the 'Alf Moon, and Pinch 'ad the—"

Sherry remained unamused. "I understand the game. I want to hear that portion of the story that pertains to Miss Rose falling out of the tree."

Dash's feet were beginning to drag. "Miss Rose came lookin' for us to wash up so we could put on a good face for Lady Rivendale. Pinch and Midge, they climbed down wi' nary a problem, but I was never a till frisker wot could do the roof work. My 'ead gets muzzy, and it's like the ground is comin' up to—"

"Vertigo," Sherry said. "It's called vertigo."

Dash nodded. "That's the same wot Miss Rose called it. Can't say if it's what caused 'er to fall, though." He quickened his pace and looked over at Lily. "Was it, Miss Rose?"

She smiled weakly. "No. Climbing a tree in a dress is what caused me to fall." Her grip around the poles of the litter tightened when the lead footman stumbled.

Sherry bit off the sharp rebuke he had for the clumsy footman and merely said, "Careful, man. We cannot manage two on the litter."

Lily's attention wasn't for her bearers. She was watching Dash's lower lip tremble as he fought tears. Sheridan had had occasion to discipline the boys before, but he had never been angry with them. There was no mistaking that he was angry now. His stride was deliberate, his jaw set, and it was evident that he was still restraining himself. He was angry with her as well, perhaps more so, but Lily suspected that her narrow brush with serious injury or even death was forcing him to find another target for it. The boys were convenient and, in a very small way, culpable. Pinch and Midge, she noticed, were looking every bit as morose as their compatriot.

When they reached the house, Sherry sent the boys to

their rooms with instructions to decide what their punishment should be. Lily's heart went out to them. They hadn't the least idea of what might be reasonable or fair. She tried to catch Sherry's eye and implore him to mete out his own correction, but he was careful not to attend to her too closely. He ordered the footmen to carry her to her room, sent one of the maids to look after her, then dispatched a servant to bring the doctor from the village.

It was Lily's opinion that fetching the doctor was rather more than was needed, but she kept this to herself as Sheridan appeared unwilling to entertain any ideas but his own. She noticed that he stood back while the maid and the housekeeper fussed over her and often glanced toward the door as though anticipating a visitor. At first she thought it was the physician he was in expectation of seeing, then she realized his vigilance was for Lady Rivendale.

Only a few days ago, Lily might have inquired after her ladyship as she had never been unduly cautious of her remarks to Sheridan in front of the servants. It was being borne home to her anew how last night's intimacy had altered communication between them. They were self-conscious of their changed circumstances and, in not wanting to bring attention to themselves, were perhaps doing just that. Still, Lily thought she should follow Sheridan's lead in this regard, and though she chafed at not being able to speak as freely as before, she accepted it as the consequence of sharing his bed.

Like the boys would surely do, she and Sheridan had crafted a punishment for themselves that was neither reasonable nor fair. She was actually relieved when he left her in the care of others and did not return upon the arrival of the physician, though she felt vaguely guilty for being so.

It was Dr. Clarkson's judgment following his examination that Lily's injury was a sprain, and she was directed to keep her ankle elevated and given a small amount of laudanum for the pain. One of the footmen remembered a pair of crutches he'd seen tucked away in the lamp room and brought them to her. The maid who had first attended her found a stool suitable for raising her foot, and the house-keeper brought a pillow to lay under her heel.

Lily was overwhelmed by the attention the servants paid her. Governesses, she had reason to know, were neither up nor down, but more in the way of betweenstairs. It could, in fact, be an awkward position, one that engaged the resentment of the household staff and the indifference of the employer. It was what she had expected upon agreeing to accept the position at Granville Hall, yet she seemed to have engendered neither resentment nor indifference.

That this was the case, Lily suspected, had very little to do with her and almost everything to do with the scoundrels. With no conscious effort on their part, Pinch, Dash, and Midge had come to be accepted by everyone. Their antics were tolerated, their incessant questions answered. In equal measures they were coddled and disciplined, fussed over and shooed away. They had been taken into the heart and hearth of Granville Hall, and as the one charged with their care, Lily had been taken in as well.

Lying back on the bed, Lily could feel the laudanum begin to dull the throbbing in her foot and all her other senses besides. She yawned widely and curled on her side, slipping one arm under her pillow. It occurred to her that she should seek out the boys and help them arrive at a just punishment, but the lethargy that made her yawn a second time also stole her will.

Burrowing deeply under the covers, Lily knew only a profound sense of contentment as she closed her eyes.

Sherry escorted his godmother from the music salon to the dining room on his arm. At her request, he had played several Mozart pieces on the pianoforte. To his own ears his fingers had lacked the lightness of touch that was sometimes remarked upon when he was pressed to play in London. It was not surprising that he had stumbled over some of the more difficult passages; since returning to Granville, he had entertained himself at the keys only late at night when restlessness compelled him to leave his bed. What was unexpected was that he had not felt the restlessness so keenly—until Lily.

"You are very quiet, Sherry," Lady Rivendale said as she was seated at the table. "I cannot help thinking that you have not been attending to me."

There was no point in dissembling. "Indeed, Aunt, I have not heard a word. Forgive me." Sherry refused the chair the footman offered. He stood beside it instead, looking toward the door where the butler stood. "I expected the children to be here, Wolfe. Why are they not?"

"I will find out at once." With a discreet wave of his hand, Mr. Wolfe dispatched one of the maids.

Lady Rivendale looked across the beautifully set table, then up at her godson. "You are scowling," she told him. "I hope you will find another expression before you sit, as that one is perfectly disagreeable."

"I do not scowl."

"You have never been kept waiting before."

Grunting softly, Sherry took measure of his features and discovered they were indeed set disagreeably. He was not so out of sorts that he could not find humor in it. The line of his jaw relaxed, and one corner of his mouth lifted in a smile rich with self-mockery. "It was not so very long ago that the scoundrels accused me of having but one expression."

"And I know it very well. Absolutely maddening, the way you can be so self-possessed and secretive. The scowl, though, is not an improvement."

His grin widened. "Your point is taken."

Her ladyship glanced toward the door. "I freely admit I was not in favor of the children dining with us, so it surprises me that I am—" She broke off as the maid returned, flushed in the face and out of breath.

Sherry gave no outward sign that he was concerned by the maid's excitement. His voice was mild, even detached, as he asked, "What have you discovered?"

"The scoundrels, m'lord," the maid said, bobbing her head.

"They're not in their rooms. I found this in Master Dash's bedchamber. I thought it might be important." She quickly stepped forward and placed a folded paper in Sherry's upturned palm. "I think that's your name there, m'lord. Is it?"

"Yes. Did you inquire of Miss Rose?"

She shook her head. "I looked in her room, but she was sleeping and the boys weren't there."

"You did well." He unfolded the missive and read, aware that everyone in the dining room would be gauging his reaction. He recognized Dash's hand. The script was painstakingly neat, and there had been a good effort made at spelling. Sherry read it silently, then read the whole of it aloud for his audience.

> My Lord Sheridan,
> We are ~~hardily hartily~~ heartily sorry for the trouble we cozed you and for the hurt we cozed Miss Rose. We ~~wood~~ would like to make a most sincere promice that it won't appen ~~agin~~ again but Pinch thinks it will anyway. Midge and me dont like it much but Pinch is ~~probly probbly~~ mostly right. Midge says if you had a dunjun it would be a good punishment. Since you dont we will bannish ourselfs and go to ~~Lunnon~~ Lundon.
>
> Your servants
> Dash Pinch Smijun
>
> Also a fish wot eats boys would be good too.

No one spoke following the reading, although the maid sniffled twice.

"What is to be done?" Lady Rivendale asked. "You will go after them, of course."

Sherry regarded his godmother with some surprise. "Did I not say they were scoundrels? What is to be done? Nothing. At least not until you and I have had our dinner."

"Sherry! That is not at all amusing."

"It was not meant to be." He sat and indicated to the butler that the first course could be served. "If they've set off for London—which I find difficult to believe—they will certainly not get so far that they can't be caught on horseback."

"If? Did you not just tell us it was their destination?"

Sherry unfolded his napkin in his lap while the maid ladled clear beef broth into his bowl. He waited until Lady Rivendale was served before he lifted his spoon. "I read what they wrote," he said. "I never said I believed it. Dash may have penned the missive, but banishment was certainly not his idea."

"The fish?"

"Yes. That's Dash. I have to believe that Pinch is the one who suggested banishment."

Her ladyship sipped delicately from her spoon. "I'm afraid I don't understand. Really, Sherry, it is all too dizzying. Have they taken themselves off to London or not?"

"Pinch is a clever fellow, Aunt, and no one's fool. I have good reason to suspect that he has talked the others into hiding at Granville."

"In the house, you mean?"

"Precisely. Right under our noses, if I'm not mistaken."

Lady Rivendale's expression was considering, then her lips quirked. "Extraordinary."

"Yes."

She regarded the empty places at the table. "They will not be easy to find."

"I know, but Cybelline and I played a good game of hide-and-seek when we were children. I think I can remember most of the best places, although I cannot hope to flush them out alone. Finding them will require a thorough search and the assistance of the servants."

"And when they are caught, Sherry? What then? I hope you do not mean to make them choose their own punishment. They are not very good at it, are they?"

He sighed. "No, they're not." Sherry knew he had come far too late to that realization, though he was fairly certain now that Lily had comprehended there was a danger. He had

seen her trying to catch his eye, and he had stubbornly ignored her. How would she have advised him? he wondered.

Chagrined, Sherry chuckled under his breath. There could
be little doubt that she would inform him of all the ways he
might have done things differently.

"Something amuses?" Lady Rivendale asked.

"It is nothing I can explain, but I have concluded that I
must needs seek out Miss Rose's counsel."

She frowned. "Are you certain that is wise? A governess
who climbs trees, even to mount a rescue of one of her pupils,
cannot possess sound judgment." When Sherry did not respond to the bait she dangled, her ladyship went on. "I cannot
think why they were allowed to behave in such a ramshackle
manner in the first place."

"I don't believe they were allowed."

"Then she does not have their respect. That they can be so
willfully disobedient does not speak well of them or the one
who has their charge. Shouldn't the children have been at
their studies, Sherry?"

"I'm afraid you will have to take me to task there, Aunt. I
declared a holiday in honor of your visit. The children would
have been in the schoolroom otherwise."

"Oh." Lady Rivendale pressed her serviette to her mouth,
dabbing lightly, as the soup was removed. She was presented
with the platter of roast lamb and indicated that she would
have some. "It cannot be good for you to indulge them."

"Probably not, but then I have only your own example to
guide me." He gave her a significant look, one eyebrow raised
the merest fraction, and saw she had the grace to blush. "Let
us agree to say no more on the matter until you have met the
lads, then I will attend to your views again. Does that suit?"

"Of course. You know it is not my way to be disagreeable."

Sherry murmured something against the rim of his glass
that might be construed as assent, then took a mouthful of
wine to forestall a reply. By the time he set the glass down,
he observed Lady Rivendale was mollified and nothing fur-

ther needed to be said. "What of the baron?" he asked. "He did not surprise you at Sir Arthur's after I took my leave, did he?"

"Oh, now you mean to be unpleasant. That is no subject fit for dinner conversation. You will ruin my appetite." In spite of that, she speared a tender slice of lamb and put it in her mouth, then waggled her fork at him. "How I wish I had not pressed for an introduction, Sherry. Woodridge is a distant relation by marriage, to be sure, but not nearly as distant as I should like. If Rivendale had not seen fit to turn up his toes so many years ago, I swear I would be taking him to task now. No husband should leave his wife a fortune *and* impecunious relations. That the baron has always held favor with the *ton* must be acknowledged, yet I find him too willing to impart advice. I cannot hang on his every word."

"Then he has not been able to ingratiate himself."

"No. Precisely the opposite."

Sherry feigned relief. "Good. Then mayhap you haven't written me out of your will."

"What makes you think I ever wrote you into it?"

"Because you asked me if I wanted the Vermeer or the Reynolds."

"I never did such a thing." There was a pause as she reconsidered. "Did I?"

Sherry chuckled. "No, you didn't. But in the event you are wondering, it is the Vermeer I have had my eye on."

"You are a villain, Sherry." From Lady Rivendale's lips, this was naught but an endearment.

It was gone midnight by the time Pinch, Dash, and Midge were found sleeping in an unused stairwell hidden between the walls of the gallery and the music salon. The passage began in the wine cellar and extended two floors above the gallery. In addition to a paneled entrance to the gallery and salon, it also opened into a drawing room and, higher yet, into a bedchamber. Sherry remembered the stairwell but did not credit that the boys could have found it after little more than two months. He had been almost of an age with them when he came across it, but he had grown up at Granville Hall and knew its place in history as a sanctuary for those out of favor with the Court. Intrigued by the stories his father told him, he had spent long hours searching for the passages and had eventually found three. That the scoundrels had discovered even one simultaneously awed and amused, and he took no pains to hide it.

Sherry picked up Midge and slung him over his shoulder like a sack of grain. Tolley helped Pinch to his feet and took care to keep him from stumbling, while Pipkin looked after Dash. As word of finding the boys spread, servants that had been part of the search began to assemble in the gallery. When Sherry ducked through the narrow opening carrying Midge, it aroused a collective sigh. He noticed that his godmother stood hovering just beyond the circle of servants, interested in spite of herself and trying not to show it.

She was a fraud. He almost said so aloud, but Midge stirred and he decided to level the accusation later.

"Thank you for your help," he told the gathering. "I am certain the boys will want to make their apology to all of you in the morning." He addressed the butler. "You will tell Mrs. Bennet that it appears the boys helped themselves to her meat pies."

"I will, my lord."

"Then these three ruffians are for bed." Sherry handed Midge over to one of the footman. "As I hope all of you will be."

The servants parted for the trio taking the boys away, then followed them out, dispersing once they reached the hall.

Sherry closed the door in the wall, using his shoulder to press it into place until he heard the latch catch. Standing back, he regarded its clever concealment in the dark walnut paneling and shook his head as he marveled at the boys' achievement.

"I believe you are impressed," Lady Rivendale said, stepping to his side. She slid her arm in the crook of his and gave it a small squeeze. "As am I."

He glanced sideways. "They are good lads, Aunt. I am sure you'll—"

"With you, Sherry," she said, interrupting him. "I do not know if I ever have been so favorably disposed to you as I was upon seeing you carry out that scamp upon your shoulder. You already own my heart, so I cannot understand how it is possible for you to have tapped this wellspring of affection, but there you have it." She sighed and leaned against him. "I think you can anticipate getting the Vermeer."

Bending his head, Sherry pressed his smile against the top of hers. "Do me the very great favor of living forever," he said. "That will be enough."

After waking around midnight, Lily grew restless as she became aware of activity in the great house of which she had no part and, worse, no understanding. Using one crutch, she hobbled to her door and poked her head into the hallway just in time to see several servants duck into the wing's rear stairwell. She called to them but did not raise her voice much above a whisper as she was loath to rouse the children.

It was rare since coming to Granville that she had not spent time with each of them when they were ready to lie down. They were unfamiliar with the ritual, but Lily had memories of her own mother occasionally coming to her room and sitting with her until she fell asleep. At the abbey, Sister Mary Joseph would sometimes sit in one corner of the dormitory and read from the Bible until every girl in the double row of beds was finally asleep.

The boys had no memories to compare to her own. Pinch and Midge could only vaguely recall a time when they lived with their parents. Dash knew his own mother long enough to understand she was a whore. They had no sense of belonging to anyone save for each other, and that belonging had been born and fostered by the desire to survive.

Lily considered that it was no different for her. The bond she had forged with them—and the children she'd helped before them—was necessary for her own survival. If she were to go on, it could not be alone.

While the restriction to her room and the bed was irksome, it was the overwhelming sense of aloneness that finally provoked her to leave. To Lily's way of thinking, the fine thread of fear woven into that feeling distinguished it from loneliness, and as she limped awkwardly toward Dash's room, fear was very much on her mind.

Finding that Dash was gone from his bed was not in itself alarming. There were times when one of the boys would cry out in his sleep, and when she went to calm the nightmare, she would discover them all in one room, sleeping side by side by side like spoons in a drawer. Since that room was usually Pinch's, Lily went there next and felt the first stirring of real panic when they were not abed.

Leaning heavily on the crutch for support as her ankle began to throb, she hobbled to Midge's room and had her breath stolen by finding none of them there.

It was a puzzle, but not a particularly difficult one once she calmed herself enough to consider it. The unusual activity, the furtive coming and going of the servants, the occasional thumping that seemed to arise from the bowels of the house and vibrate the inner walls, made Lily suspect she was not the only one aware the scoundrels were absent from their rooms. There was a search under way, and she doubted the boys were assisting in it. More likely, they were the cause of it.

If it was true that they had taken themselves off, then the responsibility for it was Sheridan's, and Lily was of no mind to wait until morning to tell him so.

Backing out of Midge's room, Lily paused long enough to catch her breath and her balance. She could support herself using one crutch for short distances, but the long walk to Sheridan's room required that she use two. With this in mind, Lily started out for her own bedchamber.

She was not yet halfway there when Pipkin and two foot-men entered the hall from the servants' stairs with Pinch and Dash in hand and Midge slung over a shoulder. Pinch and Dash were almost asleep on their feet, but not so unaware of her presence that they didn't hang their heads as they shuf-fled past.

Pipkin gave Dash's hand over to Tolley and motioned them to keep moving. He offered his arm to Lily. "Should ye be out of bed so soon, Miss Rose? Here, take me arm and I'll see you back to it."

Lily gratefully accepted the support but did not mention her intention to retrieve the other crutch and be on her way again. "Where did you find them?" she asked.

"I didn't. That was his lordship's doing."

Lily looked at Pipkin askance. "Lord Sheridan partici-pated in the search?"

"Aye. He led it. I don't think we would have stumbled across them the whole of this night otherwise."

"Why is that?"

"There's a passage behind the north wall of the gallery, if ye can credit it, and his lordship pointed it out. It's a mystery how the young masters knew it was there."

It would not be possible to maintain any appreciable anger for Sherry, Lily realized, not after hearing what Pipkin had to say. "The young masters, Pipkin? Is that how you think of them?"

He rubbed his knobby chin with his knuckles. "Oh, they're scoundrels right enough, but I see how it is between his lordship and them. He makes it easy to forget they was plucked off the streets, same as yourself, if you'll forgive me for sayin' so."

She did. "It's certainly true. We were plucked like weeds."

"That's just it, Miss Rose," Pipkin said. "Never could put my finger on it before, but you and the lads wasn't weeds in Holborn, just flowers in the wrong place. You've seen his lordship's garden, so it shouldn't surprise that he knew it all along."

Lily stopped in her tracks and brought Pipkin up short as well.

"What is it, Miss? Your foot? Do you have need of my shoulder?"

"Only to cry on." She gave him a watery smile. "You are a dear man." He was of a height with her, slightly stooped from years spent on the driver's box and with a complexion weathered to ruddiness. Lily noticed for the first time how blue his eyes were and, more important, how kind. "A dear, dear man." She caused him no small amount of embarrassment by kissing him on the cheek. Even his distress was endearing. "Thank you, Mr. Pipkin. I shall treasure your words always."

Drawing back, Lily saw the driver's eyes widen and his distress turn to mortification as his attention was claimed by something farther down the hall. Even before she turned, she knew what she might expect. As it happened, she only knew the half of it, for when she faced front, Sheridan was not alone on the lip of the landing.

Lady Rivendale was at his side.

At such a distance it was difficult to know the expression of either, but Lily did not think she was wrong that her ladyship was more amused than her godson. While Pipkin shifted his weight nervously from one foot to the other and ducked his head, Lily brought up her chin and made an awkward curtsy to soften what might be seen as impudence.

"We are interrupting, it seems," Sherry said, approaching with his godmother on his arm. "Pipkin? Was Miss Rose detaining you?"

"No, m'lord. I was helping her to her room."

"And she was demonstrating her gratitude, no doubt." He did not glance at Lily. "Are the boys in their rooms?"

"Aye. The footmen just left."

"Then go on."

Pipkin made a slight bow, spun on his heel, and was off at a brisk step. As quickly as he moved, he still managed to direct a sorrowful glance Lily's way.

Seized by the urge to bang her crutch over Sheridan's head, Lily's grip on it whitened because she restrained herself. She could not speak until spoken to, not in the presence of Lady Rivendale, so she suffered the relentless boring of Sheridan's dark eyes and waited him out, hoping it would occur to him that his response to what he'd witnessed was out of all proportion.

It was Lady Rivendale, however, who breached the uncomfortable silence. "For heaven's sake, Sherry, dismiss the girl or make an introduction. You know I cannot abide indecision."

He did not respond immediately but darted a glance at his godmother that spoke of impatience for all females. "Very well," he said finally. "Miss Rose, you will be pleased to meet my godmother, the Countess of Rivendale. Lady Rivendale, Miss Rose, governess and teacher to the scoundrels."

Having dreaded this moment since she'd learned the countess meant to visit Granville, Lily was relieved to have it done with. Using the crutch for balance, she managed another curtsy, this one deeper and less awkward than the one that had come before. "My lady," she murmured. It required some effort not to tug on the cap that covered most of her hair or tuck in the tendrils that had strayed from under it. She withstood Lady Rivendale's frank appraisal, though it was more difficult than holding her own with Sheridan.

"How are you called again?" her ladyship asked, directing her question to Lily.

"Miss Rose, my lady."

"Rose. Rose. I do not know the name. Who are your parents?"

Sherry intervened. "It is late, Aunt. Permit me to escort you to your room."

Her eyebrows rose in two perfect arches. "That lacked subtlety, Sherry. If I am not to be allowed to satisfy my curiosity, then I am for bed, and as I am not the one requiring a crutch, I will navigate on my own." She raised her cheek for

Sherry's kiss, and once he'd complied, she bid him good night.

Sherry and Lily did not exchange a word while Lady Rivendale's light footfalls could still be heard in the hallway. When she turned the corner on the landing to the west wing and all was silent again, they spoke at the same time.

"I hope you mean to explain yourself."

That they used the same words might have been cause for amusement; this time it wasn't. Their expressions mirrored annoyance.

Sherry inclined his head, indicating Lily could go first.

"You were perfectly odious to Mr. Pipkin."

"Odious? A less generous employer would dismiss you both."

It did not matter that it was true, it was not what Lily wanted to hear from him. "Is that what you mean to do?"

"Of course not."

"Then please step down from your high horse." Her voice dropped to a sibilant whisper. "I merely kissed Mr. Pipkin on the cheek; I let you have me on a desk."

Sherry blinked.

"Or did you think I meant to do the same with him?" When he blinked again, Lily hit him on the side of his leg with her crutch. "If you cannot own that you are harboring some maggot in your upperworks, I shall have to knock it loose and show you the thing myself." Lily dropped the crutch and hopped once so that she was flush against him. Slightly off balance now, she depended upon Sherry to steady her. He did not disappoint, placing his hands on either side of her waist when her arms rose to his shoulders. She rested her hands at the back of his neck and pressed lightly with her fingertips as she lifted her face to his lowering one.

She kissed him. Sweetly at first, then with passion. Nothing about it resembled the kiss she had placed on Pipkin's cheek. This was warm, then warmer, and it did indeed cause Sherry to dismiss everything else from his mind. It did not matter that their embrace was in the hall where anyone might come upon them, and it was equally insignificant that she was standing with most of her weight resting on one of his feet.

What was of import was the manner in which she held him to her, as though making a claim on him, and the way she turned in his arms, giving him the right to do the same.

When Lily drew back, it was to gauge the success of her enterprise in the cadence of his breathing and the widening of the dark centers of his eyes. "If that does not convince you of the sincerity of my affections, then I cannot think what might."

Sherry could, but he did not ask her to say the words, not when he had to tread so carefully around them himself. "It convinces," he said instead, his voice husky. "But you are welcome to repeat your argument."

She smiled and deliberately trod more heavily upon his foot before hopping off. "You will not turn me from my purpose."

"You have another purpose?"

"It does not involve designs upon your person."

"Pity." Sherry stooped and picked up Lily's crutch. "Here, put this under your arm before you topple."

She accepted the crutch, then his arm, and he led her the rest of the way to her room. "I hope I can secure your promise that when there is cause to discipline the boys you won't take it all upon your shoulders, then place it on theirs."

"Pipkin told you what they did?"

"No. Not the whole of it. I reasoned most of it out myself when I discovered they were gone. He told me where you found them." She paused while he opened the door to her bedchamber and released her so she could precede him inside. "You are master here, but you hired me as governess and teacher, and I would only ask that you permit me to perform my duties."

Sherry did not fail to notice that Lily was leaning heavily on the crutch, fairly listing to one side. When she tried to right herself, her sprained ankle bore too much weight, causing her to wince. He did not wait to secure her permission but picked her up, knocking the crutch aside, and carried her to the bed. That she did not protest told him clearly how much pain she was in.

Lily grabbed his forearms when he would have straightened and stepped away from the bed. "Please. May I have your word?"

"Certainly you shall have it. I did not expect they would banish themselves, Lily."

She smiled faintly and released him. "Is that what they called it?"

"Yes."

"I fear they are romantics, my lord. It is the house, I think. They still imagine there will be dragons to slay, and they fancy themselves your knights."

Sherry brought forth the missive Dash had penned. "You will want to see this."

She held it up to the candlelight and read, then accepted Sherry's proffered handkerchief to dab at her eyes.

"It had the same affect on the maid present at the reading," he said, taking it back. He found the laudanum on the side table and began mixing it with a glass of water. "And my godmother? *There* is a romantic. She was won over by the notion of dungeons and piranha, although she fought it with considerable gusto." He helped Lily sit up, then handed her the glass. "All of it."

She made a face but drank it down. "May I have a pillow to place under my foot?"

"Of course." He took back the glass, then made her as comfortable as her pain would allow. "Aren't you tired?"

"It will take some time for the laudanum to work. I only woke a short time ago."

Sherry was aware of Lily's quiet regard; she was studying him in a way that discomfited him with its thoroughness. "What is it?"

"You never fought being won over by them, did you?"

"No. It seemed pointless."

"Why?"

Sherry eased himself down on the edge of the bed. "You will perhaps want to hear that it was a selfless act, but I can tell you it was one of extraordinary selfishness. They are like a balm for my soul."

Lily frowned. "Is your soul so wounded, then?"

"Mayhap not so much as it was." He felt her hand slide over his. "I do not know what it was like for you when your parents died, but when mine were killed I blamed myself. It was not unreasonable, given that they were journeying to Eton at the time. I learned later that only the innkeeper and one guest survived the fire. If they had not been asked to attend me at the school, they might yet be alive."

"Attend you?" asked Lily. "Because you were being recognized for excellence? An award perhaps?"

He shook his head. "But you are kind to champion me. No, I was in trouble with the headmaster—again. I was organizing a coup that would have replaced one of the prefects. The plan—all of it committed to pen and paper by my own hand—was flawed. There were not to have been any blows exchanged, and certainly the blood was not anticipated, but I didn't know that Gordon Olin was going to leap over a banister and break his leg, nor did I think that when I butted the prefect with my head that it would bloody his nose."

"It was a brawl," Lily said.

"It was the last in a series of trials to the headmaster, thus the invitation to my parents to take me in hand or take me home."

"And they never arrived."

"No. Never."

"Is that when you began to embrace your well-ordered life?" she asked.

"What do you mean?"

"I am imagining you said or did very little after that to call attention to yourself. No more tricks. No plots. Nothing out of the ordinary. Am I right?"

"In a manner of speaking."

"And now it nettles that you have been such a model of rectitude and good sense."

"A model of rectitude." He pretended to give that serious consideration. "That is puffing the thing up a bit, for I am simply accounted to be toplofty. You cannot pretend it is otherwise because you have named me so yourself."

She flushed. "I did not understand then. I wish you would not mock yourself."

"It is a talent recently acquired and one I find with much to recommend it. You should be encouraging me, not asking me to stop. In any event, I do not believe one can properly be called a model of anything at only eight-and-twenty years."

"You are so young?"

He gave a shout of laughter. "Oh, pray, say you will never try to flatter me because I enjoy this so much more."

Lily felt a surge of heat to her face. "Forgive me. It is only that your eyes . . ."

"Yes?"

"They seem older."

Sobering, Sherry laced his fingers with hers. "Do you know that is precisely what I see when I look at you?"

It did not surprise her. She had seen it for herself in the mirror. "We are two old souls, then."

"I had choices, Lily," he said, "about the things I have done."

"You told me that before."

"Then believe it. I do not think it was true for you."

She shook her head.

"Where did you go when you left the abbey?" He held his breath while he waited to see if she would answer this time.

"Le Havre."

He exhaled softly. "Then on to England?"

"That was the plan. It would have been a smuggler's vessel, but I didn't understand that. Sister Mary Joseph gave me a young man's identity papers and a letter of introduction to her brother."

"She wanted you to go?"

Lily nodded. Perhaps it was the laudanum, she thought, that made her less cautious, or perhaps it was that Sherry had finally breached her defenses. It probably didn't matter; she was ready to tell him some piece of the truth. "Because of him," she said. "She wanted me to go because he came to the abbey looking for a governess, and he chose me. They had a party for me that same afternoon, to say farewell, because he was to return for me the following morning. I did not want to go, but I thought they were sincere in wishing me well. When Sister Mary Joseph sought me out that night and told me I should leave, I thought she could not mean it. You cannot imagine how frightened I was at the prospect of setting off on my own."

She was right; he could not imagine. "So you did leave."

"Yes. She saw me off. I walked most of the night. That is what she encouraged me to do: to walk at night and sleep and hide during the day. It would take weeks, she said, to do it that way, and she was right. I counted a full twenty-one days before I saw Le Havre."

Sherry had not been certain Lily had made it so far. He waited for her to go on, applying no pressure, not even where his fingers laced with hers.

"He was there," she said. "Waiting for me. He knew I was dressed as a boy; he knew the name I had been given. I do not believe Sister Mary Joseph gave me up willingly. She was compelled to do so by Reverend Mother or Bishop Corbeil, perhaps threatened with the loss of her immortal soul." Lily studied Sherry's features. "Do you think I am being dramatic?"

"No. I cannot imagine a nun being compelled to speak for less."

"He enjoyed some influence with the bishop, though I did not understand it at the time. It was money, I think, that held sway, not his devotion to the church. He was not a Roman Catholic, nor even particularly religious—not in any accepted fashion. What he knew was sacrilege."

"He is the one who taught you to say your prayers." Sherry thought he had said too much when he felt Lily go still. Her eyes darted away from his.

"Yes," she said quietly. "He is the one."

Sherry felt her shudder slip from her and into him. "Where did you go after Le Havre?"

"To Paris. That is where his children were. It was no fabrication that he required a governess for them, and he employed me in that position for more than ten months before there was the least impropriety."

"Then he was very clever."

She nodded. "I was frightened of him when I met him at the abbey, and those fears were borne out again when Sister Mary Joseph insisted I should go. When he appeared in Le Havre, I tried to run, but his footmen caught me and took me to his carriage. I was trembling so violently I thought I would faint."

"But he put you at your ease."

Her eyes met his again, wondering this time. "How did you know?"

"Because you are describing the sort of man who enjoys watching a butterfly in a bottle. He waits until the wings have stopped beating frantically against the glass to observe what he has caught . . . and only then does he make it part of his collection."

Lily pressed her lips together and nodded quickly. "It was exactly that. I was wary but, in the end, too naive to understand how I was being manipulated. He calmed me enough to get me away from Le Havre without further incident, then gradually wore me down over the course of the next weeks and months. The children helped, though they could not know how they were also being used. They simply made it easier for him to approach me. He visited them often when I was about. He inquired about their progress and invited them to dine with him on occasion. I was asked to attend them." Her smile was rueful. "It was considered a privilege."

Sherry listened, but he heard her words as a succession of

small blows, struck each time they pointed to how he had inadvertently fashioned the same path for her. He was humbled by her courage to extend him even a modicum of trust.

"Did he make you love him?" Sherry asked.

"No."

"There would be no shame in it."

"No," she repeated. "He had no understanding of how a thing like that might be accomplished. He was able to encourage me to lower my guard but not engender any fine feeling for him. I do not think he understood how truly innocent I was. He knew I was untouched, but he could not entirely comprehend that it was as much a matter of mind as it was a physical state."

Sherry watched Lily's eyelids droop suddenly and recognized the effects of the laudanum. "Will you not lie down?"

She smiled faintly. "Then you have heard enough?"

"I will listen to whatever you want to tell me, but I hope you will also rest."

Lily lifted Sherry's hand to her mouth and brushed his knuckles with her lips. "Will you lie with me, my lord?"

"What of your ankle?"

"It barely throbs."

He hesitated, then agreed. "Very well."

"Snuff the candle," she said quietly, releasing his hand. "There are things I must say that can never know light."

Eleven

Sherry lay on his side, propped on one elbow, and listened to the sound of Lily's quiet, even breathing. She had been asleep only a short time, and he was loath to move away and perhaps jar her awake.

It was a well-deserved respite. He understood why she required the cover of darkness to speak of what had been done to her. Though she never said she suffered, there had been suffering. In a matter-of-fact voice, Lily described the teachings of her nameless employer, the impiety of the prayers at his feet, the mock confessional where she might be locked away for hours before he came to hear her sins and require that she do penance on her back. He spoke of cleansing when he gave his seed to her belly or her mouth, and if he gave his seed to her womb, then it was because she had tempted him and was punished for it with the same scourge he used on occasion to flay his own back.

She was expected to be with his children during the day and conduct herself as if nothing untoward happened after they were abed. Like a whipping boy, she was made to accept their punishments, then was punished herself for not setting a better example.

In a voice that Sherry had to strain to hear, Lily told him

how her employer would not come to her for weeks at a time, as though testing his will over his obsession, then use her body without relent for days. It did not take long before it was the anticipation of his arrival that she came to dread more than whatever act he forced upon her.

Sherry asked if there was a wife who might have intervened or a servant she could have applied to for help. Lily told him that she knew her employer only as a widower, though some servants gossiped that his wife had fled when the younger child was yet an infant and that she was too ashamed by the use he made of her to go to anyone for help.

There were visitors to the house in Paris. Her employer entertained guests at least once each sennight. Usually these evenings were exclusively male, and the company stayed long after dinner was served. Occasionally there were cards played, but more often it was merely talk. If there were ladies among the guests, sometimes she was asked to present the children, and Lily believed it was during such an introduction that she attracted the attention of one of the gentlemen in the party.

Later that night, her employer made a gift of her to the gentleman. A sacrificial lamb, he had called her, in the cause of peace, and he had remained in the room to observe that she was obedient to every demand made on her. When he was invited to join them on the bed, he did so, and they agreed they would take her at once so that the cries that one forced on her were smothered by the act of the other.

The following day she tried to leave. It was not her first attempt at fleeing, but she had never gotten so far before. Instead of trying to reach Le Havre, she set off in the direction of the abbey, intending to apply for sanctuary. It was not her employer who found her but one of the gentlemen who was a frequent guest in his home and by happenstance was traveling the same road as she. When she realized she was recognized, she threw herself at his mercy, telling as much as she dared and begging to be taken to the abbey.

Lily described perfectly the revulsion the gentleman demonstrated for her tale and ultimately for her. To prevent her from spreading what he was certain were lies and ruining the reputation of a man of some importance, he returned her directly to her employer and suggested the asylum that once held the notorious de Sade as being a fitting place for her.

"Do you think he considered it?" Sherry had asked. In the deep quiet of the room his voice seemed harsh, though Lily didn't flinch from it. She found his hand instead and drew it just under her breast so that his palm cupped her steady heartbeat.

It was then that Sherry fully comprehended the dual purpose of the darkness she had insisted upon. It was not that she did not want him to see her face as she spoke but that she did not want to see his. Perhaps it was her experience with the fellow traveler that made her wary. Her clearest memory of her escape was not where she had been when his carriage met up with her but rather the man's repugnance as he listened to her story and his revilement when she finished.

It was what she could not bring herself to risk with him; she had taken his hand to her breast only partly as comfort for herself. It was more important to her that she ease his mind.

That was why, having asked the question, he did not wait for her reply. With his hand held to her heart, Sherry bent his head and placed his mouth gently on hers. He tasted the tears she had not allowed him to see, the ones that had given her voice a note of huskiness and forced the occasional pause in her words so that she might swallow the ache of them.

His kiss was gentle, healing, and without any expectation that it would be returned. It was what he wanted to give that prompted it, not what he wanted to take. When he drew back it was because he sensed her watery smile under his mouth and knew she was in need of another handkerchief. Because they couldn't find the one she'd had earlier, he gave her a corner of the sheet instead.

He helped her carefully change position so that she could rest her head on his shoulder and his arm would shelter her.

He thought she would sleep then, but she was fighting the soporific effects of the laudanum and wanted nothing so much as to have the whole of the story behind her.

"I think he did consider the asylum," she told him as if there had been no interruption. "But he was not willing to be parted from me yet. I learned there were other governesses before me, three in all, though none remained under his roof as long as I did."

"What happened to them?"

"I was told only that they left. I think it is more likely that the servants themselves did not know and refused to speculate in front of me. Perhaps he committed them as was suggested for me, but I know their fate was different from my own. Within four days of my return to the house in Paris, I was on a ship bound for England with the children and my employer."

"England? A Frenchman making his way to England during wartime?" It was when Lily fell quiet that Sherry found his faulty assumption and realized the truth was fraught with complications. "He is English, then, this employer of yours."

"Yes."

"And he was in Paris for so long." Sherry spoke more to himself than Lily, musing on the problem with no anticipation that there would be an answer from her. He could think of only two reasons an Englishman would have spent so many months in Paris: he was either traitor or diplomat. The fact that he returned to England made Sherry suspect it was the latter, and if it were the latter, then there was a real possibility that he was also a spy. Diplomacy and spy work, all of it in the service of the Crown. It virtually assured Lily would not know justice for what had been done to her. Her tormentor was beyond the reach of law.

It was why Sherry knew he was vulnerable to those forms of justice that existed outside it, the type that Sherry himself had been called upon to mete out before he announced that he was leaving his other well-ordered life.

"I beg you not to think on him any longer," Lily said. "I have not protected his identity to save him but to save myself and those I—" She hesitated. "And those I have come to care for deeply. He is not deserving of your consideration in any manner you give it."

"It is like demanding that I not remove a splinter from my thumb," he said. "It is bound to fester."

"Please," she implored softly. "Do not cause me to regret what I have already said."

Sherry had to make a decision, so he honored Lily's wishes and put the gentleman he would cause to be killed someday from his mind. "Was it to London that you were brought?"

"Yes. We stayed for a time there, then retired to the country. It seemed that he was less interested in me when we were at his estate. I saw him in the company of other women and was glad of it. For a few months there was talk of an engagement, but it came to nothing. I thought I should be able tolerate my life there, such life as it was, then he informed me of his wish to make me available to others. He liked watching, you see, and had discovered it when he gave me over to the gentleman in Paris. He was having a hunting lodge built that would serve but one purpose: it would be the setting in which I would entertain his most particular friends."

Sherry had stroked Lily's hair for a time, winding soft strands around his fingers, giving her respite from the effort of speaking.

"He sought my permission, if you can imagine it. It was a peculiar source of pride to him that I could be made to sanction not only my own captivity but what would be done to me once I agreed to it. I refused in the beginning, but not overlong. I deemed that too quick a surrender would have made him suspicious, while denying him might have made me a cripple.

"I left him before the lodge was completed. It was not a well-planned escape, merely taking advantage of an opportunity. I hid away in the tinker's wagon almost as far as the next village, then found a hayrick where I could burrow. I walked west to the ocean, not south, and stole aboard a ship."

"Blue Rutland's smuggling enterprise," Sherry said.

In the dark, Lily smiled. "Yes. The very same. It might have come to a bad end for me then—a woman onboard a ship of that sort is not in any way popular—but I had the good fortune to look remarkably like the figurehead, at least from the shoulders up, and they allowed me to stay and remain unmolested."

Sherry shook his head, marveling at this turn. She had escaped from a gentleman who treated her worse than any whore and found shelter with old sea dogs and smugglers who treated her like a lady. "Extraordinary."

"It was. I met Blue in London and began working at the Ruin."

"He told me he let you use one of the sleeping rooms."

"And you thought I was bedding lodgers there."

"At the time I did."

She shook her head. "It's where I taught some of the children. I helped them with their letters. Sums. Whatever I thought might be of use to them that was not part of the rough trade."

"The lads told me you were their teacher. I thought they meant you taught them the finer points of thievery." He felt her shoulders shake lightly and knew she was laughing. "It was not an unreasonable assumption."

"No, but I'm only a fair to middlin' thief myself. I learned the trade for survival and barely survived it. On two occasions the Charlies had me by the collar and were set on taking me to the assizes. Blue offered a bribe that made them reconsider the necessity of it."

"Both times?" When Lily had hesitated, Sherry broke the promise he made to himself not to press her. "You would hold this back after telling me all of the other?"

"Ned Craven," she said finally.

"I see. Then I imagine that he expected some favor for obtaining your release."

"He expected me to whore for him."

Sherry did not ask the obvious question.

"Is it that you do not want to know the answer?" asked Lily when he remained silent. "Or that you think you already do?"

"Neither. I can bear to hear whatever you can bear to tell me, but what you say must be said freely."

Lily simply lay very still in his arms. "I agreed to do it," she said quietly. "I set the terms that it was to be only once to clear the debt and I would choose my own gentleman. He said he accepted that. At the breaking of the spell in Drury Lane—that is, intermission—I found a gentleman ripe for what I was offering and led him away from his friends and into the mews. I was not expecting that Ned would follow me. I suppose he wanted to be certain he would collect what was owed him, but knowing he was there . . ." Lily's voice trailed off, and she required a moment to find her voice again. "I could not do it, not with him watching from the shadows. It was like before, with *him*."

"I understand."

"Do you? Do not be so certain. I would have discharged my debt to Ned in that alley, my lord, had he left me alone. It was only his presence that made it impossible."

Sherry could not imagine there had been no consequences. "What did he do?"

"Beat me."

"And the gentleman?"

"He tried to flee. Ned caught him and served him a worse beating than he gave me. I am not certain he survived it. He didn't move or make a sound when Ned stripped him of his valuables."

"Bloody hell," Sherry said softly. It was comment enough.

Lily turned her head slightly so her cheek rested on his shoulder. "I haven't stolen anything since. It has always struck me as a terrible irony that Ned Craven was the one who set me on the straight and narrow path, but there you have it. I could not risk being in his debt again. You know I have tried to keep others out of it as well."

"Then he accepted what he took that night as payment."

"It is still a matter disputed between us. He says I reneged on our agreement; I contend he was more than compensated for bribing the Charlies. In any event, like the other, it is not for you to do anything."

Sherry merely grunted softly, offering no promise.

"They are dangerous, my lord, each in his own way. I would not have you hurt—more likely killed—on my account. I have managed to make my own way, and I shall continue to do so if I cannot have your word that you will not interfere in my affairs."

"You want a great deal, Lily."

"I do not apologize for it."

"And I will not make such a rash pledge under threat that you will leave. You are here because you interfered in *my* affairs. Has that ever occurred to you?"

"I did not know you then," she said. "It was not interference in the strictest sense, it was—"

"Interference," Sherry said.

Lily's sharply indrawn breath transformed itself into a yawn. She pressed the back of her hand to her mouth. "It is unfair of you to make this argument when I am all but asleep."

Sherry did not believe that she was so close to sleep but rather that she was offering some version of an olive branch. He elected to accept it. "Certainly it is unfair, but I find that when pressing my point with you, I must seize every advantage."

Lily snuggled more deeply into the shelter of his arm. "Your lordship is kind to say so."

That was when he had given her shoulders a light squeeze and determinedly offered nothing else that might prolong their conversation. He'd felt her body grow heavier as she relaxed against him, and in time he sensed the change in her breathing. Waiting until he was certain she was deeply asleep, he had slipped his arm out from under her and eased himself away.

She didn't stir when he finally left the bed. Closing the door quietly behind him, he thought her sleep would be considerably less troubled than his own.

Crutches did not keep Lily from the schoolroom. Over the course of the next three days she learned to use them to great advantage when she required the attention of one of her pupils. Out-of-door activities were strictly forbidden to the boys until she was able to manage with only a cane. Even Pinch agreed this was a better punishment than being banished. They also had to help with chores in the kitchen to compensate for the inconvenience they had caused to the servants. Lily suspected they were acquiring more in the way of biscuits and scones than they were work, but she did not interfere in Mrs. Bennet's domain.

Mr. Wolfe presented her with a cane that he'd used earlier in the year after taking a spill on an icy patch outside the village church. The scoundrels had a vested interest in Lily being able to abandon the crutches in favor of the butler's gift, and they offered her considerable encouragement each time she hobbled around the schoolroom with it.

Three days of rain confounded their efforts to get her and themselves out of doors, but at the end of a sennight it seemed the planets had at last aligned themselves in their favor.

Lily was sitting on the grassy bank by the lake, observing the boys as they untangled their fishing lines, when she sensed that her week's respite was truly about to end. She saw Dash turn his head in her direction but focus his attention on something behind her. He raised an arm and waved.

"Good afternoon, m'lady," he called cheerfully. "'Ave you come to fish wi' us?"

"It is a splendid offer, young man," Lady Rivendale said, "but I think I should like to sit here on the bank for the nonce." She came abreast of where Lily was sitting and glanced down. "You don't mind, do you, m'dear? I find it is intolerably stuffy indoors today."

"No, of course not," Lily said, "but I have no blanket and your dress will be quite . . . " Lily did not finish because it was abundantly clear this was no deterrent to her ladyship's plans as she was already dropping gracefully to the ground. There was also no excuse that she could present to leave.

"I have no intention of rolling about," Lady Rivendale said. She extended her legs in front of her and arranged her dress so it fell smoothly across her ankles. In a tone that brooked no refusal, she added, "I brought this for you," then produced a parasol. "I saw from the window that your hat is not at all the thing."

Lily stared at the parasol while her hand flew to her straw hat. "I know it is not the first stare of fashion, but—"

Her ladyship's hearty laughter interrupted. "Oh, my dear, the first stare? No, it certainly is not that. One might well be struck blind by it." She thrust the parasol forward a second time. "I saw also that you seem to have no more need of the cane, but you might find this useful for traversing the uneven ground."

Lily could think of no way she might politely refuse. As soon as she removed her hat her hair would be brilliantly displayed in the sunshine. Every curl she'd tucked under the band would spring free; every heavy lock that she'd anchored with combs would be loosened. Still, there was nothing for it. There was no way to avoid bringing Lady Rivendale's attention to what was certainly her most singular feature. She would be surprised if that was not her ladyship's intent from the outset.

Lily set her hat aside and quickly took up the parasol. She had not yet opened it when Lady Rivendale offered her initial observation.

"It is striking, Miss Rose, but then I suspected it would

be. Your fair complexion and green eyes made me think you might be a redhead, though it was difficult to tell from your brows. I am not one of those who believe it is an unfortunate color, though perhaps when it veers toward orange one's choice in dress fabrics is limited."

Lily held the parasol in one hand and fumbled with the combs with the other. It seemed to her that Lady Rivendale was working her way to a particular point. Lily prepared to be stuck by something every bit as painful as the shiv she'd taken for Sheridan.

"But orange does not describe your hair, does it? Auburn, I have heard it called, yet I believe that color has not the same tone of dark copper. Nor is it so vibrantly red as Titian painted it, I think, though that may be closer to the mark. Can you credit it, Miss Rose, that I once had a friend with hair your exact shade and in all your abundance?"

Treading carefully, Lily said, "If your ladyship says you did, then I can credit it."

"Her mother also, for I knew that woman as well when I was young. She is gone now, as is my friend."

"I am sorry to hear it."

Lady Rivendale inclined her head forward, acknowledging the remark, then went on. "I was struck by your resemblance to them when Sherry made the introduction. It was unfortunate, I thought, that you spent so much time this week in your room and I had no opportunity to inquire."

It was just as Lily feared. The question her ladyship had immediately raised in regard to Lily's parentage was not of idle interest to her. Sherry had directed his godmother to the lateness of the hour on that occasion and had been successful in diverting her while Lily was recuperating, but he was far afield now and unlikely to make a timely rescue.

"So I have applied myself to this matter of your family," Lady Rivendale was saying, "and I am now firmly of the opinion that you must be a limb on their tree."

"Perhaps I am, though I think we will discover it is a very short limb."

"Why do you say that?"

"I have no brothers or sisters. No grandparents."

"Sherry tells me your parents are gone."

"Yes."

"And you were raised for many years in an abbey outside Paris."

"Yes." Lily realized that whatever story she might present to Lady Rivendale, it could not veer sharply from what she had already told Sheridan. She had hoped he would be less forthcoming with his godmother. "*L'Abbaye de Sacré Coeur.*"

"That is unusual, don't you think? An English girl being raised in a French abbey?"

"I never thought about it growing up."

"But you see it now?"

Lily could not very well deny it. She had been the only girl of English parents enrolled in the school, just as Sister Mary Joseph had been the only English nun. "Yes, of course it was something out of the ordinary, but since it was my life, it seemed unexceptional."

Lady Rivendale's comment was cut off by Pinch's cry that he'd hooked a big one. She turned her attention to the boys and watched as Pinch fought with his catch. "He is not unlike Sherry was at that age," she said as if to herself. "The dark hair and solemn eyes, all arms and legs that do not quite seem to move in concert. I wonder if Sherry realizes it."

Her ladyship did not seem to expect a reply, so Lily did not offer one. She was not so certain, however, that the words were idly spoken.

"Look at how he takes care of the others," Lady Rivendale said as Pinch allowed Midge to grasp the pole. "Sherry did the same with his sister, even before their parents died. Afterward, well, you could not often find Cybelline without Sherry nearby." Her voice turned a shade wistful. "And now she is to have a child, and Sherry . . ." She did not finish, but allowed her voice to trail off with this last thought contained.

Lily drew in her bottom lip, worrying it. Lady Rivendale's manner of speaking to her without quite addressing her directly was unnerving.

Lady Rivendale applauded Pinch and Midge when they proudly held up their wriggling fish for her inspection, and she called encouragement to Dash. "Sherry knew I would not be able to harden my heart to them," she said, turning back to Lily. "They are perfect rascals, but it is all part and parcel of what makes them so appealing. Did you have doubts when Sherry engaged you that you could teach three young ruffians?"

Lily knew herself to be in very dangerous waters now. Except for a few particulars about her parents and her abbey education, Lily had no idea what else Sherry might have told his godmother. "I am always plagued by some doubts," she said, "when I take a position, but it is never about my pupils' ability to learn that I question. I suppose that if they cannot, the difficulty lies with me."

"That is a progressive notion." She nodded slowly as though giving it consideration. "You will have noticed, I believe, that Sherry is progressive in his thinking." She did not wait for Lily to comment. "Consider your own employment at Granville. One might easily form the opinion that in hiring you, Sherry showed himself to be remarkably progressive. You must admit, Miss Rose, that you are hardly the usual thing. A tutor would not have caused comment, but a female teacher? For all his advanced thinking, Sherry does not do things that invite notice—until now."

"I was not aware there was notice," Lily said cautiously.

"*I* have noticed."

"Yes, of course, but you are his lordship's godmother."

"That is neither here nor there. It will come to the attention of others. Sherry's reputation will not suffer, you understand. Quite the opposite, I would imagine, yet I wonder that you did not think of your own when accepting this position."

"I did," said Lily. "I came to the carefully considered conclusion that I would not be compromised by relying on Lord Sheridan's good judgment. Is it your ladyship's contention that I was wrong?"

Lady Rivendale said nothing for a long moment while her light gray eyes became visibly sharper. "Sherry said you were clever."

"I should hope it is one of the reasons I was able to secure this position."

"Lillian Rosemead," Lady Rivendale said. "She was clever, too."

Lily managed to school her expression, but she could do nothing about the flush that stole over her features. Lady Rivendale was an adept at conversational sleight of hand, and Lily felt her ladyship's point being thrust home.

"You do know who I mean, Miss Rose," she said. "I hope you will not pretend it is otherwise. What I cannot understand is why you would disassociate yourself from that connection. You are from a good family on both sides. It is more than a little curious that you use but a portion of your mother's maiden name and none at all of your father's. It begs the question why."

"I suppose it does." Lily felt as if fists had been plunged into her midsection. Drawing breath was difficult; the boys' chatter came to her as if from a great distance. "But I cannot explain."

"That does not surprise. I cannot like it that you are deceiving my godson."

"I do not think I am deceiving anyone in a way that is of consequence. As your ladyship points out, I am from a good family."

Lady Rivendale pursed her lips, not satisfied with this response. "I will want you to tell Sherry the truth. He has given you a position of great responsibility. I will insist that he study your references again. I think the matter of your name is of some importance."

"You may tell him whatever you wish, but I cannot speak of it."

"Of course you can speak of it. You are being willful."

"If you like," Lily said quietly.

"I do *not* like."

It seemed to Lily there was nothing she might say to calm Lady Rivendale's nerves or temper her annoyance. An apology was unlikely to be looked upon with favor, especially since there was nothing she was willing to do differently. Lily started to rise as her ladyship made to get up but was waved back down.

"Do not trouble yourself," she said, brushing off her skirt. "I would not regard it as sincere. Good afternoon . . . Miss Sterling."

Lily could not find it in herself to offer the same in reply. *Miss Sterling.* Her ladyship had been quite deliberate in her use of the name. Lily did not turn to watch her trek across the wide lawn and through the terraced gardens; instead, she watched the boys race along the edge of the lake and carefully reviewed the plans she'd made for her departure from Granville.

Sherry let himself into Lily's room, realizing once again that in some ways she was perfectly predictable. It was difficult to appreciate this aspect of her thinking and deportment when it ran counter to his own. He stood just inside the doorway for a long minute and watched her carefully pack the valise open on her bed. It was only when he sighed audibly that he finally drew her attention.

Lily gave a little start, glancing toward the door. "Oh! You might have announced yourself."

"I thought I just did."

Her mouth flattened, and she returned to packing.

Sherry did not join Lily at her bedside but elected to take one of the chairs near the fireplace. It was in direct line of the mild breeze coming through the open window, and the air was lightly scented with the distinctive fragrance of roses. "You will not be able to take much away in that valise. Will you allow me to have a trunk brought to your room?"

"I cannot manage a trunk on my own," she said. "I am not certain I will be able to keep the valise, but I am loath to surrender all of the clothes you bought for me." She began folding a nightgown with a crisp, deliberate economy of movement that spoke of her distress. "I begged you not to purchase so many fine garments on my behalf. It was unfair of you to make me want things again. I have been reminded today that it is far better to have nothing, to want nothing."

Sherry refused to return to the argument that had engaged them during Lily's first days at Granville. What clothes he had been able to find for her came from among Cybelline's castoffs. They served for the journey to the country, but once he had engaged her as governess to the scoundrels, he decided his sister's dresses would no longer suit. He was able to convince Lily to accept a new wardrobe because Cybelline's gowns were, in fact, more colorful and finely made than those garments worn by women in her position. Sherry's own reasons for insisting on new clothes had nothing to do with their suitability. He wanted Lily to wear things that were her own and to remove any thought of his sister when he looked at her.

Glancing at what she had placed on the bed to pack, he saw only the most drab and serviceable items. There was nothing fine about anything she had chosen. "I can have trunks sent to you later," he said. "That should pose no problem."

She nodded jerkily and did not turn away from her task. "Yes, all right."

He chuckled, albeit without genuine humor. "Do you think I believe you, Lily, when you will not even look at me? Do you have any intention of telling me where you're going?"

"Not tonight, but eventually. I will write."

"I still do not think I believe you. Do you know where you're going?" When she did not answer, it was answer enough for Sherry. "Will you not sit down and discuss it?"

Lily neatly folded a second nightdress and placed it in the valise. "You said you would not prevent me from leaving."

"Discussing is not preventing, but if you are going to raise things that were said between us, then I seem to remember that you promised to inform me when you meant to go."

"And I would have done so." She glanced over her shoulder while she gestured to the clothes she'd selected to take. "I'm not finished."

He raised one eyebrow. "So you would have announced your plans with your valise in hand? That is all the notice I might have expected?" Sherry did not approve of the careless shrug she gave him. "Then Aunt Georgia was right to come to me."

"I did not expect her to keep my secret."

Even with her back to him, Sherry did not miss the bitterness edging Lily's tone or the way her hands clenched at her sides. He felt himself becoming impatient with her. Reminding himself that she was more frightened than he was—though it was probably a narrow thing—he managed to remain outwardly composed.

"From me, Lily. She could not keep it from me. It is entirely unfair of you to suppose she will tell the whole of the *ton* that she has stumbled upon Howard Sterling's daughter at Granville Hall."

"She has only to tell one person," she said. "Secrets are always given away in such a manner. Can you promise me that she will not speak of it to anyone else? What of Sir Arthur Meredith? You have intimated they are dear friends, perhaps lovers. It is natural that she will want to bring him into her confidence."

"She is entirely aware that her discovery has distressed you."

"Distressed? Yes, that would be an apt description. Lady Rivendale accused me of deceiving you, my lord."

Sherry sighed. "She is protective of me."

"I understand, and I do not fault her for it."

"Then do not fault me for it."

Lily spun on her heel. Her eyes were luminous with a mixture of hurt and indignation. "Do you think I am leaving to punish you? I am leaving because it is only a matter of time before *he* will find me. And if you believe he will not or that you can protect me in the event he does, then you don't comprehend what he is capable of." She blinked back tears and took a steadying breath. "Remaining at Granville makes me vulnerable. *You* make me vulnerable. He will exploit my affection for the boys to force my hand."

Sherry sat forward in his chair, regarding her intently. "Is that what he did before?"

"With his own children? Yes. He would not threaten to harm them physically, but I learned that he could accomplish his ends in small and subtle ways that were just as devastating."

"He hasn't that sort of power over the scoundrels. He couldn't manipulate them in such a manner."

"No, of course not. There would be no reason for subtlety there. He would see them with broken bones or broken necks first. While we were yet in Paris, he once brought a young street girl home. She had been ill used many times in her short life and thought she knew what to expect from her encounter with the English gentleman. What she could not understand was that he meant her to be naught but a lesson to me. Her sole purpose was to serve as an example."

"Lily. You don't have—"

"I must say it," she told him. "I must know that you know. She was unrecognizable when he was finished with her. Her face was blackened from the blows and the blood. He flayed the skin from her back and thighs. *That* is what he can do to someone whom he regards with the same compassion he has for a cockroach." Her voice shook with the emotion. "I can bear whatever he does to me, my lord, but I cannot bear what he will do *because* of me."

Sherry came to his feet. He stood there a moment, hands

at his side, palms out. He was unused to hesitation, even less to the numbing fear that kept him rooted to this spot. He wanted to approach her, wanted to hold her, and anticipating, dreading, that she would flinch from him kept him where he was.

It was then that Sherry understood what it was that he could not bear. "I love you, Lily." He watched her complexion lose every vestige of color. "I must say it," he told her, borrowing her own words. "I must know that you know."

Lily pressed her lips together and shook her head.

"You can refuse to believe me," he said. "Indeed, you can be angry that I spoke of it at all, but you cannot pretend you did not hear. I have such respect for you, Lily, that I will accept your decision to leave, but know that I hold you so dear that I will not allow you to be gone from my life forever. I will also find you, but I will find him first."

Lily's knees went out from under her. She might have dropped to the floor if Sherry hadn't caught her and hauled her up. Far from flinching, she anchored herself to him and held on. He didn't move; he barely breathed. Steadiness was what he offered and what she gratefully accepted.

Her eyes remained peculiarly dry, though tears would have relieved the insistent ache behind them. She pressed her cheek against his frock coat and would have burrowed under his skin if such a thing could be done.

"How is it possible that one heart can make room for both despair and joy?" she whispered. "Can you feel how heavy it pounds?"

Sherry turned his head and lowered it just enough to place a kiss on her forehead. "Are you speaking of my heart or yours?"

She raised her face. "Is it the same for you?"

He nodded. "Perhaps that's how it is done," he said. "Not with one heart, but two beating as one." He took her hand from where it rested at his side and brought it to his chest. "Does it seem as if it might be so?"

Lily did not miss the slight smile that lifted one corner of his mouth. "You are teasing me. That is a romantic sentiment, not a scientific one."

"Perhaps it is both." He held her gaze, his own darkening. His smile faded as his mouth came within a hairsbreadth of hers. "Shall we see?"

Lily's reply was a soft, surrendering moan. His mouth took hers and she held on again, this time with her arms sliding over his shoulders and around his neck. His hands secured her at the small of her back. Her body shuddered with need; he rocked back on his heels. They did not make it as far as the bed.

Impatience drove them to their knees and urgency made them careless. They could not remove their clothes quickly enough to suit. She helped him out of his frock coat. He unfastened the belt of her robe. A brass button rolled under the bed. The ruffled hem of her nightgown was rent where it was caught under his boot. The pile of clothes beside them grew, then was scattered as they lowered themselves the rest of the way to the floor.

The kiss that had been long and drugging when they were still on their feet now was a succession of kisses, each one of them a staccato burst of passion that fed their frenzy. In a bid for dominance, they rolled on the floor and tangled arms and legs. Lily's fingers caught in his hair, and she tugged, pulling him back with enough insistence so he yielded her the high ground. She straddled his hips just long enough to feel him surge powerfully beneath her, then she was turned, mouth parted, still trying to catch her breath, and brought under him again. Her hips lifted, sank, lifted again, trying to unseat him at first, then simply wanting him more deeply inside her. It was not surrender now, but the expression of her own desire.

Supporting himself on his forearms, Sherry held himself still and looked down at Lily's flushed face. Her eyes had a vaguely slumberous appeal, yet there was such purpose in the way she looked at him that he could not doubt she knew the sirens' song. He moved then, only a little, but it was enough to make her contract around him and wrest a soft groan from his throat.

"Witch," he said, nudging her mouth just once with his. "Has there ever been a more comfortable cradle for a man than between a woman's thighs?"

"You do not mean for me to answer that, I hope." She felt his quiet chuckle against her own breast. Her fingers lightly trailed along his shoulders and came to rest on his upper arms. His skin was smooth and warm, and beneath it, tension in his muscles defined their long line and strength. She sighed, satisfied, when he began to move slowly in her again.

In moments it was as if there had been no brief respite. They were both struck by the same pressing hunger as before. They did not so much as share the same breath as stole it from each other. By turns selfish and demanding, responsive and giving, they acted out despair and joy in equal measure. Rough play that made them gasp with pleasure so intense that it was almost an agony also brought them back to moments of profound quiet where it simply simmered.

Sherry suckled her breasts; her pink-tipped aureoles puckered under his teeth and tongue. She arched under him, flesh ripening. Her mouth parted, and she made small mewling sounds at the back of her throat. He pushed into her, rocking her back so her heels left the floor and found purchase against his calves, then the backs of his thighs. She held him, moved with him, then opposed him.

Above them, the window curtains fluttered in the breeze. The light fragrances from the garden mingled with the heavier scents of sweat and sex. They breathed deeply, harshly, sometimes through their mouths as though they might taste the air, then taste each other.

Lily's slight frame rippled with the strength of her pleasure. Her breath caught, and when it was released it carried the sweet sound of his name. He came a moment later, his own pleasure as powerfully realized as hers but with a hoarse cry that was wholly unintelligible.

Surprised he had the wherewithal to chuckle, he nevertheless found himself doing just that. Lily did the same, though hers was less effortless since his weight was pressing her down. Sherry eased himself carefully onto his side, then his back, bringing Lily to lie fully on top of him. "Your cradle, my lady."

Lily found the strength to lift an eyebrow but not her head. "You cannot be serious, my lord. The floor was more comfortable against my bottom than your chest is against my breasts."

"Imagine my astonishment, then," he said, "to find I like both positions equally well."

She sunk her teeth lightly into the skin of his neck. Instead of squirming under her as she thought he would, he brought the flat of his palm against her bottom. "Ow!" That small cry caused her to release him.

Sherry soothed her indignation by laying his hand over the offended portion of her anatomy and massaging it. "Better?"

"For whom?"

"I take your point." He roused himself enough to kiss the crown of her hair. "Can you reach my shirt?"

She stretched, snagged the sleeve with her toes and dragged it across the floor until he caught it with his fingertips. Sherry bunched the fabric in his fist then pushed it under his head to use as a pillow.

"We could move to the bed," she said.

"Can you not see that it looms as a veritable mountain before us?"

Smiling contentedly, Lily could see that it did. Beneath her breast she could feel the beat of Sherry's heart, perfectly synchronized to the beat of her own. "Two into one," she said quietly. "Can you feel it?"

He could. "It proves my point, I believe. A triumph of scientific inquiry."

"Romantic twaddle. But it's lovely of you to puff the thing up." Feeling not the slightest pressure to stir or speak,

Lily lay quietly for a long time. Sherry's fingertips traced a trail from the curve of her bottom all the way up her spine and back again. It was how she knew he had not fallen asleep. "I don't want to leave, my lor—" She hesitated, then said, "Sherry."

"I know."

"I will count it as the hardest thing I have ever done."

"I know that, too."

"Did you mean it that you would find me?"

"I meant it, Lily. I meant everything."

Lily could not doubt it; the quiet resolve was there in his voice. He loved her. He would also try to kill for her. "Is there something I can do to make you change your mind?"

Sherry's hand dipped in the curve at the small of her back and rested there a moment. "About loving you? No."

"And the other?"

"I don't know. You will make your choices, and I will make mine."

Lily's cheek remained resting against his chest. Her heart had begun to beat more quickly while his maintained the same steady rhythm. "Have ever called a man out?"

"No."

"And never been called out?"

"Never."

"Then you've never met a man at twenty paces."

"That's right."

"He has. In Paris once. And again, quite secretly, after he returned home. He is an excellent shot, Sherry. Both men were grievously injured. One died not long after he was taken from the field. I heard the other departed the country as soon as he was able to travel. I fear he will kill you."

"Based on what you have said, it seems there is an equal chance that he will not."

Without a word, Lily rose up and moved away. She found her shift and slipped it on, then stepped over Sherry on her way to the dressing room. She remained there, washing and collecting herself, until she judged ample time had passed for him to have gathered his own things and left. When she stepped back into the bedroom, however, she saw she had been too generous with the time she'd allotted. Her valise and all of the clothes that had been lying at the foot of the bed were now on the wing chair, and Sherry was comfortably situated in her bed looking for all the world as if he had been invited to be there. She noticed he had even picked up after himself, setting his own garments neatly over the chair at her escritoire.

"I had hoped you would leave," she said.

"Did you? Odd, that. I am perfectly comfortable here." He patted the space beside him. "Come, Lily. Have done with your high dudgeon and sit with me. In every way it would be better if you stayed the night. I cannot think of one reason that you must finish packing now and take yourself off. Your behavior suggests that you expect to be found out at any moment. My aunt has only now made the discovery. Even she requires more time to set the *on dit* in motion. She can have scarcely penned more than five or six letters to her friends with this news, and none of her correspondence can be posted until the morning. I collect that it will be—"

He dodged the first thing she threw at him, which happened to be a slim volume of poetry that was in easy reach on top of her desk. He put out his hands to ward off the next items—a crystal paperweight and a shoe—which were pitched in quick succession. When the valise came flying in his direction, he had no choice but to catch it.

While she was looking around for something else to throw, he opened up the valise and took out one of her neatly folded nightshifts. He snapped it open with a flourish and waved it over his head. Rather than signaling truce, it was like waving red at the bull. Lily came flying at him this time, catapulting herself onto the bed so fiercely that the entire frame shook. He barely had time to toss the shift and the valise aside before she was in his arms, fists raised and bent on pummeling him.

He caught her wrists and held them, though it was no

easy thing. "My little Valkyrie. Can I truly have made you so angry?"

Lily pushed at him, trying to land a single blow that would leave him in no doubt of the answer to his question. She ground her teeth in frustration when she could not match his superior strength.

"I was being patronizing," he said, "wasn't I?"

Lily's attention was caught more by his calm than what he said. She had to wait for his words to echo softly in her head before she could respond. She nodded once.

"And I was making light of your concerns."

Lily could feel some of the tension being leeched from her. "Yes."

"I'm sorry for that," he said. "I do not take them lightly. And I am sorry for the other, because you do not deserve to be spoken to as if you had no sense." He lowered her hands so they rested on her thighs. "I appreciate that you are worried for me, but I admit there is some sting to my pride when you wonder if I can manage the thing I am set on doing. I am not at all certain any longer that you are afraid I will kill him but that you are afraid I cannot."

Sherry uncurled his fingers from around her wrists. "You should not fear for me, Lily. It is true I have never called a man out or been called out by one, but that is not the question you should have asked. You want to know whether I have ever killed a man."

Lily was not certain that she did. He would not offer that information if she hadn't the courage to ask it, or courage still to hear the answer. She searched his face but could not see past his shuttered expression. Drawing a shallow breath as though bracing herself, she asked, "And have you killed a man?"

"No," he said. "I've killed more than one."

Twelve

"More than one?" Lily frowned, certain she could not have heard correctly or that she'd misunderstood his meaning. She made an attempt to present what was the most logical explanation. "I did not realize you once had a commission."

There was a time when Sherry would have seized on this interpretation, perhaps presented it as his own, but now he had to consider all that Lily had shared and decide if he was her equal in this regard. If he did not love her, he would not be considering what he might say to her, but loving her did not make it easier to say.

"I never had a commission," he said. "I have been in the king's service but not in his regiments or his navy."

Lily slid off his lap. She remained sitting, pulling her legs up tailor fashion so her shift was spread taut between her knees. Regarding him intently, she said, "I don't think I understand. How were you of service to His Majesty?"

"Not only in his service, Lily, but in the service of those who advised him. I cannot share the particulars with you. It is the nature of what I did for them that speaking of it can put innocents in harm's way. There are few people who know, and in matters such as these, it is always the fewer, the better. Aunt Georgia certainly has no knowledge. Neither has Cybelline. I have never said as much to anyone as I've already said to you."

"But you've told me nothing save that you've—" She cut herself off as she realized precisely what he'd told her. Her voice was but a whisper as she finished her thought aloud. "—that you've killed."

He nodded slowly. "That you will regard me with loathing is probably the clearest measure of your own good sense."

It was not loathing Lily felt, but confusion. "You do not mean to explain yourself?"

"I can paint this canvas only in the broadest of strokes. If that does not satisfy, then . . ." He let the sentence dangle, punctuating his thought with a shrug. "I was approached when I was yet at Cambridge. As you know, my days of leading small revolutions within the dormitories were long behind me. I was a model student, a prefect myself by then, and accounted by my professors and fellow classmates to be endowed well enough in the upperworks but completely dull in the application of it."

"So you were brilliant, but not eccentric."

His smile was wry. "Succinctly put. My tastes, I suppose you would say, were prosaic. I spoke of returning to Granville, of applying what I learned to matters of working this land, increasing the crop production and raising cattle. I considered taking a turn in the House of Lords, but even then my interests were about improving the lot of tenant farmers and repealing laws that inhibited personal industry. When I imagined living in London, as I knew that I would on occasion, I saw myself as a patron of the arts, supporting those individuals who shared my interests but whose talents far exceeded my own."

"Music," Lily said. The wistful smile that curved her lips also touched her eyes. "You love music. I have heard you play, you know. Sometimes late at night, when the house was very quiet and it seemed that no one was stirring, I could hear the strains of the pianoforte. If I went to the landing on the main staircase it was clearer yet, and I could sit there undisturbed for as long as you chose to play. To me, it always seemed too short. Did you know you had an audience?"

Sherry shook his head. "Never."

She could see that he was moved by her admission. Lily reached out and rested her hand lightly on his knee. "Go on. You were telling me about your prosaic tastes."

"Only in an effort to make you understand why I was chosen. It was the perfectly unexceptional manner in which I was conducting my affairs that garnered the attention of these men. They did not want someone who drew notice for what was out of the ordinary."

"They?" asked Lily.

"There is no name for them. I have lately come to think of them as a confederacy, but they—we—are not so tightly knit as that name suggests."

"Then you are one of them?"

"I was. From the time I was twenty until shortly before our encounter in Covent Garden. I spent almost nine years accepting and carrying out orders from them. On occasion I was the one who gave the orders."

"But I thought you said it was in the king's service?"

"Yes, but it was not always so straightforward. Sometimes there are reasons for . . . " Sherry hesitated, choosing his words carefully. "There are invariably matters that the king or his ministers are reluctant to have placed publicly at the palace steps."

"Like assassination."

Sherry did not answer. He was aware of nothing so much as Lily's hand on his knee. He wondered if he would be able to breathe if she removed it. She was not, however, regarding him with revulsion. What he saw in her eyes was deep, abiding sadness. This was not pity, but grief. "Should I have spared you, Lily? Would it have been better if I had said nothing?"

She shook her head. "Are these men responsible for the murder of my own parents?"

"I don't know. It would be difficult, if not impossible, to

discover. I was not part of that circle fifteen years ago. Howard Sterling is but a name to me. I did not know your father except by reputation. He was in France at a very dangerous time, Lily."

"He was on the king's business."

"I understand that. He was attached to the Foreign Office, I believe, and at the front of some delicate diplomacy. His death was a blow to almost a year of peace efforts."

"His death was a blow to me," she said on a thread of sound. "I was only six."

"I did not mean—"

She closed her eyes briefly. "I know," she said. "There is no need to make an apology. You did not kill him."

"No," he said, waiting for her to look at him again. "Not him." He saw Lily flinch at what he hadn't said, what he could never say. "What do you know of your father's assassination?"

"Precious little. It was the abbess who told me my parents were dead, and if she knew the truth, she offered none of it. For years I believed it was typhus that killed them until Sister Mary Joseph told me what she knew. You will have already guessed that I was at the abbey school because my parents feared for my safety, though I never supposed it was for my health. As you said, it was a dangerous time. Even at six, I understood that."

"I knew little enough about their deaths, Lily. My aunt is considerably more informed, and she shared what she remembered once she understood the connection between you and Sterling. Did you know that perhaps a year before your parents were murdered the Duc d'Enghien was executed for a plot to kill Napoleon? There were many who suspected the English of financing that plot. It is almost certain that we would have been in favor of that outcome, yet it was Enghien who was executed for it. Aunt Georgia suggests that Howard Sterling was murdered by the French in retaliation, either for the plot itself or for allowing Enghien to take complete responsibility for it."

Sherry watched a crease appear between Lily's brows as she considered what he'd said. "My aunt's memory should not be discounted. She numbered your mother among her friends and paid particular attention to the rumors surrounding her death."

"There are some who would have me believe my mother was not an innocent in what happened."

Now it was Sherry who frowned deeply. "Who? Did Sister Mary Joseph tell you something that would make you think that? Because I can assure you it was not any part of what my aunt told me."

"Not Sister," Lily said. "*He* said it."

Sherry swore softly under his breath. "Then he always knew who you were?"

"Perhaps not at the very first, not when he came to the abbey to select a governess, but I have always suspected that he knew of the connection by the time he returned for me. I do not think he would have gone to such lengths to run me to ground in Le Havre if he hadn't known I was Lillian Rosemead's daughter."

Sherry's eyes lifted to Lily's hair. "That extraordinary color."

She nodded. "I am given to understand it is a family trait. It is also likely that Bishop Corbeil told him who I was. After my parents died, the bishop had to approve my stay at the abbey. I believe it was Sister Mary Joseph who made the request."

"Why weren't you returned to England to be with your family?"

"There was no one. I am an only child of only children. My mother's mother died just before we left for Paris, my father's mother shortly after. Both of my grandfathers died before I was born. One from drink, the other from a cancer. I did not know so much then. I have since learned of the things that influenced the bishop to permit me to remain."

"Your employer again? Or Sister?"

"Some from each," she said. "Some I learned on my own."

Sherry said nothing for a moment. "Why did you never seek out Sister Mary Joseph's brother? Do you remember his name?"

"Yes, but I thought you understood why I couldn't seek him out. *He* would expect it. I'd hardly be safe there, worse, I would bring him down upon people who did not deserve it. He confiscated my papers at Le Havre. He knew where I intended to go."

"Yes," Sherry said thoughtfully. "He did. That and so much more."

Lily raised her knees toward her chest. She removed her hand from Sherry's knee so she might clasp her own. "He said my mother was a whore and could not be depended upon to keep a secret. He told me my father would have been branded a traitor if my mother had been allowed to live. They were killed in their sleep, you know. Throats slit. My father had to die, he said, because he could not control my mother. It would be different with me. He would not allow me to suffer my mother's end. I could be made to do as he wished—anything he wished."

Sherry watched her lower her forehead toward her knees. She kept it there for a time, eyes closed, face pale. She did not weep, merely collected herself, drawing steady breaths and releasing each one slowly. When she raised her face she was composed again, and her eyes were frank in their assessment of him.

"Could he have known the truth, my lord? Or was it like so many other things he told me—a lie?"

Sherry wanted to reassure her, yet he wondered if he could with no evidence. He certainly did not know what motivated the murders in Paris. His aunt had recalled the manner in which Lily's parents had been killed, but she seemed wholly unaware of any other explanation for their deaths than the one she gave him. Except for the assassin, all anyone thought they knew was merely speculation.

"I believe it is wiser not to accept anything he told you as truth," Sherry said. "At the very least, it is a kindness to yourself. You deserve that, Lily. You have done nothing to earn the other."

Lily nodded slowly. "Is it the sort of thing you were asked to do? Slit someone's throat because they spoke out of turn?"

"It is not speaking out of turn when someone reveals His Majesty's secrets. If intent is present then the case may be made for treason."

"You have not answered my question."

He exhaled sharply. "Yes, Lily, it is the sort of thing I was ordered to do."

"Ordered? You told me once that you had a choice."

He had wondered if she would remember their conversation when he alluded to the things he had done. Apparently she did. What he could not decide was if it was in any way helpful to him now. "I could always pass on an assignment, but that did not mean the assignment was not completed. If I did not accept it, there was always someone else who did."

"It does not seem to me there is much choice there."

Sherry saw that sadness had returned to her eyes. She relaxed her posture, unfolding beside him, then moved closer and rested her hand on his thigh. He realized he had not understood before, or rather he had not understood everything. The grief he was witness to did not spring only from her own memories; she was grieving for him, for that part of him that she believed he had lost.

"Ahh, Lily, you are too fine for me." He gathered her up as she moved into his embrace. "I should have left you in Holborn where you could save more deserving souls than mine."

"Do not say it." She pressed her face against his neck. "I will throw things again."

He ruffled her hair, then laid his cheek against it. "That is a threat I can respect. You would make a good bowler."

"I *am* a good bowler. What? Do you think I've never had a turn at it? There is a version of cricket that we played in Holborn. Midge is a decent enough batsman, and I am credited with holding my own against him and many others."

"Pricked your pride a bit, did I?"

"We are speaking of cricket, my lord, hardly a matter of no consequence."

Sherry's chuckle rumbled in his chest, and he felt her snuggle closer. He realized she was comforted by the sound of his laughter and wondered why it had taken him so long to comprehend it. "I should like to match skills with you sometime," he said.

"Holborn rules, my lord. You must play by Holborn rules."

"There are some, then. That surprises."

"It does, doesn't it?" She lifted her head and kissed the corner of his mouth. "Will tomorrow suit?"

He caught her chin in the cup of his thumb and index finger. "Do you mean it?"

"It is cricket, Sherry, of course I mean it."

He kissed her hard, pouring all the emotion he'd failed to express this last hour into that kiss, and when he came up for air he let her know he wasn't done. He caught the corner of her mouth, her jaw, found the sensitive hollow just below her ear. She was laughing, gasping for breath, squirming deliciously as she tried to dodge his kisses and discovered she was only offering a new sweet spot for his lips.

He whispered against her ear, tickling her with his warm breath so that she actually shivered. "We will also play the following day."

"If you like."

"And the day after that."

"I did not realize your blood ran so hot for the game." She squealed as his teeth sank into her earlobe. "Yes, Sherry, I am not leaving you. I will stay as long as you will have me, and I hope you will not regret pressing me to that rash promise."

"I will not," he said, lifting his head so he could see her face. It was bathed in candlelight, no longer pale beneath a gold and orange glow but radiant in a way that made her appear the source of the light. "Will you regret it?"

"No. I have never made regret my companion."

He believed her. It seemed to him that she could not have survived had it been otherwise. "Will you allow me to spend the night?"

She slipped her arms around his neck and began to draw him down to the bed. "You misjudge my intent, my lord. I will not allow you to leave."

Lady Rivendale thwacked the crown of her soft-boiled egg loudly enough to secure her godson's attention. "Did you not sleep well last night, Sherry?"

Shaken, Sherry rattled the paper in his hand a bit, and he lowered it the few degrees necessary to view her across the length of the table. "I did," he said. "Why do you ask, Aunt?"

Her ladyship carefully peeled back a bit of crushed shell and discarded it. "Am I mistaken, then, and you have not been yawning behind that paper?"

"Perhaps once."

"Four times by my count. Your jaw cracks."

Sighing, Sherry set his paper aside and picked up his fork. "Is there nothing that passes your notice?"

Still attending to her egg, Lady Rivendale shrugged. "Something tried once, but I tripped it and wrestled it to the ground."

Sherry's shout of laughter brought his godmother's head up sharply.

"Really, Sherry, you might cause me a fit of apoplexy when you bark like that."

Feigning contriteness, he reined in his laughter. "Forgive me." He speared a slice of tomato and brought it to his mouth. "Is there something you wish to discuss?"

"I wondered if you had spoken to Miss Rose."

"I did." He glanced at the footman at the sideboard, then at the maid hovering near the fireplace. He dismissed them both and gestured to the footman to close the door. Once privacy was assured, he said, "There is no part of Miss Rose's past that can be talked about with others present."

"Oh, surely you are—" She stopped, having been accosted by the full force of Sherry's implacable stare. "As you wish."

"I *do* wish. In fact, I must insist. It is a condition of beginning any discussion at all with you."

"Really, Sherry, I am not insensible that you require my discretion. If I thought it were otherwise, I would have upbraided you in front of the servants for returning to your room at the unseemly hour of daybreak. I might have even mentioned I saw you wearing the same clothes you were wearing yesterday."

Sherry thought he should check himself for bruises, for he was certain he had just been tripped and wrestled to the ground. He did not ask her how she had seen him. This was no conversation he wished to have with a woman who knew him since he was in short pants.

"That you can be discreet will never be called to question again," he said dryly. Setting down his fork, Sherry picked up his cup of coffee and allowed the heady aroma to finish the job of waking him. He looked over the rim of the cup and saw he had his godmother's full attention.

He began to speak.

Lady Rivendale did not interrupt his discourse with many questions. Those she asked brought him back to a salient point he had neglected to mention and kept him fixed on the most important aspects of Lily's story.

At the end, her egg was stone cold and almost as hard. She'd eaten a few bites of toast, a slice of tomato, and nothing at all of her porridge. Throughout Sherry's recitation her features had remained composed while her complexion had been gradually drained of color.

"I believe I will have my coffee now," she said as he began to refill his own cup. "And a touch of that whisky you keep in the sideboard, if you don't mind."

Sherry did not raise an eyebrow. He went to the sideboard, removed the decanter, and served his godmother her coffee exactly the way she wanted it.

"It is something more than I expected to hear." There was a faint tremor to her hands as she raised the cup to her lips. "She knows you have told me the whole of it?"

"I haven't told you the whole of it, Aunt." Sherry returned to his seat. "I doubt that she's told me everything. But, yes, she agreed that I should tell you whatever I believed was of import. She is afraid of you."

"Afraid? Of me? That is a ridiculous notion."

"No," he said. "It's not. No one has ever recognized her connection to the Sterlings before. She understood better than I how reentering society, even one so small as mine is here at Granville, might bring about just this end."

"It was like seeing a ghost, Sherry. You cannot appreciate how closely she resembles her mother. There is little enough of her father there, except perhaps for the color of her eyes, but she is Lillian in every other way. Her father's people were from Warwickshire. You know that is not such a great distance. While she has no one left on that side of the family, it is not outside all possibility that someone might eventually be struck as I was by her looks. Lillian was a great favorite there, and she and Howard were married in the church at Middlestoke."

"You are speaking of something that occurred more than a score of years ago."

"And it is indecent of you to point it out. *I* recall it well enough."

"I beg your pardon."

Lady Rivendale waved aside his wry apology. "Who is he, Sherry? I should very much like to know that."

"As I would." He noted her surprise. "Did you think I knew? She won't tell me. I have stored every piece of information that she thought inconsequential enough to permit me to have, but I have only a list of possibilities."

Her ladyship was thoughtful. "She is afraid you will do something impulsive."

"She is afraid I will do something. I believe she knows me well enough to understand I will not be reckless."

"You frighten me also, Sherry, when you speak that way."

There was nothing he could say to that. Her feelings were her own.

"What are your intentions?" she asked.

"You do not want to know."

The look she gave him was a shade pointed and a bit rueful. "I was not speaking of your intentions toward him. I can divine those well enough. I was inquiring about your intentions toward Miss Rose."

"I love her."

Lady Rivendale rolled her eyes. "Do you think I am in my dotage? On my first afternoon here I witnessed how besotted you were. However, it is good to know that you have arrived at last at a calmer place."

"It does not feel calmer."

Her smile was knowing. "No, perhaps not quite yet." She sipped her coffee. "You have not really answered my question. You cannot present her to society, Sherry, and I cannot like it that you would keep her as your mistress."

"This is something I should discuss with Miss Rose first."

Sighing dramatically, Lady Rivendale agreed. "I hope you will do so quickly, Sherry. I cannot abide being kept in the dark."

Pinch nudged Dash with his elbow, then jerked his chin in Lily's direction. He winked. Dash, in turn, did the same to Midge. That young worthy glanced up from his sums, regarded Lily for a moment, then turned to his friends and wiggled his eyebrows. This gesture signified he understood the import of what he was seeing.

All three boys bent their heads and continued their work, satisfying themselves with only the occasional sly glance in the direction of their teacher.

Lily was oblivious. She stood at the window, one shoulder resting against the corner niche it was set into, and stared out across the terraced gardens and expanse of lake. From the schoolroom, it was an angled view, but the perspective gave her an appreciation for the vastness of the park and the ribbon of road that first appeared miles in the distance.

She saw these things, but they were not what held her attention. Rather, she saw herself as she had been last night, lying across the bed, abandoned in her pose for him, one leg raised and an arm flung wide, his hands under her bottom, fingertips pressing, lifting, and his mouth—his beautiful mouth—joined to her at her thighs. This was not something that had ever been done to her before. All aspects of a woman's pleasure were new to her, but this, this manner of lovemaking had been outside her imagining.

His humid breath had made her moist; his tongue had made her wet. He drew out such pleasure in her that she'd screamed, and afterward, when she'd buried her face in a pillow, too embarrassed to look at him, he'd teased her from her hiding place with his hands and fingers and lips and made her come again. This time he'd swallowed her cries, covering her mouth with his, accepting her pleasure as though it were a gift from her to him.

He made her forget there had been anyone before him, that she had been naught but a vessel for the dirty pleasures of another. In a way she could barely comprehend, yet knew it to be true, he made her clean again.

They had slept very little. Twice she'd dozed and found herself being wakened on the brink of pleasure's release, once because he'd initiated their love play and once because she had.

He had invited her to touch him. She knew a man's body for what it could force on her, but Sherry asked that she learn it in a different way. Some things were already understood. He had a sensitive spot at the curve of his neck and shoulder that made him respond agreeably to the touch of her lips. His abdomen retracted when she let her fingertips glide across his skin from rib cage to groin. There was a peculiar rumbling sound that he made at the back of his throat each time her hand slid along the sensitive skin of his inner thigh.

What she had discovered last evening was how his body could make her so powerfully aware of her own. She lay beside him, the soft underside of her elbow curved against his waist, and was struck by the neat fit of arc and plane. Turning on her side, she drew up her knee and rested it on his thigh. Her belly was pressed flat to his hip, and the contour was so perfectly aligned that she did not so much as move later as peel herself away.

His hands formed a cup that held the full roundness of her breasts, and his thumbs were precisely positioned to sweep over the budding nipples. The sole of her foot could be arched the exact degree necessary to slide along the length of his calf as though joined to it. Where he was an angle, she was a curve. Where his body thrust, hers yielded.

She delighted in differences of texture: the crispness of the dark arrow of hair below his navel, the softness of the mat on his chest. At the nape of his neck, short strands the color of bittersweet chocolate wound easily around her fingertips. The puckered scar on his hip was surrounded by skin as soft as a baby's bottom.

His belly was hard; his erection was harder. Her hand curved around him, ran the length of him. She cupped him and heard his deep, throaty response that was more growl than rumble. Even that seemed sweetly synchronous with the purr she harbored at the back of her own throat.

She had explored him with her hands, her fingertips, and finally her mouth. Afraid of his rejection, remembering all too well how he had thrust her from him in disgust once before, she had been cautious in these first intimate explorations.

In the end, it was yet another way he invited her to learn about him. She tested his patience, his tolerance for carnal frustration, his ability to stay inside his skin when she was bent on releasing him from it. She learned what he wanted, and more important, she learned what she was willing to give.

Standing at the window, Lily felt a small shiver slip along

her spine. Hugging herself, she glanced back at the boys. Their heads were bent, each one of them working diligently on the tasks she'd set for them. Mayhap too diligently. She suspected that she'd almost caught them out at some bit of mischief.

"Do you need help?" she asked. When they shook their heads simultaneously and did not look up, her suspicions were confirmed. "You are fortunate indeed that I am of so fine a temperament this morning." Turning back to the window, Lily did not chastise them when they giggled.

They must know her attention was not on their lessons this morning. How could it be? she wondered. Sherry had promised he would seek her out sometime today, and he had left no doubt about his purpose for doing so. It was unfair of him to plant that seed in her mind. She could still feel his hands on her breasts, the weight of his body on hers. Between her thighs there was a fullness, a sense that he was yet joined to her there, and the line of her mouth was still swollen from the pressure of his kisses. It was not difficult, then, to imagine the manner in which he might come upon her later, just as it was impossible to turn it from her mind.

Midge poked Dash and rolled his eyes toward the open doorway. Dash nodded and nudged Pinch under the table, making the same gesture with his eyes. Carefully swiveling his head to one side, Pinch saw that it was Sheridan on the threshold.

Sherry actually gave a small start when the scoundrels winked at him. Impudent rascals, every one of them, and too clever by half. He placed his index finger against his lips and secured their cooperation to remain quiet, then began to close the distance to Lily's side. In spite of the fact that his tread was near to soundless, she was turning around before he had covered half the room.

"That is really too bad of you, m'lord," she said, stopping him mid-stride with her sternest look. "It is yet another example of your impoverished sense of humor and sets a poor standard for the boys."

Sherry brought his back foot up to meet the forward one and stood as though at attention. "You misunderstand. My purpose was but to show these fine fellows how easily they might be caught out." He glanced at the boys. "Did I not say she had eyes in the back of her head? I offer proof of it now."

Pinch chortled. "Sure, an' we knew that!"

Midge was gleeful. "She caught ye fairly, m'lord."

"And 'er just moonin' about," Dash said. "She'd 'ave stopped ye when ye put a finger to yer lips otherwise."

Lily flushed, but Sherry was intrigued by this last bit of intelligence. He regarded Dash thoughtfully. "Mooning about? Was she?"

"Oh, yes, m'lord. All dreamy like." He tilted his head to one side and stared vacantly toward the world map at the head of the schoolroom. Parting his lips, he offered a breathy little sigh. As his thin chest heaved, he wrapped his arms around himself.

"My," Sherry said, much impressed with this mimicry. "You belong on the stage, Master Dash."

"He belongs under the palm of my hand," Lily said under her breath. Since she had never raised more than an eyebrow at them, no one was particularly concerned by her observation. Sherry, in fact, chuckled. The dark look she gave him was blithely ignored. "You should not encourage them."

Sherry merely grinned. "Lady Rivendale is making plans to go to the village this afternoon," he told the boys. "And I am here to say she is desirous of the company of three young gentleman. Do you know any?"

"I'm quite certain they do not," Lily said wryly. "Really, my lord, how will they ever learn if her ladyship is forever indulging them with treats and trips?"

"Time spent with Aunt Georgia is an education unto itself."

"I'm sure." She regarded the boys a moment. They were sitting at attention, hands folded on the table, knees and feet perfectly aligned under it. Here was proof that unholy innocence was not simply an oxymoron. "Go on," she said. "And, pray, conduct yourself in a manner that will bring no embarrassment to her ladyship."

The haste with which the scoundrels vacated the schoolroom bordered on unseemly.

Sherry gave Lily a sidelong glance. "I was afraid you would not let them leave."

Lily put out an arm as he began to advance on her. "No, my lord. No. I am perfectly serious. No."

"What are you saying no to?"

"The glint in your eye." She took one step backward. Then another. "You are a villain to come here and disturb my lessons."

"Disturb? There you are in the wrong of it. I came to teach you a lesson."

Lily felt the window at her back. Her arm was still stiffly extended, but now her palm lay flat against Sherry's chest. "You must not kiss me here."

"Kiss you? My dear Miss Rose, that is the very least of what I intend to do."

Eyes widening, feeling a shade desperate, Lily looked for some avenue of escape. She glanced to her right and left, then saw she might evade him by ducking low.

Sherry pivoted to one side and showed her the path was clear to the door. "I am all for a merry chase."

The look Lily gave him was meant to pin him where he stood. She noticed he seemed oblivious to it. There was nothing for it but to make a full confession. "I *was* mooning, Sherry, and I cannot thank you for making me admit it. It is lowering enough that the scoundrels saw me and tattled."

Sherry took immediate advantage of Lily's falling arm and moved in. He placed his hands on the window, bracing himself on either side of her shoulders. His lips twitched. "I should like to hear more. Please say there is more."

"Well, you figured largely in my imaginings."

"That sounds promising."

"And I simply couldn't think of anything else. There, I have said it. You cannot kiss me here because it will not end there, and I will never be able to teach in this room again for thinking about it."

He grunted softly, not terribly sympathetic. "Then perhaps you can appreciate how difficult it is for me to attend to correspondence at the desk in my library."

Lily's knees sagged. The heels of her hands rested on the windowsill and kept her upright. "Do you see, Sherry? I am liquid. You really must not touch me, else I will become a puddle."

"Now there is an argument that convinces." Although his tone was mocking, he was not proof against the appeal in her eyes. "Oh, very well. I cannot be gracious about it, however, and you shouldn't expect it of me."

Finding a measure of strength had returned to her legs, Lily pushed herself up a fraction. "Are you pouting?"

He considered it for a moment. "Yes, I believe I am."

Lily's laughter was cut short by Sherry's sudden shift in attention from her to some point beyond her shoulder. She turned around as he straightened and looked for what had caught his eye on the landscape.

An eddy of dust rose up from the road where two riders were approaching from the south. Except for the obvious difference in the color of their mounts, they were indistinguishable from each other at their present distance from the house. They rode with their heads bent, the tails of their black frock coats flapping behind them. Neither possessed an enviable seat.

"Do you know them?" Lily asked, looking back at Sherry.

"Yes." Sighing, he stepped away from the window. "I will not be long with them."

"Sherry?" Lily could see that everything about his demeanor had changed. It was suddenly difficult to remember that he had been teasing her so effortlessly only moments earlier. "Will you be all right?"

He nodded. "It is nothing. An annoyance, really." Bending his head, he touched his brow to hers. "Tell me where I'll be able to chance upon you later."

She could have pointed out that if she told him, it would hardly be true that he could chance upon her. He was asking her to participate in her own ravishment. Honesty compelled her to admit she was naught but looking forward to it. "The music salon. I should like it if you'd play for me."

"Certainly." After kissing her chastely on the crown of her head, Sherry departed the schoolroom.

At Sherry's request, Mr. Wolfe showed the visitors to the gallery and brought them refreshment. Sherry did not join them immediately, but rather let them cool their heels in what was perhaps Granville Hall's least comfortable room for doing so. There was space enough for pacing the floor, but as this could only be accomplished under the watchful eyes of every Grantham who had come to the title before Sherry, it was not particularly restful. The portraits of the former viscounts were famous for the way their eyes seemed to behold one who was beholding them. Most guests to Granville reported an uneasy admiration for the impressive collection, which included portraits by Joshua Reynolds, Gainsborough, Hogarth, and Daniel Mylens, who was once court painter to Charles I.

When Sherry judged they had waited long enough, he pushed open the doors from the adjoining drawing room and greeted them.

"Forgive me for keeping you." This was said merely as a matter of form. Sherry did not mean it, and he expected them to know it. Moreover, he did not explain his absence. This also showed a lack of regard for his visitors that he wanted to underscore. "You have been made sufficiently comfortable, I hope."

"Sufficiently," the taller of the pair said. He was standing at the room's midpoint, just to the left of the fireplace mantel. Directly over his head was the portrait of the third Viscount Sheridan, a man of enormous appetite who required a considerably larger canvas to do justice to his girth.

He glanced above him, then offered Sherry a sardonic smile. "I had to stand here to get away from him."

"Then pray he does not fall on you, Gibb."

The man known as Gibb shrugged and remained where he was. He was taller even than Sherry, more hollowed out in his features. A light layer of dust clung to his clothes, but he was still nattily turned out in fawn riding breeches, a crisply folded stock, and Hessians.

In contrast, his traveling companion looked slovenly, though this was more a matter of the man's nature than a consequence of the journey from London. Mr. Conway had a robust frame that was not favored by the current fashion. No corset, no matter how sturdy the whalebone stays, could reshape his barrel chest or slim the thick waist. He sat sprawled on the chaise longue, one leg stretched toward the floor, the other set carelessly on the damask fabric. His frock coat was missing a button, and his loosened stock lay limply against his shirt. His eyelids were raised only to half-mast.

"Pray, do not think I will permit you to sleep there, Con," Sherry said. "I can suggest an inn in the village suitable for that purpose, however."

Grunting softly, James Conway roused himself enough to reveal a pair of indigo irises.

Gibb picked up his tumbler of whisky from where it rested on the mantel. He tilted his head in Conway's direction. "He has a toothache."

"Then allow me to recommend someone to look at it. Mr. Briggs. He is the innkeeper in the village."

Conway pressed his cool crystal tumbler against his jaw and smiled weakly.

Sherry regarded Gibb again. "I hope you mean to state your purpose quickly."

"Actually, Sherry, I wagered Con that you would refuse to see us. It is more than surprising we were offered libation."

"You will recall that I was gone from home when you arrived," Sherry lied. "And the libation is hemlock."

Gibb grinned, though on his thin face the effect was a trifle ghoulish. Conway could not muster more than a sour smile.

"Well?" asked Sherry.

"It's Liverpool," Gibb said. "The prime minister has specifically requested your services."

"Surely someone informed him that I am out of it."

"He wants Michel Ney, Sherry."

"*Le Rougeaud*?" Sherry made a scoffing sound. Ney's widely used sobriquet referred to not just the flaming color of his hair but the ferocity of his temper. "No, I won't deliver him to Liverpool. Let the French have him."

"The people love him."

"Didn't Napoleon call him the bravest of the brave? The last man to leave Russian soil, fighting every step of the way—all of it backward? Certainly they love him." Ney had been named a marshal of France under Napoleon, and the man was so admired by the men he led that when Bonaparte was exiled to Elba, the Bourbon king allowed Ney to retain his rank and position.

Conway lifted the tumbler away from his cheek for a moment. "He betrayed his people—and his men." He looked to Gibb to finish the rest of it.

"We know that when Boney left Elba it was Ney they sent to secure his surrender. God's truth, Sherry, the man promised Louis he'd bring Boney back in an iron cage. He might have meant it at the time, but when he saw Napoleon he laid down his sword and joined his fight again. That decision eventually cost thousands of lives. There never should have been a Waterloo."

"I don't intend to argue in favor of the man's release, Gibb. A public trial is what the French deserve. They need someone to stand in Boney's place. If he is banished, then they can vent their spleen on Ney."

"That is precisely what concerns us," Gibb said. "We don't think they will have the stomach for it."

"Badly mixed metaphors aside, what evidence do you have to suggest they won't put him to trial?"

"It ain't the trial that'll be the problem," Con mumbled. "It's the goddamn execution they'll fumble." He winced as pain spiked. "Ney should have my tooth. He'd put a pistol to his own head."

Gibb knocked back his drink and set his tumbler down. "There might be a better way to set the thing before you, Sherry, but Con's distilled it to the essentials. Ney will no doubt be afforded a trial, but it will not astonish if his fellow marshals form the tribunal. They might find him guilty of taking Napoleon's side when he should have captured the bastard, but can they execute him? He was one of them. They made him their spokesman last year and gave him the unenviable charge of going to Boney and recommending his abdication. Ney did it, clearly not for himself but for what everyone believed was the good of France and the survival of what was left of the army. Less than a year later, when Napoleon escaped Elba, he's asked—this time by his king— to perform an almost identical task. Do you think the other marshals are not sympathetic?"

Sherry shrugged. "It matters not a whit to me. Did I not already say I am out of it?"

"Waterloo, Sherry. English lives were forfeit. Allies lost. Ney betrayed all of us when he took Napoleon's side after Elba."

"Perhaps the target should be Boney." He saw Gibb and Con exchange glances. "Ahh, so that is being considered as well. Dangerous stuff, that." He held up one hand, making it clear he did not want to entertain discussion on that count. The less he knew, the better. "Why were two of you sent all the way out here to pose the question? I admit, my curiosity's piqued."

Con mumbled, "Too important to trust just one of us with it."

Sherry frowned, looking from one to the other. "No, that's not it. Or not all of it. There's something you're not telling me. Were you given some instruction in the event I refused the assignment? Should I anticipate spending the rest of my days looking over my shoulder?"

"Bloody hell, Sherry," Con said. He tossed back his drink then pressed the empty glass against his cheek again. "What do you take us for?"

"Assassins."

The single word brought a stillness to the room that had not been there before. Sherry regarded each of his guests candidly, unwilling to allow himself or them to pretend it was otherwise.

It was Gibb who finally spoke. "We came together for protection. Con was supposed to ride out alone. His tooth? That happened the night before he was set to leave. He was attacked in Vauxhall."

"Three of them," Con said. Rising to his feet, he went to the drinks tray and poured another whisky. "Knocked me about. I chased them off, but I took a bit of a bruising. Ribs and back. Cut my arm. Damn if the tooth isn't the worst of it."

"Was it provoked?" asked Sherry.

Con shook his head, then immediately regretted it. The tumbler went up to his cheek. He looked to Gibb to take up the story.

"A sennight before Con was attacked, I was almost run down in front of my townhouse. I jumped out of the way, but it was a narrow thing. One of my retainers was not so fortunate. Had his foot crushed and might still lose it. There are other incidents. Barnett. Penn. Woodridge. Merriman."

Sherry's dark eyebrows lifted in tandem. "He's one of us, then."

Gibb nodded. "So it would appear. There's always the possibility that someone has spoken out of turn and brought this down on us, but with so much at risk, it seems unlikely."

"It is curious that none of the attacks have ended in more than injury. Either he is not very good or there is another purpose. If he is indeed one of us, then it cannot be that he is not good at his work."

"Our thoughts also," Con said.

Sherry was struck suddenly by what was perhaps the true

reason for their visit. "You were told to make certain I was here in the country."

Gibb shrugged. "There was some question regarding your sudden departure from the service and what your intentions were."

"My intentions are to stay well out of it. Tell me, was the Marshal Ney assignment simply a ruse to explain your visit?"

"No ruse. As long as we found you here, we were to offer the assignment."

"Could I not be directing the assaults on all of you from here? Con said he was fallen upon by three men. If it was not simply random, but rather a single scene in the play as you suggest, then it is being directed by someone, not necessarily carried out by them."

"That's right," Con said, returning to the chaise. He did not drop to a half recline this time but sat at the foot of it and rested one elbow on his knee. "But I was only recently in town. If you were in the country, you could not have known I was back."

"I see." Sherry kept his features carefully neutral. "You mentioned others. Merriman, I think you said. Barnett?"

"Both of them. Barnett took a spill from his mount in the park. Could have been fatal, I suppose, but he had the good fortune to land on his arse, not his neck." Con looked to Gibb once again to pick up the tale.

"Merriman was accosted by footpads, same as Con. Woodridge and Penn were in bed for days with a stomach ailment. We suspect poison."

"It seems that while we are not to be eliminated, we are certainly being warned."

"We are. You are out of it."

"Perhaps not." He gave them a brief account of what happened at Covent Garden, leaving out the fact that his rescuer was a woman and that she was currently in residence at Granville Hall.

"In April, you say?" Gibb rubbed his pointed chin with

the back of his hand. "That would make you the very first. You told no one?"

Sherry shrugged. "It seemed unimportant. I escaped without injury."

"What do you make of it?" asked Gibb.

"Nothing more than you. It is proof we are all vulnerable. Did you truly think that I might be the one committing these acts?"

"We couldn't dismiss it. You know we couldn't. It is the end if we don't discover who among us is responsible. It is no secret that you have not shared our thinking for some time. Of course it was conceivable that you would decide it was not enough to merely leave, but that the whole of it must be finished."

"Except," Sherry said, "were that my decision, it would already be done."

Thirteen

Lily was sitting at the pianoforte pretending to play a piece when Sherry let himself into the music salon. Her fingers moved lightly along the keys, never depressing one with enough force to strike a single note. She hummed the song that was in her head, and occasionally her lips would part and a clear, sweet note would emerge.

She stopped abruptly, flushing brightly, when Sherry quietly applauded her efforts. Turning in her chair, she chastised him with a look.

Sherry held up his hands as though he might ward off this criticism. "I did not think it necessary to announce myself."

"You move like a cat. It is unnerving. If you cannot change your ways, you might at least tell Mr. Wolfe to stop having the staff oil the door hinges."

Chuckling, he pulled up a chair beside her. "Have you played even a single note?"

"Oh no. I could not."

"Of course you can." He took her hand and placed her fingers in position for a C chord, then pushed down. "See? You can. Now, one at a time. Fingers curved and tripping lightly up the scale." He demonstrated what he wanted her to do on keys an octave higher.

Lily followed his movements, her own fingers moving more slowly and deliberately. "You were with those gentleman longer than was your wont, I think. Are they gone, or will they be staying?"

"Gone." He manipulated her fingers again but could tell that her heart was not in it. "What is it?"

"They are from your other life, aren't they?"

He did not ask her what she meant. He supposed it helped her to think of what he had done as if it were somehow separate from the man he was now. It was not so different than how he thought of it, though the visit from Gibb and Con was an unpleasant reminder that remaining apart from that life required more in the way of determination than distance.

"Yes," he said. "They are."

Lily's hand slid from Sherry's and fell to her lap. She did not look at him. "I do not imagine you can say what they wanted."

"No, I can't. But I can tell you that I will not be joining them and that they accepted my answer."

Lowering her eyes, Lily nodded faintly. "Good. I'm glad of it."

"Were you afraid for me, Lily?" Touching under her chin with his index finger, he brought her around. "Did you think I would give them the little enough that remains of my soul?"

"Do not make light of it."

"I wasn't. It is a perfectly serious question."

"Then, yes," she said. "I was afraid for you. For myself, also. I don't know what pressure they can bring to bear. They had you once."

"Those two? No. They never had me. I was a younger man, in the grip of an idea—of ideals—when I was selected and groomed for this service to the Crown. I believed what I was told, believed in what I was doing, and place no blame on anyone save myself for what I have done since." He lowered his hand. The pianoforte made a soft, discordant sound as Sherry rested his forearm on the keys. "I think it is true for each of us in the service that there comes a time when the scales are removed from our eyes. Some do as I did and make the decision to leave. Others stay but are more disposed to cynicism in their views. Then there are those who not only remain but are compelled by a sense of righteousness or apprehension to justify their existence. They are the ones who recruit others to the very small circle. It was such a man who recruited me."

Sherry fell silent. He slowly tapped the F key three times, wholly unaware of what he was doing until Lily's eyes shifted to his hand. He mocked himself with a small smile. "Forgive me. I was thinking how remarkably easy it was for them to have me. You are younger even than I was, and I do not believe for a moment they could have you. It is perhaps youthful arrogance that permitted me to see the solution to complex problems in terms of good and evil, black or white . . . " His voice trailed off, then added even more softly, " . . . dead or alive."

Lily touched his forearm. "Does the why of it matter so much now?"

Regarding her hand curved gently over his arm, Sherry considered his answer. "Yes, I think it does. There is no end to young men such as I was, and therefore there will be no shortage of candidates. It may be true there is but one way to finish the thing."

Frowning, Lily drew his attention back to her face. "You are speaking of something else now. I can feel it."

Her perspicacity did not surprise. "Yes," he said. "I am. It is entirely possible that one of us, or rather one of the number that I recently left, is set on destroying the whole. It would seem your actions in Covent Garden did indeed interfere with an attack against me."

Lily snorted lightly. "You still entertained doubts on that score?"

"No, not the way you think. It is merely a certainty now that the attack was not random."

"Those men. They came to tell you that?"

"It was not the purpose of their visit, but yes, I learned as much from them." And more besides, he thought. It seemed to him that few in their confederacy had not been singled out. Suspicion would naturally fall first on those who were not the target of an attack, but it would be the greatest idiocy if it remained there. Sherry began to see more clearly why they desired him for the particular assignment that was pressing them now. Once cleared of responsibility for the attacks, he was the only one they trusted. The very fact that he had broken off with them was what made his participation so essential and valuable.

"You are doing it again," Lily said.

"Hmm?"

She smiled. "So deep in thought that you make yourself alone. I am still here, Sherry, and I am willing to listen. Willing to be part of whatever you will share with me."

"I know. But I am well out of it, and any lingering doubts on their part have been put to rest. There is nothing you should, or need, to know. I suspect that with one notable exception I will not see any of them again, and I will make every effort to put him from my life as well. It is unfortunate that as it regards him, the outcome is not entirely in my hands."

"A family member, then," Lily said flippantly. "It cannot be a friend or a retainer because you could always dismiss—" She stopped. It was not often that she caught Sherry so unaware that he had no time to close his expression. She glimpsed his stricken countenance in the heartbeat of time it required him to slam the shutters on it. Lily knew she should pretend she had not seen it, but her curiosity would not let her remain silent. "Never say it is Mr. Caldwell."

Sherry blinked. "Who?"

Lily almost laughed at the perfectly blank cast of his features. It was not feigned. He was still recovering from the fact that her poor attempt at levity had come so close to the mark. "Mr. Caldwell," she repeated. "You must recall your sister's husband."

"Of course I do, and it is not Nick. Do you think I would permit my own sister to marry such a one as I am?"

Taking umbrage on his behalf, Lily pushed her chair away from the pianoforte and stood abruptly. "It is remarks of just that sort that put me out of all patience with you. You insult yourself when you say such a thing; moreover, you insult me. It is really not to be borne."

Sherry did not try to stop her from stepping out of his reach. "I meant no insult."

She waved that aside. "Do you think I don't know that? It is what makes it so perfectly aggravating. To say you would not permit your sister to marry one such as you is tantamount to saying you possess no redeeming qualities. If you cannot have the sense to know your own goodness, then at least you might acknowledge that I have the sense to know it. You have nothing at all to say about whether or not I am with you. It is *my* choice, and I have chosen you for what you are, not for what you are not. I would have you show me the kindness of respecting that, please."

Sherry's brows lifted a fraction. "Do you know there is an element to your reasoning that puts me quite off my balance?"

She looked at him pointedly. "Truly? Then mayhap you should not be sitting like that."

It was then that Sherry realized he was balancing himself precariously on the back two legs of the Queen Anne chair. He had no doubt that it was the vehemence of Lily's argument that made him rear back. Grinning, he dropped it to all fours. "You are kind to warn me. I might have prostrated myself at your feet."

Lily snorted lightly. "Fool."

Sherry waved her back to her chair. "Come, I will teach you a song, then I will play for you."

Judging his offer to be sincere, and knowing he meant to put a period to her speculation regarding the family member he would attempt to avoid, Lily acquiesced graciously.

He taught her a simple country air on the pianoforte,

playing the left hand while she worked on the melody. Hesitation made her fingers clumsy at first, but with each passage that was learned and memorized, Lily's confidence grew. Delighted with the music they made, she laughed as the last notes faded away and turned to Sherry in expectation that he would join her. His look made it clear that he was entertaining a wholly different idea.

"You said you would play for me." She placed one hand on his chest as he began to lean toward her. "Sherry?"

"Later. I find myself inspired by music of another kind."

She moaned softly just before his lips covered hers. They were on their feet together and moving toward the chaise. Neither one had suggested it, but the thought was communicated between them just the same.

Sunlight streamed in the window and laid its translucent brilliance across Lily's hair, making it seem as though it were woven through with fine filaments of copper and bronze. Fire in the color made it like molten metal. Sherry dipped his fingers in her hair and cradled her head.

He kissed her. First on the mouth, then just at the corner of it. His thumbs grazed her cheeks. His lips touched her jaw, her chin, then settled in the curve of her neck. He sipped her skin and pushed at the neckline of her dress, widening it enough so that it slipped over one shoulder. He kissed her pale skin and traced the line of her collarbone.

Lily trembled under his light touch. She recognized the depth of his concentration, understood it was very much the same when he played. He was learning her like he would a passage of music, a particularly difficult piece, playing it through first, then again . . . and again. It was more than memorizing the notes that he did; it was learning the nuanced language it evoked.

And with each successive pass of his fingers, what he was able to draw out was something of himself.

Sitting on the landing of the main staircase late at night, this is what she heard when he played. She'd felt it also, but not quite like this. His music had floated up to her from the salon, had settled like a mist around her, but now he was making it as essential as breathing.

She helped him lower her gown and muslin shift over her breasts. She moved higher on the chaise so the beam of sunlight slanted across her skin. His eyes darkened, then his gaze fell. She stroked her breast, cupped the underside, and arched her spine, offering herself up to him.

He was as greedy as she'd hoped he would be. The flush of pleasure was washing over her even before his mouth surrounded her shell pink aureole. The rough edge of his tongue made the nipple bud. Heat pooled between her thighs. Her fingers scrabbled in the fabric of her dress and began to gather it up. He worked the buttons of his flies.

She was frantic for him by the time he was inside her, and she cried out softly, frustrated when his tempo changed.

Chuckling deeply, wickedly, he nibbled at her lips. "You did not expect that, did you?"

"I thought I knew the piece you were playing." That made him smile. He was beautiful when he smiled, she thought, and nearly told him so. It would embarrass him; knowing that kept her quiet. Lily smoothed his brow with her fingertips and flicked back a heavy strand of dark hair that had fallen forward. "I could not imagine this," she said quietly. "I could not imagine you. No, do not say anything. It is for me to say this time. I love you, Alexander Henry Grantham. What? Did you think I did not remember your name? Alexander. It is an impressive name. It has an impressive pedigree." She laid her palm against his cheek and ran her thumb along the line of his mouth. "Still, I like Sherry. I have never tasted it, you know. Sherry. Is it as smooth and sweet as I have always thought?" When he kissed her, she murmured agreeably against his lips that it was.

"Say it again," he said, seating himself more deeply inside her.

"Your kiss is as smooth—" She stopped because he was shaking his head.

"No," he said. "Say the other."

"Alexander Hen—" Again she stopped. He'd made another small negative shake. Then Lily understood. "I love you," she said. "Can you have doubted it? I have loved you since the scoundrels pinched your handkerchief, and you did not mind in the least."

"Ahh. If I had but known you were so taken by that, I would have let them make off with the silver."

She was going to warn him that they still might, but he stirred in her again and the words were simply lost to her. In mere moments it was as if they had never spoken. It had only been the brief lull at the end of one movement. Now it was the beginning of another.

She let him take the lead. As he had at the pianoforte, he guided her hand through the motions first, then added his own. Her sex felt swollen and heavy. Ripe. She raised her pelvis and rubbed against him. She could feel her own dampness and knew he felt it too. His nostrils flared; his lips parted. The sense of fullness that he gave her was exquisite, the heat something she was not certain she could bear for long.

He did not simply make her want him but made her want more of him. Her hips jerked, ground, and she squeezed her eyes closed as she felt herself being lifted. It was only pleasure that made her rise. His hands were not under her but holding hers. She pressed her heels into the chaise, groaning in frustration when she could find no purchase against the sateen fabric.

They adapted, changing positions, turning so that she was still under him but with her bottom raised. He knelt behind her, holding her hips, thrusting as deeply into her as he had before. Her skirt bunched around her hips, and the hard points of her nipples rubbed against the smooth chaise. Lily jammed her knuckles against her mouth. She heard the change in Sherry's breathing, the roughness of it as he pressed her harder.

It was a crescendo of pure joy that he evoked this time, each note of pleasure more deeply resonant than the one before it. Just as she had known would happen, what he was able to evoke in her became part of him. When his rhythm changed to one that was both quick and shallow, she thrust back harder, urging him toward the same release she had known.

Sherry did not surrender to the urge to shout, though considerable effort was required. It was just as difficult not to fall forward and crush Lily beneath his weight. The familiar lethargy that came in the aftermath of pleasure was upon him quickly.

Easing himself out of her, he repaired his clothing and lay down beside her. He helped her right her drawers and shift, then pushed at her dress so that it covered her thighs. The chaise was narrow, and each time their knees bumped they were in danger of falling off.

"We are like two magnets facing each other at the north end," he said. "Turn on your other side."

"And give you my south end again? I know what you did the last time it was presented to you."

He did give a shout of laughter then. Almost immediately, he felt Lily's palm clamp across his mouth. It did not sober him, but it muffled him well enough. "Alukdthadurr."

Lily frowned. "What?" Although she asked the question, she refused to lift her hand even a fraction to hear the answer while Sherry's shoulders were still shaking.

"Alukdthadurr."

"You must compose yourself, m'lord."

He struggled manfully, though he thought her unappreciative of his efforts. Her mouth remained primly flattened, and the manner in which she eyed him was a look she usually reserved for the scoundrels. When she judged his laughter had subsided enough, she raised her palm. He said the words quickly, lest she changed her mind. "I locked the door."

"What does that signify? If you bring so much attention down on us, it will not matter that no one can get in. Everyone will imagine the very worst."

"The worst? Surely not."

Lily gave his shoulders a small shove, not enough to dislodge him from the chaise but enough to make him reconsider the notion of lying there long. "Play for me, Sherry. I want to hear your music in this room." Blushing slightly, she added, "Your *other* music."

He grinned and dropped a kiss on her parted lips. "Very well, but stay just as you are. It will inspire me."

Lily thought she liked the sound of that. "It is a very pretty compliment, m'lord."

Sherry sat at the pianoforte and prepared himself by playing a series of scales, then slipped easily into a Mozart piece that he had committed to memory years ago. He did not know what had inspired Mozart, but the exquisitely complex melody, the intricacy of the fingering, and the brilliance of every measure did indeed remind him of Lily.

From time to time as he played, he glanced in her direction. She never moved. Lying on her side, her head supported by an elbow, one knee drawn up higher than the other, she might have been arranged in just such a fashion for the pleasure of a painter. What artist, he wondered, would have been able to capture the brilliant play of sunlight in her hair or the incandescent gleam where it rested on her white shoulder? Vermeer? Titian? How would it be possible to give full expression to the essence of her on canvas? Which master could do justice to her singularly splendid eyes and bring to mind the harmony of mystery and frankness that existed there?

She was an exquisitely complex piece of work and, to Sherry's thinking, worth devoting a lifetime to appreciating.

He set his palms on his knees when he finished playing. The final notes still echoed softly in his ears, and he waited for them to fall silent before he turned to her. When he did, he saw that her eyes were luminous with unshed tears but that there was no aspect of sadness in the cast of her features. On the contrary, she looked radiantly happy.

"Will you marry me, Lily?" Sherry watched her blink, then become still. What was in her face remained frozen, but there was no longer any joy behind it. "I had thought to say it better," he said quietly. "I had other words, prettier ones, in my head that would explain how you have come to be my heart, how I recognize you as both separate from me and a part of me, and how I cannot imagine my life with you outside of it. Selfish, is it not, to insist you know all the ways I will benefit." His faint smile held more in the way of mockery than humor. "Are all offers of marriage made in that same vein, I wonder? I have never made one before."

"I don't know." Lily's voice was husky and not much above a whisper. "I have never received one before."

He nodded slowly. "I cannot even say where one goes for advice on the matter. And it begs the question: what is the measure of a good proposal? Can the woman's reply be the only yardstick of its worth? If the thing is completely fumbled and she says yes in spite of that, what does it signify? In contrast, what if the proposal is intelligently conceived and she—" He stopped because Lily was rising to her feet. His heart hammered in his chest as she approached, and when only an arm's length separated them, he stood.

"It was a beautiful proposal," she said. "And my answer has nothing at all to do with what is in my heart. It is my head that will not allow me to accept."

"Don't say anything else. Not now. Think on it, Lily. Think toward the solution. I know the problems well enough. I know why you believe you cannot say yes, but do not say no. Once spoken aloud, you will find it even harder to back away from it. Perhaps you think I spoke out of turn or should have never thought of putting the question to you, but it has been on my mind, and I decided it was unfair to both of us to not give it voice."

Sherry held out his hand to her. "There was also the sunlight in your hair." He shrugged a bit diffidently. "I could not help myself."

Smiling, Lily took his hand and let herself be drawn into his embrace. "I did not know you could be so impulsive, or at least moved to it by sunshine in a woman's hair."

He tried to dismiss it with a soft grunt at the back of his throat, but his arms came around her more tightly. "Will you think about it, Lily?"

"I have not said no, have I?"

Sherry placed his lips against her hair and breathed deeply of her fragrance. He knew he had pressed her into giving him this reprieve. Depending upon the generosity of her spirit had never failed him, though he experienced a flash of guilt for doing so. "You will not be sorry."

"No, I do not think I will be."

It was Lady Rivendale's idea to invite Lily to dine with her and Sherry. Lily could think of no plausible excuse that would permit her to beg off. The boys had already had their meal and submitted to a bath with hardly a protest. When they emerged, only Midge needed a second dunking to scrub behind his ears. They'd dressed for bed in record time and waved aside her offer of having something read to them. She should have suspected then that they had already been apprised of the countess's intention, but she was still revisiting Sherry's proposal and did not see their part in the plan as it was unfolding.

Lady Rivendale's invitation took Lily quite by surprise, and there was but a single answer that she could give. "Thank you," she told the maid who came to her room with the message. "Tell her ladyship I shall be happy to do so."

Lady Rivendale received this news calmly enough. It was only when the maid departed that she turned to Sherry and allowed him to see her relief. "I confess, Sherry, I was not certain she would accept. She must imagine it will be as comfortable as having thumbscrews applied."

"That is what I am imagining, Aunt. She deuced well better find another vision that will serve. She cannot have mine." He closed the book he was reading and set it on his lap. "Please say you mean to behave yourself."

"Sherry. Is it possible you do not trust me? Of course I

will behave. I only wish to know her better. How that can give you the least pause I'm sure I don't know."

"What gives me pause is that you have been planning it all day. The scoundrels are never finished eating, bathing, and abed so early. I'd like to think it is because you wore them out, but I suspect it is because you drew them into your confidence. Cybelline is to have a child, you know. Is there not some attention you should be paying to her?"

"Cybelline is wonderfully well settled, thanks in no small part to me. You are not."

"Neither are you. I thought Sir Arthur would have visited by now. He was certainly attentive to you in his home. Why have you not invited him here? Shall I ask him to dine with us tomorrow?"

"If you do, I shall never speak to you again."

"You will have to explain why that should deter me."

Lady Rivendale laughed. "That is very bad of you. If I thought it was in any way truly meant, I would be hurt beyond reason. Arthur and I have an understanding, Sherry. He will be available when I have need of him, and I will be available as it suits me."

"It seems all the advantages are yours, Aunt."

"Yes, and that is why it suits me so admirably."

Sherry simply shook his head. It was probably not possible that he would understand women, but that did not preclude enjoying them. He might have said as much to his godmother—he certainly considered it—but Wolfe arrived to announce that dinner was ready to be served.

Setting his book aside, Sherry stood and offered his arm. "Shall we?"

Lily was coming down the stairs when Sherry and Lady Rivendale stepped into the hall. They stopped and greeted her, then continued on so that she followed naturally in their wake. Those first moments were not as awkward as she'd thought they would be, and once they were seated, dinner proceeded with remarkable ease.

They spoke of things both inconsequential and of import,

but none of it of a personal nature. Sherry listened as his godmother skillfully drew Lily out, getting to know her not by means of who she was but by means of what she thought. Her ladyship was too clever for thumbscrews. She accomplished her ends with humor and grace, by listening more than she spoke, by challenging with a well-considered question, and by remaining nonjudgmental while giving no ground on her own positions.

It was a masterful performance, and Sherry was moved to slyly salute her with his glass of wine when Lily's head was turned. His godmother's faint smile told him the gesture was appreciated.

There was hardly a lull in the conversation as dishes were served and taken away, and the only awkward moment was when Lady Rivendale suggested they retire to the music salon so that Sherry might play for them.

"Do you not wish to play?" she asked. "I confess, it did not occur to me that you would not want to, though I have heard little enough of it since my arrival."

Sherry held up his left hand and stiffly wiggled his thumb and index finger. "A recent injury, I'm afraid. Dislocation. I should rather play when it's not quite so painful."

Lily kept her eyes on her dessert plate. She had no idea whether Sherry's explanation was truly accepted by his godmother or simply allowed to pass without scrutiny. The outcome, though, was that they retired to one of the intimate drawing rooms on the ground floor.

Lady Rivendale accepted a small brandy and encouraged Lily to try the same. Sherry had a glass of port.

"Do you play cards?" Lady Rivendale asked Lily.

"No. As you might imagine, it was discouraged at the abbey."

"That is the problem with a religious order taking up the cause of education. I suppose they did not allow gambling either."

Lily swallowed carefully before answering. "No, m'lady. They were particular about discouraging all the vices."

"Do you hear that, Sherry? There was no end to the mischief at Eton, was there? Cards and gambling were the least of it." She sipped her brandy, not anticipating there would be any reply from her godson. "Do you know who I credit with being a superior card player?"

"It cannot be me," Sherry said. "You beat me regularly."

"I do, don't I? No, you are quite right, it is not you. As much as it pains me to admit it, it is that annoying cousin of my late husband's. His card play may well be the sole reason I am willing to allow him to claim a connection." She sipped her brandy as she considered the truth of that. "He cheats, you know. I am sure of it, but I cannot catch him out."

Lily asked, "Then how can you be certain he cheats?"

"Because I am accounted to be a card sharp myself, my dear. Isn't that so, Sherry?"

"It is indeed." He joined his godmother on the sofa and laid his arm across the back of it behind her shoulders. He spoke to Lily. "It is inevitable that she will know what you have in your hand before the play is fully finished. She counts cards and remembers everything that was discarded. She is invariably the only woman Hepplewhite invites to play cards in his home." Sherry chuckled when he saw Lily managed to look impressed. He was quite sure she had no idea who Hepplewhite was. "The marquess's wife gives the most excruciatingly dull entertainments during the Season, but his card games are all the rage for their unconventional wagering and elimination play. Aunt Georgia has won on occasion, though I think the last was several years ago. What did you win then, Aunt? One hundred shares in a shipping venture to China and a Turkish bathhouse?"

"Two hundred shares. And they turned out to be extraordinarily valuable. I believe I realized over four-thousand pounds. The bathhouse was disappointing since it was not in Turkey as I'd hoped, but in St. Giles. I sold the enterprise and have recently discovered it is a gentlemen's club, though perhaps not so respectable as White's." Lady Rivendale could not miss that Sherry appeared faintly appalled or that Lily was clutching her snifter of brandy, uncertain where she might look but careful not to catch anyone's eye. "Perhaps it is not respectable at all," she said, "but it is out of my hands."

"Please, Aunt, not another word about it. I beg you."

"You are a prig, Sherry, but I love you for it. Give us a kiss." She tapped her proffered cheek and smiled beatifically when Sherry leaned over and bussed her lightly. "Do you see how I love him? I cannot help myself. Is it the same for you, or have you hardened your heart against my godson?"

Sherry sucked in his breath sharply. Lily's knuckles whitened around the stem of her glass.

"I overstepped myself there, didn't I?" Lady Rivendale asked softly, looking from one stricken expression to the other. "I am vastly sorry that I have given you such discomfort. I would countenance a match, you know, for I believe you are well suited. There. It is said." Smiling, very much satisfied with herself now that her opinion had been expressed, her ladyship sipped delicately from her glass. "Do you have cards here, Sherry? I think it would be just the thing to teach Miss Rose to play whist, and you know I do not chatter when I play, at least no more than I do at any other time. That will be a relief to you, I think."

It required a moment for Sherry to collect himself. Of late, it seemed to him that he could be stunned into perfect senselessness by the things women were wont to say. He looked to Lily for direction, and as color was just beginning to return to her face, he said, "Mayhap Miss Rose will not want to play."

"Oh no. I think I should like to learn."

"There, you see?" her ladyship said. "She will be grateful for the distraction also. We can all be served by it."

Sherry rose and crossed to a round side table near the window. He rooted through a drawer and extracted a deck of well-thumbed playing cards. "These will do. Shall we play here?"

Lily and Lady Rivendale joined him at the table. Sherry set chairs in place and seated each of them before taking the chair between them. He passed the cards to his godmother while he explained the basics of the game to Lily. "Playing with only three creates special challenges because none of us has a partner. When there is a fourth, we would form pairs, and you could reasonably expect to be assisted in making seven with your partner's help."

Lily listened to these instructions but understood little of what he said. Her eyes, though, were riveted on Lady Rivendale's hands as they performed a shuffle of lightning speed. Her ladyship caused the cards to fan out between her hands as though suspended in air. She would collapse the deck, then draw it out again, nimbly spreading the cards in an arc on the table in front of her.

"Ignore her," Sherry said, bringing Lily's attention back to him. "She is showing off." He continued by explaining the rules of the deal, how trump was set, and the scoring. "We will play a few practice hands. Does that seem reasonable to you, Aunt?"

Lady Rivendale was already dealing the cards one at a time as prescribed by the rules. "Of course. And I will show you the sort of things you must look for in the play to spot a cheat."

"Meaning it is your intention to play fast and loose with us."

"With the cards, dear boy. With the cards. I have the utmost respect for you." She turned over the last card, the one she dealt to herself, and showed it to Sherry and Lily. It was a diamond and therefore set diamonds as the trump suit. Placing it in her hand, she picked up the remainder of her cards, examined the hand, and addressed Lily. "I hope you will not think I practice underhanded play as a matter of course. I merely amuse myself with it from time to time with Sherry. He does not care, you see, so it is of no consequence. I should not like to be called out for the same by Hepplewhite or his friends. Can you imagine, Sherry? I would be a pariah."

"If you were called out, Aunt, you will be more than a pariah. You will be turning up your toes."

"You would not stand in my place? That is very bad of you. I would have to call on the baron, then. He is credited to be a good shot, and there is always that rather unsettling rumor that he once killed a man at twenty paces. You should be out of my will then, Sherry, and I shall have to think more carefully about the Vermeer."

Sherry turned Lily's hand so he could see her cards and pointed to the one she should put down as her first play. "You would be fortunate," he told his godmother, "if he did not shoot you himself. It would hasten his inheritance."

"Bah!" Lady Rivendale made her play and took the first trick. "You are in the wrong of it there. He would have to put a period to your life first. You are standing squarely in his way." She gave him an arch look. "That is, unless you champion me and I do not eliminate you from my will."

Sherry rolled his eyes. "Play your next card, Aunt Georgia." To Lily, he said, "This matter of being in or out of the will is a relatively recent bone of contention. I believe my place in that document was assured until the arrival of the usurper."

Concentrating on the card play, Lily merely nodded. She dropped a diamond on the pair of spades only to have Sherry pick up the card and return it to her hand.

"You have to follow suit. You can't play trump when you have a spade in your hand. Play your queen and the trick is yours."

Lily did as she was told and swept the trick in front of her. "So you are out of it, then." She led with the ace of hearts. "Her ladyship means to give her vast wealth to the usurping cousin."

"Not bloody likely," Lady Rivendale murmured, though it was unclear if she was discussing Lily's comment or the card she'd put down. She trumped the ace with a flourish.

Sherry tossed off the three of hearts and watched his godmother gleefully take charge of the trick. "Aunt Georgia is not especially fond of her cousin, except it seems, in regard to his card play, and there her admiration is of a most suspicious nature."

Lady Rivendale placed her next card on the table. "Sherry is not telling you the whole of it, m'dear. He introduced the villain to me and—"

"You begged the introduction," Sherry interrupted. "If you recall, I was not in favor of it." He tossed off another card and watched Lily make her choice. "In any event, I did not suspect a connection to you."

Her ladyship sighed. "Neither did I. I admit, I was struck immediately by his fine looks." She saw Lily give a small start. "What? Do you think I am too old for a flirtation? I assure you, I am not. Sherry, we must stop talking about my will. It makes a poor impression." She snapped up the next trick as soon as Lily laid down her card, then set down another. "He is handsome enough, in a wicked sort of way, but now that I know he is set on making himself my heir by hook or by marriage, he is not in the least interesting to me."

"Marriage?" Sherry folded what remained of his cards and tapped one corner of the stack on the tabletop. "You have never mentioned marriage. He's proposed?"

"Twice. And I refused twice. I am currently in anticipation of another offer."

"Sir Arthur?"

"No. Woodridge again. Really, Sherry. Are you not paying atten—" She stopped as the cards in Lily's hand dropped and scattered. "What is it, dear? Go on, pick them—" She tossed down her own cards and reached across the table to Lily. "Sherry, catch her! I think she is going to—"

Sherry already had Lily by the shoulders and was keeping her upright in her chair. "Will you ring, Aunt Georgia? Ask Wolfe to bring smelling salts." He lifted Lily's limp figure in his arms and carried her to the sofa. She was pale, and her breathing was shallow. He patted her lightly on the cheek. "Lily?"

"I do not like this, Sherry," Lady Rivendale said from the other side of the room. "What cause did she have to faint? She had only a small amount of the brandy, and I did not notice that she was sickening for something. She ate well enough at dinner, though there is not much flesh on her bones. Oh, dear, you do not suppose she is *enceinte*? That can do nothing save complicate matters at this juncture." This last was said just as the door opened and Wolfe appeared. Lady Rivendale made her request, and he disappeared. "I cannot say how much he heard, Sherry. I swear he must have been standing at attention on the other side of the door. Do you suppose he speaks French?"

"I do not think it matters. He is no dolt and perfectly able to divine your meaning."

Her ladyship arrived at Sherry's side. "Is she coming around? There is a bit of color in her cheeks now. Surely that is a good sign."

Sherry stopped patting Lily's cheek and the color immediately faded. "I'm afraid I've put most of it there."

"Look!" Lady Rivendale clapped her hands together lightly. "Did you see? Her eyelids twitched."

Sherry had not noticed. His attention was caught by Lily's hand. Out of the line of his godmother's vision, it was squeezing his with undeniable, conscious strength. "Aunt Georgia, will you see if you cannot hasten the arrival of those smelling salts?"

Lady Rivendale did not hesitate. "I shall be happy to. It is always worse when one has no good purpose at a time like this."

Sherry waited until the door closed. "She is gone, Lily. You can come out of hiding now."

Lily's eyelashes fluttered open. Her smile was vaguely embarrassed. "I am sorry, Sherry. I have never done that before."

"Swooned?" he asked. "Or pretended to?"

"You might not credit it, but it was a bit of both. Real enough in the first moments but more in the way of avoidance thereafter. Will you permit me to sit up?"

Sherry moved aside so Lily could swing her legs over the side of the sofa. He slipped one arm under her shoulders and assisted her efforts. He searched her face as real color returned to it. "What happened, Lily? Why did you faint?"

"I think it must have been the brandy. I have no head for spirits. I am not pregnant."

"You heard that. I wondered."

"It was not an unreasonable assumption." She glanced down at her hands. "I would like to go to my room."

"Certainly. I will escort you."

"No." Lily quickly shook her head. "I can manage. Truly." She began to rise, and Sherry stood with her. "Please, Sherry. I am quite certain I can negotiate the way back on my own."

Still, Sherry hesitated. When he finally stepped aside it was with a reluctance that was palpable. "Very well. But I insist on being allowed to look in on you later."

"Of course." Standing on tiptoe, she kissed him on the cheek. Before he could make more of the moment than was her wont, Lily turned and slipped easily out of his reach.

Sherry watched her go. He realized he could not afford to give her long. She might very well have a valise already packed in anticipation of just such a moment. He was no longer certain he could depend on her to tell him she was leaving. She'd made the promise with the best intention and would not break it lightly, but she had her own survival to consider, and while he did not yet understand what had threatened her, he knew with absolute confidence that she believed she was threatened.

He returned to the table where they had been playing and gathered up the cards. Shuffling them idly, he sat in the chair Lily had occupied and set himself the task of reviewing their conversation, puzzling over what had happened.

By the time Lady Rivendale returned with the smelling salts, he had arrived at what he believed was the answer.

Lily did not turn when she heard Sherry's approach. As always, his tread was light, but on this occasion the crushed gravel beneath his feet kept it from being soundless. She made room for him on the stone bench, drawing her skirt aside so that he might sit with her.

"I thought I'd left it until too late," he said. "Or was I wrong at the outset, and it was not your intention to leave tonight?"

"You weren't wrong." It was a warm evening. Lily had removed the paisley silk shawl from her shoulders and laid it across her lap. She picked it up and drew it slowly back and forth between her hands. "It is always my first reaction. To run, that is. To hide as quickly as I am able. I am no longer sure it serves me so well. Circumstances have changed."

Sherry's cheeks puffed a little as he released a long, slow breath. "I am gratified to hear it. Are you still afraid, Lily?"

"Yes. Not so much now that you are here. I am beginning to appreciate that it is better when you are nearby. I do not know if I can adequately explain what it is like to live with the threat of him. It doesn't matter that he is some place distant from Granville, he is always here,"—she tapped her temple—"always here in my mind. Tonight it seemed he had joined us at cards."

"Woodridge."

She nodded. "You suspected?"

"It is truer that his name was one of many suspects on the list I had begun. I had not given him a great deal of thought, though I imagine that is because he is someone better known to me than others. Don't mistake my meaning, Lily. Knowing him does not mean that I believe you less. In fact, quite the opposite is true. I can find it all too easy to credit him with every one of the things you told me. I suppose I simply believed I would have known something about them, yet I have never heard even a rumor that alludes to the proclivities that you described."

"Lady Rivendale said you introduced him to her."

"True. As I mentioned, it was reluctantly done."

"Then you knew something about the man's character that made you hesitate."

Sherry said nothing for a long time. He leaned forward and rested his forearms on his knees. He pressed the pads of this fingertips together, making a steeple of them, tapping them lightly as he considered what he might say to her. The weight of his thoughts seemed to bear his head down. His view was the gravel path, not the lake in the distance. Once he spoke, the words could not be taken back. She would know something that no one outside the king's confederates knew and there was an inherent risk in that, the vast majority of it to be borne by her.

Sherry felt Lily's hand on his back. She ran her palm slowly across the breadth of his shoulders. With each pass there was a sense of tension easing, of warmth slipping under his skin. She said nothing at all to encourage him; she seemed completely willing to accept his silence. Even her hand was not insistent, merely supportive.

He looked up, past the hedge rows, then beyond them to the lake. Moonlight shimmered across the surface of the water, laying down a silvery path that appeared substantial enough to walk on. His chuckle was soft, mocking, as he realized he had been offered an opportunity to take a path such as that before, and he had done so without ever once testing the metaphorical waters. Remembering that was what finally decided Sherry.

"Woodridge was my mentor," he said. "He is the one who approached me while I was yet at Cambridge. He drew me out, listened to what I thought. My opinions interested him, and he permitted me to speak at length. I admit I was flattered by his attention, and certainly I was intrigued by what he had to say in turn. His ideas of governance, of what was truly required to administer the Crown's policies and assure the liberties of the people, were different than anything I had heard before—or at least in the fact that he stated them openly. He challenged the notion that reasonable men could prevail on the strength of their ideas alone. He put forth the notion that what was required was resolve."

Lily's hand had stopped moving on Sherry's back. It rested on his shoulder. "Resolve? What does that mean?"

"I did not entirely understand it then, but I do not offer that as an excuse. It means that one is willing to do whatever is necessary for the furtherance of the idea. It means that one justifies securing peace by killing, fostering the opinions of some by destroying the presses of others, and engaging the enemy in dialogue but not before knowing his secrets. Ideals, not ideas, are turned on their head. I can explain it no better than that, though I assure you that Woodridge did. Will it surprise you to learn that he is articulate, even masterful in presenting his thinking?"

Lily shook her head. "No. It does not surprise. I never thought he was a madman, Sherry. I might have been able to find pity for him in my heart if that were true. I think he is both clever and ruthless and that what he proposes as though it were reasoned and reasonable is naught but amoral."

Sherry turned his head and regarded her a moment. "Did I not say they could not have had you? You see it so clearly."

"He *did* have me, Sherry." Lily picked up her shawl and drew it around her shoulders. The evening had not grown colder, but she had. Her skin prickled, and the tips of her fingers tingled. "I did not see it at all. Not in the beginning. Not for a very long time. And even afterward, after he'd introduced me to what he thought should be a pleasure to me, I wasn't certain yet that he had done something wrong. I thought it must be me. He was able to make me believe that. Of all the things he did to me, I bear him the most hatred for that, for what he was able to make me believe about myself. So, no, I did not see it."

Sherry sat back. Lily's profile was elegant in its line, the chin lifted a fraction, the tilt of her head regal. She had not emerged unscathed by what had been done to her, but she also had not emerged bowed.

Then quietly, in the manner of a confession, she told him,

"I cannot conceive your children, Sherry. He has ruined me for that."

Sherry said nothing for a long time. He recalled asking her once if there had ever been a child; she had not answered him on that occasion because he had proved to her that he had not truly wanted to know. "How can you be certain?"

"I never conceived when I was with him. He had two children, so the fault cannot lie with him. I was glad of it then, but now, knowing I am barren, it is not a secret I can keep from you. It would not be fair."

It was then that he clearly understood why she was telling him. "We will have the scoundrels, Lily, and even if there are no other children, we will want for nothing."

She turned to him, her smile faint, a bit uncertain. "Do you mean it, Sherry? I would not have you hold out hope for what cannot be. Will we be enough for you?"

"Yes."

Lily took full measure of his features and saw nothing held back. She nodded once. "Then I should very much like to accept your offer of marriage."

Fourteen

Lady Rivendale regarded the cards in her hand with a suspicious eye, then looked at each of her fellow players in turn. They stared back, waiting patiently for her to make her first play, their features set with such perfect innocence that she was made even more dubious. "You rogues. I believe you fixed the deal, Master Dash." She turned in her chair and addressed her concerns to the pair sitting at the pianoforte. "They are cheating. Sherry? Miss Rose? What do you have to say to that?"

Sherry kept his finger on the passage that Lily was trying to master and glanced over at his godmother. "I say they cannot be very good at it yet. You caught them out easily enough."

Lily's head snapped up. "My lord! You should not say such things."

Sherry shrugged, his face cast with the same innocent expression as the scoundrels. "Try this fingering, Lily." He demonstrated it, bringing her attention once again to the lesson.

Lady Rivendale turned back to the boys, one eyebrow severely arched. "So it is Sherry who has been teaching you these tricks. I suppose he thinks it is amusing, but I do not."

Lily was listening to this scold with half an ear. "Thank you, m'lady. They should not—"

Lady Rivendale continued as if she were not the one doing the interrupting. "He does not have the skill for it, boys. Now, if you desire to learn the pianoforte, then naturally you should apply to his lordship, but if you want to learn to manipulate the cards, then you—"

"My lady!" Lily's head swiveled around. "Please do not—" She stopped because Sherry was directing her fingers to the keys again.

"Surrender," he whispered under his breath. "You cannot hope to win."

Dash gathered up all the cards and pushed the deck toward Lady Rivendale. "Show us the deal again," he said. "The one where you pull cards from the bottom."

"Of course," Lady Rivendale said with great aplomb. "It will be my greatest pleasure."

Lily groaned softly while Sherry chuckled, and the card game resumed. It was late by the time the boys were put to bed, and when Lily returned to the music salon Sherry and his godmother were already engaged in another enterprise, one she had as little liking for as teaching the boys to cheat.

"I thought we were agreed the wedding would be a small affair," she said. "Is that the proposed list of guests? It looks considerably longer than the last time I saw it."

Lady Rivendale protectively raised the list to her bosom. "I was just eliminating some names, m'dear, though I can tell you it is an onerous task when one has so many friends. Still, I will persevere." To prove this point, she dipped her quill in the inkwell and drew a line through two names. "There. It is done. Mrs. Hoyle and Lord Ballard cannot expect an invitation even though they live not far from here and might reasonably anticipate joining us at Granville."

Lily glanced at Sherry. "M'lord?"

He leaned back in his chair, arms folded across his chest, and challenged her with a single arched eyebrow. "If my opinion matters at all at this juncture, then I am for Gretna. Did I not say so at the outset? When you agreed to marry me, was I not all for going straightaway to the stables and ordering the carriage for us? A fortnight has passed since then, and we have yet to have the banns read for the first time."

Lily went to his side and placed a hand on his shoulder. "Are you pouting? I think you are pouting."

Lady Rivendale continued to study the list. "He is."

"I am," Sherry said. He caught Lily by the waist and brought her down on his lap.

"Sherry!" Lily tried to scramble off, but he would not release her. "Lady Rivendale is here!"

"And she will pay us no heed as long as she is adding names to the list."

Lily looked at his godmother and saw she was blithely ignoring them as she scribbled down more names. "Gretna," Lily said softly. "Why did I not agree?"

"Because you are a sensible child," her ladyship said. "And a kind one. Sherry would think nothing of breaking this poor woman's heart. What do you think of Mr. Armbruster? He has long been a friend to the Granthams."

Sherry chuckled. "Every compliment she gives you will increase the list by at least one or two."

Sighing, Lily slipped her arm around Sherry's back and laid her head against his. They sat in companionable silence, alternately amused and dismayed by Lady Rivendale's revisions, but offering no objections.

Her ladyship ran an index finger along the names. Satisfied, she looked up. "Now, Lily, what about your side of the family?"

Lily blinked. "My side? I thought you understood there was no one."

"Nonsense. Of course there is *someone*. Frankly, I have been troubled by the way you have cut them off, or perhaps it is they who have cut you off, though it is hard to believe. Your mama was well loved, and it seems to me that you should have been taken into the bosom of her family without a second thought after she died. I cannot think why it didn't happen."

Straightening, Lily looked at Sherry. "Did you know about this?"

"Nothing." He addressed his godmother. "I understood you to say there was no one remaining."

Lady Rivendale replaced her quill in the ink and folded her plump arms under her bosom. "On her father's side. That is perfectly true as far as I am aware, but I am speaking of Lillian, not Howard, and Lillian was better known to me. I know there was at least one cousin that was more in the way of a sister to her. Caroline. Have you never heard of her, Lily?"

Lily shook her head. She moved off Sherry's lap and chose another chair at the table. "It is not at all familiar."

"Well, it may be that you are too young to remember that sort of connection, and I do not know what happened to Caro, for I lost touch with her long before I made my own come out. I am not certain she attended your parents' wedding, though I cannot recall any comment regarding her absence. Odd, that. I remember quite clearly that John was there. That is her brother. Do you know that name? John Bingham."

Color drained from Lily's face so quickly it alarmed Lady Rivendale. Sherry also leaned forward in anticipation that she would falter. Lily caught her breath and waved aside their concern, though this was accomplished with a hand that trembled slightly. "I'm fine. It is rather more than surprising to hear him spoken of by anyone other than . . ." Lily's voice trailed off. Her slight smile mocked her almost superstitious reluctance to say the name aloud. "It should not be so difficult to say his name, yet I find that bringing him to mind is often accompanied by a strangling hold on my throat. It cannot be good that he can stop my voice so easily."

Lady Rivendale was sympathetic. Unfolding her arms, she laid one hand over Lily's. "In time, m'dear, it will be different. You will see. It is a testament of your great courage that you have revealed even a single particular about all you know. I do not think you should find fault with yourself for being unable to easily speak of him. It is a great comfort to me that you have taken Sherry into your confidence, for I know he will champion you."

Lily glanced sideways at Sherry and did not mistake the resolve that cast his features in sharply defined edges. "Yes," she said quietly. "He will. It makes me afraid for him."

"I understand." Lady Rivendale also looked at her godson. "But if I were that villain Woodridge, I would be afraid *of* him."

Sherry calmly sat back in his chair and stretched his legs under the table. "It is the nose, you know. I have it on good authority that it is fiercely aggressive. Is that not right, Aunt Georgia?"

She not only agreed that it was but reminded him that she had despaired that he would ever grow into it. This raised a small smile in Lily, and the difficult moment passed. Sherry had no desire for either of the women in his company to dwell overlong on what they had glimpsed in his eyes. It was not always possible to shield them but neither did he mean to frighten them.

Lady Rivendale removed her hand from Lily's. "How is it that you know John Bingham, Lily, if you do not know him as a relation?"

"I do not know him. Not really. He is Sister Mary Joseph's brother."

Sherry swore softly, bringing the attention of both women back to him. Hardly aware of what he'd said, he did not apologize. "Lily, that's extraordinary. Are you quite certain it was John Bingham?"

"Perhaps it is not the same Mr. Bingham, but I could not forget that name. Sister made certain I knew it. She wrote it down for me as well as how I might find him. The baron discovered it all. Some of it he knew before he found me in Le

Havre; the rest he learned from the letter I carried with me from Sister."

"Do you know what was in the letter?" asked Sherry.

"No, not the details. It was not for me, so I never read it. I am certain it was unexceptional, a letter of introduction only."

"Yes, but an introduction that identified you as someone more important to him than a mere student of an abbey school. Sister Mary Joseph is Caroline Bingham, his own sister. It explains why she was so certain he would accept you into his household."

"We are probably mistaken," Lily said. "I should have known if Sister was also my cousin. Why would she have kept something of that nature a secret from me?"

Sherry did not answer immediately. Out of the corner of his eye he saw his godmother shaking her head so faintly as to be almost imperceptible. Taking that as a warning, he spoke with a certain caution in his voice. "A desire to protect you might account for it. After your parents were killed, she wanted to keep you close. Perhaps she believed that if the connection were known you would have been removed from the abbey."

Lily frowned. "But before my parents died, Sherry? What of then? If Sister were truly my mother's cousin and dear friend, wouldn't that have come to light at the outset?"

It was Lady Rivendale who responded. "It is entirely conceivable that a familial connection would have been frowned upon by the abbess or the bishop. You might have been rejected for admission if your relation to Caro had been known, and I suspect your parents very much wanted you to be there because of Caroline." The wedding guest list lay in front of her. She ironed out the wrinkles in the paper with the flat of her hand. "In any event, it is all speculation. We cannot know what was in their mind."

"Or even if there is a connection," Lily reminded them. "As you said, it is all speculation."

"True."

Lily watched Lady Rivendale's hand press the list first one way, then the other. Her ladyship hardly seemed aware of what she was doing, as though it was the necessity of keeping herself busy in some way that was imperative. "Sister Mary Joseph was English," Lily said at last. "Did I tell you that, Sherry?"

"Yes."

"I never knew how she came to be at the abbey or even how she came to be in France. She never spoke of it. The girls talked, created stories as young girls are wont to do, but interest in that aspect of her faded as one knew her better. She spoke flawless French. That intrigued us also. Not everyone noticed she had an accent."

Sherry asked, "Did she speak to you in English?"

"Sometimes. Rarely in front of anyone. She said she did not want me to lose my facility for the language. I did not think it was so important, but she insisted."

Lady Rivendale pushed the list away suddenly and set her hands in her lap, threading her fingers together. "Percy Bingham, that is John and Caro's father, was your mother's uncle. I believe I am in the right of it there, though no one outside the family can be sure of such things. One need only to regard the havey-cavey manner in which Woodridge makes his claim of a tie between us to know the truth of that." This statement was greeted by a heavy silence, and she went on quickly. "I cannot say that I am more than passingly acquainted with the Binghams, but it seems to me that Mr. Percy Bingham's wife was French. Oh, it has been so long ago that you should not depend upon my memory. Really, I have no conviction that I am in the right of it any longer. Sybil perhaps was her Christian name. Sylvia. Sylvie. Yes, it might have been the last. Sylvie. It is pretty, is it not?"

Looking past Lily's shoulder, drawing on her memory as best she could, Lady Rivendale finally threw up her hands. "It is no good. I cannot recall her maiden name, indeed, I might have never known. One does not always know these things. It would be best, I think, if we applied to Mr. John Bingham for the answers. He must have wondered what became of you. Can you not imagine that his sister would have inquired after your arrival? And what of your own silence? It would raise many questions."

Lily remained unconvinced. "But it might be some other Bingham. It is not an uncommon name."

Sherry rose to his feet. "I am all for a drink. Aunt? Lily?" They each shook their head. "Very well." He went to the sideboard and poured himself two fingers of whisky. "Lily, there is no reason to correspond with Mr. Bingham unless you wish it, but you must realize that the announcement of our engagement will no doubt bring about the end you seem bent on avoiding. It cannot matter greatly if your John Bingham is the same John Bingham my godmother has spoken of; we shall sort it out in time, I expect. I can—"

Lady Rivendale interrupted. "I think I will have that drink, Sherry. The same as you've poured for yourself, though half as much, please."

Belatedly aware he had been pressing his point too hard, Sherry did not take exception to the interruption. He poured a single finger of whisky for his godmother and carried it to her.

Lily waited until Sherry returned to his chair before she spoke. "I don't think Sister Mary Joseph can have been my mother's cousin, Sherry, but mayhap I will write to the abbey. I do not know if she is still there, or even if she is yet alive, but no one will stop my correspondence from reaching her now. If there is an explanation to be made, it should come from her." She turned her attention to Lady Rivendale. "Please do not add Mr. Bingham's name to your list, or the names of any other relations you think I might have. I would rather there was no list at all, but if you cannot help yourself, confine the names to your dearest friends who can be counted on not to spoil our wedding with gossip about what might remain of my family."

She stood, her bearing a trifle stiff, her self-possession a fragile thing. "If you will excuse me. I am for bed." She put out her hand when Sherry started to rise. "No. I don't require an escort. Good night."

Sherry stood anyway, but he didn't move away from the table as Lily turned and left the room. When she was gone, he sat slowly and regarded his godmother. "You might have said something to me. It was rather more than she was prepared to hear."

"I did not realize how little either of you knew about her family. That she was kept so much in the dark is unconscionable. I understand not speaking of it to her when she was yet a child, but as she became a young woman . . ." Lady Rivendale shook her head and her mouth flattened disapprovingly. "And when she was sent off from the abbey, well, she should have been apprised of the whole of it then."

"I do not know the whole of it, Aunt, and neither do you. You are speculating."

"Do you think Lily is not also? She is afraid to know the truth now, and I cannot say that I fault her for it, but she has retired to her room so she might do so in peace. I doubt she will find any sleep tonight. To have been through so much, then to be confronted with the prospect of being a bastard, really, it is more than anyone should be made to bear."

"It does not matter to me if she is Caroline Bingham's child."

"It matters to *her*."

Sherry drew in a deep breath and released it slowly. "What is to be done?"

"Whatever it is, Sherry, it is not for you to do. You cannot affect a solution for everything." Lady Rivendale picked up the list, skimmed it once, then folded it neatly and began to tear it into quarters. "There. It is my contribution to your happiness."

"Thank you for that, Aunt."

She shrugged lightly. "A woman can dream." She pushed the confetti she'd made to the center of the table. "Why have the banns not been read, Sherry?"

"I have only just placed the announcement of our engagement in the London papers."

"I am not fooled by that. That is bait. Oh, do not look at me in such a manner as if I cannot possibly know what I'm saying. If neither of you desire a wedding with more than a few of your intimates present, then that announcement had but one purpose: to draw the baron out. Is it that she has agreed to marry you but will not do so until it is settled with him?"

"I am all admiration," Sherry said, meaning it more than not.

"Do you think it is wise, Sherry, to tempt him in such a manner?"

"It is necessary."

"What if he does not come?"

"He will. Do not forget that my acquaintance with the baron is far and away more substantial than your own."

"Yes, but you have never fully explained how he is known so well to you. It continues to puzzle."

Sherry's smile was purposely enigmatic. "And it shall remain so. But consider, Aunt Georgia, when Woodridge arrives it could very well be that his plan will not be to disrupt my engagement but to secure one of his own."

Lady Rivendale's eyes widened as the bent of Sherry's words became clearer to her. "With me, you mean?"

"You cannot be so surprised. Did you not say that he had proposed twice, and you were in expectation of a third?"

"Yes, but now that you are engaged to Lily, surely he would not dare to make an offer."

"Why not? Do you believe he thinks for a moment that she has been forthcoming with me?" Sherry shook his head. "No, Aunt, he will come to Granville Hall because he desires to deliver us all from Lily's wickedness. That is the true nature of the man. He believes it is his purpose to save us from ourselves."

* * *

Wycliff Standish, Baron Woodridge, regarded the *Gazette* notice for the third time since returning to his carriage and ordering his driver to make way again. He held the announcement carefully, letting it dangle between two fingers so that he would not inadvertently tear it. He had been equally cautious removing it from the paper four days earlier, sharpening the blade of his knife before he applied it to the border of the notice. After reading then rereading it, he had folded it in precisely creased thirds and placed it under his silk-lined waistcoat just above his heart. It amused him to suppose that someone privy to this gesture might mistake it as a romantic one. It was not. Woodridge was confident that his heart had no romantic leanings, that what he experienced was something more extraordinary than what other men knew.

What was in his heart was righteous passion. Sometimes his hands actually trembled with the strength of it. He had learned to draw on that strength, pulling it back into himself when that was what was demanded of him, then calling upon the reserve when the mission demanded it.

In London, when he'd first seen the announcement, he'd known a moment's uncertainty that he would be able to control himself, but by the time he'd tucked the piece into his waistcoat, he had already contained that passion. Looking at the notice now, his fingers shook slightly. He did not fool himself into believing the bouncing of the carriage lay at the root of that unsteadiness. He recognized the fever that was upon him and knew it would have to be assuaged.

It was not so much a question of when—for he knew he would always be able to pick the moment—but of precisely how he would satisfy himself. To that end, he returned the notice to his waistcoat, leaned back against the plump leather cushions, and brought the harlot Lilith Rose Sterling to mind.

She deserved rather more than had been done to her before. It was clear to him that he had not taken her in hand as completely as he'd thought. She should not have been able to leave him; she should not have wanted to. He had always been the one who set the terms of the arrangement he enjoyed with women. Even his own wife had acceded gracefully—and gratefully—in the end. He would have sent her anywhere she wished—the Continent, the Americas, even India—but she could not bring herself to leave him. Jane, his dear Jane, the mother of his children, had sworn she would rather die than leave him.

What choice was left to him but to oblige her?

Lilith, though, had been a provocation from the outset, making herself undesirable to him to turn aside his interest, then running from him when he discovered her perfidy. He'd followed her, though, and he'd won her confidence. He thought he would tire of her soon enough, as he had with those before her, yet she enticed him again and again. Debased, yet somehow never humiliated, soiled and used in every manner he could conceive, she had nevertheless seemed to remain untouched.

A virgin.

Woodridge grimaced wryly at the notion, yet understood it was not far off the mark. She served his needs too well, her purity compelling him to make use of her, and her pride fairly demanding that he make every attempt to diminish it.

Had she been something less than what she was, there would have been a different end. She would have been long out of his life, and he would not be on the road to Granville Hall now to reclaim his sacrificial lamb.

Lily snuggled more deeply against the comforting heat at her back. She was on her side facing the window, and the same cool breeze that shifted the curtains made her wrinkle her nose. She was not yet quite awake, but neither was she unaware of her surroundings. Behind her she could hear Sherry's light, even breathing. It was his arm curving over her waist, his knee that had nudged hers apart.

She didn't recall him coming to her room. It was just as well. She would have sent him away. They'd agreed on the evening she accepted his proposal that he would no longer slip into her bedchamber. At least she'd thought he had agreed. Perhaps he'd only said that his door would be closed to her.

Her nightshift was bunched around her hips and her bare bottom was cradled snugly against Sherry's groin. His erection pressed hot and hard against her cleft. She heard his breathing catch, then quicken, then he was easing himself inside her. She pressed back, accommodating his entry, and the delicious feeling of warmth, of being filled, made her murmur contentedly.

He moved slowly, without urgency. The languor of his rhythm seemed suited to the early morning hour and the sense there was more dream here than reality. Lily found his hand and drew it between her thighs. She guided his fingers to the swollen hood of flesh hidden in her moist sex and showed him what she wanted.

"Allegro," she whispered. Sherry's sleepy chuckle caused wisps of hair to shift against her nape and tickle her. She shivered as much from the prickling of sensation there as she did from his far more intimate caress.

"Ahh." Lily's hips jerked. Pleasure spiraled, scattered, then began to rise more strongly than before. Reaching behind her, she laid her hand on his hip and urged him again. She felt his mouth in her hair, just at the back of her ear. He nudged aside a curl with his lips. The damp edge of his tongue darted against her skin. He whispered something she could not quite make out, but the husky timbre of his voice communicated his purpose anyway.

Lily hummed her pleasure. He drew aside the neckline of her shift and his teeth nipped her shoulder. It made her toes curl. Her entire body arched when he kissed her in just the same spot.

"Do you like that?" he asked. Not waiting for an answer, he did it again and received the same response, inarticulate but communicating everything that was important.

Lily was not certain that either of them was fully awake until the moment pleasure shuddered through them, and even then it was so exquisite as to not seem grounded in any reality.

She did not know how much time had passed before she became aware of Sherry again. He was on his side, his head propped on an elbow as he looked down on her. She was lying on her back, the neckline of her shift restored to modesty, though beneath the sheet and thin blanket, she could tell there was a great deal that had not yet been put to right. Reaching under the covers, she lifted her hips and pushed at her shift, wriggling until the hem reached her knees. Satisfied, and undisturbed by Sherry's rather wicked smile, she asked, "Did I fall asleep?"

"We both did. Don't worry. It is not so early yet. We can lie abed awhile longer."

"I thought we were agreed that we would not share a bed before our wedding." When Sherry merely arched an eyebrow at her, Lily reconsidered. "Perhaps not." Reaching up, she brushed aside a lock of dark hair that had fallen over his forehead. "Will it be today, do you think?"

"I hope so. If not today, then tomorrow."

"I do not think my nerves can tolerate a great many tomorrows, Sherry. What if we are wrong, and he doesn't come? He might not see the notice. He might ignore it if he sees it. He might—"

Sherry pressed his fingertip against Lily's lips, silencing her. "You have never once doubted that he would come for you, else you wouldn't have hidden away these last years. Don't doubt your instincts now; they've served you well. If he misses the notice, he is certain to learn of the engagement from others. Recall that he has an interest in more than one matter here. I figure largely in the disposition of my godmother's fortune, and he has come lately to believe that he should be the heir. Failing to convince her of an entailment that does not exist, he apparently believes she can be persuaded to marry him. So his interests are threefold: you, me, and Lady Rivendale. How can he stay away?"

She nodded faintly. "You will not call him out?"

"I have already promised I will not."

Lily searched his face. "You really believe you can persuade him to agree to an honorable silence?"

"I do. It's what he taught me, Lily. Persuasion. And he taught me well. I have not left anything to chance. I will know before he does when he is bound to arrive."

Word came to Sherry that afternoon, delivered by the advance guard of two of his trusted retainers. Sherry had entertained the notion of pressing Gibb and Conway into service but dismissed it. While they had experience that could certainly help him in dealing with Woodridge, they were also too well known to the baron. If Woodridge glimpsed them on the road or at an inn, he would be immediately suspicious. He might not associate their company as having anything to do with Sherry, but it could be enough to make him turn back to London.

Instead, Sherry had selected the footman Tolley and the head groom Kennerly to travel to the inn at Westin-on-the-Narrows and remain there until Woodridge arrived or his carriage passed. It was not so far from Granville that they could not overtake him, and they would arouse no suspicion in doing so. They were, in fact, beneath the baron's notice.

When Sherry learned that Woodridge would be arriving within the hour, he cautioned Lily and his godmother that they must stay away. They could keep each other company for the time it would take him to conduct his business with Woodridge, but he would not have them presenting themselves and distracting him from his purpose.

Lily was all for not setting her eyes on Woodridge again, but her ladyship wanted the opportunity to give him the cut direct.

"Yes," Sherry said dryly, "that *would* sting him."

Lady Rivendale harrumphed lightly, but she conceded that keeping Lily company while Woodridge was at the hall put her to a good purpose. "You will report every detail, Sherry. I will not be satisfied until I know every particular."

"Yes, Aunt." He kissed her on the cheek and had something more substantial for Lily. "Do not worry," he whispered in her ear. "It will be done."

The Right Honorable Lord Woodridge arrived at Granville shortly before the four o'clock hour and was announced to Sherry as tea was being served to him in the library.

Sherry rose at his mentor's entrance and motioned him into the room. "Woodridge. What a surprise this is. Come. Come. If you are not the last person I might expect to see today, then you figure very close to it."

"Oh? And who would be less likely to arrive at your doorstep?"

"My sister Cybelline. She is expecting a child and does not travel now."

Woodridge nodded, smiling. "She fares well?"

"Yes. Yes, she does. I had a letter from her only yesterday and am assured she is in the best of health. Please, will you join me for tea? Or mayhap you wish something stronger to remove the dust of travel from your mouth?"

"Tea." Woodridge began a walk along the perimeter of Sherry's study while his host rang for more refreshment and cakes. "I have always admired this room, Sherry. Most impressive. Your collection of books must be among the finest anywhere. I am giving you a great compliment when I say it rivals my own."

"Indeed. Thank you." Sherry turned away from the door. "I admit I am more than moderately curious as to the purpose of your visit. It was not much above a fortnight ago that Gibb and Conway paid their addresses. Is it to be a parade from London or do you represent the last best hope to turn me around?"

He stroked his narrow chin, thoughtful, but made no attempt to answer Sherry's question. His slight smile was rueful. "Gibb and Con. I hadn't realized. There is much that I no longer know."

"A precaution, I suspect." Sherry's brief study of Woodridge noted the fact that he was thinner than the last time he'd seen him in London. Not only was his face drawn, but his eyes appeared to be more deeply set, the cheekbones a fraction more prominent. For the first time, he looked considerably older than his forty-two years. Sherry recalled that Gibb had said that it was likely a poisoning that sent Woodridge to his bed for a week. Was that what had ravaged the man, or was it something else? "It hardly seems prudent for them to discuss matters freely when everyone is at risk."

Woodridge speared Sherry with his incisive glance. "Yet they were not hesitant to discuss matters with you. Why is that? Have you decided to come back to the fold, Sherry?"

The extra service arrived, diverting Sherry's attention. He took the tray from Wolfe and instructed him that they should not be disturbed. The butler backed out of the room. Sherry carried the tray to the table where his own cup rested. He was on the point of lowering the tray when the pot of tea slid toward him. He bobbled the tray, overcompensating for the shift in weight and tipped it back. The china pot crashed to the floor, and tea poured onto the rug and spattered the ball-and-claw feet of the table and nearby chair. The pyramid of iced cakes toppled into the drink, the teacup took a wobbly turn on the floor then stopped, and the plate rolled like a child's hoop toward the fireplace where it crashed against the marble apron and shattered. The tray turned over twice in the air, then clattered to the floor, smashing the soggy cakes and the teacup.

Sherry regarded the mess he'd made of things. He glanced over his shoulder at Woodridge and offered an apologetic, ironic smile. "I have always counted it as a good thing that I was to the manor born. I would not acquit myself well in service. Come. We will repair to the gallery. Wolfe will make it all right in a very short time." He opened the door and ushered Woodridge into the hall.

Wolfe had not strayed far and had already summoned a maid to clean the mess. The butler opened the pocket doors to the gallery and stepped aside, then followed to light the candelabras. "Will you want a fire, m'lord?"

"I think it is pleasant enough, Wolfe. You, Woodridge?"

"It's fine." He spoke curtly, walking toward the portraits at the far end of the gallery.

Sherry requested another tray then dismissed the butler. He closed the doors himself. "Are you certain you do not find it drafty? I hope you will forgive the observation, but I noticed earlier that you are perhaps not recovered yet from your illness."

"So they shared that with you as well. I believe, Sherry, that you are better informed now than before you left us." He gazed up at the portrait from a century ago of a woman dressed in emerald satin and holding a long-haired snow white cat in her lap. The cat's eyes perfectly matched the woman's gown, but even more startling, they were the same color as the woman's eyes. "Your grandmother?"

"Great-grandmother. My father's grandmother."

"A handsome woman. She has called to me before when I've been in this room. I don't know why I've never inquired as to her identity."

"Perhaps because so much in the way of business has always occupied us. Is it business this time, Woodridge, or something of a personal nature that brings you all the way here from London? I confess, neither sets well with me, but business would be more palatable, I think. I am not at all in favor of you pressing your suit with my godmother under my very nose."

Woodridge's eyebrows lifted. "I think you forget yourself, Sherry."

"Do I?" Sherry did not miss the shift in the baron's light blue eyes that made his glance glacial. Woodridge's drawn features were even more suited to his obdurate countenance. He held himself aloof and still, the lines of his face already sharply cut as though by a sculptor's chisel. A granite bust would have imbued him with more animation than Sherry could see now. "I am no longer part of what connected us these nearly nine years past. I don't have any particular allegiance to you, and you are pressing my hospitality by arriving here uninvited. It seems to me that you are the one forgetting much."

"So that is the way the wind blows these days." Woodridge considered this for a long moment before offering a carefully measured gesture of acquiescence in the single nod of his head. "How much did my interest in Lady Rivendale influence you to leave us, Sherry? It grieves me to think my actions swayed your thinking. Frankly, I had not realized that such might be the case."

"One had nothing to do with the other. Certainly my godmother is able to make her own decisions, and I would not think of advising her regarding you. She informed me only very recently that you had offered marriage. Twice. That did astonish. I have always thought you would not take another wife. I knew when you began making noises about a connection to my godmother that your finances could not be in order, but I had not realized they were in a state of such disrepair that you would find marriage agreeable."

"If I were contemplating it in regard to any woman other than Lady Rivendale, marriage would be merely a solution to a thorny problem. It is the lady herself that makes the idea of marriage agreeable. Do you regret the introduction, then? You gave no sign of it at the time, you know. But keeping your own counsel has always been one of your most admirable traits. It made you particularly well suited to our peculiar institution."

The pocket doors parted, and Wolfe entered carrying the tray of tea and cakes. He took it to the table closest to the fireplace and set it down. "Shall I pour?" he asked.

Sherry nodded. "Perhaps you better, Wolfe." He waited until the butler finished pouring and exited the gallery before he addressed Woodridge again. "Will you have tea?" he asked, holding up a cup and saucer. "Gant's biscuits are very good also."

Woodridge approached and took the refreshment he was offered and chose one shortbread biscuit for himself. He held up the biscuit, contemplating it a moment, then did the same to his teacup. "I am all for the rituals of civility."

"It is the same for me. Will you not sit, or has your long journey merely made you want to stretch your legs?"

In answer, the baron chose a nearby wing chair and eased himself into it. When Sherry was also sitting, he said, "You have not answered my question. Do you regret introducing me to Lady Rivendale?"

"Yes. I did not want to make the introduction, but she insisted. Further proof, if any is needed, that she will have her own way in all things. It has always been my practice to keep the affairs of my family separate and private from what it is that you and others would have me do. You taught me that, you know, through your own example. You rarely spoke of your family."

"You rarely inquired."

"Again, by your example, I believed it was discouraged."

Woodridge's slight smile was cool. "I already knew the most important details of your background. There was no reason for me to refine upon them with you. I always learned what I needed to know before I approached anyone, and I kept my hand in with my special young men as they progressed in their apprenticeships. You never brought anyone into the fold, did you?"

Sherry recognized this last for the rhetorical question that it was. Woodridge knew the answer to it well enough.

"I have had cause recently to wonder why that was." He sipped his tea, regarding Sherry over the rim of his cup. "You might have mentored a student yourself before you left us. It would have been your legacy . . . as you were supposed to have been mine."

"Ahh. Your legacy. But surely you cannot mean your hopes

rested squarely on my shoulders. I am not the only one you mentored. There was Gibb before me and Barnett after me."

The baron set his cup aside. Crossing his legs, he brushed the knee of his breeches, removing a thin layer of dust that clung there. "You are better than they are. Do not shy away from it. It's not flattery. I am merely speaking the truth."

"You will understand if I do not thank you for it. If I shy away from the notion, it is not because I am flattered by it. Quite the opposite."

"So you no longer believe in our mission."

Sherry shrugged. "I no longer can justify it. Whether or not I ever believed in it is a question I'm still asking myself."

"You believed," Woodridge said. "If you arrive at any other conclusion, then you are a coward, and what you fear is the prospect of a lifetime of guilt and regret. Did I say you are better than Gibb and Barnett? You are. But you are also weaker. Introspection such as you are practicing does not serve anyone, Sherry, least of all yourself. I left you too long on your own, I think. I did not suspect your convictions were so ephemeral." He rested his elbows on the arms of the chair and folded his hands in his lap. His eyes did not waver from Sherry's, and his study was frank. "It was the Crick affair, was it not? That is when you began to make this reassessment of your purpose. I should have reali—"

He was startled into silence as the wall at the far end of the gallery seemed to shift suddenly. It required a moment for him to understand what he was seeing, then a moment longer to truly believe it. "I say, Sherry, three children just walked through the wall."

Sherry turned in his chair and saw the scoundrels scrambling to get back inside the entrance to the hidden stairwell. "Hold!" That single word, delivered in stentorian tones, was enough to halt them in their tracks. They froze in rather comical contortions and awaited the next directive. "Come here."

Pinch, Dash, and Midge obliged, though their feet dragged

so much they turned over the carpet when they passed by the edge of it. They lined up in front of Sherry with all the enthusiasm of soldiers caught in the act of desertion.

Sherry was on his feet, giving them a proper inspection. Woodridge stood also, coming closer when Sherry invited him to do so.

"I hope there is an explanation," said Sherry. "You will notice that I did not qualify it in any way. It is perhaps too much to expect that it will be either reasonable or good." The boys merely blinked at him. Sherry's eyes narrowed on the faint purple stain around Midge's mouth. He bent his head closer to the trio and sniffed. Straightening, he regarded them each in turn, shaking his head as he did so. "It is to be hoped that you enjoyed the bottle you took from the cellar. It is a wonder you are not foxed, or perhaps you are."

"We only 'ad a taste, my lord," Dash said. "Then we put it back so you wouldn't notice."

"I see. Well, I have noticed, and so has our guest. He is certain to arrive at the opinion that you are the least grateful of all young ruffians, and I can think of nothing to say in your defense." He turned to Woodridge and witnessed the baron's severe disapproval. Pointing to the boys one at a time, Sherry introduced them. "Well?" he demanded as they bent their heads and shifted uncomfortably from one foot to the other. "Did you leave your manners in the cellar with the wine?"

Like bees to a flower, they swarmed the baron to make his acquaintance in the most familiar of terms. They buzzed around him, jostling one another to be the first in line to make a bow. They never fully realized any order to their introduction as one bumped the other out of the way. No one could put a word in, including Woodridge who found himself moved off his feet by their fierce enthusiasm and competition for his attention.

Sherry reached into the huddle around the baron and plucked Dash from it. He set the boy down a few feet away, then pulled Pinch back. Midge had a firm grip on the baron's hand, so Sherry left it to Woodridge to extricate himself from it.

"My apologies," he said. "They obviously drank more than they would have me believe."

Woodridge pried his bloodless knuckles free from Midge and shook them out. "Who *are* they?"

Sherry caught Midge by the collar and dragged him to stand with his compatriots. "My wards, I am chagrined to admit. Or at least they will be when my solicitor has completed all the legal particulars."

"Wards? You're serious?" He looked at the three boys who were all wobbling on their feet. "Where did they come from? Are they relations?"

"No. No relations." Sherry started to move the boys toward the pocket doors. "Go on. Find Mr. Wolfe and tell him what you did. Don't think I will not inquire later." He parted the doors and let them make their escape. They stumbled out and took off in the direction of the servants' stairs. Shaking his head, Sherry stepped back. When he turned around, he saw that Woodridge was no longer standing near his chair but had moved to the open walnut panel. The baron was investigating its construction.

"Where does it go?" Woodridge asked, poking his head inside the dark stairwell. He looked up and down the narrow passage. "Clever. My country house has a priest's hole, but nothing like this." He drew his head back and stepped aside as Sherry closed the panel. "Does it lead outside?"

"You may have already guessed that it goes down to the wine cellar. That room is locked on the kitchen side so there is no exit. If one goes up, then it leads to a drawing room and a bedchamber."

"And on the other side of the passage? It looked as if it might open on another room."

"The music salon." Woodridge made a noise at the back of his throat that might have indicated that he was either impressed or bored. Sherry did not ask him to explain. He followed the baron back to where they'd been sitting and took up his chair. "The scoundrels are not always at their best on short acquaintance. My apologies for their interruption."

"You truly intend to make them your wards?"

"Yes. I like them well enough, and they have no one else."

"Bloody hell, Sherry. Can you not see what you are doing? It is just as I was beginning to say when they came in here. It is all about the Crick affair. Your doubts. Your judgments. Your decision to leave. Even these children are part and parcel of that business. Surely you must know that."

"Of course I know it."

"But you bear no responsibility for how that turned out."

"What idiocy. Was there someone else in the room when Ellison Crick put a pistol to his head? He killed himself because I persuaded him it was in the best interest of everyone that he do so. And do you know, Woodridge, I believed it. I could not have spoken so convincingly otherwise. He saved his family the embarrassment of a public trial. He saved the prince regent the humiliation of admitting he'd spoken too freely to his friend, the cost of which was that we were very nearly denied Napoleon's abdication. He saved the people from a painful examination of their leaders in and out of the Parliament.

"And he *was* guilty. The evidence supported his guilt, never his innocence. He was the only one who said it was otherwise, but does one truly expect to hear something different? I didn't. I never have. I was presented with the charge, the evidence, the accused, and told to make it right. I never doubted that he was acquitting himself as honorably as he could, given the circumstances."

Sherry leaned forward and made a steeple of his fingers. He regarded Woodridge intently as he presented his case. The man did not loom so large before him as he had done in the past. There was a look of dissipation creeping into his countenance. The touch of gray in his complexion was much more telling than the gray threads in his ash-colored hair. Lines at the corners of his mouth and eyes made his expression seem brittle. As he spoke, Sherry thought it seemed that Woodridge was making himself smaller, somehow shrinking in his chair, and that in time he might disappear altogether.

It was an end much desired.

"The circumstances, however," Sherry said calmly, "were wrong. They were wrong when they were presented to me, and they were therefore wrong when I presented them to him. His guilt was predicated on a lie, a lie that was told first by the man who *was* guilty, a lie that was believed and turned against an innocent man.

"Do you know how I persuaded him to kill himself, Woodridge? It was not what I gave him in facts or in choices, but what I took away. I took away his hope. He was an innocent man who was made to understand there was nothing left to him. I know the precise moment when he abandoned hope; it was the moment when he saw I was unconvinced by his argument."

"Crick was a weak man."

"Perhaps, but shouldn't that engage our compassion, not our enmity?"

"You did nothing wrong."

Sherry smiled, albeit without humor. "And that is why I left," he said. "Because you—and others like you—think I did nothing wrong. He had children, you know. Two boys. Two girls. His wife lost the child she was carrying. I have heard since that she was the one who discovered what her husband had done. He wanted to leave her a note, but I couldn't allow him to do that. What could he have said that would not have aroused her suspicions? He had no debts, no mistress, no reason to do what he did except for his melancholia of late. She had to be satisfied with that. She will go to her grave thinking her husband's despair was greater than the love he bore her.

"I will go to my grave knowing I convinced him it made no difference."

Fifteen

"Come away from the window," Lady Rivendale said. It was not the first time she had cautioned Lily in such a manner. "It cannot be good for you to stand there staring at his carriage."

"His carriage is already gone. The grooms have removed it from the drive and taken it to the stable."

"Then there can be nothing at all for you to see. Come now. It is wearing on my nerves."

Lily turned away. "Are you afraid I will leap?"

"Do not be absurd." She was on the point of underscoring this with a dismissive wave of her hand when she paused and reconsidered. "Would you?"

"No." Lily managed a small smile. "Killing myself has never presented itself as a satisfactory solution, though I have always thought the baron would have been relieved if I had done so. Odd, is it not? He led me to believe it was the only way I should ever be able to leave him."

Her ladyship shivered. She squared off the deck of cards in her hand then began shuffling them again. "Come. Won't you sit down? We'll play two-handed whist, and I promise you an honest game."

"I couldn't."

Sighing heavily, Lady Rivendale put the cards aside. "Neither could I." She glanced toward the open doorway. "What do you suppose they are doing now?"

Lily thought her ladyship was referring to Sherry and Woodridge, but when she followed the direction of Lady Rivendale's gaze she saw Pinch, Dash, and Midge were framed in the doorway, frozen in the act of tiptoeing past it.

"Hold!" Her voice did not have the same resonance that Sherry's had, but the authority it carried was sufficient to keep them from moving forward. They could not quite sustain the pose in which they had been caught out and teetered sideways so that they were in danger of toppling like dominoes placed on end. "Come here."

Their collective sigh was loud enough for both women to hear. Pinch nudged Dash forward; Dash nudged Midge. It was with palpable reluctance that they filed into the sitting room that adjoined Lily's bedchamber.

"Well?" Lily asked. "I thought we agreed you would remain in the area of your own rooms this afternoon. Did you have tea?"

Dash nodded. "Mr. Gant made sure there were extra cakes on our tray. Pinch played mother. We said please and thank ye even though there was no one to 'ear us do it."

"Truly?" Lily looked at Lady Rivendale and saw she appeared to be more disarmed than distrustful. "That is very good of you. And where did you come from?"

"The kitchen," Pinch said. "We 'ad tea in the kitchen."

At the same time Pinch was offering that explanation, Midge was saying, "We 'ad a picnic at the lake."

When Lily looked pointedly at Dash, he had the good sense to remain quiet. "I hope you do not mean to say you had tea twice," she said. "Now, where have you been?"

None of them could hold out for long against her. For once, though, it was not Midge who broke the silence. Pinch plowed his fingers through this thick hair in a gesture that was so like Sherry that Lily felt her heart being squeezed.

"We wanted to see who'd come to visit," Pinch said.

"And?"

"We were 'iding in the stairwell."

For all that his reply was mumbled, Lily did not mistake Pinch's meaning. "Not any stairwell, I imagine. You were hiding in that passage again."

Pinch hung his head. "Yes, Miss."

Lily moved her attention to Midge. His head was also hanging, but she suspected his reasons were different than his brother in arms. She cupped his chin and lifted it. "What is that purple stain around your mouth?"

"Blackberries. Mr. Gant made blackberry tarts."

"I thought you said you had cakes."

"And tarts. Dash forgot to mention the tarts."

"Perhaps because you lifted the tarts. Is that what you did? You pinched the tarts, then stuffed them in your mouths so fast you left the evidence all over your face?" She dropped his chin and took Dash in hand, inspecting his sheepish countenance. "It appears you were a bit less greedy than Midge."

"I don't like them as well."

"Ahh." She shook her head. "You will have to tell Mr. Gant what you've done. All of you. What if he blames one of his helpers? Did that occur to you? No, I can see that it didn't. Let us hope that has not already happened."

"Shall we go now?" Pinch asked.

Lily released Dash. "No. Not to the kitchen. That can wait until his lordship's guest is gone. Wash up and stay in your rooms. It is better if you are not underfoot right now." They turned quickly and started to go, but Lily called them back. "Wait. One small favor. Will you show me this passage? I want to see it for myself."

Lady Rivendale stood up, clasping her hands together. "Oh, I do not think that is wise. Another time, mayhap."

"No," Lily said calmly. "I wish to see it now. Boys?" They nodded, but Lily could see they were disinclined to obey. At least they did not apply to her ladyship to intercede on their behalf. "Go on. I'll follow."

"I think I will come as well," Lady Rivendale said stoutly.

"I should like to see more of the thing myself." She fell in step behind Lily as they filed out the door. In the hallway, Midge waited for her so that he might be her escort. "You're a good lad, Master Midge." She tousled his hair. He grinned up at her, the purple ring around his mouth making his smile even broader. She sighed. "Rascal. I think you mean to steal my heart."

Pinch led the way to the drawing room in their wing of the manor. It was a crowded repository for pieces of furniture that no longer served the style or function of other rooms. Still, in spite of the mismatched chairs and upholstered benches, or perhaps because of them, the room was entirely comfortable. It was in this room that the boys often took their meals and practiced their deportment. They also liked to see how high they could arrange the chairs without toppling them. The evidence of their failed attempts to reach the ceiling could be seen in the small scratches and nicks in the polished wood, but no one had yet discovered their game.

Everything was as it should be when they entered. Pinch went immediately to the cold fireplace and took the poker from its stand. He climbed on the chair to the left of the hearth and used the poker to stretch his reach. He ran the tip of it across a seam in the paneling directly above the ornate gilt frame of a pastoral landscape. When it caught the tip of a cleverly hidden lever, he wiggled the poker back and forth until it pushed the lever to one side.

"It is beyond everything that you could have found that," Lily said when the panel sprung open a few inches. "I can only imagine you were up to some trick at the time."

None of the boys volunteered they had been playing at acrobatics, stacking and climbing chairs when Midge noticed something wedged between the seams in the paneling. They hoped they had stumbled on an odd treasure, and it was in the course of trying to pull it out that the lever was moved to the side and the secret panel revealed itself.

Lily helped Pinch down from the chair and directed him to replace the poker. She pulled open the panel and examined the other side. "How do you boys get back to this room if this closes behind you?"

Midge stepped forward and pointed to the way the lever hooked on the interior side. "I can reach it if I'm on Pinch's shoulders."

Stretching on her toes, Lily found she could just touch the tip of it with her fingers. She moved it back and forth experimentally. "And this goes to the gallery below?"

"And the music salon," Dash said. "Sometimes we'd go down to 'ear 'is lordship play."

Lily had to smile. She'd sat on the main staircase to overhear the concert, while the boys had discovered much better seats for the same. Lily regarded the passage. She was struck by how dark it was. "Do you keep candles inside?"

"A few. But we always take one or two in wi' us. Ye can 'ardly see yer 'and in front of ye if ye don't."

Lady Rivendale joined Lily in inspecting the passage. "Extraordinary."

Lily stepped fully inside the narrow corridor. "Shh." She tilted her head to one side and concentrated on listening. After a moment, she whispered, "Do you hear that?"

Her ladyship's voice dropped to a pitch that matched Lily's. "What?"

"It is Sheridan."

"I'm sure I don't hear—"

"Shh."

Lady Rivendale fell quiet again, adopting Lily's position with her head cocked and her shoulders hunched.

Lily trusted her own ears when she heard the low, indistinct murmuring coming up from below. She didn't ask for confirmation this time. Stepping out of the passage, she addressed the boys. "When you were hiding in there earlier, where was his lordship?"

"In the gallery," Pinch said.

"And you were eavesdropping?"

"No. No, we made our escape as soon as we knew 'e was there."

"Did you?" Her tone made it clear she was patently skeptical. "Through the music salon and then to the kitchen for those blueberry tarts."

"Blackberry."

"Blackberry," Lily repeated. She looked from one to the other and saw they would not be moved from this story. "Go on. To your rooms now."

"I should close the panel," said Pinch.

"No. I'll do that. You do as you're told." They hesitated, then obliged, slinking off single file into the hall. "Well?" Lily asked Lady Rivendale. "Do you believe they weren't eavesdropping on Lord Sheridan's conversation?"

"I'm afraid not. It is just the sort of intrigue they would find difficult to resist."

"Precisely my thought. I am trying not to imagine what they may have overheard."

"Come away from there, Lily. You do not want to repeat their experience. Close the door and have done with it."

Lily's fingertips whitened where they pressed the edge of the panel. Distress darkened her eyes. "I must go," she said. "I never thought I would want to see him again, but to have this chance . . . I cannot explain it. He is here, almost underfoot, and I find I very much need to hear his voice. The years I spent in his house . . . in his . . ." She shook her head and pressed her mouth flat for a moment. These were not things she could say to her ladyship. "It does not always seem real to me; often it is as though it happened to another person."

Lady Rivendale took a step closer. "Is that not a good thing, my dear? Do you not want to put it from your mind?"

"I do not think I can, not if I do not fight for myself. I ran, you see. It was what I needed to do then . . . but now, now I think I need to do something else. I think I need to confront him."

"Confront? Oh, surely not. That is for Sherry to do."

"I know. Or rather I know he believes that."

Lady Rivendale did not attempt to hide her alarm. "And you do not? Lily, this is madness. If you must hear what is being said, if you must hear Woodridge for yourself to set things right in your own mind, then I will not stop you, but I cannot countenance a confrontation. In fact, I forbid it. If you cannot clearly consider the matter of your own safety, then I would ask that you consider Sherry's."

"I understand. I am only going to listen. Please, you said you would not stop me from doing that."

Too late her ladyship realized the trap she had set for herself. By misjudging Lily's intent, she had in effect given permission. "Not alone. I am going with you."

Lily shook her head. "No. It is too private. It would be like inviting you into my nightmares. I cannot do it . . . and you would not want to be there."

When put to her in such a manner, Lady Rivendale had to agree. "Very well, but I will wait here with the door open, and you must return immediately if it all becomes too much to bear."

"Yes."

Lady Rivendale regarded Lily, frankly dubious. "I believe you would say anything to be on your way."

"Yes."

That honesty brought home the futility of further argument. Lady Rivendale gave her attention to finding Lily a suitable candle. She found a three-stick candelabra, lighted it, and passed it to Lily. "Have a care with it, though I suppose if the scoundrels did not burn us to the ground, we are safe enough with you."

"Thank you." Impulsively she kissed Lady Rivendale's cheek, then before there was any comment regarding it, Lily slipped into the passage and started down the stairs.

Sherry noted that Woodridge had yet to show any signs of being discomfited by the course of their conversation. That was not unexpected. The baron was adept at schooling his features, and Sherry understood that what he had disclosed about the Crick affair was more of an annoyance to Woodridge than a revelation that would require him to alter his thinking or take any action.

"Do you believe in happenstance?" asked Sherry.

Woodridge sipped his tea. "Happenstance. As a matter of faith? No. Does it ever occur? Yes, but perhaps not so often as people are wont to believe. Is it a point of philosophy that you wish to make, Sherry? What has coincidence to do with poor Mr. Crick?"

"I'm not sure that it does. But you were the one who placed the assignment before me."

"As I did many others. What are you suggesting?"

"I think you knew Crick was innocent at the outset."

Woodridge calmly set his cup in the saucer, then set both aside. "You mean to present some proof, I hope."

"I have none. It is merely conjecture."

"You dare. I should call you out for that."

Sherry shrugged. "That certainly is your right." It was then that Woodridge blinked, and Sherry knew he had pricked the man at last. "I wonder what evidence I shall find linking you to Crick? I will be looking, you know, so if you have not covered your tracks already, there is time yet for you to do so. Whether your intention was to discredit me or whether you benefited from Crick's death in some way, I mean to eventually discover the truth, no matter what course the remainder of our conversation takes."

Woodridge gave a shout of laughter. "I believe you are serious! Oh, this is rich. By all means, Sherry, you must do what you think is right, but be warned that if you take this course, *you* will discredit yourself. I will not have you say later that I was responsible for it."

"I shall consider myself duly warned."

Woodridge simply grunted.

"It occurs to me that it was the introduction to Lady Rivendale that put the stone in the pond."

"Speak plainly, Sherry. What does that mean?"

"Ripples, Woodridge. I am speaking of ripples. I introduce my godmother to you, and not long afterward you suggest that some sort of relation exists that would make you entitled to a measure of her fortune. Perhaps you imagine I stand between you and that fortune; you might even believe I have spoken out against you in regard to my godmother remarrying. You put the Crick assignment before me, knowing it had the potential to go very badly, yet before you can announce that Crick was innocent of the charges, I discover the thing myself and bring it to the attention of others in our circle. I do not think you wanted me to leave our small group but rather to be placed in a position where you would have reason to watch me closely. By coming forward myself, the effect was exactly the opposite. I was given as much—if not more—freedom of movement and choice of assignments as anyone has ever had."

Woodridge rubbed his chin, his countenance unchanged by anything he heard. "This is fantastical, Sherry, but please, go on."

Sherry's darkly intent eyes communicated he'd had every intention of doing so. "In spite of what was offered me, I was prepared to leave. It was not an easy decision; I knew what was expected of me. At the time, I thought I knew what you expected of me. I stayed longer than was my wont, longer than I should have. Within a fortnight of announcing my decision to go, an attempt is made on my life in Covent Garden."

"You believe I had something to do with that? God's truth, Sherry, that limb you have crawled out on will surely break under the weight of these absurd accusations. If you talked to Conway and Gibb, then you know few of us have been spared an assault."

"But I was meant to die. The person who saved my life nearly did. The attempt on my life was the first. All of the ones that followed were intended to point to a different game. Yes, I know all about the poisoning you suffered. Easily faked, but even if you went further and took some potion yourself, I am certain you were never in any real danger. Moreover, I have no doubt there would have been another attack against me if I had remained in London." He shrugged. "Though perhaps now that you're here, you will try again."

"Bah! Now you are being ridiculous. If I wanted you dead, it would be done."

Sherry remembered saying much the same thing to Conway and Gibb. There was a difference, though, and he spoke to it. "Your mistake was in not doing the thing yourself."

Woodridge neither explained nor defended himself, but he did blink again.

"You cannot account for every particular when you hand over the work to another," Sherry said. "You taught me that, you know."

"I taught you many things, but I see little evidence of lessons learned." Woodridge's sharp chin lifted in the manner of a challenge. "You have yet to make your case. I am not persuaded by any of the things I've heard. You will not pull a confession from me, Sherry. I am not Crick. I do not yield to accusation alone. There must be proof."

"I have a name."

"Then you have a liar. Anyone who confesses that I hired him to kill you is a liar."

"He will not like to hear you have called him such. He has his standards, I believe. Call him a boman prig, and he would thank you for the honor. He wouldn't blush at being called a pimp. But name him a liar? I think Ned Craven would stick a shiv in you without blinking an eye."

The baron's blink became a twitch.

The candelabra trembled in Lily's hand. Light flickered on the walls of the stairwell and across her pale face. How had Sherry discovered Ned Craven was responsible for the attack? She'd been so careful not to reveal more than a few inconsequential details, and she'd discouraged him from speaking to Blue Rutland or making inquiries about Ned as they related to the boys. She'd always suspect that if Sherry knew Ned Craven was the one carrying the shiv that evening in Covent Garden, it would be more difficult, perhaps impossible, to persuade him that he was indeed the target of the attack. How easy it would have been for Sherry to convince himself that she had been Ned's intended victim and lowering his guard might well have cost him his life.

How long had he known? she wondered. Lily didn't think it was likely he'd come by this intelligence while yet in London. She doubted he would have left without resolving it in some fashion. That meant he'd learned of it since arriving at Granville Hall, and there were few sources of that information here in the country.

Barring the possibility that Sherry had come by the knowledge through some correspondence with Blue Rutland, everything pointed to the scoundrels.

In hindsight, it was less surprising that they had revealed the truth to Sherry than that they had never whispered a word of that revelation to her. That understanding pricked her heart a bit, and the smile that pulled at the corners of her mouth was a shade bittersweet. Lily reminded herself this was not a matter of Pinch, Dash, or Midge shifting allegiances, but broadening them. It was something to be not only hoped for but rejoiced in, and she would appreciate it in time.

Glancing around her, she noticed the candelabra's light was no longer shivering. Her heartbeat had slowed, and her hand was once again steady. She edged closer to the panel so she might pick up the threads of the conversation in the gallery.

"Will you have a stronger drink now?" Sherry asked. Without waiting for a response, he rose and went to the door where he rang for Wolfe. When the butler appeared a few moments later, Sherry asked for a decanter of Scotch and two glasses. While waiting for Wolfe's return, he observed Woodridge begin to assume a more relaxed posture. It required some effort as this bearing did not come naturally to him. It was the sense he had of his own importance that made it difficult for the baron to affect ease in his carriage.

Sherry waved Wolfe into the room to set down the tray and take away the tea and uneaten cakes. He poured a tumbler for Woodridge and carried it to him. When the baron did not reach for the glass, Sherry said, "If you like, I will drink first."

Unamused, Woodridge took the tumbler from Sherry's hand, then set it on the table beside him. "I won't be needled by you, Sheridan."

Shrugging, Sherry poured a Scotch for himself and took his seat. He casually stretched in the chair and crossed his legs at the ankles. He rolled the tumbler between his palms. "Ned Craven. Do you mean to pretend you do not know the man?"

"Not only am I unacquainted with the gentleman, I have never heard the name before."

Sherry chuckled softly. "Pray, do not lay further insult on poor Ned's head by calling him a gentleman. He will certainly not thank you for it, though he will probably not be moved to kill you." Sherry reined himself in, allowing his smile to fade. "Do you think Ned will not say a word against you? If you do, then you have overestimated your man. Perhaps you were unaware that he makes a fair living for himself in Holborn informing on others of his ilk. That they do not attempt to do the same to him is the truest measure of the power he wields there."

"Yet it seems you are a veritable wellspring of particulars regarding Mr. Craven. How can that be?"

Sherry was aware that Woodridge was getting his feet under him again. That was entirely agreeable. Pulling the rug out was only effective if the baron was standing. "You cannot truly believe I would name my informants. Protecting them is one of the inviolable rules. Another lesson learned from you."

"You are rather full of yourself, Sherry. Pride goeth before destruction, and a haughty spirit before a fall."

"Proverbs, is it not?" The smile was back in Sherry's voice, if not in the shape of his mouth. "Tell me how you decided that Ned Craven would serve you in this latest enterprise. Asking a man to do murder for you is different, I think, than asking him to procure young girls . . . or even young boys."

Woodridge's fingertips whitened on the arms of his chair, but his complexion mottled. His sharp intake of breath was audible as air whistled between his teeth.

Sherry waited for the baron to collect himself. "Am I wrong, then? Perhaps I have misremembered what I was told. Boys were never your interest, were they? It is only that Ned is well known for acquiring them for gentlemen of a certain persuasion."

"Perversion," Woodridge said tightly. "Not persuasion."

"You do not feel so strongly, I collect, about either murder or the purchase of *les jeunes filles*."

"What is it you think you know, Sheridan?"

"Have I been less than forthcoming? I am saying your association with Ned Craven began as a business arrangement in which he found girls bearing a specific stamp for you. Over time, I think you recognized Ned might be useful to you in other ways."

"Mentored him, you mean? As I did you? Made him one of us?"

Sherry gave a shout of laughter. It was loud enough to set Woodridge back in his chair. "God's truth, I hope not. That would be the outside of enough. It is difficult to imagine any candidate less inclined to accept orders than Ned Craven. But perhaps that was your experience. He has not done well by you."

Woodridge shook his head, not to negate Sherry's last statement but to underscore his contempt for the accusations leveled at him. "I am admitting none of it, you understand, but I should like to hear what sort of girls you imagine Mr. Craven procured for me."

"You are fishing, Woodridge. I am familiar with the bait you are using, but it is of no matter. I would have told you whether you cast your line or not." He watched the baron set himself to take another blow. It was subtle, this preparation, but it could be seen in the fixed way he held his head and the stillness in his fingertips as they rested on the arms of the chair.

"She would have to be a comely girl," Sherry said. "Naturally, you would want some assurance that she was without disease. If Ned plucked her from the streets of Holborn then she would have to be young. You will understand if I do not speculate further in that regard, else I should be quite ill." He held up one hand, forestalling the baron's comment. "She would be slender, in the first bloom of womanhood perhaps, not buxom or bawdy. Virginal, I think, though not necessarily a virgin. Green eyes would make her worth more to you, but what would set her price above rubies is her hair. Red hair, I am told, but not just any shade. It must be dark, as befits a deep claret rather than fingers of fire."

"Extraordinary," Woodridge said after a time. "Not any girl you say, but one with red hair and green eyes. That's remarkably peculiar of me. Does your informant say why I am so particular?"

The lightness of Woodridge's tone did not persuade Sherry to lower his guard, nor did it make him think his former mentor was truly so comfortable. It was a second cast of the fishing line. The baron wanted to learn the depth of the informant's knowledge. Sherry did not answer the question posed to him, raising one of his own instead. "What brings you here? Why leave London now?"

There was no hesitation. "To bring you back, of course. Not to London precisely, but back to our purpose."

"I don't believe that is it at all."

Woodridge shrugged. "Having been forced to listen to

you impugn my honor, I am quite aware I shall have to accept failure. As I mentioned, I didn't understand that Gibb and Con had already been sent out on the same mission. I came under no one's direction. My reasons for wanting you back are entirely personal. I have always thought you were worth the effort, Sherry. I regret it has come to this between us. So much distrust. So many things said that cannot be recanted. It does present a rather hopeless situation, does it not?"

Sherry regarded the baron consideringly. "Then you did not come to wish me happy?"

Woodridge offered a countenance creased by perplexity. "Wish you happy? My dear Sherry, until you began to regale me with an account of these alleged misdeeds, I could honestly say that I held you in high esteem, but even so, to set out on the uncomfortable journey to Granville with nothing in my mind save to wish you happy, well, it would appear you have puffed up your own consequence and the significance you have in my life."

"Lady Rivendale says the sun rises and sets by me," he said wryly. "It is lowering to discover I am not at the center of all things."

"Just so."

"Then you were unaware of my engagement." It was more in the way of a statement than a question.

"Engagement? You, Sherry?" Woodridge picked up his tumbler of Scotch and lifted it toward his host. The gesture was as mocking as his smile. "Of all the things you've said, that is easily the most preposterous, but since I am here, I will wish you happy." He knocked back a mouthful of his drink. "Tell me her name. Is she known to me?"

Sherry set aside his drink so he could reach into his frock coat and remove a piece of paper. He held it up as he opened it so that Woodridge could see it had been carefully folded in thirds and that the writing on it was not someone's copperplate hand but newsprint.

The baron's crystal tumbler thudded to the floor. What remained of the Scotch made a dark stain on the rug between his feet.

"So you do recognize it," Sherry said. He looked down at the spilled drink then back to Woodridge. His slight smile was chilly. "It is difficult to moderate one's reaction when the surprise is genuine. At least I have always found it so. Apparently it is also true for you."

The baron kicked aside the tumbler and stood. At his sides his hands clenched into fists. He resisted the urge to reach just beneath his waistcoat for the announcement he had taken from the *Gazette*, though he recognized the futility of denying he knew what Sherry held or where it had come from. "You are acting as though you think it proves something."

"Several things, actually, the least of which is that you knew about my engagement before you arrived. It points to the reason you came to Granville and offers further evidence that you felt compelled to lie about it. This last begs the question why."

"I did not think anything was served by admitting I knew. Naturally it prompted my visit. When I saw the announcement it occurred to me that my last and best opportunity to convince you to return would be now. I could not imagine the argument that would induce you to come back to us once you were leg-shackled." Woodridge shrugged. "There. Now you know the whole of it."

Sherry said nothing for a long moment, then he said quietly, "I do not think I have ever fully appreciated your genius for turning things on their head." He stood himself, unwilling to yield the high ground to the baron. "But it will not help you here. I will not be moved. We might strike a truce, however, if you are willing to make certain concessions."

"Confessions? You are quite mad if you think—"

"Concessions," Sherry said, interrupting. "Though it is interesting that you heard the other. I am proposing that you remove yourself permanently from the service and also from

London. You may retire to your country home or some other place of your choosing here in England. I would strongly advise you against attempting to take up residency on the Continent or the Americas. If you are set on traveling to foreign places, then transportation to Van Diemen's Land can be arranged. I don't think you can count on being given a government post, though. Your exile there would be considerably less agreeable than the one Napoleon enjoys on St. Helena."

Woodridge's fists uncurled. He attended to the left sleeve of his frock coat, brushing off a spot of dust on the forearm. After several swipes, his hand fell away slowly. The raised arm also dropped back to his side. When he lifted his eyes to Sherry, he was unable to keep his expression remote. Something of his consternation was visible.

Sherry shook his head, responding to what the baron would not ask. "Your blade is no longer there. I did not like the idea that you were carrying a weapon when I had none. I could have armed myself, I suppose, but this is my home, and it would have pained me to do so."

This time Woodridge did not try to be surreptitious as he searched the right pocket of his frock coat. His hand came away empty.

"Gone also, I'm afraid," Sherry said. "How a garrote would have assisted you at this juncture, I cannot say, but I have never known you to be without one. Now, if you wish to call me out, I believe arrangements can be made that will suit you. You may have your choice of weapons and opportunity to practice. I would not have there be any accusation of unfairness."

"You were always accounted to be an excellent shot, Sherry."

"Yes, but then so are you. We are evenly matched, I think."

"If you trust your informant, if you are certain of your facts, then why are you not calling me out?"

"It is a matter of honor. I gave my word."

The import of this was not lost on Woodridge. "Who have

you spoken to, Sherry? Gibb? Con? Did they make you agree to offer me exile in the country?"

Sherry chuckled. "A word to them of what I've told you and they would have planted you themselves. That is what you risk if I go to the others and tell them what I know. Even now they are trying to learn who the traitor is among them. After all I have said, do you doubt they can be convinced that it is you?"

"Even if it is not true?"

"Even then, as you have good cause to know. You have but to remember the unfortunate Mr. Crick. However, we know that is not the case here."

Woodridge fell quiet as he considered his choices. "This is not about you and me at all any longer," he said finally. "Perhaps it never was. As little as one hundred years ago we would have burned her as a witch, and who is to say we would have been wrong?" He shrugged. "She has befuddled your senses as she did mine. Can you not imagine that I would want to save you from her?"

Sherry's reply remained hovering at the tip of his tongue. Behind him, he heard the sound of the latch being turned on the hidden panel. If he had harbored any doubts that it was the panel being pushed open or who might be appearing on the threshold, they were put to rest as he watched the baron's complexion turn ashen.

"Your concern, my lord," Lily said, stepping into the gallery, "should be to save yourself from me."

Sherry did not turn but listened for Lily's approach. When he judged that she was within a few feet of him, he reached back with one hand and beckoned her to take it. He did not bring her forward to stand in front of him but kept her to one side and slightly to the rear of his right shoulder. "It was too much to hope that Lady Rivendale would keep you away, I suppose."

Lily heard no criticism from him, merely an observation. She managed a faint smile as she set the candelabra beside

Sherry's drink. "Indeed. Forgive me, but I must needs see him for myself." Her eyes narrowed as she regarded Woodridge critically. "Odd, but he is smaller than I remembered."

The baron started to take a step toward her, but Sherry immediately put out a hand, staying his advance. "Mind that your distance remains respectful, Woodridge, else the distance will be twenty paces."

One of Woodridge's brows arched. "Your word means nothing, then?"

"I did not mean to suggest I would call you out. It is the distance I can throw you."

Lily could not help herself; a bubble of nervous laughter parted her lips. She pressed one hand to her mouth as though she might be able to push it back. She flushed, embarrassed by her unseemly response. If she had been able to find her voice, she could have explained that the tension in the room had forced it out of her. Woodridge was staring at her, his eyes like ice chips. Sherry, she noted, when she glanced around his shoulder, looked as if the corners of his mouth might be twitching.

"She is changed." The baron spoke to Sherry, but his gaze remained riveted on Lily. "Disappointing, but not unexpected. Her name is Lilith, you know. The *Gazette* reported Lily, but Lilith is how she should be called. Are you familiar with the name, Sherry? Rabbinic legend says Lilith was Adam's first wife, later supplanted by Eve. Hell hath no fury . . ." Woodridge's eyes remained humorless and cold. "Then again, perhaps hell does hold such fury when it embraces one of its own. That is what Lilith became. The devil's handmaiden, I believe, an evil spirit. There are parallels, don't you think?"

Sherry waited until Woodridge's attention shifted from Lily to him. "What do you say to the terms I put before you?" he asked. "Exile or exposure?"

"I think you are offering something different from that. Isn't it exile or execution? That must be more on the order of what Marshal Ney presented to Boney."

"Do not flatter yourself with that comparison."

"Flatter myself? No comparison to the Frogs is ever flattering."

"The terms, Woodridge. Do you mean to take them?"

"You are convinced she is worthy of your protection?" the baron asked, jerking his chin toward Lily. "Knowing that, like her mother, she invites men to crawl between her thighs for the—"

He did not finish. Lily launched herself at him, moving so quickly and unexpectedly that Sherry could not pull her back. Woodridge raised his arms to block her, but Lily flew at him high. She dug her nails into his cheeks, drawing fine rivulets of blood. He cursed and shoved her aside hard. She stumbled, almost fell, then came at him again. Sherry stepped forward, not to stand in Lily's way, but to make certain Woodridge didn't strike her. Lily raised her hand, prepared to mark the baron's face with her palm print, then stayed her delivery when she saw him flinch.

She did not make the mistake of thinking it was her hand that he feared. It was what he saw in her eyes, and it was enough for her.

Lily stood facing him a moment longer, then she retreated a step. Having faced down the cobra, she still was not so foolish as to turn her back on him. When she was out of his reach, she pivoted on her heel, picked up the candelabra, and kept on walking to the far end of the gallery, exiting the room exactly as she had entered it.

"She is not changed in the least," Sherry said when he heard the panel close. "It is only that you have never known her." He handed Woodridge his own handkerchief. "Here. For the blood on your cheeks. Do not trouble yourself to look for your own."

Frowning slightly, the baron nevertheless accepted it.

"Now," Sherry told him. "I will have your answer. Choose."

"If it must be one or the other, then I will take refuge in the country."

"Very well." Sherry crossed the room to the pocket doors.

"But understand, you will not return to London. Such arrangements as must be made can be accomplished through correspondence. I'm certain your man of affairs will be able to manage the details of closing your townhouse. In regard to the Crown's business, you will write your statement here, and I will see that the best use is made of it."

Parting the doors, Sherry gestured for Woodridge to precede him into the hallway. They returned to the library where Sherry urged the baron to make himself comfortable behind the desk, then presented him with paper, quill, and ink to begin his missive. Sherry dictated the language and monitored the writing so that Woodridge penned the words precisely.

When the baron was done, Sherry examined it one more time. He set it down, gave Woodridge a second piece of paper, and said, "Another, please. Just the same as this."

Woodridge obliged, and Sherry scrutinized it as he had done the first. "This is more than I was able to offer poor Mr. Crick," he said when he was finished. "You comprehend it will be your farewell letter if you do not follow the terms exactly as I have put them before you. There can be no exception. If you go more than five miles in any direction from your estate, I will learn about it. You will not like the consequences. If you return to London for any reason, you cannot expect that you will leave it alive."

Woodridge set the quill in the ink and came to his feet as Sherry skirted the desk. The announcement of Lily's engagement lay beside the inkstand where Sherry had placed it. He picked it up, let his eyes drift over it, then looked at Sherry. "This was an invitation, wasn't it?" he asked, one corner of his mouth curling in a manner that mocked himself. "As effective as drawing a moth to the flame. I congratulate you. I did not suspect. I wonder, was it you who knew me so well, or Lilith?"

Sherry did not allow himself to be drawn into that conversation. "Your carriage, your trunks, and bags are all waiting for you at the front. Your cattle have been tended, but I would not recommend pushing them hard today. There is an inn at Westin-on-the-Narrows that might serve."

"I am familiar with it."

"Good. I'll escort you out myself." Stepping aside, he let Woodridge pass, plucking the announcement from his fingers as he did so. "I cannot let you have it, even as a sweet remembrance of this encounter."

Wolfe had taken up position in the entrance hall so that he might be at the ready for just this end. He had the baron's coat and beaver hat in hand, both of which had been neatly brushed. He also produced the baron's soft leather gloves and crystal-knobbed walking stick.

Sherry fell into step beside his old mentor and didn't hold until they reached the edge of the drive. The carriage door was already open; the driver and grooms prepared to make way. Woodridge walked ahead and climbed into the carriage without once looking back. It was as dignified an exit as Sherry thought he could make under the circumstances. Not unimpressed, but still cautious, Sherry stood on the lip of the last step and watched until the carriage took the last curve in the road at the end of the lake. When it was out of sight, he took the stairs two at a time and disappeared into the house.

Lily was waiting for him. Already halfway down the stairs, she astonished him by hoisting herself sidesaddle on the polished banister and sliding the rest of the way. Sherry acted as the newel post and caught her, sweeping her up and making a full circle that caused her gown and petticoats to billow. At the top of the stairs, Lady Rivendale clapped her hands and called for the scoundrels to come and be part of this celebration.

"Do not drop her, Sherry!" she exclaimed. "I fear she has a delicate constitution."

Still holding Lily aloft, Sherry looked up at her. "Where does she come by these notions?" he asked. "Did you not tell her you nearly flattened Woodridge with the palm of your hand?"

"It would have been indelicate of me to make too much of the moment."

He grinned, drawing her closer and letting her down gradually, keeping her pressed flush to him as he did so. Lily kept her arms around his neck. Over her shoulder Sherry saw Wolfe had been joined by the housekeeper and one of the maids. A footman was observing from farther down the hall. To a person they were smiling indulgently. His eyes lifted to the top of the stairs, and he saw it was no different for his godmother.

"We have many well-wishers, it seems," he said.

Lily nodded, pressing her cheek against his shoulder. She squeezed him hard, unable to get close enough to him to suit her.

He whispered to her, stirring her hair, "I do not suppose you could be moved to kiss me."

Drawing back, Lily took his face between her palms and pressed her mouth firmly to his. She tasted his smile against her lips. Scotch and peppermint. Fire and ice. "It is over?" she asked, her mouth but a moment from his. "We are finished with him?"

Sherry nodded. He bent his head enough to take her mouth once more, then set her gently from him. "It's done." He drew her toward the library. The servants parted to let them pass. He glanced up at the landing and saw his godmother had disappeared. "Hurry," he said conspiratorially. "By my reckoning, we have but a few minutes before they descend on us."

Lily did not resist his pull. She was happy to be pressed against the library door and have her lips given the full attention of his. It was only when he pointed to his desk that she balked. "Oh no. Not again." Then she qualified that refusal. "Certainly not when we might expect an interruption at any moment."

Chuckling, Sherry hustled her across the room. He pointed to the letters Woodridge had penned. "Please. Take one."

Lily sat in Sherry's chair while he hitched a hip on the edge of the desk. She accepted one of the documents and began reading. It was not what she had expected. "This is no resignation," she said slowly as she continued to read. Her eyes darted to Sherry's. "It's a confession."

"Indeed. Woodridge is capable of writing his own resignation. I was not certain he could be counted on to manage the confession." He showed her the other was a copy. "I will keep one here, but the second I will put in the hands of my solicitor." He took both letters and rolled them into separate scrolls. Lily helped him seal both with wax, then he hid one behind a shelf of books on agrarian practices. The other he gave to Wolfe for immediate delivery to Sir Arthur Meredith.

"Sir Arthur is your solicitor?" Lily asked.

"Yes. Why does that surprise?" He was smiling slyly as he turned away from giving Wolfe his instructions. "Do you think I would tell just anyone about you and the boys?"

Lily did not have the opportunity to respond. Lady Rivendale's shrill voice called for their attention.

"Sherry! Lily! Come quickly! I fear the scoundrels have fled!"

Sixteen

Sherry dashed into the hall, Lily on his heels. Lady Rivendale was hurrying down the stairs, one hand floating just above the banister in the event she needed it for balance. She was carrying a piece of paper in her other hand, waving it aloft like a flag of truce.

"Here! You must see for yourself. You will not believe me otherwise." She was out of breath and flush of face, and her eyes were bright with hovering tears. "I can hardly credit it myself." She thrust the paper at Sherry, then sat down heavily on the stairs.

Lily was immediately at her ladyship's side, trying to attend her but also keeping an anxious eye on Sherry as he read the missive. "What do they say?"

Sherry read,

> *Do not fret yerselfs! We are safely hid with the ~~villin~~ villain. Midge ~~sez~~ says we can't trust him to leave. He saw the bloke twice in Holborn talking to that other villain Ned Craven and no one trusted Ned even before he tried to murder our good friend*

Lord Sheridan. We will be back. We solemn promise.

Dash Pinch Smijun
Please do not cry ladies.

Sighing heavily, Sherry passed the letter to Lily. "Penned by Master Dash again, but it bears the stamp of all three."

Lady Rivendale dabbed her eyes with a lace handkerchief. She sniffed inelegantly. "What do they mean, Sherry? Who is this fellow Ned, and when did he attempt murder?"

"You will have to explain it to her," Sheridan told Lily. He motioned to one of the footmen who had come forward to offer assistance to Lady Rivendale. "Tell Kennerly I want Achilles brought around." When the footman hurried off, Sherry hunkered down in front of Lily and his godmother. He took one of their hands in each of his, squeezing lightly. "I will bring them back all of a piece. You may depend upon it. Woodridge has no use for them. If he finds them, he will toss them and leave them by the side of the road. I'll be their escort. It won't hurt them to walk back."

Lady Rivendale gave Sherry a sharp look. "I do not think I like that. Perhaps you should take one or two of the grooms with you so the lads can ride. Better yet, Lily and I will follow in the carriage. The boys can return with us."

"No." Sherry's voice brooked no argument. "Don't leave here. I will be responsible for the boys, but I would rather not have you on my mind as well."

Her ladyship's shoulders sagged. She dabbed at her eyes again. "Oh, very well. You know what is best, I suppose."

Sherry thought his godmother sounded more resigned than confident. He felt the need to extract some sort of promise from Lily. "You, Lily? Do you think I know what's best?"

Looking up from the letter, Lily nodded. "I'll wait here."

Easing his hands out of theirs, Sherry stood. "I must go. Woodridge cannot have gotten far. I'll be back soon."

"Sherry?"

He stopped and looked at Lily. "Yes?"

"How is it possible that Midge saw the baron?"

Sherry pointed to the letter in Lily's hand. "He says Woodridge was in Holborn."

"I know. With Ned Craven. But Midge *recognized* him here. When did he see Woodridge? I know they were playing in the passage and heard rather more than they would admit, but I doubt Midge would be able to identify the baron by his voice alone. When did he see him?"

"They came into the gallery while Woodridge and I were speaking."

"Is that right? They did not tell me that."

"I asked them not to."

It was as Lily had begun to suspect. "You enlisted their aid, didn't you?"

Sherry did not deny it. "Yes. They are good at what they do, and I needed their help." He held up one hand to forestall the objections. "They were never in any danger."

"Can you be so certain they are not now?"

"I did not enlist them to do this thing, Lily."

It was not precisely an answer to her question, but she realized it was not entirely fair of her to pose it in the first place. She wanted assurances from Sherry that he could not properly give. He'd tried to do so once, more for Lady Rivendale's sake than her own. She should not press him a second time. "Go on. I am sorry for keeping you."

Sherry took a few steps toward Lily again, dropped a kiss on her mouth, then strode down the hall.

Lady Rivendale watched him go, puzzled by his direction. "His horse is at the front," she said. "Why is he going—"

"His pistol, I imagine."

Her ladyship immediately stopped dabbing at her eyes and pressed her crumpled handkerchief against her mouth.

Pinch caught up to the stone he'd been kicking and kicked it again. It skittered down the road some eight feet before it stopped. "I don't see 'ow ye fell overboard," he said to Midge for the third time.

Midge had his own stone to kick. He caught it just right with the toe of his boot and sent it flying in a perfect arc. When it landed it was at least five feet beyond Pinch's. "I told ye. It jest 'appened. I ain't 'appy about it."

Dash's pace never faltered. Having no interest in kicking a stone all the way back to Granville Hall, he was able to keep his head up and his eyes on the ribbon of road in front of them. "'E 'ad an itch," he told Pinch. "'E let go of the ropes to scratch it, and then—" Dash shrugged. "Well, ye know wot 'appened then."

"Ye 'ad an itch?" Pinch stopped in his tracks. "I should kick ye back to Granville 'All instead of this stone. It 'as more sense."

"It was me balls. I 'ad to scratch."

"Oh, well, as long as it was yer balls."

Midge shied away when Pinch raised his hand as though he meant to strike.

"Stop it," Dash told them. "It's done. Anyway, 'ere comes 'is lordship an 'e's not likely to be in a forgivin' frame of mind."

Pinch looked up and saw Sherry's approach. "Wot makes ye think that?"

"'E's got no 'orses wi' 'im, now does 'e? We're walkin', lads."

"We're already walkin'," Midge said.

"Sure we are, but we only 'ad Pinch to yammer at us. In case ye 'adn't noticed, when it comes to givin' us a piece of 'is mind, 'is lordship 'as a generous nature."

Pinch and Midge sighed heavily, in agreement for the first time since they'd had to abandon the baron's carriage.

Sherry reined in his mount several yards in front of the boys and waited for them to catch up. "Hello," he said pleasantly, turning Achilles around as the scoundrels filed past. "I must say, I was not in expectation of crossing your path quite so soon. What happened?"

Pinch threw up his hands, his lip curled in disgust. "Midge 'ere 'ad to scratch 'is balls."

Sherry's dark eyebrows rose in tandem. "Really? That sounds rather like the end of the tale. I should like to hear it from the beginning."

The scoundrels began talking at once.

Lily found Sherry and Lady Rivendale in the music salon. In a reversal of the usual practice, her ladyship was sitting at the pianoforte and Sherry was the appreciative audience. Lily joined him on the chaise, but when Lady Rivendale realized it was no longer only Sherry listening, she stopped playing abruptly and turned away from the keys.

"Oh, please," Lily said. "Don't stop. I should like to hear more."

"As would I." Lady Rivendale looked pointedly at her godson. "Well, Sherry? Lily is returned, the boys are tucked in, and we are waiting to hear the whole of it." She glanced at Lily. "Unless the lads shared it all with you."

"No," she said. "I did not demand they make another explanation. I said I would hear it from Sherry. They were bone weary and prepared to fall asleep on their feet."

"Their blistered feet," her ladyship said. "Really, Sherry, you might have allowed them to take turns riding. They fairly dragged themselves in here."

"As I've noted before, they belong on the stage," Sherry told her. "And I don't think I like it that they've replaced me in your affections, Aunt."

"None of that now." She dismissed it with a wave of her hand. "Tell all. I want to know where they were hiding and how they got away."

Sherry grinned. "It was surprisingly simple for them. While Woodridge's horses were being tended, the boys climbed aboard the carriage and wedged themselves between the trunks and bags. Actually, because it was a squeeze they drew broom straws to see who would ride in one of the trunks. Midge pulled the short straw—though my own opinion is that there was some sleight of hand involved. He is the smallest, and I think Dash and Pinch got the better of him."

"Those devils," Lady Rivendale said under her breath. "Poor Master Midge."

Sherry smiled at his godmother's quick championing of Midge, though she would have said the same if it were one of the others being taken advantage of. "Indeed. The close confines of the trunk did not set well with our Smidgen, and he started to feel sick not long after the carriage was underway. He had to knock on the lid a bit before Pinch heard him and opened it. Pinch managed to get Midge out of the trunk without them being seen by the driver or the tiger, but Midge was feeling so poorly by then that he didn't have much strength to support himself. In addition, it seems he developed a most inconvenient itch."

"Itch?" Lady Rivendale asked. "What sort of—" She stopped because Sherry was shaking his head, indicating he did not mean to answer any questions in that regard. "Oh, go on, then. It cannot be important."

"Thank you," he said dryly, mocking her restraint. "Before Pinch could secure him properly, the carriage wheels hit a rut crosswise, and Midge was bounced off the roof. He caught one of the lines keeping the bags in place, but he couldn't hold on. Pinch and Dash saw nothing for it but to jump as well. They refused to be separated from him."

"Lord love them," Lady Rivendale said, putting one hand over her heart. The sincerity of the gesture overshadowed its dramatic bent.

The smile that was still hovering on Sherry's face deepened. "Oh, I think He does. Not only did they escape injury, they escaped notice." Beside him, he felt Lily shiver. "What is it?"

"Nothing." She hesitated, then merely shook her head. "No, it is nothing."

"They're fine, Lily," he said. "You saw them. I imagine you inspected them for bruises."

"There are a few of those. Scrapes as well." She turned slightly on the chaise. "I am not certain they understand how lucky they were. I don't want them ever putting themselves in so much danger on any account, least of all mine."

"They know how fortunate they were. As for the danger, they had a good number of miles to contemplate their foolishness."

"And you, m'lord? Have you considered your own?"

"Mine? What do you mean?"

Lily's lush mouth flattened disapprovingly. "Using the boys as you did."

"I thought this was settled. I told you the lads were not imperiled."

"I heard you well enough. I simply do not agree. You didn't encourage their participation because they could lift the baron's handkerchief. Pray, do not feign astonishment. I was out of the gallery but still in the passage when I heard you comment on the blood on Woodridge's cheeks. I surmised you handed him your handkerchief because you told him not to trouble himself to look for his own. I did not think much of it then, but later, when I realized the boys had most likely been in the gallery and made the baron's acquaintance there, I realized they were the ones who had pinched the linen."

Lily's chin lifted a fraction. "They are thorough scoundrels, my lord, but even I acquit them of giving one of your guests the rum-hustle without your sanction. What I want to know is what else did they take from Woodridge?"

"They didn't tell you?"

"I didn't ask them. I wanted to hear it from you."

Sherry was aware that his godmother was following this exchange with open interest. He sensed her sympathies were not with him. "I imagine this will sound rather worse in the telling than it was in the practice." He noticed that neither woman was moved to soften her expression. Seeing there was nothing for it but to plunge ahead with the explanation, he did so. "The baron carries a knife sheathed in his frock coat and a garrote in his pocket."

Lily's face fell and she moaned softly, hugging herself. Lady Rivendale was more vocal. "Sherry! I am beyond incredulous!"

Sherry wondered why the Foreign Office never engaged interrogators of the female persuasion. They were more effective at wringing a confession than a medieval torture chamber. "Midge also found an announcement of our engagement that Woodridge was carrying somewhere on his person. That was unexpected but perhaps of the most benefit. It proved that he knew we were engaged in spite of his denials of the same." When this elicited no response from Lily or his godmother, he added somewhat helplessly, "And then there was his handkerchief."

Lady Rivendale sighed.

Lily stood. "If you will excuse me, my lord. Lady Rivendale." She inclined her head toward her ladyship. "I find myself unaccountably fatigued. I am for bed."

Sherry was on his feet as soon as Lily came to hers, but he did not try to prevent her exit. She was already turning away from him as he bid her good night. When she was gone, he plunged his fingers through his hair and regarded his godmother. "I believe some time and distance are in order."

"Oh, good for you, Sherry. I estimate that time to be at least the rest of this night and the distance at better than arm's length."

Sherry understood that well enough. He would not be seeking out Lily in her bedchamber this evening, even to make an apology. "There was very little risk involved, Aunt. They are quite good at the rum-hustle, and we practiced until I was perfectly satisfied with their ability to relieve Woodridge of his—"

Lady Rivendale held up one hand. "Do not say another word, dear, else I will take my leave as well. I hope that is not an explanation you mean to offer Lily in defense of your actions. She is likely to want to box your ears."

Sherry sat down heavily. "Mayhap it is something females cannot comprehend."

"My word, Sherry. Such condescension. I believe I may be moved to box your ears myself. You will do much better if you will simply allow that you were wrong and trust that she will be merciful."

He grunted softly. "Men are stirred to these actions by their desire to protect women, and I include the lads here. I know you and Lily are of the opinion they are children, but it is only their age, not their experience, that makes them so. Lily believes she has been protecting them when the truth is somewhat different than that. They have been the ones shielding her."

Much struck by this idea, Lady Rivendale's brow furrowed. "What do you mean?"

"I cannot explain all of it to you, Aunt. There is so much that is Lily's alone to say, but I can tell you that the boys have long been aware that women of Lily's particular coloring were highly prized by a certain Holborn . . . procurer, shall we say."

"I would say pimp, but you must use the King's English as you see fit. You are speaking of this Ned Craven whose name I have heard."

Sherry sighed. "Yes. The lads did a bit of work for Ned from time to time to keep him from snaring Lily. All the while she was trying to keep them out of Ned's hands, they were working to keep her out of the same. It is hard to know if they were ever at cross purposes, but there is no question that their intentions were honorable. They stayed close to her, kept a vigil as it were. She used to disguise the color of her hair with blacking, but the boys had learned she was a redhead. They didn't want Ned to discover the same, so they made certain she was properly covered when she was out. They pinched clothes for her so that she could go into the streets as a young man. When they knew Ned was scavenging the streets, they warned her against going out or followed her if she went anyway."

"And she knows none of this?"

"I don't know what she might suspect, but they've never told her."

"Why not?"

"For the simplest of reasons: they were afraid she would send them away." He spoke to his godmother's skeptical expression. "It was a reasonable fear. If Lily thought they were doing things because of her that would endanger them, she would remove herself or remove them. Do not say you doubt it. That was her objection to this day's piece of work by the scoundrels, and she cannot appreciate that the lads and I share a different view. She would bear all of the risk, and that is unacceptable to us. She might not agree with our perspective, but I should very much like her to respect it. Pinch, Dash, and Midge did nothing more today than they've done since taking her under their collective wing. What is different is that I knew it and she didn't."

Lady Rivendale was quiet, considering this. "Lily is more out of sorts with your part in encouraging them than she is with the part they played. You shall have to set it right with her."

"You have some advice, I collect."

"I like her immensely, Sherry. My advice is simple: do not muck it up."

Lily's sleep was restless. Several times since coming to bed she felt herself drifting off, only to awaken shortly after and trouble herself by reviewing the day's events in her mind. Wondering what choices she might have made in Sherry's position did not make sleep easy to find. Twice she rose and went to the boys' rooms, not because she was concerned that they would not be abed but because she needed to believe she was doing something more than pacing off her unsettled nerves.

It was tempting to go to Sherry's bedchamber and settle with him, but she resisted, uncertain of her reception. She had taken him to task for all that might have happened—and didn't—while demonstrating precious little in the way of gratitude for what he had been able to accomplish. It was very poorly done of her, she thought, and he would be well within his rights to show her the door, or at least insist that she stay on the other side of it.

Lily was lying on her back, hugging a pillow to her aching chest and staring at the ceiling, when she heard the sound of breathing that was not her own. Her fingers tightened on the pillow. "My lord?"

"Which lord is that?" Woodridge asked, stepping away from the deep shadow beside the fireplace. "You will understand my confusion, Lilith."

Lily pushed herself upright and peered into the darkness. She could make him out as he came to stand to the right of one of the wing chairs. He leaned casually against it, resting his elbow on the high back. Eyes narrowing, Lily saw that he carried something long and slender in his hands and that he was passing it back and forth between them. It was when the object tapped against the floor that she realized it was his crystal-knobbed walking stick.

"Leave now," she said, "and I won't scream."

He shook his head. "If you meant to raise the alarm you would have already done so. You do not want to call those boys from their beds. Nor Sherry, either."

Lily screamed. It was a good effort: shrill, loud, and long. As Woodridge got his bearings and lunged for her, she rolled to the opposite side of the bed, taking the pillow with her. Before she could drop to the floor, the baron extended his reach with his walking stick and poked her in the chest. The pillow would have made the blow less punishing if it had only been the flattened tip that she'd felt, but Lily heard the revealing snap of the stick's blade being released and understood what was going to happen. She had the fleeting thought that perhaps if she hadn't known what to expect, she wouldn't have experienced the pain quite so keenly, but that first prick was as sharp as the deep thrust of the blade had been in Covent Garden.

She was not without any defense, however, and she used the pillow to keep the knife from sinking into her, deflecting the blade down and to the side. The tip rent her gown and sliced her skin along the underside of her breast, but she held on, protecting her hands with the pillow until she was able to turn and use Woodridge's forward momentum to drive the blade and walking stick into the bed.

The baron sprawled across the mattress and lost his grip on the stick. He groped for it blindly. Lily tossed the pillow and yanked the cane out by the knobbed end. Woodridge's keening, wounded animal cry startled her so that she nearly dropped the weapon before she could fling it away. All the instincts of survival served her now, and she held on long enough to pitch it like a javelin in the direction of the door.

She felt the baron's fingers clawing at her, scrabbling to get a fistful of her nightgown. Lily tore herself away, rolling to the very edge of the bed and dropping over the side. Her knees banged the floor hard. Pressing one hand to her wound, she used the other to push herself to her feet. As her head rose above the edge of the bed, Woodridge cuffed her and knocked her sideways. Dazed, Lily lay there, unable to move. She heard the baron leaving the bed and sensed when he came to stand over her. Still standing, he straddled her. She tensed as he dropped to his haunches.

His first touch was unexpected. Warm. Wet. His fingertip slid too easily along her cheek, made almost frictionless by the thin liquid film that separated his skin from hers. Not tears, she realized. Blood. His blood.

Lily flinched, but she could not escape him. He caught her on the chin, tilting it so he could run his fingertip along the underside and down her throat. She imagined the blood trail he was making, painting her face in the fashion of some ancient Celtic warrior. He continued across her collarbone to her shoulder, then turned her from her side onto her back and pinned her upper arms with his knees. There was more pressure than pain, and in very little time she was numb to the tips of her fingers.

"They didn't hear you," he said softly. "Have you realized they aren't coming?"

Because she knew him so well it was far too easy to imagine his eyes boring into her, the ice blue glance sharp enough to cause physical pain. Lily sucked in a breath, and before he could realize her intent, she screamed again.

The baron's response was immediate. He sat heavily on her chest, changing the pitch of her scream as air was forced out of her lungs. He grasped the fallen pillow and jammed it across her face, stifling her completely.

Lily struggled, kicking, flailing. She bucked, lifting her back and bottom entirely off the floor to try to heave him to the side. She hadn't the strength to sustain the effort when he would not be moved. He pressed her down and held the pillow in place. Lily could not draw a breath. She recognized the difference between the dark that had surrounded her and the terrible blackness that was absorbing her now. Inky fingers clawed at her scattered thoughts, the vision of Sherry and the scoundrels that she held in her mind's eye, and finally at her body's inability to mount any defense.

Woodridge pulled back the pillow.

Long moments passed, and Lily did not move. She had no sense of coming to awareness, only the sense that she was not dead. She sucked in air, gasping as Woodridge raised himself just enough to relieve the pressure on her chest. The sound was harsh and loud to her own ears, but it was no more than a whisper in the quiet room. Woodridge did not even threaten her with the pillow again. Watching her closely, he laid it to the side.

"Your bravado does not interest me, Lilith. I was not wrong that he has changed you, yet there is nothing admirable about what you have become. You should not have left me. I had appreciation for what you were; I did not demand that you become something you are not."

Lily's heart slammed against her chest. Her breathing was ragged. Afraid she might be sick, she turned her head so she wouldn't choke. Woodridge grabbed her chin and wrested it back. She moaned softly as her head swam and her stomach roiled.

"Look at me," he said. "Where are the documents?"

Lily frowned. She understood the words, not their meaning. The light slap Woodridge delivered to her cheek did nothing to improve her comprehension.

"Where are the documents, Lilith?"

"I don't know." It was the simplest answer until she could think of what he meant.

Frustrated, the baron plunged the fingers of one hand into Lily's hair and twisted until he had a fistful of it. "Will pain help you apply yourself?"

"Why didn't you stay away?"

Woodridge's grip tightened momentarily, then eased. "Shall I indulge you? Will that help you remember?" He did not wait for her reply. "I wonder if you fear for me. You shouldn't, you know. I am able to hold my own with Sheridan, though he would have you believe differently. He was certain he had bested me; it made him overconfident. I took a room at Westin-on-the-Narrows as he could expect that I would, then I left by means that he would not anticipate. Can you imagine me lowering myself from a window, Lilith? It amuses, does it not?"

Because he seemed to anticipate she would answer this time, Lily whispered that it did indeed amuse.

"I knew you would find it so," he said. "But then your understanding of me is very narrow. Would you agree to that?"

"Yes."

"I left the inn and returned straightaway. Sheridan would have done well to send someone to watch for just such a thing, but it has always been his weakness that he is too trusting of a man's word."

Thinking of the boys' mad scheme to follow Woodridge, Lily shuddered. The small movement made him bear down on her again as he misinterpreted it as the beginning of another struggle. She forced herself to remain calm and draw short, even breaths. "My lord Sheridan believes in honor."

"I know. He has never embraced the notion that it is merely something to be manipulated and exploited. Pity, that. For you, I mean. His failure has left you unprotected. That was never so when you were in my home. You were cherished there, Lilith. You cannot deny that it was my way to cherish you."

It was truer that Lily chose not to deny it. His words did not surprise. She had always found that his ability to view his actions in a benign, even benevolent, light to be the single most frightening aspect of his character. It was no different now. She knew he would be able to kill her and justify it to himself as necessary to free her soul.

The baron placed his hands on either side of Lily's head and bent closer. "I was not certain I would find you alone. As I waited for the house to grow dark, for the servants to retire, I tortured myself with thoughts of you in Sheridan's bed. I wondered what I would do if I found you there. I don't believe there would have been any pleasure in watching you with him. I think it would have enraged me."

The matter-of-fact manner in which he spoke of these things was chilling. Lily's skin prickled. She could no longer feel her arms below the point where he kept them pinned with his knees. She tried to curl her fingers into light fists, but without turning her head to one side to look at her hand, she could not judge her success.

"I saw you at your window before you extinguished your candle. I thought you looked lonely, though perhaps it is merely that I want to believe it. Are you lonely, Lily? Were you looking for me when you stood at your window?"

She did not respond. The lie would have cost her dearly, perhaps even more than the truth.

"Where are the documents?" Woodridge asked. "What has Sheridan done with them?"

"I don't know. He told me nothing about—"

Woodridge pressed his thumbs into her throat, cutting her off. He counted to five under his breath before he eased back. "Again," he said softly. "Tell me again that you know nothing, and I will kill you. But know that I will find the children next and kill them as well, then Lady Rivendale. Sheridan will be the last, and he will learn that everyone he cares about has gone before him. Can you imagine his suffering? He will beg for me to end it. Mayhap he can be persuaded to do the thing himself." Woodridge moved this thumbs lightly along her neck from the underside of her chin to the hollow of her throat. "Will you have that on your conscience, Lilith?"

She shook her head.

"Good. I will ask only once more. Where are the documents?"

"In the library." Because Lily could not predict how he would react to learning that one of his confessions was already in the hands of Sherry's solicitor, she chose the safer course of gaining some time and perhaps an advantage. "Do you know where it is?"

"Yes, though I don't expect he has allowed them to remain where they were when I left."

Lily heard the faint inflection in his tone that made it a question. "I don't know," she said. "It's where I saw them. On his desk."

"You will show me, then."

He stood so abruptly that Lily could not grasp immediately what had happened. Relief at being able to draw her first full breath warred with a profound sense of humiliation that she could not lift herself. Her arms and hands tingled painfully as blood flow returned, but they were still useless in supporting her effort to rise. She blinked back tears as Woodridge grasped a handful of her nightshift and pulled her upright, first to a sitting position, then to her feet. She weaved unsteadily when he removed his support.

"Cover yourself," he said.

Lily looked down and saw that her gown was laid open where he had split the fabric with his blade. She managed to close the gap with fingers made clumsy by their weakness.

"You understand what I will do," he said, "if you scream again."

"Yes." If he was unconvinced by her answer, her husky, slightly strangled voice offered further proof that he had defeated her in this regard.

Woodridge turned on his heel, unconcerned that he gave her his back, and began searching for his walking stick. He found it lying close to the door of the adjoining sitting room. It had missed being embedded in an upholstered footstool by mere inches. Shaking his head, Woodridge bent to pick it up. The deep cut in his own palm made it difficult to grasp. Blood still flowed freely from the wound, and the stick was made slippery by it. It was only when he started to rise that he realized his mistake in underestimating Lily's resolve and her ability to act on it.

Using her shoulder and the strength of her forward motion, Lily struck the baron hard from behind. Dropping the walking stick, he stumbled across the threshold of the sitting room and fell to his knees. Lily kicked the door closed, then kicked Woodridge's weapon under the bed. She ran for the door to the hall. Her fingers fumbled with the knob, and she cursed softly when she realized she would not be able to turn it quickly enough to make her escape. Turning, considering what course was left to her, Lily dove for the foot of the bed. She did not seek protection on top, but under it. Pressing her mouth against her forearm to quiet her breathing, Lily listened as the door to the sitting room opened and Woodridge stepped out.

Lily waited, alert to the sounds that meant he was crossing the room. What she heard, though, was the unmistakable sound of feet pounding down the hallway. He could not miss it either, and her breath seized as she anticipated his next action. Lily searched blindly for the walking stick and found it with her fingertips moments before Woodridge threw himself across the top of the bed and rolled to the other side, landing on his feet closer to the window just as the door to her room was thrown open.

"Lily?"

"Miss Rose!"

It was Sherry and the scoundrels. She had never held out any hope that Sherry would hear her scream from this distant wing. It was a calculated risk to rouse the boys, knowing they might choose to act alone again, but she had prayed that today's bit of heroics would convince them to seek Sherry out. Lily felt tears sting her eyes as they called her a second time. Fear that they all might advance incautiously kept her from revealing her place under the bed.

Her position was such that she could not see them, but at the periphery of her vision was the soft flood of candlelight they carried with them. She turned her head to one side, looking for Woodridge. Where was he? Why hadn't Sherry seen him yet?

"Wait here," Sherry ordered the boys. "Keep your candles high. Good." He stepped into the room. "Lily?"

It was then that Lily saw the tips of the baron's boots parting the delicate gold fringe of the velvet drapes. Behind her, she heard Sherry begin to go in the opposite direction toward the sitting room. Using her elbows and forearms, Lily pulled herself closer to where the baron was hiding. When Sherry's steps paused, so did she. If he looked for her under the bed, the baron would have all the advantage of surprise. He started again, and she crawled forward as well, this time gripping the walking stick with fingers that were beginning at last to know their strength.

When he halted a second time, she didn't hesitate. Lily thrust the blade end of the stick toward the drapes and felt the sickening plunge of it into Woodridge's flesh.

The baron cried out, grasped the drapes to steady himself, and pulled them down instead as he staggered forward. Lily withdrew the weapon and thrust it like a spear again, this time pricking him just above the ankle. At Woodridge's cry, all of Sherry's attention shifted to the window. He closed the distance in a few strides but stepped aside to let the baron fall rather than attempt to catch him.

The drapes themselves were the handiest restraint, and Sherry used them to good effect, rolling Woodridge over and over so they became his shroud. The baron struggled to free himself, but with each successive turn the fit was tighter.

"Bloody hell, Lily," Sherry said. "Will you show yourself now?"

From the doorway, Pinch waved his candlestick wildly. "Look! My lord! The bed!"

Lily poked her head out from under the bed frame, then drew her shoulders forward. She glanced up at Sherry, smiled weakly, and continued scooting out on her belly. He took her so strongly by the arms that she was lifted off her feet. His embrace was so tight that she could barely draw breath, yet she didn't think of trying to release herself from it.

"M'lord! M'lord!" From the doorway, Dash begged for Sherry's attention. He was joined in short order by Pinch and Midge. The candlelight danced as the boys jumped up and down. "'E's gettin' out!"

Sherry looked over his shoulder, saw that the baron was indeed making a good attempt at wriggling free, then motioned the boys forward. "Guard your lady, lads." He set Lily from him. His face lost some of its color when he saw the condition of her shift and the bloodstains outlining the tear at the front of it. "Here, take this." He swept one of the coverlets off the bed and thrust it at her. Go with the scoundrels." When she hesitated, casting her eyes once in the direction of Woodridge, Sherry nudged her toward the door. "Go. Give the boys this moment." His dark eyes became implacable. "Give me mine."

Lily did not mistake this for a request. Had it been one,

she would not have denied him. "The walking stick," she said softly. "It's what he—" She stopped because Sherry was nodding.

"I see it," he said. He kissed her forehead and turned her in the direction of the scoundrels. They were waiting at the foot of the bed, darting anxious glances between Lily and Woodridge. "Wait for me in the schoolroom. I will come for you when it is finished here."

"Yes." Lily stopped worrying her bottom lip and released it. She skirted the edges of the undulating drapery as Woodridge flopped and twisted like a netted trout and let Dash take her in hand. The boys quickly escorted her out of the room. Midge set his candlestick on a side table before he closed the door.

Sherry's slight smile was rather grim as he bent and picked up the walking stick. He examined it experimentally, twisting the crystal knob clockwise and watching the stiletto blade retract into the shaft of the cane. Turning the knob to the left made it appear again.

"A clever instrument," he said, jamming his boot against the small of the baron's back to keep him from making another roll in that direction. "I am talking about the walking stick. I did not suspect the blade, else I would have taken it from you as well." Stepping aside, he gave Woodridge a light kick, encouraging him to keep rolling. When the baron didn't move, Sherry taunted him. "You are shy, perhaps, Cleopatra? She presented herself to Caesar in such a fashion, I believe. Or is it the terrible ignominy of your position that gives you pause?" Sherry set the walking stick on the bed and dropped to his haunches beside Woodridge. Taking a handful of drapery in each fist, Sherry yanked hard, forcing the baron to roll out. While Woodridge lay facedown on the carpet, Sherry picked up the stick. With the blade retracted, he poked at his former mentor until he turned over.

"Ahh," Sherry said, looking at the blood pulsing from Woodridge's closed hand. There were stains as well on his trousers at the calf and just above his ankle. "I see she got some of her own back. That must rankle." He tapped the blunt end of the stick lightly against the floor. "Is this what she used to make you reveal your hiding place?"

Woodridge said nothing.

Sherry pressed the tip against the wound in the baron's calf. "Is it?"

"Yes!" When Sherry removed the stick, Woodridge repeated himself, more softly this time. "Yes."

"Will you get to your feet?"

Nodding, Woodridge began to rise. His injury caused him some difficulty, and he held out his hand to Sherry for assistance. When Sherry took a step backward, the baron responded with a humorless smile. "You do not trust me, Sheridan? I told Lilith it was a flaw in your character that you were too trusting, but perhaps you have corrected it at last." He finished straightening, holding his injured hand close to his chest. He glanced down at it then back at Sherry. "It's a grievous wound." He showed Sherry that he could not flex his fingers smoothly. "It may well be that I will not have the use of it again."

"I don't think that matters," Sherry said quietly.

Woodridge's slender mouth curved in a parody of a smile. "No, I don't suppose that it does. How will you do it?"

"Quickly."

"That's good of—" He broke off because it was already done.

Sherry took a step to the rear, sharply removing the stiletto from the baron's chest. He examined the stick once before he retracted the blade and tossed it aside, then he turned away, his expression like his eyes, dark and remote, and exited the room without a backward glance.

Epilogue

L'Abbaye de Sacré Coeur, Décembre 1815

Sherry came to his feet, inclining his head politely as the two women hurried past. They acknowledged him courteously, serene smiles fixed but curiosity in their surreptitious glances. He watched them bend their heads toward each other once they were out of his hearing and could easily imagine they were discussing him. It was more difficult to imagine what they might be saying, though he distinctly heard one of them titter. Until this moment it had never occurred to him that nuns might be given to tittering.

Lily made certain she had impressed upon him what a solemn place the abbey was. While she'd shared stories of her own sly misdeeds and efforts to bedevil the sisters, she was equally careful to paint a picture of women embracing long hours of contemplation and prayer. According to Lily, footsteps were what one heard in the hallowed corridors, not voices, and no one ever hurried. She had failed to mention there might be tittering.

Sherry returned to the hard bench. Positioned as it was outside the Reverend Mother's study, Sherry could not quite shake the sense that he had been called up to explain some misdeed of his own. It harkened back to his days at Eton where the headmaster had carefully prepared lectures on a variety of offenses that students were wont to commit. Coming to stand before him had always seemed serious business, fraught with certain anxiety and embarrassment, but Sherry decided it paled in comparison to making the same stand before the abbess.

That was why he was relieved it was Lily inside with the Reverend Mother and he who was cooling his heels in the hallway. Grinning widely, unapologetic for encouraging her to go in alone, Sherry leaned back against the cool stone wall and stretched his legs in front of him. He warned Lily at the outset that he had too many sins to atone for to be strictly comfortable in the presence of so much piety, but he was all for accompanying her to the abbey.

It had been, in fact, his idea.

Their wedding trip, he had explained, would be to Paris, and Lily was so overwhelmed by his generosity that she failed at first to comprehend that pleasing her was not his only motive. She was not long in coming to the understanding that he was maneuvering her, and she did not thank him for it. They had words, many of them exchanged the morning after their wedding night, so that when they appeared at breakfast and barely spoke to each other the tension at the table was discomfiting. His godmother and the scoundrels tolerated it as long as they could, but then they began to twitch. Pinch elbowed Dash, Dash kicked Midge under the table, and Midge poked Lady Rivendale with his index finger. They volleyed glances, wiggled eyebrows, and whispered to each other in asides that were perfectly audible to the people they were talking about. He and Lily had surrendered to them, and it was then that Lily had agreed that whatever his motives, a trip to Paris was just the thing.

They were married in September as soon as the inquiry into Woodridge's death was behind them. The wedding was a small affair, just as Lily had wanted, with only a few family members and close friends attending. Cybelline and Nicholas had been present, Cybelline still slender as a boy from the back but burgeoning alarmingly from every other angle. His godmother honored Lily's promise to abandon her list and invited only those dearest to her. His own friends made the long journey from London and settled in Granville Hall for a fortnight, finding great delight in teaching the scoundrels a host of tricks they didn't need to know and losing a considerable sum of money to his godmother at the card table.

Lily had not been ready to make the acquaintance of her own family, if indeed there was a connection as Lady Rivendale suspected. Following the wedding, she found one reason after another to put it off, and Sherry realized finally that his intrepid, seemingly fearless wife was actually quite afraid. In the end, she had no choice, not because he forced her to it but because her family did.

Lily received a letter from John Bingham in October, some three weeks following the wedding. The missive introduced himself and made cautious inquiries after her own family. Lily set it aside for more than a sennight before she decided she would answer. Sherry believed he demonstrated considerable restraint by not offering his opinion, even when it was requested. He was beginning to learn when Lily was truly desirous of hearing what he thought and when she merely wanted to hear him agree with her. Marriage, he was finding, was filled with hidden snares such as that one. Sometimes he was able to sidestep them; on occasion they snagged him so sharply he went head over bucket.

Sherry never minded landing at Lily's feet. She was too generous of heart to let him lie there long and too smart not to realize that he quite enjoyed the manner in which she made up to him.

Lily invited John Bingham and his wife to visit Granville Hall, thereby delaying—quite purposely, Sherry thought—their Paris trip a few additional weeks. The visit lasted a fortnight, and the Binghams proved to be the most excellent of people. Arriving with the family Bible, they showed Lily the lines that connected her mother to John and Caroline Bingham and confirmed that Caroline was indeed Sister Mary Joseph of *L'Abbaye de Sacré Coeur*. Never once during their visit did Lily ask directly if Caroline Bingham had given birth to her, and neither John nor his wife volunteered information to suggest that this was true. Sherry did not press Lily to make the inquiry, respecting her wishes not to discomfit their guests. If it was a secret, John Bingham had determined it was not his to reveal. If it was simply not true, Lily's cousin might find offense in having the question put to him.

For himself, Sherry allowed he was curious, but whether or not Lily was a bastard was insignificant to him, except as it mattered to her. Lady Rivendale opined the same view, but her curiosity was so great Sherry was afraid she might wheedle the information from the Binghams regardless of Lily's desire to let the thing rest.

It was with some relief that the Binghams finally departed, but by then Cybelline was close to delivering and everyone was in agreement that London was the place to be. The Paris trip was again delayed, and Sherry could not very well accuse Lily of bringing it about when nature was merely taking its course.

A slow course as it turned out. The infant showed no signs of being in any hurry to make the acquaintance of its parents or the world at large. It was a week past the expected arrival when a runner delivered the message to Sherry at his townhouse that his sister was now confined to her bed. His beautiful niece was born just as day was breaking. Lily attended Cybelline and afterward came downstairs to announce the birth. Later she would be moved to tell him that he and Nicholas looked far worse for the experience than Cybelline did.

Some five days later, with Cybelline insisting that she was in the best of health and relying on the good judgment and experience of the nurse—and the well meant but less reliable advice of Lady Rivendale—Sherry was prepared to finally embark on the Paris trip with his bride.

The scoundrels were perfectly happy to be left in the care

of their Aunt Georgia. She had impressed upon them the necessity of addressing her as such or risk giving the gravest offense. They had become her devoted followers, and Lady Rivendale enjoyed it shamelessly. Sherry was certain they would be spoiled beyond bearing by the time he and Lily returned, but he had survived much the same treatment at his godmother's generous hands and had not been irreparably damaged by the attention.

Sherry came to his feet and out of his reverie as the door to the Reverend Mother's inner sanctum opened suddenly and Lily stepped into the quiet corridor. By nature, Sherry was not given to fanciful notions, but when he saw Lily it seemed to him that the very air around her shimmered. She looked not merely happy, but beatific, profoundly serene and yet moved by an excitement that simply could not be contained. He had thought she was surpassingly lovely on her wedding day, coming toward him down the center aisle of the village church attended by the three scapegraces, but what he saw in her now was something altogether different. She did not merely glow; she was radiant.

"Sherry?" Lily said his name uncertainly. She held out her hand to him. "Are you unwell?"

He blinked. "You have not decided to join the convent, have you?"

She frowned. "Pardon?"

"You do not mean to become one of them?" The inflection in his voice betrayed his uncertainty.

"One of the order, you mean?" Lily's eyes widened a fraction. She looked away from Sherry and surveyed the length of the corridor to be confident it was empty, then she threw her arms around his neck and kissed him soundly. His hands came around her waist and supported her as she stood on tiptoe. "You foolish man," she whispered against his mouth. "I cannot imagine what put that maggot into your head, but if I have not already proved to you how unsuited I am to that life I will set about the thing directly." She kissed him again, this time flicking her tongue across his upper lip.

Sherry jerked his head back and put her from him, holding her securely at a distance. "You are depending on me to show at least a modicum of good sense. That is not fair, Lily."

"You have never disappointed."

His dark eyes darted toward the room she had just exited. The door remained closed, and Lily's smile was teasing him almost beyond bearing. "Bloody hell, but you tempt me."

"Sherry! You forget where you are!"

At first he didn't understand, then he realized she was referring to his language. It didn't seem to matter that she had put him to a blush with that kiss. He was moved to offer the wry observation, "I am wondering why my slip of the tongue is worse than yours."

Now it was Lily who was put to a blush. "You, my lord, are a perfect rogue." She found his hand again and began pulling him toward the door. "Come. I promised Reverend Mother I would bring you directly, and frankly, Sherry, you have put me off my task."

Flashing Lily a rather satisfied, superior smile, Sherry allowed himself to be led away. He noticed her slight hesitation when her fingers fell on the door handle. "Lily?"

She looked up at him. "She is the very best of women, my lord. I hope you will not think—"

Sherry reached around her and placed his hand over hers. He exerted enough pressure to turn the handle. "I expect I shall like the Reverend Mother enormously."

The door swung open. The Reverend Mother stood on the other side of the threshold. "I believe Lily Rose is more desirous that you like her mother, Lord Sheridan."

Sherry's glance absorbed the Reverend Mother's slightly anxious expression, the way her head tilted to one side, the small vertical crease between her brows, the set of her delicate features framed by the wimple, then his eyes flew to Lily's and he saw the identical expression there. It was not the similarity of coloring but one of manner that put the connection between the two women firmly in Sherry's mind.

Lily slipped her arm in Sherry's and said softly, "My lord, I would very much like you to make the acquaintance of the recently appointed Reverend Mother of *L'Abbaye de Sacré Coeur.*"

The last niggling doubt was removed. Inclining his head, Sherry spoke the name that had been often on his mind of late. "Sister Mary Joseph."

In their Paris apartments that night, Sherry dismissed his valet and went to find Lily in her dressing room. She was sitting at the vanity, her eyes closed, her head tilted slightly backward, as her maid ran a brush through her hair. Sherry caught the maid's attention and gestured toward the door with his chin. He held out his hand for the brush, and they smoothly switched places. The maid departed the room with such stealth her skirts did not rustle. Still, Lily's deeply satisfied sigh indicated she knew quite well who was pulling the brush now.

"What gave me away?" asked Sherry.

"Your touch is infinitely more gentle than Beecham's." Without opening her eyes, Lily reached behind her and laid her hand over Sherry's, patting it lightly. "Pray, do not let that affect your work, my lord. I find your way of doing things has much to recommend it."

"You will understand that I am gratified to hear it."

His wry tone made her smile. She let her hand fall back in her lap and her smile gradually faded. "Beecham tells me that *Le Rougeaud* was executed this morning. I confess, I did not think it would happen. I thought the marshals would save him in the end."

"Perhaps they did. There is already a rumor that it was not Ney who faced the firing squad."

"Oh, that cannot be. I was told he gave the order to fire himself."

"And that does not make you suspicious?"

She frowned, at once suspicious, but not of the courage shown by *le brave des braves*. "Sherry? What do you know about this?"

"*Rien*. Nothing."

"Nothing?"

"I am well out of that intrigue, Lily, and it is only happenstance that we are in Paris at the time of his execution. You know very well our trip was delayed."

"I am not certain I believe in happenstance where you are concerned. You have an extraordinary talent for getting what you want."

"You are kind to say so."

Lily could not help smiling again. He was always provoking her to that end. She made a small murmur of pleasure as he lifted her hair and ran the brush through the underside. The bristles tickled the nape of her neck. She shivered delicately.

Sherry was not proof against the invitation of her parted lips. He bent and kissed her mouth. The brush dangled from his fingers, then clattered to the floor. Without breaking the kiss, he drew Lily to her feet. His fingers threaded in her hair while hers settled at the small of his back. They held each other in just such a fashion for a long time, their mouths moving with aching slowness as they enjoyed the thoroughness of the kiss.

In the end it was Lily who danced Sherry in the direction of their bed. When the back of his knees bumped the edge of the mattress, she pressed her fingertips against his chest with just enough force to topple him. She followed him down, covering him with her body. The room was far too chilled for her to enjoy that position for long. Lily was quite happy to be rolled under, happier still, when Sherry made a cocoon for them with the blankets and warmed her feet with his own.

"Shall I add coals to fire?" he asked.

Lily fingers tightened on his shoulders, keeping him close. "Attend to this fire first, *s'il vous plait*."

Chuckling wickedly, Sherry obliged. With exquisite attention to detail, he proved he knew her body as intimately as his own. Each touch elicited a response. He felt the pulse thrumming in her neck, heard the small cry at the back of her throat. She seemed to fairly vibrate with need and her skin retracted in anticipation of his mouth following the same path as his hands. What pleased her pleased him as well. When her fingertips trailed down his spine, he felt a shiver that went much deeper than his skin. She cupped his buttocks, settling him against her, cradling him with her thighs. Parting her legs, she made room for him there, then held her breath, releasing it with the same measured slowness as his entry.

For a moment it was as if they shared the same skin, a single heartbeat. That fusion was deliciously intense for as long as it lasted, but the most satisfying pleasure lay in what made them distinct and complimentary, and to that end, they engaged each other like fencers, thrusting, parrying, appreciating that first one could be the aggressor, then the other.

Lily felt herself contract around him, and even when Sherry found his own release, she did not want him to move. They lay on their sides, bodies flush, legs tangled, still joined as their breathing quieted. Lily nudged Sherry's lips with her own. She hummed her contentment against his mouth and felt the shape of his lips change.

"Are you smiling, my lord?" she whispered.

"Can you doubt it?"

They fell silent. Sherry's fingers sifted idly through Lily's hair. Lily traced the line of his collarbone. When he moved a second time to ease himself from her, she didn't stop him, but rolled onto her back and repaired her nightgown while he remained propped on an elbow on his side. Candlelight flickered across Lily's features. Sherry's were more shadowed.

Searching out something in his face that would give her ease, Lily asked, "You do not mind?"

Sherry was not entirely surprised by the question, only that she had waited so long to ask it. The few times he had tried to draw her out after leaving the abbey, she had politely changed the subject. It seemed she was determined to have the conversation now that they might have had hours ago. "You will have to say all of it, Lily," he told her gently. "If you mean to be sure of my answer, then you must ask all of the question."

She drew in a shallow breath, bracing herself. "You do not mind that I am a bastard?"

"No."

Lily waited. "You have nothing else to say?"

"No."

"It is not a ridiculous question, Sherry. There are husbands who would find it unacceptable and reason enough for divorce."

One of his dark eyebrows lifted. "Trust your judgment, Lily. You did not marry one of those witless fellows."

She smiled a little at that. "I am your viscountess, though. It seems to me that I should be—"

Sherry placed his index finger perpendicular to her lips. "A touch higher in the instep?" Removing his finger, he kissed her. "Very well, I will cede that position to you. It was deuced uncomfortable."

Lily was torn between relief and amusement. Her sigh vibrated with a bit of a chuckle. She was quiet for a long moment, then added in a voice not much above a whisper and filled with emotion, "It was good of you to suggest Paris."

"Was it? You have no regrets?"

Her heart swelled a little when she heard the uncertainty in his voice. She found his hand. "None, Sherry. You always made it my choice. This morning, when we were going to the abbey, even then I didn't know if I would put the question of my birth to her. I could not have told you then how I hoped she would answer. To discover Sister Mary Joseph was now the Reverend Mother quite took my breath away. If

I had known—if Mr. Bingham had breathed a word of it—I do not think we would have crossed the channel, but once I saw her, or more accurately, once she saw me, the truth simply was there between us whether we said so or not. It seemed we might as well say so."

"It was difficult for her?"

"Not so much as you might think. She was rather more relieved, I thought. She had never denied me in her heart, Sherry. That is what she said, and I believe her. Had you realized who my father was?"

"I did not know that she was your mother, Lily. Not with any certainty. I confess, I gave no thought at all to your father."

"Howard Sterling," she said as though for the first time. "Odd, is it not, how things are resolved in a family? An indiscretion with his fiancée's cousin has the consequence of pregnancy; she keeps the secret until after he is married, then begs a favor of him and Lillian to raise her child. The three of them travel to Paris for her confinement, and after she gives birth they return to London, and she retires to the abbey and takes up a life altogether different than she might have known."

Lily shook her head, marveling at the caprices of human nature. "So I am raised by my father, while the woman who became my mother never knew the truth of it."

Sherry was not entirely certain this was the case, though he did not raise the question. It was quite possible that Woodridge had not been lying about Lillian Sterling's adulterous affairs or her giving up her husband's diplomatic secrets. A liar sometimes told the truth, he knew, just as a good woman could be moved to betray others when she believed she had been betrayed herself.

He merely said, "So Caroline Bingham never told Lillian?"

"No. She said my father loved Lillian and that she could not bear to come between them, not when she loved Lillian as well. He only sought her out because he had had words with my mo—with Lillian." She frowned a little. "It's all very confusing. Caroline is Sister Mary Joseph. Lillian is my mother, yet not my mother, and my mother is the Reverend Mother. Has there ever been such a muddle, do you think?"

"In the royal family, certainly. But as for the rest of us, I don't believe so, no."

Lily gave him a soft poke in the ribs with her elbow.

"You meant it to be a rhetorical question, then," Sherry said, pretending to nurse his ribs. "I wondered."

"I was not conceived in love, Sherry, but by way of consolation. I am not certain what to make of that."

"I should not be surprised if that isn't more often the way of things. You cannot doubt that they loved you."

"No, not at all. At every turn, they were moved to protect me."

"Perhaps that is why you are similarly moved to protect others."

"Do you think so?"

"I think the scoundrels would agree with me."

Lily bolted upright. "Sherry! The scoundrels! They wrote to us."

Sherry made a grab at her nightgown but came up with a fistful of the sheet instead. Sighing, he sat up, and watched Lily hurrying across the cold floor on tiptoe. "You might have taken a moment to put on your slippers," he called after her. "Your feet will be like ice. Do not think I will allow you to warm them against me." He thought he heard her low chuckle from the dressing room, but he could not be certain. It might only have been the rustling of paper as she rummaged through her reticule.

"Here it is!"

That announcement preceded her bounding back to the bed by only seconds. Sherry barely had time to raise the blankets. Lily dove under them and immediately began to rub her icy toes against his calves. "Your heart is as cold as your feet," he said.

"I know. It is shameless how I abuse you, Sherry." She gave him the letter. "Here. You must open it. It arrived before we left this morning. You were out making arrangements for our carriage. I put it away so that we might read it together on the journey, and then . . . "

"I understand well enough what happened then." He recognized his godmother's stamp as he broke the seal. "They had some help from Lady Rivendale. Perhaps some encouragement also. I did not expect they would write." He unfolded the paper, saw it was Dash penning the thing again, and read aloud.

Dear Lord and Lady Sheridan,
    We hope you are having a jolly good time in ~~*Perris*~~ *Paris and desire you to know there is no need to hurry home.*

"That does not sound promising, does it?" Lily said, edging closer.

Aunt Georgia is in fine health after taking a turn on the banister and nipping her ~~*arse bottom*~~ *derry aire on the newel post. Pinch heard her remark it was only her pride that was broozed. We are all agreed that she must needs win at cards tonight as it will go a long way to unbroozing her.*

"Oh dear," Lily said.

We can tell you now that Mr. and Mrs. Caldwell are also in good spirits after learning their dotter did not swallow Aunt Georgia's pearl earbob. Dr. Harris came to the house and there was a great dust up, but Midge found the earbob in Aunt Georgia's ~~*bosum brests*~~ *bodice and he was acclaimed to be a hero by all.*

"Have you noticed the spelling is improved?" Lily said weakly. She slid a bit lower when Sherry cast her an incredulous sideways glance.

We hear from Blue that Ned Craven has come to a bad end. Ned got a taste of his own when someone informed on him. Two blokes took him out of the Ruin at night and Blue sez we won't see him again. Ever, he sez. The long and short of it done the deed. He sez we should tell you that most particular.

Lily frowned. "The long and short of it? What does that mean? And what are the boys doing in Holborn?" She felt Sherry shift slightly, communicating his sudden discomfort. "Sherry?"

"I doubt the boys were in Holborn."

"Sherry."

There was nothing for it but to explain. It was a bad piece of luck the thing had happened while he was gone from London. "I had an arrangement, shall we say, with Blue to relieve Holborn of Mr. Craven's presence. The long and short of it—"

Lily sunk her nails into his forearm, stopping him. "Those men. The ones who came to Granville. One was quite tall, and the other was most definitely not. They are the long and short it."

He sighed. "Yes."

"It will be transportation, won't it?"

"Yes. Van Diemen's Land."

She had to consider it only a moment. "Good. Go on. What else do they write?"

We are pleased to tell you that Sir Arthur Meredith has been a visitor but not pleased to report he is toplofty. He sez we are your awards now and that means you will be our keepers ~~becoz~~ because we are badly in need of keepers. Pinch told him that was fine because we already decided we are keeping you.

Warmest regards,
Dash Pinch Smidgen

Sir Arthur sez we must have new names now not meazurments. We like Peregrine, Beowulf, and Thor.

Lily and Sherry stared at the letter, then at each other. For a moment neither of them spoke, the import of this final notation being rather more than they could properly take in.

"How soon can we leave?" asked Lily.

"Morning," said Sherry.

"Will you mind?" This last they said almost simultaneously, then quickly shook their heads in unison.

Sherry set the letter aside, blew out the candle, and slipped deeper under the covers to join Lily. She snuggled against him, fitting her bottom neatly in the curve of his thighs and drawing his arm about her waist.

"Do you know, Sherry, I think I like the idea of the scoundrels being our awards. It seems fitting somehow, more distinctly appropriate, as if we earned the right to name them that."

"It occurred to me also. They know how to turn a phrase."

"Twist our hearts, you mean."

"Just so." He bent his head and kissed the curve of her neck. "My reward," he said quietly, his mouth hovering above her fragrant skin.

"Hmm?"

"My reward, though I am quite certain I haven't earned you."

Lily smiled sleepily, threading her fingers through his. "It is quite enough that you think you must."

Sherry chuckled, tickling her with his breath as it stirred her hair. He felt her hand tighten in his, then slowly relax, and he was careful not to disturb her again.

Lily listened to the cadence of his breathing change. She nested more heavily against him as sleep pulled at her as well. Spreading his palm across the gentle swell of her belly, she held it there. The warmth of his hand comforted her. "No reward at all here," she whispered. "But a blessing."

His suspicions confirmed, Sherry's mouth curved in a tender smile. His arm tightened the merest fraction. He would wait until morning to tell Lily the truth he had learned in this moment: that holding her made him doubly blessed.

She would be naturally dubious, of course, but then she'd smile at him as if she'd swallowed the sun. He did indeed have an extraordinary talent for getting what he wanted.